D1448303

013847772X

FAR, FAR THE MOUNTAIN PEAK

Peter Savage, civil servant and mountaineer, is a man of ruthless will and ambition from his Cambridge days to his time of near glory in India. His motto is 'at all costs'. He wins the love of a woman who both understands and fears him, and the friendship of an English peer and an Indian patriot, but his friends are chosen because they are essential to his design for fame and greatness – he is indifferent to his destructive effect on them as human beings.

When tragedy reveals his own false values, he has to find the way to self-redemption...

FAR, FAR THE
MOUNTAIN PEAK

FAR, FAR THE MOUNTAIN PEAK

by

John Masters

WARWICKSHIRE
COUNTY LIBRARY

CONTROL No.

Magna Large Print Books
Long Preston, North Yorkshire,
BD23 4ND, England.

British Library Cataloguing in Publication Data.

Masters, John
  Far, far the mountain peak.

  A catalogue record of this book is
  available from the British Library

  ISBN 0-7505-1661-5

First published in Great Britain in 1957 by Michael Joseph Ltd.

Cover illustration © Colin Woods by arrangement with Swift Imagery

The moral right of the author has been asserted

Published in Large Print 2001 by arrangement with
the Estate of John Masters care of Laurence Pollinger Ltd.

All Rights reserved. No part of this publication may be reproduced,
stored in a retrieval system, or transmitted in any form or by any
means, electronic, mechanical, photocopying, recording or otherwise
without the prior permission of the Copyright owner.

Magna Large Print is an imprint of Library Magna Books Ltd.

Printed and bound in Great Britain by
T.J. (International) Ltd., Cornwall, PL28 8RW

FOREWORD

This book is entirely a work of fiction, and no reference is intended in it to any person living or dead, though a few historical characters are mentioned. Some of the 'country' is real, some imagined.

From the beginning I have been encouraged, and advised on technical matters, by John Hedley, Dave Harrah, Hugh Ruttledge, and Tom Longstaff. This note expresses my thanks to them, and my hope that *Far, Far the Mountain Peak* lives up to their belief in it. There will, nevertheless, be mistakes and inaccuracies in the work and for these, as for the tone and structure of the whole, I alone am responsible.

J.M

For
MARTIN
my son

CHAPTER 1

So this was being grown up: to sit straight-backed in this uncomfortable old chair in the lounge of the Appleby Hotel in Cambridge, her neck strangely cold because her hair was piled on top of her head instead of falling in pigtails down her back; to glance carelessly at her own image in the mirror behind Daddy, and know that the slender young woman there, the one with the auburn hair and the grey eyes and the cold, clear, sophisticated gaze, was herself; to look secretly at Peggy and try to suppress the laugh of excitement when Peggy caught her eye; to talk in a low, even voice about nothing, while they all waited in the lounge for the three young men.

A small, dark room. A Victorian room, terribly cluttered and out of date for 1902. Daddy's tails were out of date; he'd probably had them since *he* was at Cambridge. So was his beard. Mally – ah, she always looked wonderful. '*She* is the cat's mother, Emily, not your own.' Mally was her mother. Forty-one. As beautiful and graceful as a gladiolus.

She thought: Why don't I suggest a game of ring-a-ring-a-roses, or kiss-in-the-ring? They were sitting in such a perfect circle – her mother, her father, herself; Gerry and Peggy, who were brother and sister though no one would be able to guess *that* from looking at them; Joan Gordon,

9

invited to the ball because her great-uncle had been Mally's godfather, or something. All waiting for the three young men.

Emily Fenton sat up a little straighter. They should have let her come to the ball last year. Surely they could have allowed her to put her hair up at sixteen instead of seventeen. Many parents did. But she and Peggy might have found it harder, perhaps impossible, to hold back their laughs (which her mother called 'giggles'), and to keep their voices pitched in this melodious key and the subject of their conversation to the correct nothingness. The Gordon girl could do it all perfectly; but she was nineteen at least; nineteen and a half, Peggy thought.

Emily peeked at the grandfather clock in the corner, and her mother said: 'They are only five minutes late, Emily. Ten is polite. And, you know, the ball won't start any earlier, however soon they get here.'

Gerry laughed, and Emily wished Gerry's friends would hurry up, all the same. Mr Walsh, Mr Khan, Mr Savage. She rehearsed their names and wondered what Mr Khan was Khan of. After they came there'd be fifteen minutes more of polite talk here; a glass of sherry for the young gentlemen, another glass of lemonade for herself, Peggy, and the Gordon girl. Then they'd go in to dinner. Then at last, at last, to the ball. But the ball wouldn't begin until ten o'clock, and it was only – another careful peek – just after eight.

The May Week Ball at King's College, Cambridge, in the year 1902 – June 1902, to be exact, but of course May Week was always held in

June. Everybody knew *that.*

Gerry said: 'Mally, now that we know you're not going to Zermatt, do you mind if I ask Peter – Peter Savage – to spend a week or two at Llyn Gared? I thought July would be best.'

Emily Fenton's mother's name was Mary, but ever since Gerry and Peggy Holcombe first began to spend so much time at Llyn Gared, the Fenton's home in Wales – and that was when they were all very small – they had all compromised by calling her Mally. Gerry and Peggy's mother, who had been Mally's greatest friend, died young, and Mally had promised her to do all that she could for them. It had worked out well, the three children becoming a single family group, because Emily's father had found a son in Gerry, and she a brother. She and Peggy were like sisters, too, and that had been important, but never quite so much, somehow.

Now Mally said: 'I think you'd better wait till I've had a chance to meet Mr Savage, Gerry. It isn't often that we disapprove of your heroes – but it has happened.'

Emily's father said: 'Ray, Raymond Consomething. Young whippersnapper. Wanted his behind kicked.'

'Conderwell,' Gerry said, grinning. 'He wasn't as bad as all that, Uncle G, though he *did* get sacked from Eton. It was only for making a book on the Derby. But you'll like Peter.'

'So you have told us, several times,' Mally said, picking up her sherry. 'But I'd rather wait. I'll tell you later this evening.'

'I think it would be nice,' Peggy blurted out

11

suddenly. The girl Joan raised her eyebrows. Peggy looked at the floor, shuffled her feet, and went scarlet.

Mally said: 'We'll take that into account. What do you find so wonderful about this young man?'

Peggy mumbled: 'Oh, he's all right. He's a jolly good dancer.'

'How nice!' Mally said. 'Even though there are no opportunities to dance during July in Llyn Gared.'

'Oh, don't tease her, Mally,' Gerry said. 'She likes Peter, the same as I do.'

'Where does he usually go?' Mally asked.

Gerry said: 'He spends most of his time with his grandfather, an old retired General with white side-whiskers. He's a nice old bird, but Peter won't want to spend the whole Long Vac with him.'

Mally said: 'Where are his parents?'

Gerry said: 'His mother's dead and his father... Well, Peter doesn't talk about it but I believe he disappeared years ago. It wasn't anything disgraceful.'

'Did he tell you that?' Mally asked languidly, but the veiled violet eyes were suddenly sharp.

'No,' Gerry said, 'but I'm sure.'

'Of course, dear,' Mally said gently, and Emily stirred comfortably. Oh, what a wonderful man Gerry was. She'd never heard him say anything unkind about anyone. She and Peggy would talk gossip and scandal occasionally, but when Gerry was there he'd be so obviously unhappy that they would stop – until he went away. But gossip was mean all the same, even if it was so much fun.

12

Gerry was right. Gerry was always right when it came to knowing what was right and what was wrong. Perhaps this Peter Savage would be nice, after all. But Gerry wasn't always *quite* so right about people – or was that only herself being mean?

Her father said: 'It's a pity you aren't going to spend July with your father on the Grand Tour. Why did he change his mind?'

'I think the doctor said he'd better not,' Gerry muttered, and now it was he who did not look up at them but spoke at the faded carpet under his shiny pumps.

'He's been promising you that trip for ages,' Mally said warmly. 'You must be terribly dis-appointed.'

'Not really,' Gerry said, 'though I suppose I ought to see Florence and Venice and all those pictures some time – just so that I can talk intelligently about some of the stuff we've got at Wilcot. I'd much rather come to Llyn Gared.'

Emily thought: The earl is a selfish old humbug. He just doesn't want to disturb himself. When the countess died he had been delighted to shuffle off all responsibility for Gerry and Peggy on to the Fentons. He passed his days in his big London house, not caring for anyone or anything except his study of words and the long letters he wrote to professors and people who printed dictionaries. He never appeared in the Lords except about once every five years when he thought the Lord Chancellor would let him make a speech about the state of the English language; and he left the management of the Wiltshire

13

estates entirely to Mr Mervyn, the agent. He saw Gerry and Peggy only two or three times a year, on their short holiday visits, and even those bored him.

'Savage is not a climber, is he?' Emily's father asked casually, while Mally turned to talk to the third girl.

''Fraid not,' Gerry said. 'Cricket's his line. He'll get his Blue next year, sure as eggs, though he really wasn't much good when he came up.'

Her father said: 'When you ask him, I suppose you'll let him know that we like to spend a good deal of our time on the hills, eh? I mean, we don't want him to be bored at being left behind, eh?'

Gerry said: 'He'll come with us, I'm sure. But I thought I'd spend most of the time fishing with him – or sailing. Something he'd like.'

Emily watched her father subside, pulling at his heavy, grey-flecked beard. She thought that he was not keen on having this strange young man come to Llyn Gared. He would prefer to have Gerry to himself, so that the two of them could scramble on Cader Brith, ride the ponies across the moor, take the boat out on the lake after trout. Often she and Peggy would go with them, but her father didn't mind that. They didn't count – they were girls.

And her friend and almost-sister Peggy, Lady Margaret Cowley Holcombe, had a mash on this unknown Peter Savage – deceitful of her to have concealed it since Christmas; rather clever, too, much cleverer than Peggy usually was; perhaps it was an important mash. Gerald Cowley Holcombe, Viscount Manningford, also had a mash on Peter Savage, or whatever you called it when men became great friends and each thought the other was the most marvellous, wonderful person on earth; but Gerry hadn't tried to hide what he felt; so he wasn't deceitful, but he was modest, and untruthful, because if Gerry himself was the most wonderful man in the world, and of course he was, then how could Peter Savage be?

Gerry said: 'Here they are. Only one. It must be Walsh.' He jumped to his feet and hurried to the doorway. Before he or the hotel porter got there it was pushed open from the outside, and a young man came in with a slow, firm step. He was short and broad of shoulder, narrow-hipped in the tight tail-coat. He had a square jaw, deeply cleft, and thick, tightly curled brown hair, and the sun had tanned his face so that small wrinkles already made tiny white lines round the deep-set, deep-blue eyes.

Mr Harry Walsh, Emily said to herself. Another new friend of Gerry's. Son of the managing director of Walsh and Drummond, stockbrokers. Went down from King's last year, Gerry's first at Cambridge; so he must be about twenty-four. Old. Very keen on climbing. It was strange that they hadn't met in Switzerland – well, there were other climbing centres besides Zermatt, where their own party always went. A *very* nice-looking man – beautiful teeth; polite; not awkward. Honest – more honest-looking than anyone she knew, except Gerry. The introductions began.

Now, past Joan Gordon, she could see two more blurred faces appear beyond the rough glass of the door. This time the porter got there in time, and ushered in two young men. They were in evening dress, with white silk scarves at the throat and white gloves in the hand.

Gerry turned and hurried towards them. When he came back his hand was resting on the shoulder of one of the new arrivals, a tall man, but not as tall as Gerry; thin-faced, with rather a wide mouth, thin lips, and bright pale-blue eyes.

Gerry said: 'Mally, here he is.' He was beaming, and his hand fell away from the other's shoulder with a small, almost involuntary pressure. Emily suddenly felt very grown-up.

Gerry said: 'And here's Adam Khan.' This young man was slight, not very tall, and his face was the colour of wheat with the sun on it, and his eyes were deep, soft, and black.

Mally said: 'I think some more formal introductions would help, don't you, Gerry?'

Gerry said: 'Oh, yes, of course. Well, Mally, may I present Mr Peter Savage – and Mr Adam Afzal Khan?... Peter – Mrs Fenton. Adam – Mrs Fenton... Uncle George, may I present Mr Peter Savage – and Mr Adam Afzal Khan?... Peter – Mr George Fenton...'

Emily waited, immobile, mentally rehearsing the gracious smile, the small bow of the head; the hand ready in her lap to offer, swan-like and limp, if one of the young men was gauche enough to grab for it.

She was introduced, and relaxed. Her mother said: 'Lady Margaret tells me you are a very good dancer, Mr Savage.'

Emily glanced at Peggy. Peggy was blushing

16

furiously again. Now why did Mally say that? It made it awkward for anyone if you praised them the first time you met. Mally knew that – had told Emily, in fact; so Mally *meant* to make Mr Savage feel awkward, probably to see how he would get out of it.

'Lady Margaret is wrong,' Mr Savage said. 'We dance well together, that is all.'

Emily thought: Well, that's a flat statement – rather rude, really. His voice was light and full, the tones hard-edged and clearly defined, like an operatic tenor's.

Mr Savage went on: 'Adam Khan's the best dancer among us three. I don't know about Mr Walsh.'

Mr Walsh smiled and said: 'Count me out.'

'Gerry's *very* good.'

In the short silence Emily realized with a small shock that it was herself who had spoken. The young man with the pale eyes was looking at her.

'Adam's better,' he said.

She wanted to say that she would wait and decide after the ball who was the best dancer. That would be the right, cool answer to Mr Savage's cool assertion; but it would sound wrong, so she said nothing, and soon they went through to the small dining-room and sat down at the reserved table that was loaded with flowers and cut-glass and ornately folded double damask napkins.

At dinner, while the bent old waiter sucked his teeth deferentially in her ear and Mally signalled that she could have two glasses of Château Yquem, no more, she found herself sitting between Mr Walsh and the Indian. Mr Khan spoke very good English, she was vaguely disappointed to find, although with a slight blurring of Bs, Vs, and Ws so that the three sounds, as he made them, were almost identical. His tail-coat was as impeccably cut as the others', and his high collar looked as if it would choke him, just as theirs did. She was disappointed because she had expected some Oriental splendour, perhaps a huge ring on his hand, or on his head a turban with an egret plume and a glittering diamond; and that his conversation would be of elephants, slave girls, and tame peacocks.

Instead, while on her left she heard snatches of mountaineering talk between Mally and Mr Walsh, Mr Khan gave her a lot of information about Cambridge's town drainage. Mr Khan seemed to know a lot about drainage, or at least to be fascinated by it.

This was surely not quite the sort of conversation to have at a dinner party before a May Week ball? Well, gentlemen talked about strange things, as Mally had told her, and it was her business to steer the talk into other channels if she didn't approve. *Drainage* channels, perhaps?

'Drainage is a serious problem in Rudwal,' the young man said. 'That is why I am interested.'

'You live in – Rudwal?' she asked. 'In India?'

'In the Punjab,' he said. 'Rudwal is our nearest town, though my father's estate is a few miles outside. You see, if we could get proper town drainage in Rudwal, we could make the Maghra there into as beautiful a river as the Backs here –

though it is somewhat bigger.'

'As big as the Thames at Oxford?' she asked.

'About seven times as big as that,' he said dryly. 'You see, the Backs could not be used for anything until the drainage was completed, in nineteen hundred, I think, just before I came up. There was sewage in the stream, you see. That was why it was not pleasant.'

'Yes, of course,' she mumbled.

Sewage! But Mr Khan was right. It wouldn't have been nice to go on the Backs – she had seen them for the first time this afternoon – under those circumstances. Well, right or not, it was time to ease the conversation away.

'Do you go to Calcutta very often?' she asked.

Now it was the young Indian's turn to stare at her, his lips suddenly tight. He said quite curtly: 'Calcutta is about one thousand one hundred miles from Rudwal by rail, Miss Fenton. I have only been there once, when my father presented me to the Viceroy, Lord Elgin. I was eighteen.'

Thank heaven, Peggy, on Mr Khan's other side, said something then, so that he turned to her, and Emily could relax. Mr Walsh was looking at her with admiration. She turned away... How was she expected to know that Rudwal or the Punjab was so far from Calcutta? India didn't seem very big on the map. Why had Mr Khan looked at her almost as though she had hurt or insulted him? Well, perhaps he thought everyone ought to know where Rudwal was. She remembered an old gentleman Daddy had brought to the playroom at Llyn Gared once, when she was about twelve, who'd been terribly cross because none of them knew where Hellion's Bumpstead was. But perhaps Mr Khan was annoyed because India belonged to England, which meant to her, really, and still she didn't know. Daddy had sacked a groom only last year because he didn't know where the trap ponies were at that moment. But oh dear, there was such an awful lot of the Empire. She knew plenty about other things, and no one had called her stupid. Perhaps she'd better not raise any subject unless she knew it very well – just listen to Mr Khan, and agree, and try to pick up what she could. What had she learned now? Rudwal was in, or on, the Punjab. It was eleven hundred miles from Calcutta. They had a big river called the Maghra. When would she need any of *that* information again?

Near the end of the meal Mally turned to Mr Savage, on her left, and said: 'Mr Savage, Gerry would be very pleased if you could come and stay a week or two with us at Llyn Gared in July. We'll all be there – and Mr Fenton and I will be delighted if you can come.'

Emily sat up. So Mally had made up her mind that Mr Savage was acceptable. All she could have seen in this short time was that he knew how to use a knife and fork, and cleaned his fingernails.

Mr Savage said: 'Thank you, Mrs Fenton. It's very kind of you, but I'm afraid I had made plans to go to Henley with Adam.'

'What a pity,' Mally said pleasantly.

'Henley?' Gerry cried, interrupting himself in the middle of a sentence. 'What are you going to

20

do after that?'

'We thought of going back to London and staying with my grandfather,' Peter Savage said.

'London in the second week of July!' Gerry cried in mock horror. 'You can't do that. It's a desert! Unless you're going to spend your time at the Tivoli and the Gaiety. There won't be much competition in July, eh?'

Peter Savage smiled suddenly, and Emily saw that Peggy was blushing again. Oh, don't be silly, she thought to herself. They're just talking; that's the way they have to talk to show they're men, not boys, the same as we put our hair up.

Peter Savage said: 'It wasn't me who threw that mash note on to the stage on New Year's Eve.'

'You didn't, Gerry!' Oh dash, damn, bother! There she went again, and everyone round the table laughing at her.

Gerry was laughing, his voice high with sheer excited pleasure. Well, he'd had at least three glasses of wine by now. 'Peter dared me to,' he said, 'and I did – but *he* was the one who bought the drinks for her in the Tivoli Bar afterwards.'

Emily sniffed and said: 'I don't see anything funny in that at all,' but they were all laughing, and Peter Savage was looking at her with the strong, electric light sparkling in his pale eyes. She smiled. What fools men were!

Gerry said: 'Come to Llyn Gared! You too, Adam. Think what a good time we can have, Peter. You've often told me you wanted to learn dry-fly fishing, and you know how you talk about the sea. Well, we've got both!'

'I'm sure Mr Savage would come if he could,'

Mally said with a slight warning in her voice.

Peter Savage said: 'I would like to come, Mrs Fenton, and I'm sure Adam would, but I know that your main sport is mountaineering. Gerry has often told me about what a good time he and Mr Fenton have on the mountains. Neither Adam nor I can climb – so we'd just spoil it for you, wouldn't we, Gerry? If not for you, then certainly for Mr Fenton.'

'Nonsense,' Emily's father growled. 'Delighted to have you both.' But Mally was looking at Mr Savage in quite a different, almost appreciative way, and Emily thought: He is a strange man; there he is again, saying something that is right but that people don't usually say.

'Of course it's nonsense,' Gerry broke in eagerly, and was about to go on, but this time Mally said firmly: 'Now, Gerry, I won't have Mr Savage bullied. The invitation remains open, as we're not thinking of asking anybody else. You talk to Mr Savage and Mr Khan later and see if you can persuade them – but not now. George, don't sit here too long. We shall be waiting in the drawing-room.'

The men pushed back their chairs, and Emily rose to her feet in obedience to her mother's light, sweeping glance. Up one flight of stairs to the ladies' room; wash her mouth carefully, bite her lips, bite, bite, bite; wish she could put on just a tiny bit of something to make her cheeks redder than they were; downstairs, remembering to move the feet so that she swept, the gown gliding with and around her – but no one there except the old porter to admire with narrowed eyes, man's eyes, and he reading a newspaper; on into the drawing-room, sweep, rustle, shirr of organdie; cup of coffee, no milk, no sugar: correct.

The men joined them ten minutes later, and almost before they had sat down Gerry said: 'Peter and Adam *will* be coming to stay.'

Emily's father explained: 'They're going to have a punt race along the backs, before the ball. If Savage or Khan wins, Gerry will go where Peter decides, but if Gerry wins, they'll come to Llyn Gared.'

'Whose idea is this?' her mother asked coldly.

'Mine,' Gerry said, grinning.

Mr Khan said: 'You must excuse us, ma'am. It is not as rude as it sounds, to decide your kind invitation this way. I have poled a punt but three times in my life, and Peter only twice – and Gerry, as you know, is an expert.'

'It's just a way of letting off steam,' Emily's father said. She thought he would have liked nothing better than to join in.

'No, it's a bet,' Gerry said, 'and each of us is going to have one of the girls as passenger.'

'You'll do no such thing,' her mother said automatically.

'Oh, yes, *please*,' Peggy said. 'Please, Mally! It'll be such fun.'

Emily saw her mother glance at her father. He shrugged. 'No harm in it, dear. They can all swim, and the Backs are hardly deep enough to worry about even that. It's the men who'll fall in, if anyone's going to.'

Mally said tartly: 'Well, Gerry, it's a strange way

of getting someone to accept an invitation. And of course I won't permit it to be binding, but if you–'

'Oh, it will be binding,' Peter Savage said calmly.

Emily's mother went on, with a look: 'But if you want to make exhibitions of yourselves, I suppose I can't stop you.'

Gerry kissed her quickly on the cheek and swung round, his eyes dancing. 'Dolbys will have the punts at the foot of the back lawn by now, won't they, Peter?'

'Yes,' Adam Khan said, 'I saw them, on our way here.'

'Well, let's take three down to Clare Bridge, start there, and race to Silver Street Bridge.'

'All right,' Peter said.

Gerry said: 'Now, who's going to go with whom? I choose Emily. She's the lightest.'

'What charming manners you have, Lord Manningford,' Joan Gordon said mockingly. 'And haven't you forgotten about Mr Walsh?'

The short young man, who hardly seemed to have opened his mouth since he came in, said: 'Sorry, I'm not in this race. I won't be able to join you at the ball till about eleven, either, I'm afraid. I have an appointment with the Vice-Provost.'

'On ball night?' Mally said.

Gerry cut in at once. 'Yes, Mally. About the Chapel. Harry has something he wants to do for the Chapel. Business. He couldn't get down any other night. I'm sure I told you about it.'

'I'm sure you did not,' Emily's mother said decisively. 'That will leave us with even numbers, and I had carefully planned to have an extra man.'

'I hope I won't be kept after eleven,' Harry Walsh said, and again Gerry cut in. 'It's a dashed shame, Mally, I know, but we'll see the girls aren't wallflowers, and...'

He rattled on while Emily looked at him suspiciously. She knew Gerry very well indeed, and he was telling a fib. The honest-looking Mr Walsh was not comfortable, either. She saw that her mother, too, had sensed that something was being hidden but decided not to press it now, and allowed Gerry, who heaved an almost audible sigh of relief, to return to the business of allotting passengers for the race.

'I'll take Peggy,' Peter Savage said, and Peggy said, 'Oh, yes!'

'Peggy' now, Emily thought. They must have seen a lot of each other in London at Christmas.

'Then it looks as if you and I will bring up the rear of the procession, Miss Gordon,' Mr Khan said cheerfully. 'How are we going to get to the Backs?'

'Walk,' Gerry cried. 'It's only a couple of hundred yards. Fine evening. We don't need a chaperon for this, Mally.'

Her mother said: 'No, but I will be waiting on the lawn and will expect to receive these young ladies in good condition as soon as this nonsense is over. George and I shall go in a hansom.' She laughed suddenly and gave Gerry a big hug. 'Enjoy yourselves! And may the best man win.'

'Don't say that,' Gerry said. 'Not the best man – just the most expert waterman. And that's me!'

CHAPTER 2

'Ready?' Gerry called.

Peter Savage, on the right, answered: 'Yes.' Adam Khan, on the left, called: 'Wait a minute, Gerry.' Emily snuggled down on the cushions and waved happily to Peggy a few feet away. This was ridiculous, not at all what she had expected of her first big dance – but exciting; and there were several men peering down at them from the bridge. 'What are they doing?' she heard one ask.

'Racing, of course!' Gerry called back. If she or Peggy had thought of having a boat race in evening dress, Mally would have been very firm and mean about it, but because it was Gerry's idea it was all right. Not fair.

All the men looked handsome really, once you got used to Adam Khan's darker skin, but Gerry was the most handsome. For a moment she felt her heart flutter as it had two years ago when she was fifteen and suddenly the boy who climbed trees with her and rode across the hills with her was a member of Pop, and going to Cambridge, and she knew she'd miss him for something more than his lost companionship. She remembered cursing her pigtails and her straight figure, and the serpentine ladies her mind conjured up, only half envious, for him to squire. Well, her hair was up now; and her figure was not so straight.

She strained her ears to hear music but could hear nothing. The water made no sound as it slid past, and the twilight slid down the buildings on her left and it was dark under the arches ahead. She could smell a cigar, and there were roses at her breast.

Peter Savage stood poised on the stern deck of his punt, the foot of the long pole just touching the water. He had a strange face, all hard angles; and his eyes, so bright and pale, glittered in the dusk; and he was not smiling. Anyone would think his life depended on winning, but really it was only a question of who decided where they spent a week or two of the summer – as if the summer didn't last for ever, and then the next summer after that – as if he *could* win, anyway. And Peggy was looking up at him with lips parted, devotion written all over her. She was coiled like a spring, in sympathy with him. But Gerry just stood there, so gracefully, and Adam Khan said: 'Ready now' and the funny thing was that everyone, including herself, was looking at Peter Savage.

'Go!' Gerry called.

The poles dipped into the water, all together, and she felt the surge of power pushing the punt away from under her as it leaped forward. They glided together under the arches and shot out on the other side. Gerry slid his pole easily up and forward, dropped it into the water, leaned back on it. The punt moved faster; the pole lifted, dripping, forward again.

He smiled down at her as he pushed the pole in. 'Hope I'm not splashing you.'

'Gerry's drawing ahead,' she heard Peggy scream.

But Peter Savage wasn't going to waste breath answering. Looking across at him, Emily thought he probably hadn't even heard. Gerry was three or four yards ahead and Adam Khan another yard behind Peter. The water hissed merrily, and she put her hand over the side to trail her fingers in it. It was cool, and lovely to touch, like velvet, and the bubbles that fled back from her fingers were green and gold and silver. Now there were lawns on the left, and men and women in evening dress turning to watch the race, and a looming, immense building, but they shot under another bridge, and there she just caught a strange, fierce grin leaving Peter Savage's face. He had been looking at her hand trailing in the water. Ah, she was slowing Gerry's speed that way, and that was why Peter's teeth had gleamed in a smile, a spider's smile. She pulled her hand out of the water quickly.

It was quite frightening to think anything so small could matter so much. Peter's forehead was beaded in the summer night, and his punt rocked with strong, ungainly jerks as he forced it forward, while Gerry's glided on, steady as a liner, graceful as a swan. But Peter was gaining. He was only a yard back; and it *did* matter. They shot under another bridge. Gerry mustn't allow himself to be beaten.

'Queen's,' Gerry said conversationally. 'The next one's Silver Street.'

'You're gaining, Peter,' Peggy screamed.

'Faster, faster,' Emily found herself yelling at

28

Gerry. He smiled as the pole slid into the water. 'Don't worry,' he said. 'Only ten more and we'll be there.' Effortlessly he stepped up the pace, still the punt rode the water like a swan.

A yard, two yards back, Peter hammered at the lead. Fascinated, almost appalled, she watched him. He didn't look strong, like a strong man in the circus; he was lean, leaner than Gerry, and a little shorter, too – five foot eleven or so to Gerry's six foot three. He didn't know much about poling a punt, so he wasted his time and his strength in ugly, needless movements – but his boat jerked forward, gaining on them. Whence came the sudden fierce release, like a bowstring, as he rammed the punt forward? From nervous strength alone?

She sighed. He was going to win. Gerry was trying with all his might and all his greater strength and skill, but Peter Savage was going to win. The square bow of Peter's punt edged past and with a final plunge lurched ahead as they shot under Silver Street Bridge. The men eased the poles into the water to brake the speed.

Adam Khan glided alongside on her left. 'Congratulations,' he called across to Peter. 'I don't know how you did it. *I* kept back to rescue you in case you got stranded on the pole.' He laughed, and Emily saw that he was as delighted with Peter's victory as if it had been his own.

Gerry said: 'Peter, how on *earth* did you do that? I didn't think there was a man on the river who could beat me.' They were turning the punts slowly and heading back downstream. The girls were smiling at each other, Peggy as proud as –

as a hen that's hatched a duckling!

Peter Savage said: 'I wanted to win.'

Gerry said: 'But Peter, don't you want to come to Llyn Gared?' He sounded distressed, and Emily thought: It's not fair, turning a joke into a battle and then winning.

Peter's face had relaxed a little, as much as it could, and he looked quite ordinary again – not a bit handsome really, his nose a little too long and his jaw too long and his cheekbones too high. He said: 'I don't know yet – but I thought I'd prefer to make the decisions. Now you're going to spend those two weeks where I say.' He was looking across at Gerry, and she could not for the life of her tell whether he was joking or not.

Nor could Gerry. He mumbled unhappily: 'But Peter, Mally and Uncle G will have their noses put out of joint if I don't go there.'

'It wasn't my idea to race,' Peter said. 'You'll still have the rest of the Long Vac at Llyn Gared.'

Then they reached the bank at the back lawn of King's, and Gerry handed Emily out. Mally and her father were waiting there. 'How much did you win by?' her father asked. 'A length, and going away, when you passed here.'

'I didn't,' Gerry muttered.

Emily saw her mother look at Peter, again with that surprised, calculating glance. She looked at him herself, because she had made up her mind that she did not like him. Gerry and Peggy might be unhappy that he wasn't coming to Llyn Gared, but she wasn't. Only … Gerry would be doing what *he* wanted him to, and that wasn't good.

She turned away. The ball had begun, and she was going to have a wonderful time. She took Gerry's arm and squeezed it. 'Take my programme and write your name in it lots of times,' she said.

They were walking up the centuries-old lawn, the smell of the cut grass in her nostrils, towards one of the most lovely buildings she had ever seen.

'Gibbs,' Gerry said. 'Isn't it marvellous? Peter's rooms are in there, on L staircase. Mine are in Chetwynd.'

His face cleared in the glow of light from the windows, and he began to laugh. 'The biter bit! I ought to have known you can't get the better of Peter when he's made up his mind. Well, I'm sure he'll think up something wonderful for us to do. Let's have a look at that programme.'

They had passed through a deep-arched passage under the building, and now on her left she became aware of a vast presence, King's College Chapel. She turned, and although she realized she had seen it twice before, this evening, she found herself sighing in wonder. Beside her the tremulous wall of stone and glass soared up into the summer night, and above again the pinnacles were haloed in summer stars, so thick and close that they seemed to have been set there by the hand of the same sculptor.

After a time she turned away. She could hear the music of the ball very plainly now; but these years of organdie and sipped wine seemed so small, with the towering mystery of the Chapel behind her, that she was ashamed to be enjoying

31

them. This time was only a vestibule or ante-room to life, and though there was fun here it was not, surely, what she meant by happiness. Happiness must be bigger and higher – and deeper – as when you had responsibilities, and knew sadness. Then perhaps she would become like her mother, tall and beautiful and deep-rooted in the walled garden of Llyn Gared, as the foundations of the Chapel lay deep under the velvet lawns.

And her father there, would he be the model for Gerry? He was forty-five now, and he did not have 'fun.' Most of the time he seemed more worried than happy, yet she knew he was content. When he was at Llyn Gared he thought of Zermatt, and oiled his ice axe and fondled his climbing ropes and rubbed saddle soap into his boots, and read and reread Whymper and Freshfield; and when they were at Zermatt he was soberly grateful for the good days on the mountain, but when the clouds came down and it was impossible to climb, he thought of Llyn Gared and wrote letters about the management of the home farm, and wondered whether Preece's wife had had her baby yet.

It would be good to know what happiness was, exactly, before she reached out for it; also, to have grown big enough for it. She could not yet, for instance, be happy with her mother's kind of happiness. That meant she didn't even want to be married yet. With a queer, cold sense of doing something wrong she examined her mind as it was and not as it was supposed to be.

She did *not* want to be married yet. That was

the truth. She prayed with sudden passion that Gerry would wait a few years before asking her. If he didn't, heaven knew what she might have to say or do. Her mother's life was beautiful, and so was her father's in its way, and more beautiful still the way they had made their lives one; but she knew there was more yet, and that she was not old enough, or was too taken up with the present, to find it. Her mother and father were rooted in Llyn Gared, but the Chapel went down deeper than the soil. It stood, and towered so against the stars, because its foundations were in the history of Cambridge University, and that meant in something very old and deep, which had nothing to do with comfort or happiness. The builders must have found some purpose or fire to give them the power to raise that magic tower of stone and crystal. Somewhere there must be such a purpose for her, and such a life as much beyond happiness as happiness was beyond fun – not for her alone, for her and Gerry together. But if she talked about it to him, he would laugh and be a little embarrassed. That was why she knew he must wait. *He* must understand, and she must be ready.

CHAPTER 3

She was dancing at last, and with Gerry. This was what it had all been leading up to, putting up your hair and biting your lips. This– She swayed away from him, felt his hand firm at her waist, and looked at his face.

'Is it what you expected?' he asked her.

She nodded. Yes, it was. She was not feeling quite what they had expected for her, perhaps, but *she* had known she would feel things differently when she was grown-up.

She said: 'Now tell me what Mr Walsh is really doing.'

Gerry shot her an astonished look, so that she laughed and said: 'Don't be an ass, Gerry. You're the worst actor in the world.'

'I can't tell you,' he said in an agonized whisper. 'Not now. Don't ask me. It's a secret, and I've promised not to tell till I'm allowed to.'

'I see,' she said. 'Does Peter know?'

Gerry shook his head. 'No, I'm not allowed to tell anyone.'

She laughed gaily. Heaven knew what they were up to. It didn't matter, but it made her cheerful to think that Harry Walsh had a greater hold on Gerry than Peter Savage did, at least in this case. Perhaps that was what had made Peter so angry; well, not exactly angry – determined, as though he were going to show Gerry whose opinion really mattered in the end, and why it really mattered – because he could win by sheer determination.

Gerry said: 'Peter's jolly nice, isn't he?'

She said carefully: 'I'm sure he is. I don't really know him, do I?' It didn't always do to tell Gerry exactly what you thought. She didn't want an argument.

But now Gerry had made her think of Peter Savage again, and she'd promised herself she wouldn't. In the lounge of the Appleby he had been a dim figure, Gerry's friend, nothing more. In the dining-room he'd spoken a few sentences that showed he was a person in himself, and rather a disconcerting one. She had come out of the hotel quite liking him, and admiring the way he was allowing himself, rather gracefully in the circumstances, to be forced to change his plans and come and spend a couple of weeks at Llyn Gared. Then, during the race, everything had changed – his face, his manner, the circumstances, the whole situation. And he had changed them all. He wasn't nice; he wasn't allowing himself to be politely manoeuvred into anything. On the contrary, he had forced Gerry into a position Gerry hadn't wanted to be in. Peter Savage wasn't a gentleman.

Gerry said: 'Peggy wants him to come to Llyn Gared, rather badly. That's why I thought up the race. I could hardly tell him Peggy has a mash on him, could I?'

'He knows, I am sure,' she said dryly. The music dipped and swung, and the old gentlemen on the walls peered benignly down on her from

35

their heavy frames.

She said: 'What's he going to do – Peter – when he leaves Cambridge?'

'I don't know,' Gerry said earnestly. 'He hasn't made up his mind yet. The last time we talked he was thinking about taking the exam for the Indian Civil, but I tried to persuade him it would be an awful waste. He could be prime minister if he set his mind to it.'

'Can he afford to go into politics?' she asked.

'I don't suppose so,' Gerry said. 'I don't think the family's well off. In fact I'm sure they're not. But dash it, it's a shame. Anyway, he could go into law and make a fortune while they were giving him hopeless seats, and then he'd be ready when they could give him a good one. But I'm really afraid he's almost made up his mind to go to India. Most of his people seem to have gone out there for donkey's years. Well, whatever he does, he'll know what he's *going* to do. Wish I could say as much for myself. I say, what about a glass of champagne cup?'

'If you like.' They swung out of the dance, and at the edge of the floor she glanced at the programme now dangling from her gloved wrist. She had the next dance with Adam Khan. Very nice. But Gerry had said something odd…

'What do you mean?' she asked as they wended through the crowd, walked out across the lawn to the marquee. 'You know what you're going to do – much better than any of them, as a matter of fact.'

Gerry said: 'Of course, but – well, a chap's life seems rather pointless when everything's going to come to him. I mean, some day the old man's going to pop off, and then I'll be the Earl, and there'll be the estates, and the House – not that I know anything, but I suppose I ought to go and say my piece when they're talking about something that's going to affect the tenants. Plenty of money that I haven't earned. Whacking great mansion. Town house. Deer forest... There.'

'Thank you... It's not a crime to be heir to an earldom, Gerry – even to have a lot of money. We've got enough, I suppose, but Daddy's never felt that he ought to be anything except what he was born to be.'

'No. Wish I could be like Uncle G. But – well, here's Peter probably sailing off to India when we go down next year, and he'll have something to *do*. I mean, things won't be the same after he's lived as they were before, will they? And whatever he does, whatever he becomes, it'll be his. But a hundred years from now no one except some oldest inhabitant's youngest grandson is going to know or care whether I was the fifth Earl or the sixth. Dash it, there won't be any difference between me and the old man, except that his name will be mentioned with thanks in the preface to some enormous dictionary as the chap who gave the proper derivation of "postliminical" – and then half the readers are going to think it's me. I tried to persuade Peter to go into politics here. No go... I've a dashed good mind to go to India.'

'What?' she said sharply.

They had wandered out on the lawn, where she could listen to the music of the orchestra and

37

look at the Chapel. Horses' hoofs clopped past down King's Parade.

'Oh, not seriously,' he said quickly. 'It was just something Peter's grandfather, the old general, said that made me think of it.'

'What did he say?'

'He asked me, when we were first introduced, whether it hadn't been a relative of mine who was Governor of Madras or Bombay or somewhere, I can't remember where, in eighteen-seventy-three. It was, as a matter of fact, though we'd all forgotten about him. It made me realize I could be something that I made myself, if I wanted to be, instead of just being what came to me.'

She hesitated, for it was impossible not to feel that perhaps this, in Gerry, was the same need for a purpose that had come to herself so short a time ago. But this was all wrong; she felt it in her bones and knew it in her head. This wasn't Gerry's purpose, but something he had caught from Peter Savage, like a disease, and now was trying to persuade himself that he needed.

She said slowly: 'I don't think that would be right, Gerry. The relative you're talking about wasn't the Earl, was he? Well, you will be. Is it any better to look after some Indians whom you don't know, than your land and your tenants, whom you do? *I* wouldn't want to go to India – if I were you,' she added hastily.

Gerry said: 'You're right, Em. And I wouldn't be making my own way even there. It would be just that some governors practically have to be peers, according to Peter. It would be an awful sweat, and a long, long time, before I could hope to become Viceroy.'

'Who said you could?'

'Peter. He was only joking.'

'Oh,' she said. But privately, she added: Was he? She didn't think that Peter Savage made jokes of quite that kind.

They returned in silence to the ballroom and stood together under the balcony, waiting for Adam Khan to claim his dance with her. She saw Mally and Daddy up there on the dais, among ranks of chaperones and fathers. Goodness, how those old people did talk, fans waving, heads nodding, eyes darting here and there. And there was Peter Savage, sitting with Joan Gordon. And here was the Indian, with the delicate bones and the understanding eyes. He was in front of her, his white gloves touching at the tips as he bowed rather lower than was usual. The music had begun.

'Miss Fenton, I think I have the honour...?'

She held out her hand. What was it this time? Another waltz. It was time someone invented a new dance.

'Do you know anything about the mystery of Mr Walsh?' Adam asked her at once, as soon as they were fairly launched on the floor.

'Hasn't he come back yet?'

'No. Your mother is quite annoyed, I fear.'

She said: 'Gerry knows, but he's promised not to tell. I suppose we'll find out some time.'

They danced without speaking for a time. He *was* good. She half closed her eyes and tried to judge whether, if she had not known whom she was dancing with, she would say he was better than Gerry. But it was impossible because his hand felt different, and the rhythm of his movement felt different. Dancing wasn't something that you could really take by itself; you and your partner and what you thought of him were a part of it. But he was a beautiful dancer.

He said: 'It was very kind of you to invite Peter and me to your home. I am–'

'I didn't,' she said. 'Gerry did.'

Then she really blushed, scarlet with mortification and shame. 'Oh! I'm sorry.' She gasped. 'Of course I didn't mean… We … I would be – have been – delighted, only–'

'There's no reason why you should pretend to be overjoyed,' he said with a smile. 'We would have deprived you of Gerry's company for many days if we had come. I was going to say that I will try to persuade Peter to release Gerry from his wager.'

'It won't help,' she said. 'Gerry's promised. He'd be miserable if he thought he was being let off something.'

The young Indian looked at her thoughtfully. 'You are quite right. Well, now we are all in Peter's hands. He will decide.'

She said: 'And you'll – let him?'

She thought: That's not quite polite, implying that he has no will of his own. But she might as well speak as frankly as he did. It was exciting to say what one thought.

Adam nodded. 'Yes, I shall let him. Partly because I have already agreed to be his guest at that time, so I am in his hands, but really because he knows where he is going. It is always exciting to go with Peter, even on a walk through the streets.'

She said: 'Gerry just told me he *didn't* know. He thought he hadn't made up his mind... I mean, about what he would do when he left Cambridge.'

'He has now,' Adam said, 'this evening. We were out on the lawn for a few moments while you ladies were in the cloakroom. Gerry had disappeared – on his secret service, I suppose. We were looking at the Chapel, then at the ladies and gentlemen walking up and down. There are four sons of cabinet ministers here, you know, and a score of earls and dukes and heirs to peerages. There is a wealth here such as there was at our Mogul courts, though not so obvious. Peter said, "I'm not going to hang around begging these people for favours. I'll come back able to demand what I want. I'll take the Indian Civil." That was all. I hope he will stay with us in India and forget about coming back here. But I suppose, when you feel that there is nothing you cannot do, it must seem much greater to be prime minister of England than lieutenant-governor of an Indian province – for Peter, I mean, not for me. I am an Indian.'

Emily said: 'He didn't mention Gerry, did he? Any idea that Gerry might go to India too?'

Again Adam looked at her thoughtfully, and again the music and the moving faces blurred behind him, because this was important and he understood. He said: 'Gerry? No, Miss Fenton. Peter didn't mention Gerry at all. I hope Gerry never thinks of India. He could be a Presidency governor, and quite soon, if he decided he wanted to be – but I don't think he is suited to the life.'

She felt better. Adam Khan was an ally. She said: 'You're going back, I suppose. Oh, of course, you're going to put new drains in Rood – Roodbar.'

'Rudwal,' he said with a quick smile. 'Yes, and plenty more besides, I hope. If Peter has really made up his mind to go to the I.C.S – it will be wonderful! My family is very old and respected, Miss Fenton. If I can persuade Peter to come to Rudwal as D.C – why, between us there is almost nothing we could not achieve, because he has the power and I know the people.'

'It sounds wonderful,' she said untruthfully. She didn't know what a D.C was, and the only wonderful thing was that Peter Savage was going to sail away and leave Gerry alone.

The music stopped.

'That is the end of our dance,' Adam said, bowing slightly.

She saw Gerry and Peggy standing together at the side of the floor, close beside one of the doors that led out under the gallery into the cool, summer-scented ante-passage. Gerry was beckoning her with a surreptitious motion. Adam saw too, and they walked over together.

As they reached Gerry's side from one direction, Peter Savage and Joan Gordon came up from the other. Gerry said: 'Listen – which of you girls wants to practice her skill as a houri?'

'What's this?'

Emily swung round with a start and found her

mother at her elbow, and, behind, her father.

Gerry muttered: 'Shh, Mally, it's important. Quick, which of you wants to be a temptress for fifteen minutes?'

Mally said: 'Gerry, I am chaperoning these young ladies. I forbid it – whatever it is. You have been behaving like a very inferior Doctor Watson ever since dinner. Now tell us what your stupid secret is.' She spoke sternly, but it didn't work. Emily, watching her, knew that she loved Gerry too much, and had spent too many years entering with them into the spirit of just such childish games as this.

Gerry said: 'Mally, I can't tell you, exactly. I can't tell *anyone*.' He glanced pleadingly at Peter. 'Not just yet. But we must have Bennett, the lay dean, kept in Hall for the next fifteen minutes. Everyone else is being looked after. Bennett's the man over there with the thick black hair. Got his blue in 'eighty-eight. He's handsome, isn't he? Isn't he, Peg?'

'I suppose so,' Peggy said dubiously, 'but–'

Peter Savage said: 'Mrs Fenton can do it best.'

Gerry started and said: 'Mally? But she's–'

Mally said: 'Mr Savage! I shall do no such thing!' But her eyes sparkled with pleasure.

Gerry gabbled: 'Oh heavens, time – it's urgent. I promise I'll tell you all as soon as I can – five, ten minutes. Peggy, you do it. Dance with him – talk, flirt, sit out. I'm going to get him now, introduce him.'

'Gerry!' Mally called, but Gerry had gone.

The music began, and Emily found Peter Savage standing in front of her, his pale face cold

43

and reserved. 'This is my dance,' he said.

'Wait a minute.' She fumbled for her programme and read it through carefully three times. Then she looked up with a dazzling smile. 'So it is – I had made sure it was somebody else.'

'I will be happy to give it up, if you wish,' he said.

Gerry led Mr Bennett into the group. Emily had been hoping to play the role of seductress herself, since it was for Gerry's sake; but she could hardly get rid of Peter Savage that way, now that Peggy had been named.

'It doesn't matter,' she said, and took Peter's arm; and then, when they were dancing, she said: 'What is the secret? I'm sure you know,' because she knew he did not know.

'I don't know,' he said.

'Isn't it thrilling?' she said.

The pale eyes suddenly focused on her. They were the colour of the sea on a cold, clear day – blue-green and strangely lighted, brilliant. She felt that he had never seen her before, that she had been a mere speaking doll, an obstruction in organdie, but that now he weighed her as a person.

He said: 'Men don't usually have that kind of a secret between themselves when they are grown up, Miss Fenton.'

She could afford to ignore the barb about being grown up. Mr Savage made you angry, but he didn't make you blush. She said calmly: 'You have secrets from Gerry, I'm sure.'

He thought a moment and then said: 'No.'

Well, damn Mr Savage! She had spoken to annoy him, expecting him to answer with a mocking evasion. But he'd answered the question exactly and, she was sure, honestly. That put her in a bad position; now she would have to explain herself further or be thought of as a coy little girl. She said: 'What about your decision to join the I.C.S, or the Indian Civil?'

'Same thing,' he said. 'The Indian Civil Service. That's not a secret. I haven't had the opportunity to tell Gerry yet. I only made up my mind tonight, and he's been disappearing like a jack-in-the-box ever since.'

He ought at least to have wondered how she knew and then after a few minutes of fencing she would have told him, and then it would have been the end of the dance and she would have been the winner. Now she was left holding the dead body of a secret that wasn't a secret.

There was Peggy, smiling nervously at Mr Bennett. She was almost as bad an actor as Gerry, but in a way it made her performance more realistic – with her face flushed and her big blue eyes blinking in obvious confusion. Emily smiled to herself, while keeping her face impassive in case Peter Savage should think she was smiling at him. Peggy was her best friend, but it was no good pretending that being a houri was in her line, or ever would be. She was big, for one thing – not heavy in an ugly sense, but strong – and her skin was fair but marked by small freckles and healthily brown with the veneer of wind and sun and rain. It was easy to see that she spent more time in the saddle of a Welsh hill pony than in a ballroom. Her hair was her best physical feature – strong, of a brown like oak leaves in October. Mr Bennett was preening himself and looking terribly important and talking all the time. Men!

Peter Savage did not dance very well. That was just what he had said. She said: 'Do you think Gerry will go out to India too?'

He looked full at her again; and she thought that though perhaps he kept no secrets, there were secret parts of his mind, where ideas and thoughts whirled and grew, and that she had touched one of them.

He said: 'No. He might be happier if he did, though.'

'And it would be nice for you too, wouldn't it?' she said.

He said: 'Not for a long time. He'd have to start by working in politics here for several years, and when he went out he'd go to a Presidency. I shall go to the Punjab. A non-regulation province is the best if you're in the Indian Civil. We wouldn't see much of each other, and we wouldn't be able to help each other for years.'

Ah, she thought – help each other. You mean, Gerry can help you. Things are beginning to be a little clearer. Over Peter's shoulder she saw Gerry duck into the ballroom from a far passage and hurry towards Mally and her father on the dais. Then he slowed his pace to a carefree stroll, and then, as they turned, Peter saw him and said: 'Gerry's signalling us. He's going to let the cat out of the bag.' Suddenly he smiled, his face crinkling and his bright eyes flashing. 'He's an ass. Let's go and help him squeeze the most out of the great moment. Someone's probably painting the Founder's statue green.'

They gathered in a group in the corner, and the music had stopped. Now what would Peggy do? She was waiting in the middle of the floor, looking frantic. The band struck up again. Mr Bennett had no alternative but to ask her to continue the dance. Mally said: 'Someone has bribed the band, I see. Gerry, if you don't tell me what's happening I shall burst.'

Gerry looked around cautiously and lowered his voice. 'I'm allowed to tell you now because he's up and probably starting down. Someone's climbing the Chapel.'

'The Chapel!' Mally gasped. 'He'll kill himself! Gerry, this is dreadful! Do you mean to tell me that Peggy is unwittingly–'

Emily thought of the soaring wall of stone, and her head swam. She had been a climber and mountaineer since she was eight, but this was different. What was there to hold on to? How could a man possibly get up there?

'By George, I'd like to see that,' her father said. 'I was looking at it before the dancing began and wondering, as a matter of fact, whether it would be possible. Who is it?'

Gerry said proudly: 'Harry Walsh. He'll be the most famous man in the University tomorrow.'

Her father said: 'By God, you're right! If he should finish up as prime minister, this will still seem the greatest moment of his life – unless he finds and climbs a new mountain.'

Emily glanced at Peter Savage. His expression

47

had narrowed and become almost as tautly concentrated in listening as when he had stood poised for the start of the race.

Gerry said: 'I'm sorry I couldn't tell you about it, Peter, but I'd promised not to–'

Peter Savage interrupted. 'I want to see him coming down.' He had been put out – jealous, perhaps – because Gerry had held the secret from him; now that was past and done with, and his voice was urgent but not excited.

Gerry said: 'We'd better wait a bit. We might attract attention, and then–'

Peter said: 'Walsh is a senior member. What can they do to him? We can stroll out without being noticed. Are you coming, Mr Fenton?'

'Yes, certainly, I'd like to – but won't the others in the party get into trouble if they're caught? Some of them must be undergraduates.'

'They'll be rusticated,' Peter said coldly. 'But if they're caught it won't be any fault of ours. I'm going.'

He walked away, and Emily thought no one would suspect he was in a hurry, but actually he was moving very fast.

Gerry said doubtfully: 'I don't suppose we can do any harm now.'

'I'll stay,' Mally said. 'I have to keep an eye on Peggy. And I don't want to see it.'

'Nor do I,' said Joan Gordon with a shudder.

'Then we can sit out with Mrs Fenton,' Adam Khan said.

Emily followed Gerry out of the hall, with her father at her heels. As soon as they were out on the lawn Gerry muttered: 'Round the far side of

48

Gibbs. They're on the north-west pinnacle, north face.'

They passed the great west door of the Chapel, and then, in the darkness under the wall, with high railings to the side and the loom of blank-windowed buildings beyond, and all the sound of the ball deadened by the bulk of Gibbs and of the Chapel itself, she saw the shimmer of white shirt fronts, and a voice muttered: 'Manningford? Keep close in under the wall. How's that girl doing with Bennett?'

'He's safe for a few minutes. She's my sister. Where is he?'

From beside them Peter Savage's low voice answered: 'There.'

She craned back and saw, sixty feet up, a darker shape against the shadows of the turret. Staring hard, with her heart beating and her eyes aching, she soon made the climber out more clearly, for age had weathered the stone to grey-white, and the stars were bright. He was wedged into the vertical shaft between the end of the north wall and the turret that stood out from the north-west corner. He had his back against the wall and his feet against a projection, only a few inches wide, that marked the first angle of the turret. A lightning conductor ran down in the angle beside him, and he had one hand on it as he came on down, 'chimneying.' She had done that herself for a few feet in the beginning of the North Crack on Cader Brith: you held yourself in place by pressing your back against one surface and your feet against the other; you went up by pushing down and back with the palms of your hands on the surface behind you, and by straightening your knees; when your arms were stretched and your knees straight, you moved one foot as high as it would go on the opposite wall, then moved the other up to it; then repeated the whole process; coming down, you did the same in the reverse order. You never had less than three points of support, even without a hand-hold, and Harry Walsh was keeping himself from falling sideways by a light grip on the lightning conductor – but here, at night, the walls of the Chapel falling like stone curtains to the ground and the surge of the organ shaking the whole mighty fabric as the Music Scholar inside played his farewell to Cambridge... She clutched convulsively at Gerry's hand and heard herself whispering: 'He's been to the top! To the top of the pinnacle!'

Now she saw that they had put a small ladder against the wall, reaching up the first twenty feet to the point where the 'chimney' began. Peter Savage had forced a little forward and stood among the men at the foot of the ladder, but he did not touch it.

An undergraduate hurried up and muttered: 'Bennett's getting suspicious. He's heading this way.'

A voice from the ladder said: 'Wilson, go and stop him. Be drunk, hit him. Anything.'

'I'm going to fail anyway,' a languid voice answered. 'I'll look after him.'

Harry Walsh had almost reached the ladder now, his movements as smooth and effortless as Gerry's with the punt pole. He was dressed in light-coloured trousers, a dark wool jersey, and tennis shoes. The white shoes looked like small animals finding their own way down the stone cliff, seeming to have nothing to do with the dim face above.

The feet stepped on to the ladder, and Gerry muttered: 'Done it!'

Emily let out her breath in a long, hissing sigh, for her chest hurt. Harry Walsh jumped the last six feet and sprang lightly erect. A shower of whispered jubilant congratulations fell on him, and a dozen hands reached out for his.

'Well done, Walsh!' her father cried, bursting forward to grab his hand.

'Thanks, sir. I tried seven times when I was an undergraduate, but– Well, we've done it. Thanks, everyone.'

'Bennett! Run!'

'See you in the marquee at supper. Half an hour!' Walsh cried, and then she was alone with her father, for Gerry and the other young men had disappeared, taking their ladder with them.

They walked slowly back past the west door. Then she noticed that Peter Savage wasn't with them. Looking back, she saw him standing away from the Chapel, staring up at the western pinnacles and the garland of stars around them. The organ thundered on, and a faint medieval luminosity stained the glass windows.

Peter Savage turned and came towards them with quick strides. Mr Bennett passed, frowning, going in the opposite direction. Her father said: 'One fellow climbing the outside of the Chapel and another playing a Bach fugue inside. That's

51

Cambridge for you.'

Peter Savage shot him a quick look. 'They're compatible, sir. Are we going to supper now?'

Her father pulled out his watch and examined it carefully. 'I believe so. Gerry should be getting a table for us, if he is free yet.' He chuckled happily.

They found the huge marquee only half full, and all the party except Gerry waiting for them. 'Here's our table,' Adam Khan said. Seemingly oblivious of their existence, Peter Savage stood frowning down at the gleaming white cloth while they took their seats.

'Champagne,' he said suddenly. 'We need champagne!'

'Coming, coming!' Gerry cried cheerfully from behind him. '*And* the chicken and lobster. *And,* in a few minutes, the hero of the hour.' He sat down, and waiters opened magnums of champagne and set plates of cold food before them.

Emily began to eat ravenously. Then she remembered and pecked daintily, hungrily, at the lobster. Peter Savage said: 'Why do people climb – mountains or chapels?' His knife and fork lay beside his untouched plate.

There was a silence. Her father cleared his throat; Gerry said: 'Er'; she herself wondered how one would begin to explain.

Peter said impatiently: 'But you're all climbers. You must know why you climb. Gerry, why do you climb?' A sharp smile robbed the question of offence, but left no doubt that a sensible answer was expected, quickly.

Gerry swallowed his food hurriedly and said:

'Fresh air – exercise – wonderful views. Dash it, Peter, it's wonderful. You'd know if you climbed yourself.'

Her father said: 'An element of teamwork, Savage. Some danger – that's important. I can't see a man devoting himself to *lawn tennis*.' He poured a heavy scorn into the last words.

Peter said: 'Don't you climb to get to the top?'

Again there was silence. At last her father said: 'Well, one does one's best to get to the top, of course, but that's not the important thing. Not the most important, at least.'

'Would you all have been so pleased and excited if Walsh had failed, sir? He's going to be famous, you said. The most famous man in Cambridge. But that's only because he got to the top. He's failed seven times, he said. They didn't make him famous – and he didn't find whatever he found this time.'

The silence was longer and deeper. There was something awfully wrong in what he was saying, but Emily couldn't for the life of her find words to explain what it was. Nor, apparently, could anyone else.

At length Peter Savage said: 'Let's drink to Harry Walsh.' He took up his glass.

'Hear, hear,' the men muttered, and Gerry said: 'We'll toast him again when he comes in. Harry Walsh!'

They drank, and for a few minutes the conversation became general and insubstantial. Then Peter Savage, opposite Emily, leaned across to Gerry and said: 'Gerry, I'm going to give up cricket.'

Gerry swallowed his wine the wrong way, gasped, spluttered, and finally managed to get out: 'You can't do that! You're going to get a Blue! After that, a county cap.'

'What county?' Peter said harshly. 'Rudwal? No, I'm giving it up. There's no summit to it, and nothing you can make or find for yourself. It's a game, that's all. Cricket doesn't affect the man himself, and through him his work and his whole life. Climbing would. Or small-boat sailing, or big-game shooting, perhaps. What do you need to become a good climber?'

'Nothing much,' Gerry said almost nervously. 'Keep reasonably fit. Train your nerve and eye a bit. Learn a few techniques with the rope and ice-axe and so on. But–'

'To get to the top, always, of any mountain,' Peter insisted. 'Where no one knows the dangers and no one's ever been before? You need more than that, don't you? Surely it's a question of will?'

Her father, who had turned to listen, said seriously: 'To a certain extent, Savage. Of course any climber must have the will to go on when he's tired, but it's got to be balanced by something else, just as his legs have to be balanced and controlled by his head. Take that Chapel climb, now. Walsh is one of our good young mountaineers. I've heard about him, and the experts are predicting that if he develops the way he's been going he could become our best in a few years. He's strong, and courageous – and he has a wise head on his shoulders. I doubted that when I heard about the Chapel, but when I saw him on it I had to agree that there's nothing foolhardy about it. Remember, he's turned back seven times for one reason or another. We can't doubt he had the will. But something else, something more important, was in control.'

Peter Savage suddenly relaxed the intensity of his expression. With a quick smile of great charm he lifted his glass once more. 'Gerry – we'll drink to Walsh again in a moment. But he is not going to be the greatest mountaineer of his time. We are.'

'What?' Gerry cried. 'You mean you – we are going to take up climbing seriously?'

Peter nodded. 'Yes. And now I'll tell you where we're going to go in July.'

'Oh, dear.' Adam Khan groaned cheerfully. 'I am a plainsman, Peter.'

Gerry said: 'Zermatt? Chamonix? Peter, you *can't*–'

Peter said: 'As we're going to the top, we must start at the bottom. We're going to Llyn Gared – if Mrs Fenton will have us.'

'Oh!' Peggy cried, and a radiant smile transformed her healthy face to beauty.

'Delighted. Of course,' Mally murmured politely; but Emily could see that she was not wholly delighted. Gerry's face was alive with happiness, and he had jumped to his feet and grabbed Peter's hand across the table; but Emily felt a slow, thin knife pricking at the skin of the back of her neck.

CHAPTER 4

They paused for a breather when they reached
the top of the hill, and Emily turned to look back
into the valley where her father's house stood.
Llyn Gared was big and grey, its rough stone
weathered by three centuries of Welsh rain so that
the surface seemed smooth, and caught the light,
and shone like a house of gold in the sun, and of
silver in the moon, but in the days of mist the
house was itself a thing of mist, pierced with the
darkness of windows, streaming water. From
here the dark firs on the east side half hid it, but
the thin sun winked at them through the
branches, and smoke curled from many
chimneys.

Beyond, the pasture lands of the home farm
filled the valley beside the winding stream, and
there to the west, between low headlands, the sea
swept back and forth against a sandy shore.

It had promised a fine day when Jennie had
brought Emily her early-morning tea, but when
they left the house clouds were edging over the
shoulder of Cader Brith. Here at the head of the
valley the mist hung just above their heads and
the road was shiny with moisture. The sun could
only gild the droplets of water hanging from each
blade of grass, and Cader Brith had disappeared.

His pipe lit and drawing well, her father started
off again with his long, easy strides. 'I think it's

going to clear,' he said, 'but it looks as though we'll have to wait an hour or two before we can tackle the South Crack, Gerry.'

Gerry nodded. 'We'd better not count on starting until after lunch.'

'I hope we can get it in. This is going to be your last day on the hills for some time, isn't it? Real climbing, I mean. I suppose you'll be pottering about with your friend Savage after that.'

'Potter! You don't know him, Uncle G.'

'No, I don't,' her father said seriously. 'He's rather a cocksure young man, isn't he? You'd better keep a tight rein on him when you get him on the mountain – if he hasn't changed his mind. A bit slapdash I should call him, eh?'

Peggy said: 'Oh, no, Uncle G!' Emily turned and raised her eyebrows in mock surprise. Peggy fell silent, blushing hard.

Emily's father said drily: 'I take it you think Mr Savage has no faults? Well, we shall see. What's to become of Mr Khan? He doesn't seem to be interested in mountain-climbing.'

'He'll come along with us,' Gerry said. 'He'll be happy wherever he is, as long as he can talk to Peter about India.'

'Oh,' her father said, and added some time afterwards: 'Good.' And, some time later again: 'Is your father well? You had a letter this morning, didn't you?'

'He's all right,' Gerry said indifferently, and fell silent. Emily thought again, with the same familiar but always new pang, what it must be like to have no mother, and a father who had washed his hands of people and the pains and loves they involve. She still remembered Gerry's expression once, many years ago, when he and Peggy came back to Llyn Gared after a visit to the big town house in Berkeley Square, and he told her that his father had been too busy writing a letter to see them off at the door. Gerry shook off the mood that mention of his father always imposed on him. 'Uncle G,' he said cheerfully, 'are we going to Zermatt next summer?'

'I hope so,' her father answered. 'Do you think you'll be ready to tackle the Zmutt ridge of the Matterhorn by then, Emily?'

'Oh, yes,' she said. 'Peggy and I, guideless.'

They all laughed, for this was an old family joke. The usual way up the Matterhorn was via the Hörnli ridge, which fell north-eastward from the summit into Zermatt. But the first time she had seen the mountain, as a child of eight, she had insisted that the Hörnli ridge looked too steep and that when she went up she found the Zmutt ridge, which fell north-westward to the Zmutt glacier and the Schönbühl Hut. She had learned soon enough that the Zmutt ridge, which had no artificial aids or fixed ropes, was, in that virgin state, considerably the more difficult of the two. The Zmutt ridge was, in fact, attempted by few men and none but the most expert women, and then with the best guides; but it had remained in her mind as one of those stars, sparkling brighter as increased knowledge set them ever farther from the possibility of attainment, which beckoned to her from above her comfortable world. Most of these dream-constellations had nothing to do with mountains or mountaineering. For a year now she had longed to inhabit, however briefly, the soul of the mysterious veiled lady who always accompanied the Archduke Paul to Zermatt – but not to the mountains. Since she was ten she had longed to lead a revolution and hang people from lampposts, in some good cause. At fifteen it had suddenly flashed into her mind, while eating a breakfast kipper, that there existed people who heard more in music and poetry, and saw more in paintings, than other people did, and that these extra-feeling people somehow achieved great unhappiness and lived disordered lives thereby – yet she longed to go with them, at whatever cost, just as she would go up to the Zmutt ridge and risk the fall, the accident, even death, to discover what it was that beckoned her so strongly to the attempt.

That star dimmed. She was not a very good climber, and her two ascents of the Matterhorn via the Hörnli ridge had stretched her nerve and her strength to a point where the attainment of the summit had brought only new and greater fears of the descent.

'It's clearing,' her father said and paused to relight his pipe. He was a man of habit, and his pipe always needed attention at this point, where the footpath to Cader Brith left the main carriage road. A moment later they set off in single file across the moorland. Twenty paces farther on, Gerry, in the rear, stopped and cried: 'Wait! Listen!' She heard the crunch of wheels and the rapid clip-clop of hoofs on the main road, and then round a curve of rock came a trap, the two horses going at a hard canter. There were three men in it, two on the driver's seat and one perched on a stack of luggage behind.

'It's Jones the station trap,' Gerry cried. 'And Peter! Peter's got the ribbons. Hey! Stop, stop!' He ran at breakneck speed across the broken ground, stumbling on heather roots and sliding over damp stones, until he reached the road. The rest followed him more slowly. The trap drew to a stand, and the occupants jumped down.

'My, but you are the gentleman to drive the horseflesh,' Jones muttered, standing at the horses' heads. 'Look, here is Mr Fenton himself, and the young ladies and all.'

Adam Khan stood by, looking spruce and calm, while Gerry pumped Peter's arm. Peter's black hair was dishevelled, and beads of mist made his face shine as though he had just come out of the sea. 'We caught an earlier train, sir,' he said cheerfully.

Her father said: 'We weren't expecting you till the evening, but Mrs Fenton's down at the house and Jones knows the way. Go on down and get settled in.'

'Indeed, yes, Mr Fenton, but I'll drive, myself, down the hill, young gentleman.'

'Why don't you come along with us?' Gerry cried eagerly. 'Let Jones take the luggage down. Uncle G and I are going to do the South Crack. We've got enough lunch for Peter and Adam, haven't we?'

'Oh, *yes*,' Peggy said. 'Tom's bringing it up on the pony, but Bertha always sends out enough for ten people.'

'Well, what do you say?' Gerry was like a big golden retriever begging to be taken for a walk.

Adam Khan said: 'Just as you wish, Peter.'

Peter Savage was glancing down at his thin shoes. Finally, 'All right,' he said.

Peggy said: 'Good!' Emily said nothing.

So they left Jones the trap to take the luggage on down to Llyn Gared, and again set off across the moor. Peggy had cut in just ahead of Emily and behind Peter Savage, who walked behind Gerry. Adam Khan was behind Emily's father, who was leading, and that left her at the back.

Daddy was trying to talk to Adam Khan. He'd better be careful. What did he know of India? What did any of them know? – except Peter Savage, presumably. The less Gerry knew, or came to learn, the better she'd be pleased.

Peggy was pointing things out to Peter's back, naming for his benefit each of the mountain shapes that now climbed slowly out of the mist ahead, and the headlands and the sea behind. Peter answered briefly or not at all, for he was slipping and stumbling on the wet stones as he tried to keep up with the sharp pace set by Emily's father in front. She thought, looking at the backs of Peter's ears, that he would break his leg rather than ask for the pace to be slowed, that he was furious with himself because he could not keep his balance. Her father usually went at a slow, all-day pace. She wondered if he was going so fast on purpose, to vent some of his distaste for Mr Savage, or his jealousy of him. Or perhaps to show Gerry that Peter Savage wasn't a natural-born genius at *everything*. She flushed lightly –

that would have been her own idea; but it wasn't Daddy's or Gerry's.

'A little slower, Uncle G,' Peggy called. 'Peter doesn't have any nails in his shoes.'

'I'm all right,' Peter said shortly, and Emily saw him look briefly at Peggy; but her father apologized and they went on at a more reasonable pace until they reached the *cirque* below the east face of Cader Brith. It was twelve o'clock, and the mist had risen from the crest. The sun shone athwart the mountain, forcing the crags and promontories into sharp relief against the purple shadows in the gulfs and crevices.

'The sun will be off it by three,' Gerry said thoughtfully. 'Do you think it'll have dried out enough for us to start after lunch?'

'I think so,' her father said. 'There's Cader Brith for you, Savage. There are eleven ways up this face. According to these modern gradings, five are easy, two moderately difficult, three difficult, and one very difficult. Look, there's the Spire route...' He had sat down on a rock, the three young men round him, and was off on his favourite subject – after the Matterhorn – the beauties of Cader Brith.

The arrival of Tom with the lunch went almost unnoticed, and Emily and Peggy unpacked it and spread it out. 'Lunch, Daddy!' Emily called at last, and then they gathered round and began to eat.

She found that Adam Khan had placed himself next to her. Peggy, Gerry, and her father were taking turns in explaining more about the mountains to Peter Savage and snatching mouthfuls of food between sentences. Tom ate by himself a little distance off, listening to the mountain talk and occasionally throwing in a piece of local lore. She and the Indian might have been on Mars.

After a long silence she said, smiling: 'Can you see the Himalaya from Rudwal? I found it on the map.'

Adam Khan said: 'Wonderful! Yes, we can see the snows all the year round.'

She said: 'How beautiful! And when you come down from King's next year you'll go and live there all your life? Just like Gerry going to Wilcot?'

'Not quite. As a matter of fact, my father is going to be quite angry with me. He is old-fashioned, but he did convince himself that the I.C.S was the best thing for me, and for the family. He had me educated at the Prince's School, and then sent me to Cambridge. I was to take the examination next year. My tutor thought I would stand a good chance.'

'There's a lot of competition, though, isn't there? Daddy said so. He wondered how Mr Savage – Peter – could be quite so sure he was going to get in.'

Adam said: 'Oh, there is no doubt of that – but I have decided not to sit for the exam. at all. You see, I had hoped to get the Rudwal district, though it was very unlikely they would post me there, since it is my home. But Peter wants to go there and I realized that I could do more by helping him in Rudwal than by becoming a D.C myself in some other place. Peter and I have talked it over a lot since May Week. But, as I said,

I fear my father will not be pleased. He will not give me much responsibility for the estate, so I shall be hanging about.' He shrugged with a suddenly very un-English gesture of the hands.

They glanced over at the other group; her father was pointing, Gerry explaining rapidly, Peter Savage standing, silent, staring up at the jagged rocks.

Adam said: 'I think he was wrong to give up cricket. A Blue would do him more good in the I.C.S than a First. That is the English custom – ours too. Our people remember the champions at *kabaddi,* and the great hunters and wrestlers, when they have forgotten the subadars and lieutenant-governors.' Now they were both staring at Peter Savage's back – as though hypnotized, she thought angrily. Adam said: 'It is an exciting thing to be a friend of Peter's. But a little frightening, too, sometimes, Miss Fenton. We have a proverb: "When the lightning plays about a man's head, stay close – that the rain may also fall on you." The proverb doesn't say anything about being struck by the lightning.'

For a time they ate in silence. Then Adam said in a low voice: 'My father thinks I am a weakling because I talk with the cultivators on our land, and argue, instead of telling them what to do. But I think that I too have a destiny – no, that is a bad word – a fate, Miss Fenton, just as Peter *knows* he has. He knows what must be done, and he says: "Do it," and the people do it. But if we Indians are to grow, to fit ourselves into this modern world, the people must know *why* they do it, and they must agree that it is good, and *understand.* I

64

am an Indian – I keep telling you, do I not? but it is very important. When Peter says: "Do this," *I* can make the people understand, so Peter's work will be done properly. Later, many years later, it can be the other way round, so that the people will say: "Do this," and men like Peter will do it – but that will not be in my time, I think, or perhaps in my son's.'

'Your son!' She gasped. 'I mean, I didn't know–'

He looked at her quizzically. 'I am twenty-four, Miss Fenton. I was married at the age of eighteen. She was not a child bride – that is a Hindu custom – and our son was born three years later. He is called Baber, after the first Mogul emperor, who was also a poet. He is a very beautiful child – but it is a long time since I have seen him.'

'Haven't you finished eating yet, Emily?' her father called. 'Tom wants to get back.' She got up with a start and hurriedly helped Peggy repack the hampers. Adam Khan, a father! No wonder he seemed more mature and spoke of large, important things in such a serious way.

'Now,' her father said, 'Gerry and I may as well start up. Are you all going to stay here? Or watch from the side? Savage, what about you?'

'I'll go up,' Peter Savage said at once.

'The grass is pretty slippery.'

'I'll take my shoes off.' He glanced at Adam Khan and asked: 'Are you going to stay here with Miss Fenton?'

'I'm coming up,' Emily said shortly and waited, looking somewhere else, until they were all ready.

65

For a time they followed Gerry and her father up the detritus slope at the foot of the *cirque*. Peter Savage's feet must have hurt on the sharp rocks, but he didn't give any sign of it and climbed up steadily and with increasing speed, until he was at Gerry's heels.

After half an hour's strenuous but gradual ascent they reached the foot of the cliff. A slope of grass and occasional rock continued on up, though more steeply, to the summit seven hundred feet above. To the left stretched the black cliffs of Cader Brith, six hundred feet, almost vertical, not smooth, but split by fissures, crevices, and narrow chimneys.

Gerry and her father roped up, Gerry leading. The rest of them, led by Peter, scrambled on up the grass until Peggy called breathlessly: 'There, Peter! That's the best place to watch from.' They sank down in a group and looked across the face of the cliff. The pair of climbers was already a hundred feet up above the detritus, and going fast. 'They're on an easy pitch,' Peggy said importantly. 'Each separate part of a climb is called a pitch. The next one's easy too. The one after that, level with us, is the bad one on that route.'

'They all look difficult to me,' Adam Khan said cheerfully.

'Gerry and Uncle G are good climbers,' Peggy said.

'I am sure. But why do they climb by a difficult route when there is an easy one?' Adam Khan asked.

'For practice,' Peggy said a little impatiently.

'Practice for what, Lady Margaret?'

'The Alps.'

'Ah,' Adam Khan said, but Emily thought: There's a snag in that answer somewhere. It's plausible, but it's not really true – and what were people in the Alps practising for?

Peter Savage said: 'It's not for practice. It's so they can be afraid.' He was lying on his stomach where the grass verge hung over the cliff, chin on his cupped hands, intently watching the two men on the rope.

Peggy said eagerly: 'I see what you mean... This is the difficult pitch now. See, where that ridge of knobby rock gives out they have to work up that tiny crack – the South Crack. Gerry and Uncle G have done it half a dozen times, but it's always exciting.'

Emily's breathing quickened as it always did when she saw any climbers reaching an obstacle that was going to test them near their limit. And these, to her, weren't 'any climbers.' They were her father and Gerry.

Gerry had edged his fingers into the crack and placed his feet against the wall on either side for the sake of what little friction they could find. He went up slowly, and she could see the painful grimness of his expression as he relied almost wholly on his fingers to get him up. Her father, twenty feet lower down, had belayed the rope round a buttress of rock and then over one shoulder and out under the other arm. Slowly he paid out the rope towards Gerry, so that there was always enough but never any slack.

'Why doesn't Mr Fenton give him more rope?'

67

Peter asked suddenly.

'Because if Gerry should fall the extra slack would jerk tight and make it more likely that the rope would break,' Emily said, trying to make it sound like an obvious answer to a foolish question.

'What's the breaking strain of that rope?' he asked then, at once.

'Oh, I don't know, about–'

'Three hundred pounds, I think,' Peggy said.

'It'll break anyway, then, if Gerry falls. There'd be all the distance between him and Mr Fenton as slack. Twenty feet.'

'The leading man *mustn't* fall,' Peggy said, repeating the lesson that had been drummed into them over and over again.

Peter Savage said: 'No.'

Gerry was sweating, although the sun was almost off the rock and there was little heat in its rays. Now his face showed no sign of strain, though when he took one hand out of the crack to reach for a hand-hold Emily saw that he had to press down so hard that his fingernails went white. He wasn't afraid, she realized suddenly, thinking of Peter Savage's remark. This had been a difficult place to him once, but it was so no longer. Of course he had grown several inches since he first tried it, and his physical strength was much greater. Then, looking down, she saw in her father's anxious concentration that with him time was moving the other way, past the crest and down towards the valley. He *was* afraid, and he was overcoming it.

A pause, another long, slow reach up – like a

caterpillar moving – and Gerry edged himself wholly into the top of the widened crack. Only the outward pressure of feet and back held him there. He raised one leg, pressed it firmly against the opposite side, and then raised the other to join it. Pressing down and back with his hands and gradually straightening his arched back, he crept upward.

'Chimneying,' Peter Savage said. 'That's what Walsh was doing. Gerry could climb King's Chapel.'

Gerry reached the top of the chimney and made a firm belay round a low, thick pinnacle of rock. Peggy cried: 'Well done, Gerry,' and Emily sighed with relief.

Peter Savage rose quickly to his feet and said: 'Now, can't we do something?'

Emily said: 'Wait a minute. Daddy's still climbing.'

'He's all right. I don't think he could have led up there, though.'

'Oh, yes, he could,' she said. 'He has, lots of times.'

Peter Savage turned his head slightly and looked at her as he had in the ballroom at King's, the sudden switching on of a powerful electric lamp that stripped away not the clothes from her body but the polite shawls from her thoughts, so that she knew she feared him as well as disliked him – and that he knew it. That look, without words, repeated her last phrase, with a deadly emphasis on the word 'has.' She had to admit that her father could not *now* lead up the South Crack of the East Face of Cader Brith. The sullen inner voice went on to repeat another prime maxim of mountaineering: 'If you can't lead up a climb, you have no business to be on it at all.'

But Peter turned away without any word. Her father reached the top of the crack, and then he and Gerry began to work quickly towards them along a broad grass ledge that traversed the cliff a little above the head of the crack, and soon joined them on the grass. As soon as Gerry had sat down, and while he was drinking copiously from the flask of hot tea that Peggy carried slung round her shoulders Emily said: 'Gerry, when you've rested let's go up the Spire – you and Peggy and I.'

Gerry nodded as he handed back the flask. 'Thanks, Peg. That's a good idea. Uncle G, do you want to come?' Her father shook his head, and Gerry turned to Peter. 'The Spire's not so hard as the crack, and you can see more clearly what's going on.' He pointed to a gaunt ridge of rock and shale that rose up on the far side of the grass slope. The ridge towered into a pinnacle almost a hundred feet high that stood away from the side of Cader Brith like a chimney from a gable roof. 'You and Adam can watch from here.'

'I'd like to come with you,' Peter Savage said.

Exasperated, Emily turned to flare at him. He was looking exactly as he had just before the punt race. He was going to 'win.' But he was on the wrong track now, because there was no 'winning' in mountaineering. Her father came to her help. He said gravely: 'That's not an easy climb for a beginner, Savage. And you don't have any boots.'

'I'll go in my socks,' Peter said, 'the way I am now.'

Her father moved his shoulders uncomfortably. He had made his opinion plain, and this young man had no business to press his own against it. It was not done; it was bad manners.

But Peggy said: 'Peter will be all right, Uncle G. It's not a *hard* climb.'

And Gerry said: 'I'll turn back if there's any need, Uncle G. Leave it to me – only, four's too many on the rope. We'd have to make two parties.'

Emily said at once: 'I'll stay.'

Gerry said: 'But Emily, it was you–'

'It doesn't matter. Mr Savage will only be here for a few days.'

'Well, in that case… That'll be all right, Uncle G, won't it?'

Her father hesitated a moment longer, then said gruffly: 'Very well. You're not children any more. We'll watch from here. Peggy, you'd better give me that flask.'

Gerry sprang to his feet and picked up the rope. 'Now, Peter,' he said, 'you've got to learn how to tie the rope.' He uncoiled it carefully and, smiling happily, showed it to Peter. 'The rope is to save other people in case of a slip – *not you*. When you are moving, you must imagine that the rope doesn't exist. Now, the end-men tie themselves on to the rope with a double-knotted bowline, like this.'

'Wait a moment,' Peter said. 'Let me practice that.' He untied the knot and retied it; then again, twice more.

'Jolly good,' Gerry said enthusiastically. 'Anyone not at the end uses a triple butterfly, or a double bowline – so.' Again Peter practised, never making a mistake, the first knot tied slowly, the second a little faster, the third almost as fast as Gerry's experienced hands had been able to make it.

'There are other knots for special purposes,' Gerry said, 'but we don't want to go into those now. The only other things you must know about now are the belay and the anchor. Did you see that when Uncle G was coming up the crack after me I was pulling in the rope so that it came in under my left armpit and then over my shoulder before I let it coil?' Peter nodded. 'That was a body belay. But before it got to me at all it came round a knob of firm rock? That was a rock belay. The idea of all that was that *if* Uncle G slipped, the strain wouldn't come directly on me or on the end of the rope where the coils had run out. There would have been friction brakes, first round the rock and then round my body. Those belays were on the rope between me, a stationary man, and Uncle G, a man in movement. We call any piece of rope like that "live" rope. Then, did you see that I'd used the length of rope left behind my knot, the end piece, to loop round the same knob of rock? That was "dead" rope, because it didn't lead to a man in movement. I'd anchored myself to the rock with it.'

Peter said: 'A man not in motion should tie himself on to the mountain if necessary. But only with dead rope. That's an anchor. A man at either end of a live rope should pay the rope out round his body, round rocks, et cetera, to the man climbing. That's a belay.'

'Jolly good,' Gerry cried, beaming. 'Now, suppose the leader's climbing and there are three on the rope. Can Number Two use some of the rope between himself and Number Three to make an anchor?'

Peter said: 'Yes. If the leader's in movement, Two and Three should not be. So all the rope behind Two is dead.'

'Dead for the time being,' Gerry said. 'Good. All ready? We won't be long, Emily.'

They trudged off across the grass towards the foot of the Spire. Emily lay on her side to watch. She knew her father would have liked to say something about Peter Savage, but with Adam Khan there he could not. Instead he got out his pipe and began the ritual of lighting it. Adam Khan said thoughtfully: 'Peter has really made up his mind to be a mountaineer.'

'He has the determination, all right,' her father said. 'Climbing in thin socks, on that rock! He'll never get to the top – but everyone has to learn their lesson some time. It comes harder to some than to others.'

'Yes, sir,' Adam Khan said softly, 'but all the same, I think the mountains had better look out for themselves.'

Her father flung away his tenth match and said between puffs: 'The mountains – have to be – loved, too.'

Three hours later they were all striding back down the rough path towards Llyn Gared, and the sun had long since left the valleys. There was, unfortunately, no doubt about one thing: Peter Savage was going to be good. At first, on the Spire route, he had seemed to be imitating Gerry's movements, for he put his hands and feet exactly where Gerry did. Later his method changed, and for a time, as Emily stared up at them on the rock, she could not make out what was so distinctive about these new movements – a distinction which would have enabled her to pick him out from farther away than she could recognize his features. It was Adam Khan who put the words to it, saying: 'Look at Peter now. He's dancing.'

That was it: when his turn came to move, he now moved with a rhythm so pronounced and ceaseless that it was almost comical – never stopping, never checking, seldom taking long strides, the whole giving the impression of a professional dancer's grace, a little exaggerated, flashy perhaps, but none the less powerful and real. Twice he slipped, though not in bad places, and after that she noticed that he did not use hand-holds at all. She said to herself reassuringly: 'It is an easy climb.'

But it was not really easy, though, it called for nerve more than for technique or physical strength. In one place the traverse along a narrow ledge, though amply wide enough for a man to stand on in comfort, had to be made while facing out over a sheer hundred-foot drop. In the middle of the traverse Peter Savage stopped. At once she heard Gerry's voice, calling down to him, hollow and suddenly loud in the high *cirque:*

'Keep moving, Peter! You're doing fine. Look up, look up!' Instead Peter leaned out (while Gerry's voice echoed from the great face of Cader Brith behind, 'Up – up!'), and slowly bent his head until he was looking straight down the drop. Then, as slowly, he straightened and danced on along the ledge.

The fool! He might have been overcome with giddiness; even the best were, sometimes. But it was obvious that he had not found fear there. She had thought for a moment that he was wearing tennis shoes with red rubber soles, and that was why he went so surely up the sloping rocks. Then she remembered that he had no shoes on, and what she saw were his bloodstained socks.

When they all came down he washed his feet carefully in the steam and Peggy said: 'They must be awfully painful.'

He looked up at her, his wide mouth creasing his face in the sudden, brilliant smile. His feet were turning blue in the bitter water, and the purple stain thinned in the current as the cuts froze. He said: 'They are. It was worth it, though.' Peggy was very solicitous and proud. As soon as they reached the house she had hurried to fetch iodine for him, and reminded him to put it on at once.

Now it was after dinner, and Emily and her mother and Peggy were sitting with coffee in the drawing-room, waiting for the gentlemen to join them. The deep murmur of their voices filtered through the house from the dining-room where they were still gathered, half an hour after dinner, over their port and cigars.

Her mother suddenly said: 'Peggy, if you want *that* young man to like you, don't make calf's eyes at him quite so obviously. I don't think he has much use for doormats.'

Peggy sat up with a start, spilling her coffee into the saucer. 'Who, Mally? I haven't been making calf's eyes at anyone.'

'You know who I mean,' Emily's mother said in a gentler tone, smiling. 'There's nothing wrong with liking him – but don't be a doormat. A man standing on a doormat can only reach an inch or two higher than he can without it – and Peter's a climber.'

'He will be,' Peggy said breathlessly. 'He's *marvellous*, Mally. The very first time on rock, and he's nearly as good as Gerry already.'

'I didn't mean that kind of climber,' her mother said. 'I know it's not fashionable to warn young ladies about their behaviour these days, but I'm not going to leave you to your own judgement without a word of advice. You're in love. *You* know. *I* know, because this is the first time. Emily's had twenty mashes since she fell in love with Jones the post when she was twelve – but not you. Also, I'm afraid that you've got to remember that you have a "Lady" before your name, an earl for a father, and can expect a very large private income.'

'What difference does that make?' Peggy muttered unhappily, and Emily stared at her mother in astonishment. Mally had never spoken like this before. Peter Savage loomed suddenly as a brightly-coloured and fierce man-eating tiger, that he could have caused this outburst.

Her mother said: 'It makes no difference to you, dear, because you are a sweet girl. But there are plenty of men in the world, gentlemen even, to whom it would make a great deal of difference. Peter has no private means. In fact, he's penniless, and I really don't know how his grandfather can afford to keep him at King's.'

'How do you know all this?' Peggy asked feebly.

'Because I took the trouble to find out, after what I saw at the May Week ball,' Mally said, nodding her beautiful gladiolus head. 'As you know, he has no parents. His father disappeared most mysteriously in India. I hope he was not mentally deranged. His mother died of cholera some years later.'

'It's awful for him,' Peggy said. 'He's an orphan!'

Mally looked at Peggy with exasperation; then her expression softened and she reached out and caught the girl's hand. 'And you're only seventeen, Peggy. It's time we spent a season or two in London.'

'I think Peter's nice,' Peggy said slowly, 'but he won't take any notice of me. I'm too young.'

'I should think so. And he has a career to start on. *And* we will now talk about something else.'

'We're almost as old as Adam Khan was when he married,' Emily said suddenly. 'Probably two or three years older than his wife was.'

'That nice young man, married!' her mother exclaimed. 'It's not fair on mothers of daughters – Indian mothers, of course. But they'd know, wouldn't they?' She struck a hand-bell on the table beside her. Alice, the parlourmaid, hobbled in. She was thin and forty, always wore shoes too small for her, and believed herself to be the object of the unbridled lust which inhabited all men.

Mally said: 'Alice, go and tell David to tell Mr Fenton that we've sat here long enough.'

Alice's grim face relaxed into a gloomy satisfaction. 'Yes, madam,' she said, and hobbled out.

Soon afterwards the men trooped in, Emily's father tugging at the lapels of his dinner-jacket, Gerry self-consciously straightening his tie, Adam Khan silently laughing, and Peter Savage smiling. 'Sorry, my dear,' her father growled. 'Forgot the time. We were having a most interesting talk.'

'Well, have it here,' Mally said.

Emily's father sank into his favourite chair, the one he disliked least among the Chippendales in the drawing-room. 'We were talking about next summer. Peter is really taken by the idea of climbing, and Gerry's very keen for us to meet in Zermatt – Harry Walsh is going to be there – immediately after the boys come down from King's. Or we might all go out together.'

'Mr Khan too?' she heard her mother say in a low voice.

'No, he'll be sailing for India.'

Emily watched her mother pondering, her eyes sweeping from Peggy to herself, then to Peter and Gerry talking comfortably in a far corner. Her father had succumbed to Peter somehow, too, or he would not have broached the subject in public, making it difficult for her mother to refuse.

Her mother spoke at last. 'I think that might be a good plan, George.'

Emily turned to look at Gerry. She examined him closely as he talked to his friend, and wondered: Why do I not feel the same about him as Peggy does about Peter Savage? He is tall, handsome, brave, generous. I have never heard him say an unkind word or seen him do an unsportsmanlike thing. He can climb and ride and fish and shoot. His eyes are brown and gentle, and his face handsome and not weak.

Peter Savage's eyes were flashing, and his hand lay light on Gerry's sleeve. There was an eagerness in Gerry's grin and a lift in his voice as he said: 'Peter, Whymper's the greatest climber who ever lived! I'll introduce you to him in Zermatt.' And Peggy's face was alive with colour.

'Books! I'll read all of them.' That was Peter's clear, light tenor – and the others, laughing: 'You can't! There are hundreds.'

Adam Khan's low voice beside her said: 'You know, Miss Fenton, he likes Gerry just as much as Gerry likes him. David and Jonathan. Don't forget that.'

She whispered: 'Why do they laugh so? I didn't see anything funny in what he said.'

He was looking down at her gravely. 'To him everything is brighter, harder, clearer than it is to us. While you are with him, he can make you see it the same way.'

She got up quickly. It was true. Already she knew it: he had made the rocks of Cader Brith a luridly lit theatre, and in this drawing-room every colour shone more brilliantly – unnaturally brilliant to her eyes. But somehow she must find the strength to fight him, because soon Gerry, her Gerry, the Gerry she hoped desperately that one day she would fall in love with, would be made into someone else. How soon? Peter and Gerry would have only another year together. To become the best climbers in the world? They would need far more, just for that alone, or Peter would have to admit failure – or give up the whole idea. He didn't give up... David and Jonathan. What happened to *them?*

CHAPTER 5

They spent so little time at 27 Minden Square that to Emily the little Georgian house behind Oxford Street always seemed to belong to some other family. But it was summer again, 1903, and there was a familiar smell in the unfamiliar rooms, and for the moment the place had become a kind of extension of home. The packing was done, but she could still smell new rope and old wax; the sweaty, greased leather of her father's favourite climbing boots; the heavy sweetness of the linseed oil on the shafts of the ice axes. The clop of hoofs and the animal creak and grind of London traffic filled the house, roaring aloud at all the opened windows, to intensify her excitement with their pointless urgency.

'George, it's time we went,' her mother said. 'You've read *The Times* twice already. Do you suppose the old gentleman will give us curry?'

'I don't know. Why should he?' her father grumbled, laying down his paper. 'He's a member of the Athenæum. Harvey!'

'Sir?' Her father's valet appeared at the door with packing straw twined in his thin hair.

'You'll have all the heavy baggage in the guard's van, and you'll meet us at the barrier, eh?'

'Yes, sir,' Harvey said mournfully.

'The Chatham side at Victoria, and we'll be

there at three o'clock sharp. Can't remember what platform.'

'Yes, sir,' Harvey intoned.

Her mother said: 'Really, George! Harvey and Rhondda know perfectly well what to do. They've done it ten times if they've done it once. It wasn't Harvey who went to Waterloo that year.'

'The cabby misunderstood me,' her father said heatedly. 'I told him quite plainly, Victoria, and the damned fool—'

'George! Are you ready, Emily?'

'Yes, Mummy!'

Her mother's perfunctory, motherly glance became suddenly a sharp appraisal. She said: 'You're growing up fast, too fast. You look about twenty-five.'

'Oh, Mally!' She couldn't help glowing with pleasure, while adding to herself: Twenty-five? It doesn't exist; sixteen I know, and eighteen I know, because I alternate between them; but twenty-five, that perfection seven impossible years away – never.

In a moment they were in the cab and clattering through the park towards 243 Nashe Street in Kensington, on their way to have lunch with Major-General Rodney Savage, C.B, Indian Army, retired, the grandfather of Peter Savage, B.A (Hons), now a senior member of Cambridge University. Yes, they'd all got through, Gerry and Adam Khan with good seconds, Peter with a brilliant first.

'I suppose Harry Walsh will have been up and down the Matterhorn by five different routes by the time we get out to Zermatt,' her father said, peering mistrustfully out of the window at the Albert Memorial. 'Good boy, Walsh.'

Emily thought: Yes, Harry Walsh is nice, and Mally hopes that Peggy will get a mash on him to take her mind off Peter Savage. What a hope!

Her father went on: 'Walsh is nearly as attached to that mountain as I am. And much more securely.' He chuckled delightedly and rubbed his hands together.

'I don't doubt it,' her mother said. 'How long has he been in Zermatt already – three weeks? Don't people's stocks and shares require *any* attention these days?'

'The future owner of Walsh and Drummond needn't sit over a desk like a clerk,' her father said. 'And even if it is business he's thinking of – which he isn't, he's a gentleman – he'd do better to meet people in Zermatt, so that they get to know and trust him, rather than learn anything about stockbroking. Walsh and Drummond act for a good many members of the Alpine Club, and we aren't all paupers yet, though–'

'Number Two-forty-three?' the cabby said. 'Here you are, sir.'

It was not a big house by London standards, but Emily found herself thinking, as they waited after ringing the bell, that it must seem empty to an old man living by himself, however many servants he had. It would be lonelier still when Peter had sailed for India. A little of him could make quite a large house seem full – overfull.

After a moment the door was opened, and a man of medium height with thick grey-white hair and snapping blue eyes faced them from the doorway. He stood very erect, and his jaw was lean, though the flesh fell away below and at his collar his neck showed like an old cockerel's. That was almost the only sign of age about him, but he was old, she knew – seventy-five, eighty perhaps. And poor. To open his own door to invited callers!

'Mr Fenton?' he said. He had a light voice, a little rasping, and the eyes were darker blue than his grandson's, but with the same icy quality. Now other footsteps ran quickly, lightly down the stairs, and there were Peter and Adam Khan.

'Grandfather, may I introduce you to Mrs Fenton? Mrs Fenton – General Savage... Mr Fenton... Miss Fenton...'

The old man was staring at her, like an old hawk. Her mother said: 'Have Lord Manningford and Lady Margaret Holcombe arrived yet? They were coming direct from their father's.' She glanced meaningly at the door.

The old general grinned suddenly, a grin that made him look for that moment younger than his grandson and said: 'My apologies, Mrs Fenton. I was admiring your daughter. She is no longer a child, so I can say that she is beautiful.'

'Oh, you mustn't say that in front of her, General,' her mother said amiably. 'She will get a swelled head.' They were in the musty hall now, and Peter was helping Emily out of her travelling coat.

'I am a very old man, Mrs Fenton,' the general said. 'I was born in the reign of King George the Fourth, and I can say anything, particularly to young ladies.'

84

They climbed a flight of stairs and entered a large drawing-room full of bronze and brass and heavy curtains. It was a typical room, one of several Emily had seen like it, but made different, lifted completely out of its class, by four oil paintings on the wall opposite the windows. They were portraits, and as she sat down she eyed them surreptitiously. One was of an Indian woman with a veil across her forehead and huge dark eyes, one of a child of about two and a half with fair curly hair, one of a woman in her late twenties, the fourth of a man in dark green uniform. The man held a big shako loosely in his right arm; his careless, strong left hand rested on a silver sword; his hair was thick; and black, black whiskers curled flamboyantly across his cheeks, and his eyes were snapping, glacier blue.

Adam Khan handed round sherry. Peter, who had been sitting next to her on an ottoman, looked at his watch and said: 'Gerry and Peggy ought to be here by now, Grandfather.'

A bell rang, clanging heavily in the lower reaches of the house. The general said: 'Go down please, Peter. Ashraf's still busy cooking.'

Peter left the room, and Emily began wondering how he was going to be able to afford these two months in the best rooms the Monte Rosa Hotel had to offer, with all the expenses of guides, picnics, and excursions that would also fall on him. There was no money to burn here. But perhaps her mother was wrong and he had money of his own somewhere, though she doubted it. Once or twice during his stay at Llyn Gared last summer he had said something that showed he had no expectations – and was perhaps a little over-conscious of the fact.

The door opened, and Peggy came in. Peter Savage, at her shoulder, introduced her quickly and then turned abruptly to Mally. 'Peggy says Gerry's sick, Mrs Fenton. He ran a temperature this morning, suddenly. He thinks he won't be able to come with us.'

Peggy said: 'He feels *awful* about it, Mally. He says he'll follow on in a few days, when he's better.'

'What about you, Peggy?' Emily's mother asked. 'Are you going to stay with him?'

'I feel I ought to. He says I mustn't. Father's there, and the servants of course.' She turned to Peter and said apologetically: 'He's really feeling rotten, Peter.'

Peter had gone taut; his eyes were narrower and his voice tinged with an edge of sharpness. He said: 'I'll go and see him, Grandfather. At once. Now. Do you mind?'

'You'll be missing a good lunch,' the old man said calmly, 'but run along. He's your friend, and you ought to see him before you go off to Switzerland.'

'I'll meet you all at the train,' Peter said from the door. 'I'm taking my things with me now.' The door closed behind him.

Peggy sat down slowly at Emily's side. 'I don't know what it is,' she said miserably. 'The doctor should be there by now, but—'

'It's a shame,' Emily said. She wondered if she too should ask to go and see him; but her mother would not permit it.

Then a tall, white-bearded Indian, older than the general and wearing a long white coat and a white turban, stood, bowed with age, in the door and shouted in a loud and cracked voice a few words in a strange language; and the general answered him; and they went in to lunch. Emily found herself at the foot of the table with her father on her right and Adam Khan on her left.

Beyond Adam Khan her mother was saying: 'Since Peter is not here, General, I suppose *I* can say, though I was not born in the reign of King George the Fourth, thank you, that he's a brilliant young man.'

'He'll go a long way,' her father said, nodding heavily.

The old general agreed abstractedly. 'Yes, Peter's got brains. You have to have brains to get into the I.C.S these days. And brains will get a man on – these days. But a man isn't remembered in India for his brains. Character, I suppose you'd call it, is what makes a man retire feeling he's *done* something, regardless of how high he climbed. He's applied for the Punjab Commission, Adam. And then he's going to try for Rudwal. But you know that.'

'The Punjab is large, sir,' the young Indian said with a smile, 'but we both hope he can get it.'

'Didn't you say there were mountains near your home, Khan?' her father broke in. 'If there are, Peter will get there somehow. He's a most determined young man – and a really amazingly gifted climber.'

'I would hardly call them "near",' the general said with a slow smile. 'The crest line of the range is about a hundred and twenty miles in – but of course it climbs all the way from the plains in ridges and valleys, each one grander than the last. Magnificent country. There are five peaks over twenty-one thousand feet in that area, and the lowest pass over into Parasia and western Tibet is thirteen thousand, eight hundred. *I* know. Went over it in 'sixty-seven, after *ovis ammon.* Isn't the Rudwal District one of the largest in India, Adam?'

'Yes, sir. And with almost the smallest population. Apart from Rudwal City and the belt of villages along the foothills, where the Maghra comes out of the mountains, there's really nothing. I believe actually the district is far the largest in India – because there's no inner boundary.'

He smiled happily at Emily. He was thinking of his own country, his own land, and she felt happy for him and with him, though her imagination could conjure up from these strange words and names only a vision of some vastly magnified Zermatt.

'Ah, yes,' the general said, equally happy, 'the Tibetans have never agreed on a boundary commission. The last time I saw Younghusband he told me – Mrs Fenton, I do apologize. Indian shop talk, at my age! Are you sure you wouldn't care for a little more meat?'

'No, thank you,' her mother said. 'And I was not at all bored. In fact, I'd like to know just what a member of the Indian Civil Service does. I have tried to get Peter to tell me, but he didn't seem to have the time. He was too busy on Cader Brith or Snowdon or Cader Idris.'

And, Emily thought, going his mysterious, locked-in way at other times. It was now July, 1903, a year since his first visit to Llyn Gared. There had been ten days at Llyn Gared over last Christmas, a couple of debutante dances, three theatres, a visit to the zoo, and finally May Week at King's again – she and Gerry, Peggy and Peter; but she didn't know any more about him than when she had first met him, nor did Peggy. They had learned as much as one learns of a steam engine from being hauled around the countryside by it.

The general laughed and said: 'You tell Mrs Fenton about the I.C.S, Adam.'

Adam Khan slowly crumbled a piece of bread on his side plate. He said: 'Once Parliament has decided what to do in India, and the Secretary of State in London has sent a letter to the Governor-General in Calcutta telling him to do it – there is the matter of getting it done. The Governor-General – who is also the Viceroy – tells the governor or lieutenant-governor of each province. They are mostly of the I.C.S. The governors tell the commissioners of each division – all I.C.S. The commissioners tell the deputy commissioners of each district – all I.C.S. There are about two hundred districts in India, so I suppose they must have an average population of a million each. The man the people see the most of, the most important man, is the one at the bottom, the district officer – the deputy commissioner. He controls the police through a superintendent of police. He is the district magistrate and can give sentences up to two years. He can try revenue and settlement cases. He assesses and collects taxes. He tells us how to improve the breed of our cattle and the drainage of our fields, and what crops we should plant. He builds roads and bridges and schools. He is the government. He is very nearly – God.'

Mally had been listening with surprised interest. Now she said, but slowly and with a half-glance at the general: 'It sounds very autocratic. What do the people think of it? What do *you* think, after Cambridge?'

Adam Khan said: 'It is no different from what has always been. Only the I.C.S are honest, and the Mogul and Sikh officials were corrupt. The I.C.S are also foreign – most of them. That doesn't mean Indians dislike them, Mrs Fenton. It was the Sikhs whom we hated, but even while we hated them we could understand them. I doubt if there are more than a handful of Indians, in India, who don't believe, now, in the I.C.S and the I.C.S system, especially if they know or have heard what India was like for the last hundred years or so before Warren Hastings. But the I.C.S have never tried very hard to get across this barrier, that we think differently. That is what I am going to try and help with. That is why I am not going into the I.C.S.'

'What are you going to do?'

'My father thinks I am going to lead the life of a young nobleman until he is dead and I have the estate to look after – but I have other ideas. In a few years, if our plans work out right, Peter will become Deputy Commissioner of Rudwal. You

90

cannot imagine what we can do together – the people knowing what is being done and why, all of us striving to make Rudwal something new in India, leading the way! And then, as Peter goes up, perhaps I could go with him. To Lahore, capital of the Punjab. To Calcutta, capital of all India! Why not? There has not been a Viceroy from the Indian service for a long time, but why not? Peter could be another Warren Hastings. He was the first Governor-General of India – and the last who really understood India.'

For a moment Adam's animation, the frank eagerness of his expression, and the poetic fire in his voice made Emily stare open-mouthed at him, as though he had shown her one of his own secretly held visions.

Then the general said: 'By God, I wish I were going with you two. But heaven had better be with you when you try to explain all this to your father, Adam, if he's anything like the same man I knew in the 'seventies. That was the life, Fenton – a Punjabi Mussulman gentleman with land of his own and a huge *jagir* for services in the Mutiny. Twenty farms on it! Ghulam Afzul Khan, that's Adam's father, used to live like a baron in the days of King John – hawks on his hand, hunting dogs at his heel, a big sword at his waist. He'll think you've become an anarchist, a revolutionary, Adam.'

'Nothing has changed for my father,' Adam Khan said quietly, not smiling. 'But I am not a revolutionary. There are no serious Indians today, that I know of, who want independence now. A few want to go faster than others, but

that's all. Indians who think about it – not many
have the time or the education – want India to
become like England, and they know that they
will need England's help – guidance – for some
time. That's what Peter and I are going to do. But
– where is there a place for one of King John's
barons? The barons are dead, and all their way of
life with them. I sail the day after tomorrow. I
shall be glad to see my family again.'

His eyes suddenly filled with tears. The others
turned to one another and began to talk, but
Emily watched from the corner of her eye while
he got out a big silk handkerchief, carefully
wiped his eyes, and then arranged his fine-drawn
features into the controlled interest proper to a
Cambridge man.

The talk drifted about, pleasant and formless.
No one mentioned India again, and with an
effort Emily dismissed from her mind the gaudy
phrases, as arresting as strains of music heard
while passing a gypsy encampment, that had
stuck in her memory since Adam Khan and the
general had been talking. The old man was a little
tired now, she saw, and seemed to have
withdrawn from them to some restful place
where only he could go, an old man's bench
beside the flowing conversation. Then it was time
to leave, and they were gathered in the hall
downstairs, the stained glass in the upper panel
of the front door marking diamonds of red and
blue on her mother's back. The old general was
holding out Emily's coat to her.

She squirmed into it, and his light voice said in
her ear, not whispering but addressed so directly

to her that no one else listened: 'Don't let Peter bully you. It's better for everyone.'

'No,' she said, startled and off balance. 'I'm sure—'

Then they were outside and her father was hailing two cabs, and soon Peggy's cab dashed off at a hard gallop, Peggy leaning out of the window and calling: 'All my things are packed, Mally! I'll be there at the station – with Peter.' Emily settled back in the other cab, opposite her parents.

Her father said: 'A fine old gentleman. Did you notice those paintings, dear? I wonder who—'

But Emily was thinking: 'Don't let Peter bully you.' The general should have spoken to Peggy and laid yet more emphasis on those last words: 'It's better – for everyone.'

She closed her eyes, for she felt exhausted by the thought of what would have to happen to Peggy before she could stand up to Peter Savage – and it wasn't until she could do that that she would see him in his true colours. It was impossible to imagine Peggy doing it. If he'd the mind, he would make her what he chose to. It was none of her, Emily's, business, yet Peggy was her closest friend, although new barriers were growing up between them, and a mysterious sense of distance was destroying the old instantaneousness of contact. She loved Peggy as much, but she found herself standing back and saying: *This* is going to happen unless Peggy realizes *that;* and now it was impossible, as it had once been possible (lying on their stomachs on top of the walled garden, eating June strawberries and watching the grown-up visitors at tennis), to whisper in Peggy's ear: 'Isn't that man *awful?* He gives me creeps up and down my spine.'

'Wake up dear. We're here.' Her mother was tapping her on the knee, and the cab was clattering into the station yard at Victoria. There was a great bustle inside, and crowds of people passed to and fro, in and out, up and down, without pattern, under the grimed glass arch, and shafts of dusty sunlight struck down among them in solid bars. They joined a little river winding slowly towards the boat-train, the women's dust-coats and long skirts hiding their feet so that they flowed rustling on, and the men moving jerkily, in strides, like rocks and tree trunks caught in the current of the stream.

'Dover, Calais, Paris,' her father read aloud. 'Here we are.'

'There's Harvey,' her mother said.

Then they were on the platform, and the crowd was less, and Harvey was explaining with gloomy satisfaction that everything was in order, but Lady Margaret hadn't sent her luggage yet, and what was to be done about that, sir?

'Lady Margaret's on her way,' Mally began, and then Emily saw Peggy, hurrying clumsily down the platform towards them among the people. Her eyes were wide with excitement. 'Mally!' She gasped. 'Gerry's here!'

'What! I thought–'

'When I got back I found they'd gone. They're here!'

'The young gentlemen are in the next carriage forward, madam,' Harvey said. 'Lord Wilcot's man came about an hour ago and obtained a

94

private compartment – not without difficulty, ma'am. I thought you would know–'

Peggy whispered in Emily's ear: 'For heaven's sake, don't say anything, but they think Gerry is getting measles.'

They followed Emily's parents up the platform. 'Here, sir,' Harvey said. Peering into the compartment, Emily saw that the blinds on the far side were drawn and Gerry was lying at full length on one of the seats, covered with a travelling rug, a pillow under his head. Peter was sitting on the opposite seat, talking to him.

'Well!' her mother said sharply. 'What's the meaning of this?'

Gerry raised his head and waved weakly. 'Hello, Mally. I'm all right, really I am.'

'You don't look it,' her mother said. 'Oh dear, what it is to have a son who isn't your son. If I were your mother I'd take you straight back to bed at home.'

'I wouldn't go,' Gerry said with a wan grin. He glanced up at Peter as if for confirmation, then caught Emily's eye and said: 'Hello, Em. I'll be all right tomorrow.'

Peter looked at her then, and for a moment she held his stare before turning away. A fierce outflow of will was beating over her, over Gerry... Don't say anything, we're going, we're going! It was he who had made Gerry get up, though Gerry thought it was his own will. It was he who was scattering disease germs among them, and he who had used the coat of arms and the title to turn people out of this compartment. But there was nothing she could do about it now.

The guard walked down the platform, murmuring: 'Take your seats, please.' A whistle shrilled, and Emily said suddenly: 'Peggy and I'll get in with Gerry, Mally. We'll come back to you in a minute.' She opened the door and got in, followed, after a moment's hesitation, by Peggy. Her mother began to say something, but the whistle shrilled again, more insistently, and her parents hurried down to their own compartment. The train began to move, sliding gently along the platform, out into the brilliant sun, clanging over the river, winding importantly into the tangle of brick to the south-east.

Emily put her hand on Gerry's forehead and said: 'About a hundred and one. You *are* an ass, Gerry. Well, now you've done it I suppose you expect me to nurse you, and then I'll get measles.'

'Oh, no!' Gerry said. 'I never thought of that. I don't want that. Go on back to Mally and Uncle G, both of you.'

'It's done now,' she said, smiling brilliantly at Peter as she sat down beside him. 'Sit here, Peggy.'

But of course she'd been a fool and Peter had won again, because if she caught measles now it would not be at the same time as Gerry, but later – at the same time as Peter.

Peter said: 'We couldn't let measles stop us. Measles! We're on our way–'

'To the Matterhorn!' Peggy cried.

'By the Zmutt ridge!' Emily retorted; and then they were all laughing, and Emily could not stop herself from joining in, because after all they were on their way, and Gerry was with them.

CHAPTER 6

She stood on the steep slope of snow, the young sun warm on her right cheek, the ice-axe dug firmly in beside her and the tail of the rope from her waist anchored round it. Twenty feet diagonally up the slope the guide stood in exactly the same attitude, his goggled face turned up, the rope firm but not taut between him and the man, twenty feet up again, who was cutting steps. The step-cutter was standing in an awkward position, one foot directly behind the other in steps he had already cut, as he wielded the ice-axe with both hands. That was Peter Savage, leading the first rope up the south-east arête of the Wellenkuppe. She glanced back. The second rope – Harry Walsh, Peggy, and Gerry – was waiting a hundred feet down the slope and well behind.

'Not so fast, Herr Savage,' the guide growled. 'There is no hurry. But more small steps, *bitte*. The *Fräulein's* legs are not so long like yours.'

She glanced up again. Peter had been hitting so hard that the dislodged snow fell out in big scoops over the slope and hissed down, glittering in rainbow crystals as the sun shone through them. He appeared to have lost his balance from the force of his blows, just before Christian called, for he was steadying himself against the slope, and Christian was muttering something in *Schwyz-deutsch*.

There's no hurry, she repeated to herself. Come to that, there's no need for him to be in the lead on this slope, cutting these over-big steps as though the people behind him were wearing snow-shoes. But that was Peter; he *was* in a hurry, whatever the time of day; and he had to be in the lead because that was the only way he could learn what it felt like. They had argued in the hotel quite late the evening before, until finally Gerry gave in. 'All right,' he said, 'I don't suppose there's really much danger, with Christian behind you.'

Then Harry Walsh suggested that he make third on the rope. That would have made a very strong rope indeed, for Harry was as good as any of the guides – better, perhaps, in dealing with the unexpected. But Peter said: 'No, thanks. I'd feel as if I was being carried up in an armchair. Why not make it a *cordée* of two, Christian and I?'

'Four on the second rope?' Harry Walsh asked with a smile. 'That's not much fun.'

What a fuss, she thought, when only Harry and Christian Holz were going above the Wellen-kuppe anyway. Holz moved forward, and when she had moved up to where he had been, Peter turned and began another diagonal. Down the hill, Harry followed suit.

'Two hands on the axe, Herr Savage,' Christian said. 'With one hand it is impossible – nearly.'

'That's what I want to find out,' Peter grunted, in time with the blows of his axe. She saw that he was now using the axe one-handed.

She sighed and watched impatiently. It was tiring being harnessed like this, literally now, to

Peter's continuous relentless effort, even for a couple of hours. It must be about nine o'clock in the morning. They had started from the Monte Rosa Hotel at four. Now the sun was up and the long morning shadows climbing fast out of the valley towards the mountain-tops. The sun laid a line of fire along the eastern crest line – on the mountain Monte Rosa, sprawled across the head of its glaciers; on the Strahlhorn, the Rimpfischhorn, the Allalinhorn, the Täschhorn, the Dom. Turning to glance over her shoulder, she saw the sudden torrent of sunlight cascading down the east face of the Matterhorn where, caught between the soaring Hörnli and Furgg ridges, the mountain leaned like a breaking wave over the trench of the Zermatt valley.

Peter's thin upper lip was pearled with sweat, and his mouth was set in a tight, straight line. Did he feel anything for the mountains, for the beauty of them and the tremendous, sweeping generosity of their horizons? She had not heard him say anything in that sense in the three weeks since they had arrived. He had something, though, some vividly known emotion towards them, and it had even communicated itself to her. She had recognized it in that first joyful day when they'd discovered that Gerry didn't have measles – was, in fact, quite recovered by the time they reached Zermatt (only now there was another area, knowledge of the state of his own body, wherein Gerry trusted Peter rather than himself) – and had gone up on the Gornergrat railway to renew their friendship with the mountains, as by saying hello to them, one by one, from the edge of the cliff over the Gorner Glacier. Gerry and Peggy pointed them all out to Peter, speaking eagerly in turns, with an air of ownership and gift. There! These were ours, now they're yours: take them. Peter's deep, pale eyes were cold and fiery against the blinding glare off the glacier below. He stared long and silently at each peak as they presented it to him, and suddenly the mountains were different to Emily too. They were no longer magnificent friends whose sight filled her with affection and awe. They were the walls of enemy cities, turreted with ice and scarred by the lances of the wind. They were burnished castles, on whose summits the foeman stood, thunderbolts of rock in hand, on guard over the formless glow of an unknown grail. Affection left her for that moment, and a leaping, violent desire filled its place.

Then Peter said: 'Have they all been climbed?'

'Yes,' Gerry answered, laughing. 'Not only that, most of them, which the pioneers lost their lives on, are reckoned to be "an easy day for a lady".'

Peter turned his back then and said: 'I'll learn a lot on them. Let's go into the hotel and have some coffee.'

The next thing he had done was to go out of his way, taking Gerry with him, to attach himself to Harry Walsh. Harry was a good-tempered man and had been very generous in giving up some of his days, which he could have spent on difficult climbs with mountaineers in his own class, to bear-leading Peter up simple ascents and answering his uncountable questions. The girls saw little of them during the daylight after the first week, but on the two occasions when they had all at least started out together from the hotel, later to separate, Emily had been struck with the thought that the three young men were like so many knights of the Round Table. Gerry was Galahad, of course, and Harry Walsh was King Arthur, the undisputed leader, quiet-spoken, easy-moving, and expert. Peggy ought to have been Guinevere, especially since Harry obviously liked her and might have showed it more if it had not been for Peter. She herself would be – who? Galahad didn't have a lady, did he? 'Because his heart was pure.'

And Peter was Sir Lancelot, the black-avised knight whose presence altered the character of every endeavour, whose smile was always a threat. To Harry Walsh a mountain was a mountain. He set out and, if conditions were at all possible, he got to the top. If he did not, you knew that for that day, or that season, or for ever, that climb wouldn't go. It was impossible. But Peter Savage would stare at some precipice and ask: 'How do you get up that when there's ice on the rocks?' And Harry would say briefly: 'You don't'; and Peter would shake his head almost involuntarily and keep on staring.

'*Gut,*' Christian said grudgingly. 'It was better than I hope.' They had reached the level summit of the Wellenkuppe. She began to unrope, and a moment later the second *cordée* had joined them.

'We'd better go straight on, Christian,' Harry said in German, and the guide nodded. Harry turned to Gerry. 'Sure you don't want to come on with us?'

Gerry looked longingly at the ridge leading up to the Obergabelhorn and regretfully shook his head. 'Peter wants to practice glissading.'

Harry said: 'We can all go on in two ropes. We've got plenty of time.'

'Oh, yes,' Peggy cried impulsively, 'and down over the Untergabelhorn!'

'Thanks,' Peter said shortly, 'I'd love to, but I must practice glissading. It's important.'

'I don't really care one way or the other,' Peggy said.

Emily slipped up her goggles and crinkled her eyes in the strong glare. Harry was looking at her, and she had a good mind to accept his invitation, but as third on the rope with Christian and Harry she would have been nothing but a nuisance. She shook her head and watched without speaking as the two men roped up and set off along the ridge towards the Obergabelhorn. The rest of them had work to do and must forgo such aimless pleasures. They must watch Peter Savage teaching himself glissading. She lowered her goggles with a snap and said: 'Let's rope up.'

They went fast down by the way they had come until Peter at the rear said: 'This is the place I'd picked out. There's snow on the slope here, and then we can have some short runs on the ice, near the edge of the glacier there.'

The girls went on by themselves until they found a rock in the sun and sat down to watch the glissading. They were too far away to hear the men talking, but Emily saw Gerry gesturing, crouching with the axe held by his right side, his left hand on the axe head, his right holding the shaft down near the point. Then Peter, in the same position, pushed off directly down the slope. He was trying to ride on his feet over the snow, knees bent, with most of his weight back on the point of the axe. Snow rose in a cloud under his boots, and flew, like a feather at the bow of a ship, from under his axe point. Faster and faster he went. Then something caught. His heels shot up behind, and he went flying out like a sack over the snow, landed, bounced, rolled, bounced, turned over on to his stomach, dug the pick into the snow, and slowly came to a stop.

Emily clapped her hands with delight and shouted: 'What a beautiful fall! Do it again.'

'They can't hear you,' Peggy said reproachfully.

'He's all right,' she said. 'He won't come to any harm. Let's have a smoke.'

'A smoke!' Peggy gasped.

Emily winked. 'Why not? That awful Mr Kennedy in the hotel gave me two cigarettes yesterday, and I've brought them with me. And a box of matches I stole from Daddy's room.'

They lit the cigarettes inexpertly and leaned back against the rock. Emily thought the smoke tasted foul, but composed her face to show appreciation. Peter had fallen again. It was a lovely day.

'He's awfully patient,' Peggy said, carelessly stubbing out her cigarette.

'And determined,' Emily said. 'When is he off to India? Didn't he say the other day that he was expecting to get a sailing date any moment?'

'October the twelfth,' Peggy said.

'And then he won't be back for years,' Emily said, still feeling very cheerful in spite of the cigarette. She had exaggerated her fears. Peter might be a dangerous sort of man, but he was going out of their lives as surely as Adam Khan.

Peggy's voice was small and choked as she repeated. 'Years!'

'You can write to him,' Emily said heartlessly.

'Oh, I will. I don't know whether he'll have time to write back much. But I'll write anyway. Four or five years, he thought it would be, before he could come home on leave. Emily, we'll be twenty-two by then!'

Twenty-two, Emily thought. Many of their friends would have married and had two children in that time. And herself? She gazed at Gerry with the grown-up feeling of distance, of appraisal, watching as he waited, patient and faithful, at the foot of the snow slope down which his friend was sliding for the twentieth time.

She jumped to her feet and said: 'Let's go down to the hotel. My feet are getting cold.'

Peggy said: 'Well–' She was pink but determined. 'I thought I'd ask Peter to take me down across the Gabelhorn glacier and the Hühnerknubel. I've never been over there all these years, and I know you have, so I didn't want to bore you, and–'

'That's a good idea, Peg,' Emily said heartily. 'And, after all, I haven't seen much of Gerry this trip either.'

'No, of course not!' Peggy burst out. She smiled, and the colour died away from her face and neck, leaving her calm, drained, and more

grown-up than Emily had ever seen her before –
than she would have believed possible.

Emily turned and yelled: 'Gerry, Peter! We're
tired of sitting here, and it's nearly twelve. Come
on down!' This time they heard her and saw the
gesturing of her arm. Gerry waved back, and his
voice reached her a moment later. 'One more.'
One more it was, and then the men plodded
along the hill to join them.

After they had eaten the lunch they carried in
their rucksacks, Peggy and Peter set off at once
and were soon out of sight over the ridge. Gerry
began to tidy up, but she stopped him with a
wave of her hand. 'There's no hurry,' she said
slowly. '*We're* not going across the Gabelhorn
glacier.' Gerry sat down again. She stared
thoughtfully at the point where she had last seen
Peter Savage – new boots, new axe, plenty of the
best rope, good clothes.

She turned on Gerry and said suddenly: 'Who
paid for Peter's trip?'

'I did,' Gerry said absently. 'What did you...
Oh!' He swung round, and now his brown eyes
were troubled. 'I mean... I don't know. He paid
for himself, of course.' He looked bravely at her,
and she saw that he was trying to make himself
angry and outraged. 'What do you mean, asking
such a thing?'

'What's the point of lying, Gerry?' she said.
'You've never lied in your life, have you? Unless
Peter has made you sometimes. You're paying for
his holiday, aren't you? Does your father know?'

Gerry shook his head miserably.

'Or Peggy?' She spoke very gently.

'Of course not.'

'You don't think Peter has told her?'

'He might have. I certainly haven't. Why should I? Why should he? I only lent him the money, but damn it, I don't want it back, and I told him so. I've got more money than I know what to do with.' He hated to think about money and was embarrassed whenever the subject came up, but now he was plunging angrily on – as he had once when they had talked about the physical aspects of sex. 'I suggested we should all come here, at Llyn Gared. Later, Peter told me he didn't want to come. Heavens, what a thick-skinned ass a man can become when he has always had money to buy whatever he wants! Then one day we were having lunch in a pub outside Cambridge, and I wanted to have a big blow-out to celebrate something, I've forgotten what, but he insisted we have bread and cheese and beer. It made me think.'

I bet it did, my poor Galahad, Emily thought, and I bet Peter knew exactly what you would think and what you would do.

'I didn't say anything at the time, of course,' Gerry went on. 'It would have been insulting. But a few days later I took the bull by the horns and asked him straight out if he'd come to Zermatt as my guest. I told him I would have a miserable time if he didn't come. That was true enough. He's such a wonderful chap, isn't he?'

Emily nodded.

'Well, finally he said all right, but he'd only borrow the money. He wanted to let everyone know – you, Uncle G, Peggy. But I wouldn't agree to that. I couldn't have stood it if people thought he was a sort of hanger-on here, when really... I mean, half the time it's the other way round, isn't it? It's Peter who thinks what's to be done every day. It's Peter who makes rocks and climbs we've done twenty times suddenly become new and exciting again, more than they ever were – gives everything a kind of challenge, so that leaving the hotel every morning is as exciting as something you thought would only happen once, like walking out of the pavilion at Lords, first wicket down, in the Harrow match.'

'Let's get on down,' she said after a time.

'You mustn't let anyone even guess about this – the money,' Gerry said when they were ready to go. 'You won't, will you?'

'No,' she said. She swung into place behind him as he set off down the ridge. The patches of snow grew scarcer and thinner with each step they took towards the bright valley far below.

She wondered why she was not more annoyed or outraged at Peter. She acknowledged that she had been on the look-out to find things wrong with him ever since he unfairly won the punt race, and now here was a fine, damning piece of evidence – for of course Peter had no more intention of paying back the loan than Gerry had of allowing him to – and she could not feel triumphant, not even when she realized, tramping along at Gerry's heels, that the episode of Gerry's suspected measles now shone a new and more unpleasant light on Peter's conduct. Obviously, if Gerry couldn't go to Zermatt, Peter couldn't, so he had willed Gerry to get out of bed, regardless of the severe complications that could have set in if he had had measles – regardless of *all* consequences.

Regardless of consequences. She thought that was why she was not angry – that, and the reminder that he was going away on October 12. Regardless of consequences. It was like a cliff, uncompromising, appealing, but tremendous, whose black rim skirted their path. Peter Savage had to do what he had to do, regardless of consequences. Gerry never moved or spoke without thinking of the consequences, of who might be hurt, of who might be insulted. The edge of the cliff had a fearful fascination, drawing her near to peer down. What on earth, or off it, would happen to someone who stepped over?

'Have you made up your mind what you're going to do, now that you're a B.A?' She addressed the broad back ahead, forcing herself to speak lightly.

Gerry spoke over his shoulder. 'No. Country gentleman? Mervyn's doing a better job with the estates than I ever could. But I thought I'd spend the winter at Wilcot, hunting, and get ready to take over the hounds from old Slade-Carter the year after. Only I think a Master ought to know more about animals, veterinary stuff, farming – everything, really – than I do. Spend the summers here in Zermatt. You'll all be coming every year, won't you? Then of course Father's not getting any younger, and when he pops off I'd have to spend more time in town – to go to the House. It would be a sort of duty, wouldn't it? and Mervyn could tell me what to say. I thought

I might go to India some time. Big game.'

'And meet Peter?'

'Oh, yes, I suppose so. Don't know whether there'll be any tigers or elephants where he'll be.' The stones crunched rhythmically under their boot-nails for a few moments as they came to a level place. 'Travel – I'd like to climb in the Caucasus. Harry Walsh thinks he could take six months off next year or the year after. South America. The Andes. I won't be able to go far afield after I inherit. Won't want to.'

He stopped and turned to face her. 'I mean, I'd want to stay at home. With you. I mean, would you like to marry me?'

'Now?' Emily said. The sun was hot, and she was sweating, the salt, hot drops bitter in her eyes. She felt cold.

'Now? Well, if you like, of course,' he said. 'Of course – I'd thought of getting more fit for it. Worthy. Growing up. Finding something to do, something big.'

She stood looking carefully at him, and her gaze reflected straight back from his worried eyes so that she was looking at and into herself. If she accepted it must be for 'now,' so that he and she could come to grips with their life together before they had settled into different ways, before the years and other friendships had changed them both. But there was in her this same doubt of purpose. If she were a good, proper girl, Gerry himself would be her purpose; but she couldn't accept that now. She didn't love him – everything else, perhaps, but surely not love. If he took her in his arms now and kissed her hard, passionately, she would laugh, because she would know that it was not what he really felt. Nor she.

Then to say: 'Yes – some time?' That would be the easy way. She couldn't do it.

She said: 'I think we'd better wait, Gerry. Ask me again when you mean "Now."'

He said: 'Exactly. That's best.' He turned round with a last shy, embarrassed smile, and strode on down the path. Soon he began to throw words and phrases back over his shoulder at her. 'No life for a woman to sit at home while her husband goes off to the Caucasus, India – no life out there, either. Bugs. Fever. Snakes.'

True enough, she thought, but what you mean is that if you have a woman with you, you can't try out the limits of your own strength and skill, and that's what is important to you now, because Peter has made it so.

Gerry said: 'I used to think being Manningford, later Wilcot, was enough – good and sufficient reason for living. Now I'm not so sure. Got to get that out of my system. Dash it, I'll feel completely at a loose end when Peter's gone. That's not right, is it?'

'No,' she said.

She thought angrily: Gerry never used to think there was any need to define a purpose for his life, but he probably could have if he had tried. Now he could not, and he was uneasy and doubtful of himself because of it. For over two years he had been close to Peter Savage, to whom nothing was going to come of its own – and if it should, Peter might use his will to force it away and wrench his life towards some other purpose (how much merely to exercise and increase the power of that will?); the way he had given up cricket, at which he was already in the first class, in order to face the unknown peaks of mountaineering, was an ominous example and portent.

Well, one thing was certain: Peggy would come to Peter without any effort on his part. So he might deliberately sweep her out of his way? He would not do that; Peggy was a rich girl, and would be richer when she was twenty-one.

She said to herself: 'Cat!' and wished that thought had not come to her. She was as rich herself, perhaps richer, for she was an only child, and her father had inherited industries as well as land. She could not know what it felt like to a man like Peter to be poor. The sooner Peter went to India the better.

When he came back Peggy would be waiting for him, grown up and calm as a freckled madonna. She herself would wait for Gerry, but it would not be the same. She was like Peter in this at least – she could not accept something *only* because it was coming to her. Now she was supposed to wait for Gerry to find a purpose so that he could see in himself the same kind of worth that he recognized in Peter Savage.

How could she help him there? By urging him to go to an agricultural college and fit himself to run the Wilcot estates by himself? Perhaps, but Peter had turned his mind away from the unspectacular victories of a farmer and landowner. By firing him with political ambition, so that he would aim his life at the prime ministership or the Foreign Office? Perhaps. Only, Gerry would never be a politician. Eton and Cambridge were behind him, Peter going away, herself standing aloof. He was like a climber without a map, in a strange country.

Oh, dear.

Four years might not be enough. Or too long.

CHAPTER 7

LETTERS FROM INDIA

January 5th, 1904
D.C's CAMP, RUDWAL DISTRICT
PUNJAB

Dear Gerry,

The address above will always reach me. If we are not actually in camp, which we seem to be during a large part of the year, the letters will be delivered to me in Rudwal City. I have a small bungalow there, but have hardly seen it since I arrived. The train got in at midnight and by noon the next day I was on horseback, riding hard across country, trying to reach the D.C's camp before nightfall. He was on his cold-weather tour of the Southern Tehsils, and if you don't know what that means, nor did I!

You asked me in your letter to tell you about my work. It will not be easy, because there are no real limits to it. At the moment I am 'under instruction,' which means that I do anything that seems to need doing, or that Philipson tells me to do. Philipson is the D.C, and so my lord and master for the next year. He has been here a long time and does not seem too fit. I cannot tell yet whether he is efficient or not, as I do not know the ropes myself, but I should say not. He seems to be a slow thinker, a plodder and pipe-smoker, and one would say that 'Anything for a quiet life' was his motto, except that he is apparently always on tour, when he might be living in great comfort back in Rudwal (where he has a huge bungalow and fine garden), and things do somehow seem to get done. Mrs Philipson is here in camp with us. She is tall, thin, and dried up, and has no other interest than Philipson.

The third day after I joined the camp – I hadn't learned a word of Hindustani, let alone of the Punjab dialect they use here – Philipson took his pipe out of his mouth and suggested I go and judge a couple of cases. I felt like protesting, not because I was afraid to give a ruling but because I didn't see how I could do justice when I couldn't understand what anyone was saying. Philipson must have guessed what I was thinking, because he said: 'Ahmad Ali is a good interpreter. Just do your best.' Then he put his pipe back in his mouth, got on his horse, took his gun, and rode off to a snipe *jheel* twelve miles away. The court was in the open air, under a huge tree, and as I walked over to it, and realized that I was alone, I felt better. I had something to do, on my own, and it was a beautiful morning. The people's faces all shone in the sun and the Maghra – we were camped on the bank – was like a river of beaten gold behind them. Ahmad Ali and the rest of them thought I was going to fumble and stumble. I could see it in their faces – just as Emily and Mr Fenton and even you did, that first day on Cader Brith, so – I showed them!

Most days I go round with the *patwaris,* who are a kind of junior official, while they check the field records. The records show what crop is grown in every field in the district. I also inspect liquor shops, count the money in the sub-treasuries, listen to complaints, decide what to do about them – and do it. Philipson never asks what I have done or offers any advice, and, when he is dealing with these things and I am there, he never discusses them with me but just gives his decision and leaves me to guess why he gave that one and not some other. I think that when I get a district I shall make my views clearer to people who are working under me. As it is, I do not know what Philipson is trying to achieve here – if anything.

I have met Adam Khan once or twice. His father was furious with him for not going into the I.C.S, and the row has not really died down yet. Adam looks strange, at first sight, in his Punjabi dress, but after a time you get used to it, and certainly it is what he should wear if he is to keep touch with the peasants and towns-people here. You know we have a plan to work together when I finally get this district myself. Well, we've been discussing the details. He will form a group, ostensibly to discuss politics and local problems, but really to explain what I want and ensure that everyone works together to get it done. His father will be a snag, though, and would have to be dealt with somehow. He is about sixty-five and is called the Old Captain everywhere, though his real name is Ghulam Afzal Khan, Khan Bahadur. He is easily the most influential person in the district. I have not talked with him about our plans, of course, but it is clear that he is against all change of any kind, and cannot understand why Adam Khan wants to talk with lawyers and clerks and peasants 'with ideas above their station,' as he says. He is a magnificent-looking man, with a bright orange beard and white eyebrows. His house is a great rambling affair with courtyards and outhouses and scores of babies and servants, sitting in the middle of his thousand acres, about four miles west of Rudwal. I didn't see Adam Khan's wife, as the Old Captain insists on full purdah in his house – they all live there – but I saw his son, who is just five. He's a good-looking, strong child, and the Old Captain is obviously a good deal prouder of him than he is of Adam. He orders Adam about pretty roughly, and made him fetch and carry for me during my visit. Adam will have to make up his mind not to be bossed about, or he will not be of as much use to me as I had hoped.

I have definitely decided that this is the district I want, not because of Adam so much as for the mountains in the Northern Tehsils, and over the border in Parasia. It is not generally considered a 'promotion' district, I find. Philipson is only the fourth D.C since we took over the Punjab from the Sikhs in 1849, and of the other three, two died in harness and one retired after twenty-six years in the district. This suits me well. I could change the face of this district in ten years, and then get a transfer or promotion on my own terms, with something actually done to point to. This is a much stronger position than to allow oneself to be picked as a 'promising youngster,' after three or four years, and put into the secretariat, because one will then never be able to get the respect and support of the men one will have to rely on to get things done – the D.Cs. Philipson positively hates the secretariat and all the quill-pushers in it, as he calls them. It is the only strong emotion I have ever seen him express, and there will be many Philipsons to work through. I doubt, incidentally, if Philipson's health will stand up more than another three or four years, which might suit very well, as I should then be ready for a district.

I do not know when I will get long leave, but when I do I promise you we'll have a long season in the Alps together. I will get shorter leaves before then, of course, and will spend them in the Himalaya. I have a feeling that the Alps are going to be merely a training-ground in future, and that real fame will come only to men who find and conquer new peaks here. When you see the view from the foothills of the Southern Tehsils, you will understand.

I wrote to Peggy yesterday. I hope you all had a good Christmas at Llyn Gared, and thought of me eating Christmas pudding in a tent, with the Philipsons wearing paper hats, at a temperature of 75°.

Yours aye,
Peter

January 6th, 1905
D.C's CAMP, RUDWAL DISTRICT
PUNJAB

Dear Gerry,

I have three letters of yours, dating back to September, which I have not answered, and now

I fear this must be a short letter, too, as I am packing up to leave the shelter of the Philipsons' wing and set up on my own. Philipson has been asking for twelve years for a resettlement of the Southern Tehsils, and now they have given in, and appointed me settlement officer for the duration. Settlement is the process by which we map the district, try and find out who every piece of land belongs to, and decide what its basic rate of tax should be. For fifty years we have been working off a very rapid settlement made by the first D.C, one of the old school, who knew a lot more about fighting and Punjab-style wrestling than he did about law or mathematics. It has worked in a rough and ready fashion ever since, but there have been endless disputes, and now Mr Peter Savage, I.C.S, is going to put it right. It will take about three years of fieldwork, I estimate. The Lt-Governor told me, rather pompously, that I was the youngest officer ever to be appointed to settlement work, and that I could thank Philipson's report for getting such a chance so early in my career, even before passing my departmental exams. I thanked him politely, and later Philipson also, but have privately made up my mind that I shall use the job to make sure that I get Rudwal when they see fit to give me a district. It would be a criminal waste, which even the secretariat must see, to send me somewhere else when I shall have gathered such a unique knowledge of Rudwal. My address, till further notice, will therefore be Settlement Officer's Camp, Rudwal Dist, Punjab.

118

Adam Khan is still trying to form his group of people interested in good government, and is getting in worse favour with his father the Old Captain. The latter does *not* believe in democracy. When you look at people and see what fools most of them are, I don't see how any sensible person can, but the Old Captain does not realize that in the long run you achieve more by getting the people, fools and all, to work for you than by just having the power to force them to do what you tell them to.

You ask what I think about the idea of your going to an agricultural college and then taking over the full management of the estates from your agent, Mervyn. It would cut into your mountaineering quite a bit – you remember telling me that Mervyn never found a minute to leave Wilcot except for a week or two in mid-winter – but of course a duty is a duty, even though you didn't ask to be born with the title hovering over your head. Mervyn would be pretty cut up for a spell, too, I suppose.

Give my regards to Emily, and let me know whether you are still hoping to get out here after big game next cold weather. We have nothing larger than leopard in Rudwal, but they're exciting enough for anyone. I shot two last month, which had been taking goats and sheep in the foothills. The mahseer in the Maghra run up to 65lb, and fight like salmon (only I've never fished for salmon!). I'll write again soon.

Yours aye,
Peter

July 26th, 1906
P.O HARKAMU
RUDWAL DISTRICT

Dear Gerry,

There is no need to tell you what I have been doing, as you saw for yourself during the cold weather. I won't tell you again how wonderful it was to see you out here, because I told you at the time, and in all my letters since. I was on resettlement then, wasn't I? Well, I still am, but I have taken a month's leave and am living in the Forest Rest House here in Harkamu. It is the 'capital' of the Northern Tehsils, and contains at least 1,000 people in the winter. In the summer 700 of that number go higher still with the flocks. Harkamu is just under 8,000 feet, in the upper valley of the Chakdi. The Philipsons were up here a week ago, the old man trying to shake off another go of malaria. I have escaped that so far.

Thanks for sending the *Alpine Journals* on to me when you have read them. That was an interesting piece of Harry Walsh's in the last number. He seems to be making a considerable name for himself, while I sit here in a log hut in Harkamu. Still, I have been over 19,000 feet on the mountains immediately north of here, and suspect that sheer altitude is going to raise problems which the Alps will not prepare one for. You must keep right up level with Walsh, Gerry, so that when I get back you can show me what's been done, and how, and we can go after him. Whatever he's done, we'll do one better.

I find myself wishing again and again that you were here – or I there. I've met a lot of people,

120

Gerry, but I've only got one friend.

I think, and am beginning to hope, that we'll have a special reason for getting ourselves to the top of the heap. A Survey of India man who came through Rudwal a year ago dropped mysterious hints about Parasia, and now more light is beginning to emerge. Parasia is an enormous area, officially a province of Western Tibet but actually just about as much without a ruler as it is without a population. The Survey of India apparently seized the opportunity, while Younghusband was beating some sense into the Tibetans' heads a couple of years ago, to send a pair of agents into this end of the country. They confirmed what everyone has suspected for years – that Parasia is the most desolate, wild, and useless country in the world; but they also reported that they had seen and measured a very high mountain in the middle of it – 27,000 feet. They have tentatively called it Meru. There have always been legends in Asia about a sacred mountain somewhere in Western Tibet, and it has always been called Meru, though no one has ever definitely found it, and many people have thought it was another name for Kailas; but Kailas is too far to the east (81° 18′ E, 31° 04′ N). So they are going to call this one Meru, in the hope of settling the controversy, perhaps. They have not mapped it properly, as they can't get closer than fifty miles without a lot of trouble. From Government's point of view they have found out all they want to know, but for us – this may be it, Gerry, our private mountain. The best thing of all is that its mere existence is going to

121

remain a matter of gossip for a few years yet, as Government doesn't want it spread abroad that agents have been all over Parasia. So be sure not to breathe a word of this to anyone at all, or I will get into trouble.

Peggy writes regularly. She seems to be very bored with life in London, and is always longing to be in Llyn Gared or Zermatt, and holds quite a grudge against Mrs Fenton for not letting her come out here with you. I hope Emily is well. I have not seen much of Adam Khan since you left, which is probably as well, as it is beginning to be clear that he must not seem to be too close to me if he is to have real influence with his group. They have got a name now – the Rudwal Committee for Good Government.

I was fool enough to give Philipson a hint of our plan for using the group – we call it the C.G.G – as a lever to get things done. As I might have guessed, he was dubious about where it might lead. The Old Captain would send you his salaams if he knew I was writing to you. After you had gone he told me that you were a real *bahut bahut pakka sahib,* and why didn't you come to India as Viceroy? Do you remember my mentioning something like that, years ago? It's an idea, you know. If you haven't found anything else to do, why not think of it seriously?

Yours aye,
Peter

P.S – I had sealed up this letter when the post office *chuprassi* brought your telegram. I am sorry for your sake, Gerry, and can only hope that you will not take it harder than is – well, true. Your father had really been dead for a long time, as far as you are concerned, the way mine died for me when I learned as a child that he had disappeared. Please give my sympathy to Peggy. I sent off a letter to her a couple of days ago.

October 15th, 1907
SETTLEMENT OFFICER'S CAMP
RUDWAL DISTRICT
PUNJAB

Dear Gerry,

You and Walsh seem to have had a wonderful time in Peru, except for that fall. You need me with you.

This resettlement job is nearly finished now, and Philipson has promised to do his best to get me the Rudwal District when he retires – or dies – one of which is bound to happen within the next two years. He seemed surprised that I wanted it so badly, because he had thought I would prefer the secretariat.

I see in the *A.J* that Barnwell and Ingram failed to make the north-east wall of the Weisshorn. They say the weather turned against them late in the morning, but I can't help wondering whether a determined go, then, might not have done the trick. You remember we had a good look at it in '03, and we decided then that really weather and skill would be much less important than nerve – guts, to be frank. We'll mark it up as another first for the team of Savage and Manningford – sorry, Savage and Wilcot.

The existence of Meru has not been officially

revealed, and will not be till '09, I hear, but it *does* exist, and its height is 27,141. I spent a month at Harkamu and beyond, working out details of supply and transport for an expedition that could at least make a full reconnaissance of it. Another good thing is that the only approaches to it are through Rudwal, and since Tibetan bandits shot a traveller in the Northern Tehsils ten years ago, the D.C Rudwal has to be applied to before any journeys can be made north of the Lakho La.

You ask what I think about the proposal that you go into politics. It might be a fine idea, provided you had some definite purpose. When I made the remark about your becoming the Viceroy, you had not succeeded to the title. Now you have, and the idea is much more than a castle in the air. It is perfectly feasible, though it would take time. Curzon was thirty-nine when he took over, and that was very young, but it still leaves you thirteen years in hand. On the other hand, the three Presidency governorships – Bengal, Madras, Bombay – are also reserved for the likes of you, and though it would not be easy for me to transfer to any of them, it could be done. Together in one of those provinces we could make such a mark that you would be certain of the Viceroyalty in due course. In the meantime you would have to study India and its problems, and speak from time to time in the Lords about them. I could give you a lot of 'inside' information and advice and you could make a visit out here every year.

I do not think personally that your suggestion about aiming for the prime ministership or some other cabinet office is feasible, or would suit you. You don't think so yourself, I am sure, or you would not have phrased it in that jocular fashion. It is no good thinking of one's purpose in life in jocular terms, Gerry, and you did so because you know that you would have to dirty your hands in home politics, and get down and fight like an alley tough with all kinds of dirty demagogues, for any post in the cabinet. But the Viceroyalty is within your reach. The choice for it is limited to rich noblemen, and you're one. Not many such want it – but for you, well, you could do something for India. Remember telling me you never imagined that people could live in conditions like this? – and asking, what can be done about it? We *are* doing what we can, but you could do more, a great deal more. Very few rich noblemen have your love of people, Gerry. I suppose that's what has always made me like and admire you so much, though I can't be the same. I try, but it doesn't work.

I think we've reached an age when we must really decide what we want to do with our lives, what is worth while doing. I have chosen India as my field, and for Adam Khan there was really no alternative. I must get to the top, to get things done, and now I am sure that with you and Adam and some patience I can get there. We can all get there together. Then we can set to work to change the face of India. We will abolish disease and poverty, and make a new India where every Indian is the partner of every Englishman. We three, or whoever will join us, will decide what must be done. You will explain it to England,

Adam to India, and I will build and run the machine that *does* it.

Meantime I am going to stay in Rudwal, putting some theories to the test, and awaiting the Hour. I don't know how long we'll have to wait. None of us does. The signal might be your getting the governorship, it might be something quite different – a famine, rebellion, even a big war – but I think I'll recognize it when it comes. It won't be dull, because my grandfather's experience is always in my mind. He was just feeling bogged down in the routine of army life here when, out of nowhere, came the Mutiny. I think of the Mutiny as a hurricane of wind blowing over India, that separated the chaff from the straw, but who knows what our hurricane will be, or when it might come? Grandfather told me he never found life dull after the Mutiny, although it probably was, because he took nothing for granted and was always ready for anything. He never counted on the sun rising tomorrow, so when it did he was thrilled.

Then there is our mountaineering. It will be of great help to us in our plans if we become known as really great climbers, *a team,* especially if our greatest feats are done here in the Himalaya. Later we shall be too old and too involved to do anything big, so we must go all out in these next ten or fifteen years. Mountaineering is far more than a hobby to us. It's a way of thinking, of training ourselves. We know where we're going – to the top. We're going to get there. We have a purpose, all the time.

Sorry to be so serious. Just pretend we are back

in my rooms at King's, settling the fate of the universe over mugs of porter! It's sad to think that in a few years we'll all be respectably married men and there won't be any more of those long bachelor sessions such as we had at Cambridge and here, beside the Maghra. Still, it won't be for some time in my case, as I can't afford the luxury of a wife just yet, and I'm not sure that I'm ready for the responsibilities when there is so much else to do here and in the mountains. Perhaps I'll reconsider the situation when I get home on long leave – 1909 is now indicated as the year.

Yours aye,
Peter

June 4th, 1908
CITY MAGISTRATE'S HOUSE
KOLHAPUR, PUNJAB

Dear Gerry,

Jolly Boating Weather, what? Not here, though. This place has more flies than any other place in India, and it is today 124 in the shade. The incumbent has gone to England on long leave and I sit in his seat and hope there won't be a riot – not very hard, though, as a suitable riot might start the full striking of the Hour!

Adam Khan is having trouble with his C.G.G in Rudwal. They are such a mixed crowd, some ignorant and honest, some intellectual and fuzzy, some crooked and sharp; some concerned with getting rich, some with the preservation of the ideals of Islam under our Christian yoke. He has visited me once here since I came to Kolhapur in

March. He came in secrecy, which must sound strange to you, but is caused by the circumstances of what we are trying to do. His group are not anti-British, like some of the other similar groups that have sprung up around the country since the Morley-Minto reforms were published, but neither are they willing to hear what we have to tell them, salaam, and then go away to do it. This is fine in itself, but it does mean that Adam Khan has to pretend to be more remote from me than he actually is. I am not sure how much stamina he (Adam) is going to show in this business, and am tentatively looking round in Rudwal for someone who would be able to keep the thing going if Adam somehow failed us. He looks increasingly harassed, and confesses that he is finding it more and more difficult to keep the control – rather the moral dominance – over the C.G.G that is essential for our purpose. Then, affairs at his home are going from bad to worse, and the Old Captain has to all intents taken the care of the child, Baber, out of Adam's hands. So Adam has put his father and his son out of his mind, and identified himself more strongly with his C.G.G – and in the process has become too involved with all their problems and weaknesses, and of course is very unhappy about his son.

It is definite that I am coming home on leave next year, and just about definite that I shall get Rudwal when I return here. Philipson is going to stick it out till then, though the doctors tell him he ought to go now.

I have found out a little more about Meru from

one of the surveyors who went into Parasia, a P.M havildar whose home is in Rudwal. He says it is a more or less triangular mountain, with long ridges leading up from south and east to a tremendous summit cone of about 3,000 feet. The ice cliffs on the west face he estimated as 7,000 feet almost sheer.

I'm glad you found my note on the land-tenure system useful. Don't forget that what I wrote only applies to this part of the Punjab. In a week or two I hope to send you a detailed note on the problems of the provincial police forces. I should be chary of using it for anything except to gather information – I mean, don't make a speech based on it in the Lords – as there are widely differing views on the proper solution, and you don't want to get committed to any particular one just yet.

Yours aye,
Peter

January 4th, 1909
18, CIVIL LINES
LAHORE, PUNJAB

Dear Gerry,

Sir Louis has dragged me in here as assistant bottle-washer until I go on leave – May 23rd, on the *Ravi* from Bombay. I'll go overland from Marseilles and spend a few days with Grandfather in London, calling on the Sec. of State, etc, before coming to Zermatt. If you go out about the middle of June you can have all the arrangements made by the time I arrive, and we won't waste a day. I am working out a really big eight-week tour of all the big peaks in the Valais, the Bernese Oberland, and the Hautes Alpes, and will send details of it to you as soon as it is ready. I want to combine a wide variety of experience with the maximum amount of climbing – and let us pray for good weather.

In a way it is a good thing that the Fentons can't get away till August, as it leaves us free to get the really serious work done before Emily and Peggy arrive. Mrs Fenton has invited me to spend a week-end at Llyn Gared as soon as I arrive in England, but I fear I shall have to refuse.

Rudwal is definite, and in writing! I go direct there on my return from leave. The *C & M* had an account of your maiden speech in the Lords, on the Morley-Minto reforms. It was good stuff, and was well received here too, though H.E expressed some rather unflattering surprise. If I were you, I would be less diffident with my statements. Say such and such a thing *is* so, and let the other fellows disprove it if they can.

I have decided that the first things to be done when I take over Rudwal are to establish a co-operative stud farm for the improvement of the cattle, combined with some kind of practical farm school on a small scale; an irrigation scheme to use the Maghra properly; and the establishment of a hospital in Rudwal, with a nurses' school attached to it. The women are going to be very important to us. It will need money and pressure, but I think I can find both.

I am already beginning to get shivers up and down my back at the prospect of seeing the Matterhorn again. We'll go up the first day after I reach Zermatt. I am exercising hard, especially to get my arms stronger. One's legs and wind are in pretty good shape anyway, with the kind of life we lead.

Yours aye,
Peter

March 12th, 1909
18, CIVIL LINES,
LAHORE, PUNJAB

Dear Gerry,

Many thanks for your letter in reply to my last, and for the suggestions about the route we ought to take on our Swiss expedition.

The only way I can answer your letter is to say what *I* think we are trying to do during this summer. Well, first we're going to spend a week in Zermatt acclimatizing and getting used to each other's climbing styles all over again. Then we're going to set off on this eight-week tour of the major peaks, and finish up back in Zermatt, by which time, about August 15th, the Fentons and Peggy should have arrived.

Your letter seems to assume that the chief purposes of the trip are to get me into the Alpine Club, and to improve our climbing technique. I understand that to be eligible for the A.C I will have to have made about twenty first-rate expeditions spread over at least three seasons.

Now, I want to become a member of the Alpine Club, make no mistake about it. It will make our future climbs easier to arrange and to publicize, through the *Journal* – but it is not essential, and it is really vital not to allow the winning of this 'honour' to interfere with our real purpose.

Election to the A.C (with apologies to one Noble Member) is like being certificated as a good chap by a lot of other good chaps; but good chaps often don't get to the top.

The improvement of our technique is more important but not as important as you seem to think. If we are going to make new conquests, go higher and farther than anyone has ever gone, it must be in the Himalaya. These last years have convinced me that in the Himalaya technique must take third place behind stamina and something which might be called will-power, or just 'will,' in both senses. In the Alps there are few peaks that cannot be climbed in a day and a half, including the return. In the Himalaya, this isn't so. I went over 20,000 feet climbing out of Harkamu and as I told you, height itself showed signs of becoming a major difficulty – and it can't be conquered by ice-axe or rope, however skilfully used. In the Alps we choose difficult routes to test our skill; in the Himalaya a leader must always choose the easiest route, and though there will occasionally be real technical difficulties, the easiest will be hard enough, because of its sheer size.

So, although we must of course try to improve our skills, that is not the main object of the tour. That object, I am sure, must be to test and improve our stamina, our powers of physical endurance, and – above all – our mental stamina, our will.

I want us to put ourselves in the way of hard and dangerous decisions. In each case I want to take the hardest, the most dangerous among all the even faintly feasible possibilities. By taking the hard way, hour after hour, day after day, we will so train our wills that when we reach the Himalaya – specifically Meru – with a party, we will be quite clearly the most determined members of it.

But Gerry, this training of the will is not only for the purpose of climbing. You've started on a course which should in due time bring you out to India, first as Governor of a Presidency and then as the Most Honourable the Earl of Wilcot, G.M.S.I, G.M.I.E, G.C.M.G, etc, Viceroy and Governor-General of India. To get to the end of this road – the top, if you like – whatever the conditions, we have to develop our wills – and, especially, you. You usually seem to think you are no better than anyone else, and therefore have no right to force your will on them. But you have to, and there will be occasions when we cannot work as a team; when you, as the chief, will have to overcome opposition on your own. So on this trip you've got to make the decisions, the deliberately unpleasant ones, just as much as I have.

Well, the immediate purpose of enlarging our will-power is to give us something most climbers don't have. To them climbing is a sort of game, like cricket, only played on steep mountains instead of levelled meadows – in which one displays skill, sportsmanship, and good manners, and does or does not get to the top as circumstances permit. But every now and then, even in cricket, someone comes along who does not really think of it as a game – at least, not once he gets out there with the ball in his hand. He wants to win, and because of that he usually does.

We must want to get to the top. But, and this is very important, we must live the *whole* of 'wanting to get to the top,' not just half of it. Getting to the top is worthless if you don't want to; wanting to is worthless if you don't achieve it. The 'wanting' is damned important in terms of life because no one can know what 'the top' will be like. When mountaineering, we climb on because we have faith that the summit will be there, roughly as expected, when we reach it. In life, I am not so sure. I cannot help suspecting that while we are engaged in our desperate assaults on the lower cliffs God may change the landscape, so that when we arrive everything is quite different, so much so that we may not even know we *have* arrived. I told you about Grandfather, and the Mutiny giving him a permanent sense of pleasure in the expected, if it happened. There was another effect, that, when he awoke, his ambition had been turned upside down. Instead of trying to rule, he found himself trying to heal.

So – we are hoping to do something great for India and the world. We see ourselves organizing, administering, directing the flow of energy. But we've got to remember that our particular summits, when we get there, may turn out to be something quite different – moments perhaps in which one of us is killed saving the other; or when we are thrown to the wolves by the blindness of those we are trying to help; or when we father sons who will do what we have been prevented from doing. This untrustworthiness of the Deity must not prevent us from going on towards the top as we see it, because the journey itself must also be our desire – as it is in climbing.

Why do we climb? Because we want to, and to get to the top. And, in my case, *because it is easier not to.*

The pinnacles of Chapel, the shape of the Matterhorn, the pyramid of Meru – which we haven't even seen – tower up in front of everybody. They are there for everybody. The mass of men say that one should stay at the bottom, looking up – admiringly, perhaps; and it is clearly more comfortable there. *Therefore,* I say, I will go up. An usher at school used to call this attitude of mine 'contrariness.' It wasn't, and isn't, that at all. It is a fixed policy I decided on as long as I can remember, to take that course among alternatives which would keep in my own hands my own mastery over myself, other people, and, if you like, fate. They're all alike – fate, people, your own untempered inclination – in exerting a steady, permanent, downward pressure. They're like gravity. It's easier to fall than to climb, easier to lie than to stand. They're like mud, holding us still so that we never move outside the one tiny corner of our total capacity for living where we happen to find ourselves if we accept what fate, people, or our own laziness seem to decree.

Do I have to tell *you* this? You were born to be Earl of Wilcot – but you're going to be a different Earl, one that you made yourself. You, because you've climbed Cader Brith by a hundred different routes, know that the place one gets to by the easy way is not the same as the place one gets to by the hard way – even though they are the same place.

It hasn't taken me as long to write this as I had expected. I felt shy, I suppose, at saying things that I have never said to anyone before. But I never trusted anyone before, and, though we are 'only twenty-eight' in one sense, in another, we are 'over twenty-seven.'

Yours,
Peter

He laid the pen down slowly. The ink was nearly dry already. He crumpled the extra sheet of paper he had placed under his hand to write on – it was the third since he had begun – so that the sweat should not stain the letter to Gerry; and threw it into the waste-paper basket. He felt exhausted, not from the heat but because he had made a great effort. Not for anyone else, he thought savagely, and not again even for Gerry. It was like ripping out his entrails.

Yet he ought to have gone further – caught a firm hold of his heart and pulled that out too, so that Gerry would perhaps understand something else that would have to be decided this summer in Zermatt. But this he could not do, if only because it would really hurt Gerry. This was where you could talk to only one sort of human being, a woman; and to only one sort of woman, your wife; and to only one sort of wife, the right one, yours, loving wholly, wholly loved. That was what it was about.

He had to decide, during the coming year,

whether he was going to marry Peggy Holcombe or not. If he'd been speaking aloud to someone (inconceivable thought), or even writing to Gerry, he would have had to say: 'Whether I shall ask Peggy to marry me.' But to think in such treacly phrases would be the kind of hypocrisy he was fighting against on his own and Gerry's behalf. Everyone who knew them knew that he had only to ask, and Peggy would say yes. Therefore – should he ask? Or, to be clean and straight and hard, should he marry her?

She was as handsome a girl as most. She was well born, rich, pleasant-natured; and she loved him. Everybody except Gerry was convinced that he somehow had no alternative but to marry her because he had written to her once a month or so for seven years (but never as a lover or prospective fiancé); because she had waited for him and naïvely let it be known why she was waiting; and, above all, because his ambition would be greatly served by the marriage.

By God, he thought, with sudden fierceness, do they know me so little that they imagine I cannot resist having Lady Margaret Holcombe, sister of a future Viceroy, as my wife?

It would be the obvious, easy, comfortable, and wise thing to do.

The hair rose along the back of his neck as it had when Gerry suggested the punt race. Was the world going to compel him – or he the world?

But there were more important considerations. If life was a climb, marriage was another, going on within and yet separate from it. If every married couple was a cordée, did he want Peggy as his partner on that rope? Could she follow where he led? Could *she* lead?

He didn't know, but he doubted it. He doubted it particularly because of the extent of his domination over her. He also dominated Gerry, but a man's relationship with a woman was different because there were certain areas where the man could not 'lead' or 'do the thing better.' In these areas a man was physically or spiritually incapable of being more than an equal partner: in the raising of children, for example, and in the physical act of love. Because these areas existed, and were important, his wife must have vision and will and courage equal to his – equal but independent.

He had really learned this when he first lay with a woman, and every succeeding experience had confirmed it and made it more clear that both his wife and he would be unhappy unless she had the same kind of drive – to seek the unattainable, perhaps, in her own field and way – that he had.

He needed women. It was fifty years since the I.C.S had even inferentially countenanced liaisons with native women, except in Burma, and he had lived with scrupulous asceticism when in the Rudwal District. But when away he would frequently send for some dancing-girl-cum-prostitute to attend him; and in Lahore he often slipped away to the old city when he should have been drinking *chota* pegs in the Pig. He attained a physical release in these affairs, at the cost of a gradually increasing mental tension, because he was always moved to try to put more into the relationship – in this case the mere act of

138

union – than it could in those circumstances contain. He felt, and strove for, an increasing, wild kind of lifting up. He would feel that God was only a little higher, if only he could get there. The union of physical and spiritual ecstasy that animated the most sexual of Hindu temple sculptures became real and present. But on, on, there must be more!

But he could not go alone, and the girl's physical companionship was not enough. Once a woman's large eyes had stared suddenly into his, and she had sobbed: 'Not here, not here!'

She was right, although he could not, would not believe that it was not anywhere. But he was almost sure that it could not be with Peggy, because she would be only the mirror of himself, whereas his wife must be an entirely separate person, female as he was male, alight not with the reflection of his purpose but with a female vision of her own that would join his, and thus make the single, greater realization.

So although one of the objects of marriage, as stated in the marriage service, was the avoidance of fornication; although this particular purpose was of great importance to him; although Peggy was a woman and could serve as well as any other female – that was not enough, even sexually. He could not be content to rest on a comfortable platform less than halfway up what he knew to be a great mountain. And there were other peaks altogether which this cordée of marriage, and only this, could scale. In marriage too he would go to the summit, and his wife must be able enough and strong enough to lead as well as follow.

He lit another cheroot, opened another bottle of beer. Perhaps he would fall in love. It was not in human power to control the arrival of circumstances, only to master them when they had arrived. He had not made Meru, or even had any hand in bringing its existence to light – but now it was there, and he was going to conquer it. Who knew but what some woman would be revealed, as suddenly and with as startling an effect – a woman as worthy of every sacrifice, as inspiring, as this Meru which, also, he had never seen? Perhaps she would be married (as, perhaps, other climbers would lay claim to Meru); let her be. To reach her, nothing would stop him, nothing.

CHAPTER 8

'It's Savage, isn't it?' The surprised voice was at his ear.

He turned; his mind raced: Cambridge, King's – the memory, the face came into view at the same instant.

'Darrell,' he said.

The man had a smoking pipe in his fist and looked startled at what he had just said. So he should, Peter thought grimly; he was one of the majority who cordially disliked me at King's. Now the fellow was letting his expression cool into distant recognition as he tried to retreat from his initial mistake of recognition. Peter had a good mind to exude bonhomie, sit down beside the fool, and relate endless Anglo-Indian stories all the way to Zermatt, not forgetting to make them also unintelligible by the proper use of *chota, bara, mofussil,* and the rest.

Secretly he grinned. It would be good fun, but not worth the trouble. He needed the time to go over the maps for the last time before he met Gerry, and to lean out of the window and survey in silence, alone, some of the mountains he had come to make bow their heads to him.

So, after a brief exchange of platitudes, he turned his back, politely but definitely, and went to one end of the first-class carriage on the little train, while the man entered it at the other end.

He caught a half-concealed grin on the face of a foreign climber, probably French, who followed them into the same carriage. Here in Visp it was quite a local custom to gather in appreciative silence and watch a trainload of the English, who had travelled together from London the day before, emerge in separate, gelid groups on the main line platform, wander over to the narrow gauge, and there, still separate, enter this tiny train for the great Mecca of mountaineers, Zermatt – Edward Whymper's Zermatt, Zermatt of the Matterhorn.

Soon the train started, and Peter lit a cheroot and began to study his maps. That took an hour. Then he looked out of the window, missing nothing, until the train neared Zermatt.

In a few minutes now, if he looked out of the left-hand window he would see the Matterhorn rising slowly out of the near Hohbalmen ridge. Time for the final tidying-up of his thoughts.

Of the recent past – nothing to waste even a moment over now. The Secretary of State had been carefully cordial, guardedly commendatory. Grandfather was well.

In two months he was going to meet Peggy. That would have to wait. It was no good planning too far ahead, making up your mind too definitely about situations, especially those that involved people. Otherwise you would be caught helpless by a change in conditions, or in the people.

So there were only the mountains and Gerry, as he had hoped it would be; as he hoped it would be for many years to come: those two, and, binding them, bound by them, making a single unit of power with them, their work.

Gerry would be waiting on the platform. There would be something of strangeness in the meeting. They had written faithfully to each other, and they had spent those weeks together in India in the cold weather of '05–'06. But, in truth, letters were written as much to conceal as to reveal, especially by himself. Only once, on that ghastly night at the beginning of the hot weather, had he tried to explain not things or facts but himself, and he did not know how well he had succeeded, or whether the letter, successful or otherwise, had had the intended effect on Gerry. From Gerry's acquiescent reply, probably; but it would be foolish to be too sure. Gerry was malleable, as the finest gold is malleable, but he did have his own standards, and, however foolish or hampering they might be, it was no good pretending they didn't exist. And then he might have showed the letter, or talked about its content, to Emily.

She was a different kettle of fish altogether. God help Gerry when he married her. God help all of them, come to that, because that girl was deliberately competing with him, Peter, and would continue to do so. It might be necessary to do something drastic if Gerry did marry her, or perhaps even if he didn't, to make sure the poor chap wasn't torn in two between them.

It would be honest to talk more openly with Gerry. Why hadn't they ever really talked about women, for one thing? Well, gentlemen didn't, not even about whores. But *he* wasn't a gentleman, by his own definition, because a gentleman was someone who would rather do the wrong thing gracefully than the right thing brutally. Gerry went to tarts occasionally, very secretive and obvious. He was desperately ashamed of himself on these occasions, because he thought he had somehow betrayed his own upbringing, Emily, and the purity of womanhood in general. In fact Gerry's motive, acknowledged or not, was to take the edge off desire and so prevent himself from harming any of the innocent young ladies who put themselves in his way, and, of course, particularly Emily. Gerry wouldn't actually seduce a nice girl, whatever or from whomsoever the provocation; but he didn't know that, because he was a modest man. In Emily's case he was probably making a mistake, from his own point of view, if he loved the girl. That flawless ivory skin and those cold grey eyes were sheer deception, nature's protective devices, or he was a damned fool. Perhaps it was the auburn hair. Perhaps it was Gerry's self-protective instinct that kept him off her. Damn it, this was judging others by himself, which was an idiotic thing to do. Gerry just knew what was right, and lived up to it.

At Zermatt, Gerry would be waiting on the platform, and he'd be near tears of happiness. Gerry would want to hug him, but would not be able to overcome the training which told him that that was an emotional and ungentlemanly thing to do. Worse, it was un-English. But *he* would like to hug Gerry because he trusted him, and only him in all the world now; because he had suddenly realized how lonely he would be without him; because Gerry was a bar of most perfect gold; because that ass Darrell back there would be watching with a sneer hidden just behind his face; and because it would be easier, less embarrassing not to – and, oh God, because he loved him as David loved Jonathan – *he* would hug Gerry.

CHAPTER 9

August 24th, 1909, a brilliant day, one of an endless succession that had followed them throughout the eight weeks. All around the peaks shone in the sun, thrusting up far above that high point where they stood, on the summit of the Obergabelhorn. Peter looked around slowly, feeling as he did when he used to look around his settlement office at the end of each week's work and recognize each file and volume, and mutter to himself: 'Done, dealt with, put away, mastered.'

There was not a single major summit in view that they had not climbed, sometimes – usually – in this blinding clarity of sun and snow and Alpine wind; sometimes with the heavy mist surging around and the weeping rock as slimy as seaweed; sometimes clinging to the mountain while the outraged summit wind shrieked in their ears and the coats beat like snare drums on their backs; once at least in a passionless snowfall, when very large, mysterious snowflakes, wet and solid, drifted like globs of ice cream into their eyes for an hour on the ascent.

That was when Holz lost his nerve. He was a good teacher, a good guide, but he didn't have the thing inside. That had made it the second most important moment of the whole expedition, there in the snow, the loom of the Jungfrau above and the strange snow coming, the sky dark under its glutinous whiteness, the mountain vanishing underfoot. Holz said: *'Heute geht es nicht, Herr Savage.'* Today it won't go. But it had to go today, because there was the Eiger tomorrow and the Mönch the day after, and, above all, the will to be tempered. By God, he, Peter Savage, had been afraid! Fear was outside him and inside him, in all of them, caveman fear, straddling the precipice over the abyss, dark, full of that circling snow, the light dull green and fading.

'It'll go, Christian,' he said, and stared into the guide's eyes, waiting for the hate to burgeon like a spark.

That was two weeks ago. He'd been watching Christian's eyes from the beginning because he wasn't going to have the guide, who was an expert, water down the strong liquor Gerry and he were drinking. They had changed, those eyes, very soon after the party left Zermatt, the deep-set grey of them, guide's eyes, slowly coming alive as the man behind them began to live – through fear and anger. First, after a dozen arguments, the realization that he could either do what he was told or go home; the anger, growing from the spark, then; the man saying, professional though he was: 'I'll show the young devil.' The next four weeks had been the best, because Christian was a good climber, and they had much to learn from him. He'd gone hard and straight at the mountains till Gerry's mouth used to tighten each time they got up at two o'clock to light the lanterns, and his face grew thinner than it had ever been, the bones showing and the soft flesh

147

falling away. Twice Peter had fallen when he was last on the rope; once the rope broke and he went two hundred feet down an ice slope; but the glissading practice helped to save him – that and destiny – and he lived. Something hurt in his chest when he got up and began to cut steps back towards the others. But Gerry was as white, as unstable as the pulpy snow that came later on the Jungfrau.

'It'll go. We're going up,' Peter had said that morning on the Jungfrau, and that was when anger turned to hate in Christian's eyes, and with it was the dull realization that this was no ordinary English-gentleman-Alpine-Club climber; and something else. Not admiration – that there would never be, because, for one thing, the word did not fit. Awe, perhaps.

So they had stood for a while, Peter looking at Christian Holz and Gerry silent and troubled behind him. Christian Holz was a guide, tough, hardy. He could endure a great deal. But they were going up a little-known, difficult route; the conditions were terrible. They ought to have done what Holz peremptorily advised. They didn't. Holz had had enough. After a minute's staring he began to unrope.

Peter turned to Gerry. 'It's not the Jungfrau that matters, Gerry' – so reminding him with no more words of their talk in the steam bathroom at the Monte Rosa. Easy enough there to say, 'At all costs,' to talk about hard, high purpose, unbreakable resolve, unflinching determination – but here was where they became reality, and Meru was where they would bear fruit. And here

Christian Holz had reached his limit. 'It is murder,' he muttered. 'Murder, murder!'

They left him, Gerry looking back twice although the snow had already hidden Holz, until Peter said, trying to sound harsh but speaking gently: 'Even if he won't come up, he'll be able to get down.' Then they went on, and after an appalling half-hour the snow stopped, and the sun shone, and they reached the summit. On their way down they saw no trace of Christian, and in the valley they were told he'd gone – arrived, taken the train to Zermatt, gone. A German climber told them he'd seen Holz waiting on the platform, shaking his head, not in wonder but like a man with palsy; and all he would say was: 'It won't go.'

Peter reflected grimly that he had received much silent praise for not saying anything against the guide, who, it seemed obvious, must have lost his nerve in a bad place and left his employers to find their own salvation. This was not fair on Christian; but Christian had tried to break Peter, and had lost the battle.

Winning that battle was the second most important time. The most important was on the Dent d'Hérens two days ago. They'd had no guide since Holz left. Gerry had argued feebly that they ought to hire someone anew in each village, but Peter could not agree. There would be no guides on Meru, and besides, all their judgement needed training. The will could be made to go on to certain death. Yes, but they were not steeling themselves for suicide, but for victory.

So they had been alone in the thunderstorm on the Dent d'Hérens. Lightning split the sky and seared the rock. Peter led, so that Gerry's faith in him should be made absolute, so that Gerry should almost believe that the lightning and the cannon blasts of thunder were his servants, that he – *they* were unconquerable. He led on gently up the steep, and Gerry followed. Gerry never showed a sign of fear, but Peter, who knew him, understood that the silently screaming strings of his nerve might snap at any second and leave them helpless and doomed. And himself – he was so afraid, his fear was so overpoweringly strong that each moment of conquest of it, each movement of hand or foot up the ice wall, was like a separate sexual ecstasy.

They reached the crest. The storm never let up. The lightning shivered through the snow. They could not speak for the *click, crack, flash* of the bolts around them, and then the appalling blast in the ear, to right and left, down, above, faster than a bombardment, and the black rock smoking under the snow. All the time the heads of their ice-axes hummed in a piercing minor key.

When they were down again Gerry's hair was grey at the temple – a dusting of silver so that at first Peter had thought it was snow; but it was not.

Now, on the Obergabelhorn, Zermatt lay like a fat sheep asleep in its sunny valley below them.

'We've done it,' Gerry said and held out his hand. They looked at each other for a moment. Peter thought, I don't suppose I'll ever know a better man; I don't suppose there is one. He said:

150

'I don't know what I'd do without you, Gerry.'
He meant it.

Gerry grinned. 'My heavens, Peter, you're going to be the greatest mountaineer that ever lived. You *are,* dash it!' He had taken off his hat, and the touch of silver sparkled in the sun; that and the paring down of the flesh were the only changes in him, but Peter knew he'd need time to rest and put on a little fat, physical and spiritual. The main purpose had been achieved. Gerry now knew that the limits of his will were much further beyond 'normality' than he had thought.

Peter said: 'Let's go down. The Fentons must have arrived last week. We'll take a day or two off, and then do some ladies' climbs.'

'The Furgg ridge of the Matterhorn?' Gerry said with a grin.

Peter laughed, and they set off down the north-east ridge towards the Wellenkuppe. When he reached the gendarme blocking the ridge Peter saw that the slope to his left, which they would have to traverse to get past the gendarme, was in poor condition – two inches of wet snow on a thin, icy base. He began quickly and carefully to cut steps, keeping high up on the slope, only a few feet below the lip of the snow, where there was the usual bergschrund between the snow and the warmer rock of the gendarme.

Half-way across, while Gerry was moving forward to join him and he was drawing in the rope, Gerry slipped. For a fraction of a second he seemed to be suspended there, away from the mountainside, both feet a few inches in the air and the head of his ice-axe glittering like

Mercury's silver staff in his hand. Peter's own ice-axe was stuck deep into the snow and his 'dead' tail of rope was anchored around it. He was not belaying Gerry towards him round the axe, but simply holding the live rope in coils in his hand as Gerry came on. This was fortunate, as it was unlikely that the snow could have exerted sufficient friction to hold the axe in position when Gerry's full weight came on to it, however well he had used the belay to ease the jerk.

When Gerry fell, instead of trying to belay, Peter flung himself up the slope towards the lip of the bergschrund, letting go the coiled live rope as he did so. He supposed Gerry fell like a stone down the slope – he did not see, for before he had reached the end of the rope Peter had dived head-first over the lip of snow and into the bergschrund. Then the jerk came, but instead of exerting its power in a straight line along the rope, it came over the angle of snow, and forced the rope to cut deep into the lip of the bergschrund before Gerry's full weight, and his, came on it. By then they were static, and the rope held.

After a minute's struggling, Peter managed to turn himself right way up. Hauling on the rope, he reached the lip and peered over. Gerry was lying flat on the slope, his head downhill, the rope still firmly tied to his waist but also caught in a loop round one foot. He had his ice-axe in his hand but was not moving at all. He did not seem to know what was holding him, nor whether he dared change his position in the slightest to find out.

Peter called: 'Anchor yourself with the axe, Gerry, then I'll free the rope from your foot.'

After a long time Gerry's voice came up, small and far away. 'All right, Peter.'

So they did it, and in five minutes they were back on the steps; in another fifteen, off the slope. Gerry threw himself down in the snow and lit a cigarette.

'Pheeew!' he said, and then, later: 'What a damned fool I am. Perfectly good steps, snow nothing worse than we've crossed a hundred times – might have killed you too.'

That was true enough. The slope was very steep, and about a thousand feet below were cliffs, rocks, and the head of the glacier. Peter did not know why Gerry had lost his footing, but it would serve no purpose to reproach him. He told him instead not to be an ass.

Gerry got up. 'Thanks,' he said. 'I must concentrate more. I suppose I was thinking of being down, of meeting Emily and Peggy again, hot baths, food… Lead on, Macduff.' Peter saw that he was favouring his left foot, and his ankle seemed to hurt a bit.

It seemed a long way down, over the Wellenkuppe, down the long ridge, along the edge of the glacier, down into the rocky valley, past the Trift Hotel with the people sitting out in the late-afternoon sun, their climbing boots changed for shoes; on down in steep zigzags beside the shouting Trift River, into the trees. Gerry was in front then, and they could see, through the pines, the back of the Edelweiss Hotel, and beyond it the blue-gold air and then the farther slope.

There, just after they entered the trees, when the river's noise was silenced and their boots fell quietly on the pine needles, Gerry stopped short and gasped: 'Peggy, Emily!' The two girls were coming towards them, and saw them, and broke into a run.

For a moment they were all running together, the girls high-coloured, Peter and Gerry sunburned nearly black, all fit and young and running easily. Then two of them, Emily and Peter, stopped running at the same time, so it was the brother and sister who met first, and hugged each other happily. Then Peggy came on towards Peter much more slowly, her lower lip trembling and her hands out. Now was a moment when, by simply taking both those hands and looking into those moist blue eyes, he would commit himself to her.

He held still; she walked more slowly, and at last they shook hands as friends. 'You haven't changed a bit,' she said tremulously.

Beyond her he saw Gerry hugging Emily with the same kind of boisterousness he had used to Peggy; then he swung her round at the full stretch of his arms, her long dove-grey skirt whirling in the air, but she was only smiling, not laughing, and when he set her down, she said: 'You're thinner, Gerry.'

'Of course I am,' he cried. 'Lost pounds of useless fat. Feel my muscles.' He held out his flexed arm, but Emily did not touch it or even look at it; she was looking at Peter. 'Hello, Peter,' she said. 'You look just the same. What happened to Gerry's ankle?'

'I sort of sprained it,' Gerry said. 'It's nothing – but it's getting stiff. Let's go on down.'

They started on again, Emily Fenton in the lead, then Gerry, then Peggy, and himself last. He recalled that he had not said a word in all the interchanges, and still he could not, though Peggy, walking directly in front of him, kept glancing back at him with a smile.

Emily said: 'Did you do all that you said you were going to in that letter you wrote just after Peter arrived?'

'Yes – and more,' Gerry said. 'Didn't we, Peter? Twenty-three major peaks in fifty-three days, sometimes two a day, and in all weathers.'

'Any narrow squeaks?' Emily's voice was casual.

Gerry fell into the trap and said eagerly: 'Oh, yes, two or three. You see, we've been taking calculated risks all the time, pretending that each mountain, however unimportant, is Meru. The worst was today – and solely due to my carelessness. Peter saved my life.'

It was Peggy who stopped and swung around, exclaiming: 'Oh, Peter! What happened?'

He told them simply how Gerry had slipped and how he'd jumped into the bergschrund. Gerry cut in to repeat that he'd been careless and that he owed his life to Peter's quickness. Peggy said: 'Thank you, Peter. He's my favourite brother.'

'And that awful Cousin George would have inherited, too,' Gerry said. But Emily said: 'Surely the slope must have been in a bad condition? Why didn't you go down the south-east ridge, instead of over the Wellenkuppe where you have to get round that gendarme?'

Her voice was sharp, and Peggy said at once, almost as sharply: 'How can you ask questions like that, Emily? You weren't there to decide.'

And Gerry said suddenly in a loud voice: 'On Meru there won't be any south-east ridge.'

'That's the second time you've mentioned Meru,' Emily said. 'Where is it? I've never heard of it.'

The existence of Meru was now 'official,' and there was no reason why Gerry shouldn't have told Emily about it at least six months ago. When he answered, his voice was defensive, 'Surely I must have told you?' he said.

'No, you didn't tell me,' Emily said.

'It's a mountain, in Parasia – between Western Tibet and the Karakorams, I suppose you'd say – twenty-seven thousand, one hundred and forty-one feet high. Peter and I are going to climb it.'

They were swinging on down the rough path all the time, and by now had reached the top of the open fields directly above Zermatt. The sun had dipped behind the Matterhorn, and the valley was in deep, barred shadow.

Gerry took off his hat and wiped his brow. Emily chose that moment to turn and speak to him, but she said only: 'Gerry–' then stopped. Peter thought: She's seen the silver in Gerry's hair. Her eyes lit with a sudden brilliant flare and slid to him and for a fraction of a second held his. She looked really beautiful.

Gerry stopped and put on his hat quickly and said nervously: 'What's the matter, old girl?' But by then Emily had turned again and started to move faster than before, and she only answered: 'Nothing. I thought I saw something up the hill.'

Soon they were in Zermatt, and Mr and Mrs Fenton were hurrying forward across the hotel lounge to hug Gerry, and Peter was shaking their hands and smiling and laughing among them all, while Emily stood a little aside, an expression on her face which he recognized, for he had seen it often enough on his own while standing in front of the mirror, thinking, the shaving brush in his hand. She was deciding that she could no longer drift, that she had to do something, that whatever she did was going to be hard. He could have sworn that she was also, still more like him, forcing herself to the realization that the hardest course might be the best. She looked magnificent, wholly alive. Peter thought that even Christian Holz had never been more fully alive than *he* had made him, through hate.

They arranged to gather in the coffee-room for a big supper in a couple of hours' time, and then Peter made his excuses and went up to the room reserved for him, undressed, and sank back with a sigh into a large hot bath.

CHAPTER 10

He had left the bathroom window a little open so that the steam would not fill the room, and through that tiny crack, flowing in amongst and between the cloud-banks of steam, came the music of a waltz. He listened idly, but wholly committed, his eyes closed and his hand with the scrubbing brush waving in time to the lilt of the music – *Tales from the Vienna Woods*. He heard the band, and in his mind saw the narrow street and saw the people sitting out there. Mostly they had evening dress on by now, at least outside the Cervin where the band was, and were sipping wine and apéritifs, but among them were a few men just down from the mountains, their big boots set four-square under the small tables, and the veined glasses fragile as crystal flowers against the coiled rope and the hard glitter of the axe heads.

The Archduke would be there, with the veiled woman; the Archduchess never came to Zermatt, and the veiled woman never went to Cannes, it was said. A sensible arrangement. The Crown Prince and Princess would be there – an earnest, childless young couple; and the Black Macdonald, the saturnine laird who always climbed in full Highland kit; and the Spanish grandee with a hunched back, and a name two sentences long; and, in a class by himself, the Old

158

Man – he who had brought wealth to this village and Switzerland, and was the high priest and first prophet of mountaineering.

He began to scrub his fingernails.

Peggy had never looked better. Also, she had turned into a woman during these seven years, not so much in any change of figure, though she had lost her puppy fat, as in a quality of ripeness. When he was at Cambridge she had always seemed less *ready* than Emily. The dances, the expeditions to London, the theatres, the discussions on Art and Life, always seemed enormous undertakings to Peggy, almost as though she was afraid of anything with horizons wider than the confining (but sheltering) walls of the play-room. Her admiration for him had the same quality. She was like the twelve-year-old girl who crouches in worship of her brother, aged fourteen, who comes from a mysterious, dangerous world and stands in a lordly manner in front of the play-room fire, legs apart, hands in pockets, and talks about swots, lines, tannings, gatings, coll pre's. Peter thought that in her private heart Peggy had felt the same awe for the ordinary world, towards which she had been growing up. She had not then been ripe for it. Now she was, as Emily had been even then.

He got out of the bath and began to dry himself. The faint music still filled the room, but now he was seeing Peggy as mistress of his bungalow in Rudwal – the D.C's house with the big garden and the staff of fourteen. She was ready for that: calm – no, placid; her happiness like water in a well, deep, its quality unguessable;

159

motionless. Peggy in camp? Yes, there too, unchanged. She would admire the startling sunsets and exclaim when the cough of the leopards sawed the night; but the circle of lamplight in the tent would give her no vision of the dark beyond, only of what it so warmly, tenderly embraced.

Then suddenly it was Emily across the table. For her it was the enormous unknown of the darkness beyond that held the secrets of ecstasy, not the closed circle of the light. And when the sun had sunk, round and burning yellow, with tongues of fire leaping from the rim and the western trees like black fingers across it, it was not the streaked sky nor the bowl of dusty, visible glory that she stared at, but beyond the sun, and into the uttermost depths of the sky, where there was night, a blue and swimming sea of night, and a million flares, unseen, unknown.

There was an unease at the pit of his stomach, such as he always felt when alternatives began to take shape and he knew that soon he must do what he must – reach out across the ice cliff, where the bottom waited silently for him, and a great river was a flash of thin light below; step up into the wind; clench his fist and strike at the armed giants that barred his path.

A low voice said: 'Peter, are you dressed?'

He raised his head. It was coming from the door – a woman's voice. He went over and answered as quietly: 'No.'

'I want to come in.' It was Emily Fenton.

'Wait a moment.' He pulled on his trousers, a shirt, and his dressing-gown, and opened the door. Emily stepped in quickly. He left the door open; she was an unmarried girl. She made a short gesture that he should close it. He did so.

'The people aren't in the rooms on either side,' she said. 'I saw them both downstairs.'

He waited, surveying her as he had not done since the first time they met. After a time, to break the taut silence in which she was staring at him with her eyes gleaming and her lips tight, he said: 'Do you mind if I smoke?'

She shook her head, and he lit a cheroot. 'It's a habit I got into in India,' he said, looking at her over the top of his cupped hands. She was in evening dress, a cloak thrown over her shoulders, and her pale skin ivory. Her eyes were very grey and her hair a deep, thick auburn.

She spoke suddenly. 'You've got to let go of Gerry.'

The tension in her face relaxed. She'd got it out at last; it had been hard, almost incredibly hard for her, but she'd done it. She had taken the difficult course.

'Why?' he said.

'Because you'll destroy him if you go on the way you are,' she said. 'He's not like you, and he never can be. Climbing – this idea of his – yours – that he should prepare himself for India and become a governor – all you'll do is break him.' She was standing close to him, speaking fast but firmly. 'Can't you see that you're breaking his nerve now? You talk about strengthening it, but all people aren't like you, thank God' – this with sudden real viciousness. 'He's a gentleman. It's no use trying to make a Napoleon out of him because he isn't one, and I don't want him to be one. Nor does he.'

He felt himself rising to the challenge, his personality coming together from the diffused state caused by relaxing in the bath, the long tour done and the mountains conquered.

He said: 'Is Gerry a child? It's easy enough to untie the rope.'

'Like Christian Holz?' she said. 'Oh, yes, I've heard. He's given up working, poor man. No, it's not easy for Gerry to untie the rope.' She made a small movement of her hand that dismissed the anger that had been growing between them. This was too important to be angry about, it said; we are talking in an area where the rules of good manners don't apply – just as I have passed beyond another set of rules by being with you, in your bedroom, behind a closed door.

She said: 'I was angry with you today. You saw. I suppose I've always been jealous of you, too, because since he met you you have meant more to him than – anything or anybody. I'm not angry now, because I've had time to think. I don't really hate you, Peter – I admire you and wish I could be like you, just as Gerry and Peggy do. But I've got to speak before it is too late. Gerry simply does not have the nerve, the will-power, whatever you want to call it, that you have. He's not like you. He's good and gentle and considerate.'

'Nothing like me,' he said, coldly because that was his nature, but not denying her statement.

'No,' she said flatly, 'you are different. Whatever you are, it's not "good and gentle." It may be something much greater, but it isn't like that.

162

You're tuning Gerry higher than he can go. I felt when I saw you both today that he was a 'cello that someone, a god or a devil but not a person, had taken because he liked the shape, and was tightening the screws, stretching the strings tighter, trying to make it play the score of a violin, at the top of a violin's range. It can't be done! Something's got to break, shatter, all of a sudden. His hair – at *twenty-eight!* You know he went out and bought some dye as soon as you went upstairs? So no one knows except us three – Peggy didn't see, and after that he kept his hat on, even in the coffee-room. That wasn't the result of any one day, any one incident, whatever you or he think. It was something that began the moment you met him and began to turn the screw, raise the pitch – at first so little that no one noticed; and then, when they did, it was exciting and wonderful and good, because he used to be understrung, he had no purpose at all. When are you going to Meru?'

'Reconnaissance in nineteen-eleven, climb it in nineteen-thirteen,' he said. They had talked it out thoroughly in a score of Alpine huts.

'Oh, God,' she said, and she did not use the words lightly. She sat down slowly and put her head in her hands. He looked at the closed door; listened, disembodied, to the faint creak and pad of feet moving along the corridor, the lilting music of the band outside the Cervin, almost opposite. And inside this room this woman and he were talking about things that Gerry would not really understand, because they were beyond the limits of what he wanted to understand. To

163

Gerry all was a question of duty and courage only – one was brave, or one was not; one found what one's duty was and did it.

'Why don't you ask him to marry you?' he said suddenly.

She started violently and went pale. She said: 'You know why.'

'Because he'd have to say yes?'

She nodded.

He said: 'Would you have to say yes if he asked you?'

She stared at him, and her face became aware, alive again, but not angry. She said: 'No.'

He said: 'Would Peggy have to say yes if I asked her?'

She nodded.

'And I, if Peggy asked me?'

She shook her head.

'I'm not talking about pressure from outside, or who is capable of standing up against convention,' he said.

'I know,' she said, and she did.

He walked away from her slowly and stared out of the window at some white furnace, hanging in the darkness to the south-west, that might have been a strange cloud, or a new dim constellation in another universe, but was the Matterhorn. He returned to her.

'Gerry's my best friend,' he began.

'Oh, I know, I know,' she said quickly.

He said: 'No man knows what he can do until he tries. No man knows what's behind a door until someone opens it.'

She was listening, but at the same time

pursuing a parallel line of thought of her own, so that when she spoke she was not answering him but making a response, as in a psalm. 'No one but me really sees what you're doing.' She spoke, very low, almost whispering. 'Peggy – nothing, because it's you. My father and mother – a little; but for every worry, for every time they notice a new line around his eyes, something different about his mouth, they see the new strength, the expertness, the decision.'

'Those are real,' he said.

'Of course – but he's not Gerry any more.'

He felt there was nothing he could say that could lift the two of them out of the mud in which they were struggling. If he could speak with the same force that he could act or think, it would be different. That was it. He had to act.

He said: 'Do you want to know what's happened to Gerry?'

'Yes,' she said, 'of course. But–'

He said: 'Tomorrow. Come with me tomorrow, and we'll climb the Zmutt ridge of the Matterhorn – guideless. Are you fit enough?'

She stared at him. She said: 'Yes. How did you know that was my dream – the Zmutt ridge, guideless. And arrive at the top by dawn.'

He didn't answer. She said: 'It's a dream, but it's not actually impossible. Only, the amateurs good enough to take me wouldn't do it because it wouldn't be safe. I might lose my nerve.'

'I'll go with you tomorrow,' he said, 'but I won't *take* you. *We* will climb the Zmutt ridge, guideless – and reach the summit at dawn, and come down the Hörnli.'

Her grey eyes began to take on an extraordinary, vivid life of their own, perhaps some reflection of the light from her hair. 'All right,' she said.

He said: 'Gerry's got a sprained ankle.'

She said: 'Peggy's got a headache – migraine.'

He said: 'I'll find out in the morning who's going up to the Hörnli, and arrange to join them. That'll fix the chaperonage. I'll tell your father we've got a guide. But we'll go to the Schönbühl.'

'What about the people we're supposed to join at the Hörnli?' she said calmly.

'I'll send a boy up with a note,' he said, 'telling them we've cried off.'

She nodded, her eyes still aflame. She stood up suddenly. 'I've got to go. I'll get into awful trouble if anyone finds me here.'

But he hadn't finished. He wanted to keep those eyes alight with their deep, wondering fire, to keep the lips parted in her wide, strong mouth. He said: 'What else are your dreams, that you think you can never make come true?' She was a flamingly beautiful young woman. How could he have known her so long, and even suspected the Spanish fire under the over-bred calm of her manner, and still have stood away and aloof? For Gerry, of course... She was a courtesan, one of those who have turned kings into heroes – and ruined empires. He said: 'Haven't you ever wanted to make the Archduke offer you one of his detached houses in Budapest?'

Now she was breathless, and her eyes were fixed on his as though she were hypnotized. 'Yes, yes,' she whispered. 'But–'

'You shall,' he said, 'so that you can say "No!" when he does – not angrily, but inevitably. So that he'll *know* you're going to say no, but still he must try. Have you ever heard an ice-axe humming from the electricity in the air?'

She stood braced, as though pushing him away from her. Then she broke and hurried to the door. 'Tomorrow,' she whispered.

CHAPTER 11

She awoke with an almost terrifying surge of consciousness. It was midnight, and someone was scratching at the door of the women's bunk-room. Peter. She was in the Schönbühl hut. She stepped out and up in one motion and whispered: 'All right.' She heard him move away as she bent down to find her boots. The midnight awakenings in huts like this should be purgatory, a sour taste in the mouth, the muscles like lead, the stomach queasy, and ahead the heavy hours of slogging across a hummocky glacier, the lantern swinging in the guide's hand, and at the end a 'good climb for a competent lady.' This was different. She was aware of the night and the silence and Peter a few feet away, and over there the Zmutt ridge of the Matterhorn.

She dressed quickly. The night air crackled against the window panes; the moon was in the third quarter; the stars powdered the sky. A long veil of silver hung in a down-arching curve from the crest of the mountain.

She went out to him and by the light of the lantern he checked her clothes, boots, rope, ice-axe, and all the articles in his own light pack.

'Take your skirt off,' he said. She obeyed quickly, turning her back, though under the skirt she wore heavy tweed breeches.

'Where shall I put it?' she asked. Usually

women left their skirts under a rock near the foot of the ascent and put them on again on the way down; but they would not be returning this way.

'Under the bunk,' he said.

Then she followed him into the moonlight and they began to walk quickly across the Zmutt glacier. Half-way across, suddenly, she found the source of the tremendous power that moved her so effortlessly across the glacier, that made every step a vivid affirmation of life. It was fear.

She stopped and said it aloud. There was no need to pretend to Peter Savage – also, it was doubly dangerous. She said: 'I am afraid.'

He stopped and faced her, the moon-glow softening his face, so that he looked like a tensed, patient Apollo. He said: 'Look at me.' She was looking, but now she looked harder, trying to find some kind of anxiety lurking in the lines of his face or buried in the winter blue of his eyes.

'We're not going to fail, or fall. I've been up here twice, and I know it – and I know you. You're not going to lose your nerve anywhere, whatever happens. You're not a lady' – he grinned, and his teeth flashed momentarily – 'you're a climber.'

She considered, and knew it was true. There could be no fear today; and, in fact, looking for it again, she found that it had gone.

They began climbing. At the difficult places he held the lantern in his teeth as the guides did, but that too he had practised. Her own legs were long; there was need, for in places the stretch was long between foot-holds.

They came to such a place. She watched,

169

waiting. He reached up, crept his fingers into a rugosity of the rock, and held hard. The cold seeped inside her coat and the bleak wind soughed across the face of the ridge. A steady pull; then he leaned away, held by balance alone; a short step and he was up, digging his ice-axe into the snow, anchoring the rope around a rock, the lamp set down in snow under the rock. She looked up at him, past him at the falling ridge of ice and snow, beyond again at the unreachable stars. Not tonight unreachable, though. Tonight she could touch them. Her hand went up, stretching. She could not reach the place where he had taken his first finger-hold. In a second she must step down and wonder: What now?

'I can't reach,' she said, but as she spoke she felt a gentle pressure in the rope, and: 'Now,' his voice spoke, lifting her. A long stretch, and her fingers gripped the rock, and: 'Now,' he said again, and she caught the rhythm, holding the mountain away as she held a partner in the waltz, stepping quick and neatly up until she joined him.

Oh, Gerry, she thought; poor Gerry!

Always he was waiting for her, but as she climbed she knew that they could walk side by side – if this were not a mountain – for his waiting was not impatient, nor was his leading the leading of a guide. She was his companion, and as the blood flowed free through her veins she was his partner. The darkness below was a sea of land, of wishes, of talk, but they were on the mountain, the granite wave whose crest brushed the stars. On, on, let the minuet last for ever, a thousand feet an hour, and in the dawn they'd step on the summit and bow, and then–?

'Rest,' he said, and blew out the lantern and set it on a stone to cool. He opened his pack and handed her the bottle of cold unsweetened tea. He had a pint of brandy in there too, and half a bottle of champagne. That was the custom – the brandy to keep out the cold, the champagne for the summit.

He put the cold lantern in his pack and stood up. They went on, for a few moments her legs stiff and inexact. Then she heard music and thought the exhilaration had actually lifted her off the mountain; but it was Peter humming an Indian tune, and when she asked him what it was he said: *The Wounded Heart.* Then the rhythm came back, and with each step and each light breath it was the tune of *The Wounded Heart* singing in her ears.

...a long diagonal cleft of rock, the snow powdering his shoulders and falling in icy spangles around her head – up to him, now with him, for he took her hand and led her slowly forward. The summit.

'Here,' he said. A silent minute when she heard her own breathing, deep and steady under the wind; then the wind died, and they stood close in utter silence, and her knees began to shiver and the pit of her stomach to draw small and tight. She remembered no details of the climb, only the circle of lamplight, a little rock, she and Peter, strength and certainty.

'The stars have gone,' she whispered, her voice trembling. Six thousand feet in six hours; the

171

Zmutt ridge, guideless; she, a woman – any one of these was enough to explain the quaking of her heart, yet all of them together could not explain it.

He did not answer, and in the quietness the dawn marched up out of the darkness of Italy with saffron banners flying and trumpets calling and drums beating.

The wind rose and as the light touched the mountain an avalanche began somewhere out of sight below them, among the precipices at the head of the Furgg Glacier.

He said: 'Ready to go down?'

Ready? Since she could not go any further up, here, she must be ready. She remembered the champagne and told him she wanted to share it with him, here and now.

He undid the gold foil from the mouth of the bottle and pressed up under the heavy cork with his thumbs. The cork flew out, and the golden wine spurted twenty feet across the snow.

'Oh, Peter!' she cried. 'Is it all gone?'

He held the bottle upside down, and the last drops fell on the snow. 'Yes,' he said. 'It turned out to be a libation instead. Are you ready?'

Now down, the rope coiled in his hand and she moving fast down the Hörnli ridge ahead of him. She had been up and down here five times now – so now was the need to be doubly careful. On the north face, near here, the rope had broken that July day of 1865, and four men died, perhaps because they too, coming down from the first ascent of the mountain, were filled with wild elation.

What now? What next? She wanted to turn and ask him, but she could not.

Ah, but the next thing would be the Potters and their guide coming up. Some of the elation left her. They would not be alone on the mountain for long. She wondered what Gerry was thinking. From below the Solvay hut she scanned the ridge and could see nothing. The Potters would be in sight if they were coming. Then they weren't coming. They had turned back because she and Peter had not appeared at the Hörnli hut last night. In two or three hours they would reach Zermatt, and then there'd be excitement and everyone wondering what had happened to them – until the boy delivered Peter's note to Gerry. But that wouldn't help either, because then they would convince themselves that the pair of them lay dead somewhere below the Zmutt ridge. And everyone would be sure Peter had somehow forced her to go with him on this insane adventure, for his own glorification. It was unfair, unfair! Only Gerry would understand, and Gerry would be argued down because everyone knew he was Peter's slave – she had said so herself. The peak was behind them, and down there in the trench of the valley was life, muddy with a swirling, heavy ground-swell of opinion, custom, and prejudice. As soon as they passed the Schwarzsee she'd be caught back into it and whirled heavily around until all this miracle was washed out of her mind, until she could believe it had never happened; or that if it had it shouldn't have, that there was something inherently wicked about it; but it had, and there wasn't.

She set her jaw and moved faster still. Wait till they saw her striding into Zermatt without a skirt! Oh, just wait! For the sake of a skirt they would deny truth?

Peter was a silent man, and she could not tell him what she wanted to. After a while she was sure that there was no need.

At the Hörnli hut they found signs – the warm ashes of a fire, some paper, a cork still smelling of fresh wine – that someone had been there the night before. In another hour they passed the Schwarzsee and entered the forests as the path zigzagged down. The sun shone directly on their backs, throwing long shadows ahead of them, and it was morning, the cow-bells tolling slowly in the fields and little children walking silent behind the cows, and the sound of hammering as they pegged each animal to its chain and to its appointed place.

'Let's rest,' Peter said. He turned off the path, where it ran down the steep slope above the Zmuttbach, and led back along the hillside. She followed quietly, because Zermatt was near and she was growing afraid of facing it. He stopped beside a tall tree near the edge of a low cliff, and he was looking at her as she came into the place. It was quiet there, though the stream whispered silkily at the foot of the cliff. Through the feathery, lightly moving boughs of the tree the Matterhorn filled the sky, leaning over, ready to engulf them.

She stopped a couple of feet from him, holding her eyes steady on his face. She had something to say, and if she waited she would say it, for the words were welling up like water from an overfull spring. 'I never knew you, Peter. I'm sorry. I understand – but Gerry doesn't and never will.'

He looked tired for the first time that she could remember. She was not afraid of him, and it was true, as it had always been, that he was destroying Gerry, but only because he was looking for a companion, such as he had found in her for these few hours when she had been his partner. But what now? If she took Gerry away from him, as she could, it was Peter who might be destroyed. He was diabolically brilliant – but brittle. He needed Gerry more than he knew. And in fact, could Gerry return to the cattle and the footmen at Wilcot after this man had breathed discontent into his nostrils?

They were at an impasse, and no way out except surrender. Forget it had happened, deny it, pretend it wasn't, because any other course was too dangerous, too bright with chances of ecstasy and passion – and hell.

He stepped forward and took her in his arms, reaching down with his mouth for her mouth, placing his lips on hers, and seeking her.

This was the first time any man had even tried to kiss her, except Gerry. Why? Because she was a lady, and beautiful, and did not invite men to share anything with her. But this was not Gerry, and this was not Gerry's kiss. She put her arms round his neck and stood relaxed against him, wondering. His hand slid up deep into the hair at the nape of her neck.

But this would not answer anything. It was more strangely wonderful than her most fierce imaginings, and he must not stop now. But it would not solve anything, it would only make everything worse.

Slowly, as slowly as the realization of a tide rising between the rocks, she knew that he was not going to stop until all was done. So now she must break away from him, because he was insulting her. He was not a gentleman. He wasn't fit to clean Gerry's shoes, who treated her so gently, who stood so humbly before her womanhood. Then, and suddenly, as suddenly as the beginning of realization had been slow, she knew that this *would* answer everything, solve all problems. He was not insulting her any more than he had when he asked her to go up the Zmutt ridge with him. He would never treat her gently or stand humbly before her. This that was happening to her was real. This was the mystery she had dreamed about as unattainable, not even knowing the shape of it. This that was growing inside her before their bodies touched was the union, of more than bodies, which she had tried to tell herself did not exist – because she knew, seeing Gerry as her husband, that it never would. But here, now, it was real and urgent, as violently desired as the menacing promise of the Zmutt ridge; all real – the ridge, the summit's unknowable reward – but oh, guarded by what cold edges of night and virgin fear.

She was afraid, as vividly afraid as she had been on the glacier; and, as then, she tried to stop, stiffening in frantic unreason, fighting away from him, her eyes glazed and dull.

'There's no escape backward, ever,' he said.

She heard, and knew that for him there wasn't; nor for her if she went with him; and that she knew she would do, because she loved him. In spite of knowing him, in spite of anything, because of everything, she loved him. She went to him, and he was not gentle with her.

The act of love was nothing like what she had expected, and they did not reach any great summit together, though she matched Peter's desperate strivings, but she knew when it was done that they had together set their feet on a great mountain.

They sat side by side, hands tight clasped. The sun shone directly through the branches, and the sound of the torrent came louder to her ears. Peter got up and pulled her to her feet. When she was upright he said: 'Emily, marry me.'

She nodded. Her lower lip trembled so that she had to bite it with her teeth, and her eyes were full, and the far trees were blurred in the bright sun.

'"For better, for worse,"' he said slowly.

'"For richer, for poorer,"' she said.

'"Till death us do part." Come on. We'll go straight to the hotel and tell Gerry.'

But a minute after they had crossed the rude bridge over the Zmuttbach she saw five men hurrying towards them – her father, three guides, and Gerry, all carrying ropes and ice-axes, and the guides also loaded with heavy rucksacks. Gerry, in the lead, saw them first of the party. He yelled: 'Peter!' and ran forward, limping and waving his ice-axe in the air.

'Peter,' he babbled, 'are you all right? Where in

hell have you been? Mally's in a frightful stew, though I told her nothing could go wrong with you. How was it, Emily? He took you over the Zmutt ridge, did he? Well, well, no one else could have done it!' His eyes shone and his teeth flashed and his sunburned face crinkled with pure joy.

Mr Fenton came up and said gruffly: 'Well, Peter, what's the meaning of this?'

Oh, God, let's not say anything now – later, later, when we are calm and this joyful excitement's over and Daddy's not angry.

Peter said coldly: 'Uncle George, Emily and I are engaged. We are going to be married as soon as possible.'

She kept her eyes on Gerry then, beseeching him to understand that what had happened to him had happened to her, only she was a woman and his sister. Now she recognized it. Gerry was born to be the brother of mankind. Abel – Jonathan. David had taken her. She heard her father gasp; heard a muttering from the guides as they mumbled that they'd better be getting back; heard the crunch of the boots going away down the path; behind her the roar of the Zmuttbach.

'This – this – is impossible,' her father said at last.

'We're in love,' she said, speaking at Gerry's frozen face.

Gerry turned away and hobbled down the path towards Zermatt, stumbling as though he could not see. Peter took her hand and held it loosely.

'It's better,' he said.

Her father said: 'Who will tell Peggy? Is your

mind really made up, Emily? It's unbelievable, it's fantastic. Yesterday you hated him. Today–' He drifted into silence.

'I'll tell Peggy,' Peter said.

She stirred then. Her lover was unafraid, and when the way was difficult they all fell back and left it to him, so his courage grew a hard, bitter edge.

She said: 'No I will.'

He turned on her, ready to speak, his eyes glittering. She smiled, and after a moment he bent his head and kissed her hand.

CHAPTER 12

LETTERS FROM INDIA

D.C's CAMP
RUDWAL, PUNJAB
January 12th, 1910

Dearest Mally and Daddy,

It is only a month since we settled into the house – I must remember to call it a bungalow – at Rudwal, but already we are out of it again, and in camp. I was just getting used to the bungalow. It is huge, with great deep verandas all round, and eight big rooms with high ceilings and a big garden. The staff is about fourteen, of whom five are with us now in camp. I say 'about' fourteen because every time I tried to count them I got a different answer – someone had brought a friend to work and someone else had gone off to visit his mother in another part of India altogether.

Camp is wonderful, though, and if Peter had his way I don't think we'd ever be in the bungalow. We move nearly every day, and it is not a bit hot – in fact it is very cold at night, and at midday only hot in the sun. The mountains are covered with snow right down to the foothills twenty miles behind Rudwal, and you have never imagined such mountains! Nothing prepares you for them. They make everything we know seem very insignificant – except the Matterhorn, of course, but even that would look puny, too fierce for its size, like a ferocious little pygmy, if it was set out there in the great range a hundred miles behind us.

Peter is very busy. I hope he doesn't try to keep up this pace all the time because no one, not even he, could do it. The D.C before him was a man called Philipson. He was here for about twenty years, and then died in the Suez Canal on his way home. The trouble is that there are no limits, and a man seems to be able to do as much or as little as he feels like. There are a few things which are definitely the D.C's business. But there is literally nothing which can't be *made* his business if he wants it – leopards worrying the cattle, diseases that might be contagious, all kinds of crime, political movements, flooding rivers, new crop plantings, taxes, school curriculums, everything – and all over an area about the size of Wales. Believe me, Daddy, you're lucky only being squire of Llyn Gared.

I have seen Adam Khan once, in the bazaar. We exchanged a few words but he seemed very distrait, and is even thinner than he was, with great hollow eyes. His father is an absolute dear, but rather overpowering, I imagine.

I am very happy, Mally. You have got to understand that. There was a part in your first letter where you told me to take care of myself and not to worry, I could always turn to you. Mally, I am *not* going to have a baby, and if anyone's going to look after me, Peter will. You know how awful I felt about the way things happened, and it still hurts terribly that Gerry was so wounded. One *never* knows people. I just didn't think he *could* be so hurt. The trouble is, Peter feels it twice as much. But I really think everything had to happen that way. I know you don't like Peter, but it's no good blaming him, because it was my fault too ... I mean, my doing. Anyway, I love him and you'll have to think of that, always, or we shall only quarrel, or worse. I will write every week now that I am getting settled, and can find where the writing paper is kept, even in camp.

All my love,
Emily

D.C's BUNGALOW
RUDWAL, PUNJAB
October 26th, 1910

Dearest Mally and Daddy,

Yes, we had heard that Harry Walsh and Peggy had been married. There was quite a lot about it in the local paper, the *Civil and Military,* because Peggy is the sister of 'Lord Wilcot, whose informed interest in Indian affairs seems to be leading him towards the proconsulship of one of our Presidencies,' as the paper said, and lots more in the best newspaper jargon. We wrote, and sent a present too, though the latter will not arrive for some time. I hope they will both be very happy, and I can't help hoping too that this will help Peggy forget what is past. We have not heard from her since we were married.

Gerry wrote Peter a wonderful letter a couple of months ago, apologizing for what he called his caddishness, congratulating us, and saying the best man won. It made me feel like a prize cow or something, but I cried with happiness, and I thought Peter was going to, and you know what his self-control is. He wrote off at once, and I believe they are closer than ever now.

Yesterday we got another long letter from Gerry about plans for next year. He is coming out late in the cold weather, about the first of February, and will spend three months in Madras with the Lawleys before coming up here, and then he and Peter are going off to make a reconnaissance of Meru, with a few Gurkhas from the 13th at Manali. Peter thinks Gerry will learn the basic facts of Indian administration during his time in Madras, but I am not so sure. I am afraid he might only learn that he is un-suited to the life. Peter and I nearly quarrelled when I told him that. Well, we shall see, and I'm glad I shall be present when Gerry comes up here.

I saw Adam Khan again the other day, this time while I was riding, alone, miles from anywhere, and he was out walking all by himself in the middle of a very hot afternoon. He tried to pass by with a word, but I wouldn't let him, and once he started to talk he seemed to want to tell me everything. The main thing worrying him is the secretiveness that there has to be – well, Peter says there has to be – in his contacts with Peter. I told Peter about our talk later, and he said: 'Adam doesn't know what he wants. He'll have to make up his mind.'

Anyway, though I can see why Adam is un-happy, it does seem to be working. We have much more co-operation between the officials (meaning Peter) and the educated Indians here than they have in most districts. The district board, which is quite new, is really doing very well and taking a lot of work off Peter's shoulders. Peter's big problem now is the hospital and nurses' school he wants to get founded, and there the C.G.G is really being helpful. The old-fashioned people and the farmers, who are in the big majority, are quite happy the way things are, and do not have any use for the agitators – but because they are old-fashioned they wouldn't dream of sending their daughters to the nurses' school even when we get it started, and that's going to need a lot more money and the enlargement of the hospital first, as nurses can't learn properly just in a classroom.

No more now. Peter's superior, the Commissioner of the Dogra Division, is coming on the morning train, and I have to be hostess at a big mixed Indian and British tea-party, mostly Indian, and some of the C.G.G won't come because they don't think the Morley-Minto Reforms went far enough. They have written very polite notes making it clear that they do not wish to insult the Commissioner himself. The Old Captain is furious and swears he won't speak to any of the C.G.G who *do* come. It's more complicated than when Dai Jones wouldn't play his flute at the Diamond Jubilee fête unless they sang *God Save the Queen* in Welsh.

All my love,
Emily

Dearest Mally and Daddy,

Gerry arrived a week ago, looking very well. It was the first time I had seen him since Zermatt. I was a little nervous just before he came, in spite of all the letters and everything seeming to be just as it used to be, only more so.

I should have known better. Gerry is a dear all through; there is nothing mean in him, nor ever was, and nothing seems to have altered between him and Peter. They plunged into calculations for their expedition almost at once, and I hardly got a chance to talk to Gerry till the next day. They are off next Tuesday, and will be gone for six weeks. Right up till Gerry came we were thinking that I might go home while they were away, but in the end we decided it would be better if I stayed here. I shall go up to Manali for a week or two in June and be a gay grass widow, only I shall behave myself, not like the women in *Plain Tales from the Hills*. The sad thing is that it will not matter whether I behave myself or not, people will always be found to believe that I have not. It all depends on yourself and your husband. The thought that I might flirt never crosses Peter's mind, of course.

Peter's been in court all day today, as usual, and Gerry and I have had a wonderful talk and went round the bazaar together. He is really quite miserable about his time in Madras, though he tries hard not to show it. He saw how the government is run, and what can be done to improve

185

things, and he doesn't mind the pomp and ceremony. But all he is really thinking of, all that really occupies his mind both there and here, is the poverty and the disease. He reacts to them as though he personally is responsible. Peter doesn't, but he does a great deal to improve conditions. Gerry *feels* more, but can't face the pushing and threatening and struggling that are necessary to change things. I hope they have a good talk while they are on the expedition, and really thrash out what is best for Gerry to do. He seems to be very drawn to India – and, of course, to Peter. He sends you his love, by the way, and promises to write you a long letter tomorrow. He pretends to be moonstruck over a girl he met on the boat, but I'm afraid that's only for my benefit.

All my love,
Emily

D.C's BUNGALOW
RUDWAL, PUNJAB
July 5th, 1911

Dear Mally and Daddy,

They're back yesterday! And they are sure there's a feasible way so that at least they can get a good chance at the summit. It's a huge pyramid apparently, irregular and split by ridges, with short glaciers between. Most of the ridges seem to end in tremendous ice cliffs, but they are sure they can get round at least one of them, on the south-east. They didn't try to force their way up any particular route, but went round the mountain at 19,000 feet, more or less, looking through a telescope, making sketches and taking

186

bearings. Then the weather broke and they had to do double marches most of the way back. Gerry is looking fitter than I have ever seen him. There was no 'big' climbing, only hard effort and planning for the future. Peter is just the same, I do not think he would look any different if he fell off the top of Meru.

They are going to make the big attempt in 1913, and have decided to ask Harry Walsh. I hope he accepts, and that Peggy can come out with him and stay here with me while they are away. She has written a couple of times since getting our wedding present, not as she used to, but politely enough. I am sure we can be real friends again if she would come here, especially with Peter away.

There had been no change in Gerry's plans, and, seeing him again, I wonder if I was imagining things before, when I thought he would not be happy as an Indian administrator. Being with Peter has put new life and determination in him, and he has everything at his fingertips. He is going to spend a lot of time in the Lords between now and the expedition, and he has already been promised the Parliamentary Under-Secretary-ship for India by 1914, and a Presidency a few years later, depending on who retires and who succeeds Lord Minto at Calcutta.

Peter has plunged straight back into his work as though he had never been gone. The C.G.G had a reception committee for him, complete with garlands and a speech about how they were loyal to the King Emperor, and that their function was that of loyal opposition and that he, Peter, was a great man and they hoped he would rise to great heights for the good of India. I thought at first that Adam Khan had been the moving spirit behind the reception (for of course it will be reported in the *C & M* and will put Peter's stock still higher) but he wasn't – it was spontaneous. One gets so muddled when some people insist that the C.G.G are practically anarchists and others that they are loyal constitutionalists. I think Peter is the only Englishman in this country who really knows what he wants to do, and why.

All my love,
Emily

D.C's BUNGALOW
RUDWAL, PUNJAB
December 23rd, 1911

Dearest Daddy Darling,

I don't know what to say. I sent off a cablegram as soon as I got yours yesterday, and I will try and write some more soon. Everything seemed to happen so suddenly but I suppose, it being what it was, that you must have known some time ago and didn't tell me because of Peter's being away and then he and Gerry having fever. They are both well now and Peter is going to write when he comes back from a short tour. He left this morning. He shouldn't have gone, but nothing would stop him because he thinks he will be able to talk the big land-owner out there into giving half a *lakh* of rupees to the Hospital Fund – with the half-promise of a Rai Bahadur as a bait. Oh Daddy, I'm going to have a baby. I would have waited to let you know till a little later – she isn't due till July – but now I want you to know. Put some primroses on Mally's grave for me as soon as they are out.

Peter told me to tell you that if you would like to come and live with us out here for a time he'd be honoured to have you, and you know I'd love it.

All my love,
Emily

PS – Gerry is too cut up to write just yet, but he will.

D.C's BUNGALOW
RUDWAL, PUNJAB
July 22nd, 1912

Dearest Daddy,

Did you get Peter's cablegram? In case you didn't, it was a boy after all, just as Peter said it would be, and we're going to call him Rodney after his great-grandfather, the old general. He weighed 7lb 14oz, and began making a terrible noise right after he was born – that was last Saturday week, very early in the morning, soon after I got to Lahore, and was the old surgeon grumpy at having to leave the Pig at that hour! I was feeling very exhausted for the first few days and only now that I am back with Peter in Rudwal can I really understand what's happened, that I'm a mother, that I have a son. I wish Mally could have lived just this long.

Perhaps he'll be a mountaineer, like his father. But I hope not, really. For one thing, Peter won't leave him any mountains to conquer... I don't like that word but have got used to using it. Peter is silly about him. He was lifting him on his knee and asking me when he was going to be able to walk – at ten days! He has big ears rather like yours, but the rest of him is all Savage as far as I can see. He is a very greedy little baby, too, and I almost have to smack him to tell him that it's the end of dinner-time.

Peter is doing very well. He was officially commended by the Lt-Governor the other day for the way he dealt with a very complicated religious dispute we had here between the Dogras and the Mohammedans. And a few days earlier Peter's judgement in a civil case was appealed to the high court in Lahore and the plaintiff hired the most expensive lawyer there, an Englishman, but the judge said that the ruling of the district magistrate in the case (that was Peter), 'although at first sight so unexpected as to be almost startling, on deeper study showed itself to be most penetrating of the real intent of the framers of this singularly obscure piece of legislation' (I am copying from the *Civil and Military!*) 'and that it must stand, as it probably will for generations to come, as a model of clear, forceful, and original thinking.'

It's just as well, as he has already written the letter telling the Commissioner he intends to take twelve weeks' leave next year, for the big attempt on Meru, and will need a hot-weather replacement here. Junior men in the I.C.S just don't get that much leave every two years, but Peter made it clear that they are going to have no alternative, except to throw him out, and they know that if they even thought of that there'd be a terrible outcry here – and, of course, from Gerry in the Lords. He is asking one other Englishman besides Harry and Gerry, someone called James Lyon. You may have heard of him. Also two French guides, Lapeyrol and Cadez, from Chamonix.

The household staff has been increased by an ayah and the ayah's little girl, aged three, since I came back with Rodney. I have always had an ayah, of course, a sort of personal maid (aged fifty), but she wouldn't stay because she said she didn't like babies. Actually I think it was too dull for her here, and I didn't have gentlemen friends calling as soon as Peter went to the office, which I understand was the custom at her last employment in Simla – from which she got enormous tips.

The heat was appalling this year, and now the rains have broken and mould starts to grow on clothes if you leave them for more than a few days in the wardrobes.

All my love,
Emily

PS – A letter has just arrived saying that an assistant secretary and another man are coming up from Madras to look at the co-operative breeding station Peter started here a year ago!

PPS – Please tell the broker to sell another thousand shares of Central Copper for me, please, and credit the proceeds to my account at Martin's.

Dearest Daddy,

Just a hurried line as the expedition has reached Bombay and telegrams are flying back and forth about lost kit and stuff being held up in customs. *The Times* has sole rights to the story, and Peter's been writing a long article describing the preparations. I do hope they succeed as it will be terribly disappointing for him otherwise, especially the way he has been writing, as though there is no chance of failure, but the weather is not subject to anyone, not even Peter, and there are times when no one could climb Meru, or even Cader Brith.

We are so much looking forward to seeing Gerry again. He has been doing splendidly in the Lords, from what we read. But I hope he has been able to keep fit, too. Peter spends his days in court, but is in training all the time, I don't know how.

Rodney is screaming his head off and I must see that ayah makes his bottle right. I caught her one day putting a little gin into it when he had been very fretful with his teeth.

All my love,
Emily

But when she had laid down the pen and sealed up the envelope she did not go and supervise the making of Rodney's bottle. Outside it was raining, and Peter was at court, and she sat quietly, thinking how little, in all her letters, she had told of the truth of her marriage or even of her life. This failure, which she felt amounted almost to concealment, was yet not deliberate. Only how can you tell even parents whom you love about the inwardness of marriage? Mally would have been able to read more between the lines, but when she died there was only Daddy, and to him you had to speak directly – and that she could not do. She had wanted to make them understand that her marriage was going as she had expected, for she had known very well that Peter Savage could be no ordinary husband, but there was no way of telling them, or anyone, without making them think the opposite.

There had been chilly, almost silent battles with Peter – about Gerry, about Adam Khan, the Old Captain, Rodney, housekeeping, a hundred things. She never won, in the sense that he gave in to her; but often, after she had been roused to the same high pitch of intensity that was normal with him, she had made him see that she was right, and then he had agreed with her and done what she wanted him to. He never held these 'victories' against her, as she knew that many husbands did; and, best of all, he never said that something was not her business. If she chose to argue with him about farming, or the Moslem inheritance laws, he would listen and treat her with no more and no less abruptness than he used to the Commissioner.

That was good; and the sense of climbing was good, for there could be no doubt that he was brilliant as well as ferociously determined. If he merely sat back and took what was coming to him the service would soon waft him to its highest pinnacles. But of course he would not do that. That would be the easy way, and he would take the difficult, the impossible. Because no I.C.S man had been Viceroy of India since John Lawrence in 1860 – because it had been, since that time, a foundation of government policy that no I.C.S man *should* be Viceroy – therefore Peter would be Viceroy. She knew now that that had become his intention. He had even decided when it should happen: in succession to Gerry, probably about 1930. 1930! Seventeen years ahead! The good Lord alone knew what might have happened in India by then – but Peter intended to meet the destiny of India at that point, and from there on take it into his strong hands, with Gerry, by then translated to the India Office, guarding his back against the politicians at home.

There was excitement in the vistas he described to her. When they were alone in the bungalow late at night, and the work done, he would talk; better still, in the big tent on the cold-weather tours, with the flap raised and the stars flaming over the remote snows. All the Presidency governors were going to be Indians, instead of lords from home. Each province would govern itself according to the customs of its people. The Himalayan torrents would be harnessed to give the country electric power. An Indian Sandhurst would train Indian officers; and there would be ten colleges of engineering and agriculture for every one there was now. He would re-create the

Indian middle class, and give its members training, work, and responsibility. He ... he... All these and a thousand other seeds lay in his mind, ready to flower.

Then she remembered that in Lahore they were already calling him (but not to his face, for they too knew where he was going) the Koi-Hai Napoleon, and the Duke of Rudwal, and the Lord of All Asia. Remembering, she felt a pang of savage contempt for them all; then she shook her head. Peter held no one in contempt; he believed most literally that God had made man in His own image; it was man's fearful refusal to recognize his tremendous destiny that he despised.

Only – that was not true, not in the way Peter believed. He would break a hundred men before he reached his own horizons and however greatly she valued him she could not think the price worth paying. She thought that if she could make him see only that, she would have fulfilled the purpose of her life, far more than in giving birth to Rodney or being her husband's wife and lover.

Soon Gerry would be here again, and he and Peter would go off on that other journey of mountaineering where she could not be a partner because she was a woman and when she reached the physical ends of her strength they would still be no farther than at the foot of the garden. It would be wonderful to have Gerry close even for a few days, wonderful and nerve-racking. She had spent the best part of twenty years seeing him as a husband and lover, and he had never been in focus. Then Peter gave the lens one fierce twist, in that moment of discovery under the loom of the Matterhorn, and showed her the truth. Gerry was her younger brother, even her son. She wanted to look after him, and when she saw him going about with Peter, unchained, beside him, it was about Gerry's safety that she thought – as it would have been if Peter had suddenly tried to eat the baby Rodney. But (she smiled ruefully) baby Rodney could look after himself. He seemed to need nothing from her, now that she had weaned him. He had an almost appalling determination, and knew many ways both of protecting himself and of getting what he wanted. If Gerry and that baby were left out in the sun it would not be Gerry who would find, crawl to, and occupy the only piece of shade.

And Harry Walsh would be here. It was a pity that Peggy had not been able to come. Next time, perhaps – but there must not be a next time. Peter had set his feet on the mountain Meru, and if he did not climb it the earth would fall, and she and Gerry and Adam Khan with it.

CHAPTER 13

Tonight, because the expedition would be with them tomorrow, she had had the long candles lighted in the dining-room and put on her best evening dress and told the bearer to serve champagne. She could still afford that, she thought ruefully, although she – and Peter – were certainly making a hole in her money.

It was a hot night, but what else should it be in the middle of May in Rudwal, where her husband worked and where she had made a home? The smell of wood-smoke drifted in across the city, across the polished English table, reminding her among the crystal and the damask that all over the country and the world men and women ate together, being married, and their babies slept in another room, and in those things alone achieved the fullness of human destiny.

Across from her, Peter looked almost relaxed, sitting a little back in his chair, the candle lights rippling with the irregular breeze from the punkah, moving in waves across his white dinner jacket and black cummerbund, glowing in points of dull gold down his shirt and at his cuffs. All her gifts, she thought with a secret smile – those, and the expensive wines, and the Shiraz carpets, even the expedition to Meru – all paid for by her money, and yet not exactly gifts, for Peter had merely taken the money and got what he – or they – wanted. Three years ago she might have thought it somehow wrong that he should, but not now, any more than she had thought it wrong when she began the pregnancy that gave her Rodney.

Tonight he looked less like a hawk than he had for a long while, and she smiled again. Tomorrow the mountains would be upon them, and that great peak which might claim Gerry's life (she could not believe it would take Peter's; it might *try*). Tonight she would show him that between them, as a by-product of three and a half years of marriage, they had created a world with satisfactions and triumphs as great as anything Meru could offer. She looked lovely, and she knew that she did, and tonight in the luminous darkness of the veranda, looking out across the flowers and the rooftops, Pachmann would play for them and they would sit with fingers touching, their son asleep under the dim, barred twilight in his room; and without words she would show Peter that this too was the intention of God. Perhaps he would remember on the mountain, in the cold fury of those hours when the world would not bend to his will and men broke in his hands.

When the meal was over, silently he walked round the table to her, stepping like a cat, and bent down and kissed her ear. She stood up, leaning a moment back against him, and they went together, hand in hand, through the drawing-room, through the opened French windows, and out on to the veranda. She began to wind up the gramophone (hers, but who could listen to it as Peter could?).

Peter said: 'Chopin,' and she smiled at him. The music began, the notes falling as clear and clean as white pebbles into the silence. She sank down into one side of the conversation chair she had had put there and patted the other half. Peter had lighted a cheroot, and for a moment she thought he would not come but would pace silently up and down the long veranda behind her, listening to the music with the intentness of a piano-tuner. But after a while he stood over her, and the glow dimmed on the end of the cigar; he sank down. She reached out her hand and touched him. Peace, with love, was so very near, and coming nearer in the joining of their fingers.

'*Huzoor sahib!*'

'No!' She found herself on her feet, her eyes dry and angry, glaring at the doorway. It was the office chuprassi who stood there, his red coat like fire in the night.

'A visitor has come for the Deputy Commissioner Sahib,' the chuprassi said serenely in Punjabi, secure in his government coat against any chatterings of women.

Peter turned slowly. She knew, miserably, that she had been very near success, for he turned unwillingly; his face was still soft and his voice, when he spoke, as tender as the kind of love she had been leading him towards.

'Who is it?' he asked.

'The Old Captain's son, Adam Khan.'

He stood a moment longer against her, then put the cheroot back in his mouth. The spark began to burn, and his voice hardened. 'I'll see him in the study.'

When he had gone she sat down again and heard the rhythmic scratching of the needle at the end of the record. She turned it over without thinking, wound the machine, and sat down again.

Time passed, but she did not know how much until she felt Peter's hand on her neck and his fingers pushing up, widespread and angry, into her back hair.

'Is he all right?' she asked at last, wishing she did not have to worry about anything except themselves, but knowing she could not gain any peace, let alone lead Peter towards it, unless she knew what had driven Adam Khan here at this hour.

'No,' Peter said.

'What is the matter?'

He sat down. 'The C.G.G, I suppose. Only it isn't. It's Adam.'

'I thought he wasn't supposed to come to you.'

'He isn't. But he came tonight because he doesn't believe he's fit to guide the C.G.G any more. He's lost his confidence. Put it another way – he doesn't believe that his ideas are better than theirs. Put it still another way – he's finding it damn cold and lonely being out by himself. He wants to get back into the pen with the rest of them. He doesn't trust himself as a leader any more. He wants to be one of a committee of privates.'

Now he was pacing up and down as he spoke, taking short turns, the cigar dead in his hand.

She did not speak. Poor Adam. Poor Peter.

He went on, speaking in a low, hard voice. 'Oh, I talked him out of it. But what kind of India are we going to make with men like that?'

'It's democracy, I suppose,' she said hesitantly.

'It's democracy without a head,' he said coldly. 'Democracy has to have the last say, as to whether it agrees or disagrees, but it won't – it can't *lead*. Did Abraham Lincoln lead, or was he pushed? You know he led. Pitt led, England followed. A leader's no better than his followers, of course, but by God, followers without a leader are no good at all.' He sat down abruptly in the chair and said: 'Let's forget the C.G.G now, and even Adam.'

She turned to the gramophone. Peter's face was taut as he sank into the chair. Still, perhaps in time she could coax him back to the place where they had been, especially as he seemed to have found it so hard to drag himself away from it.

'*Huzoor sahib!*'

This time it was Peter who jumped to his feet, his voice edged like a razor. 'What?'

'*Sahib log a-gye.*'

Peter said: 'What sahib log? At this time of night? *Kitne?*'

'*Panchh, huzoor.*'

'Five!'

'Lord Wilcot – sahib.'

She said wearily: 'I know what's happened. It's the expedition. They caught the Mail from Lahore.'

Then she heard Gerry's voice from the front steps– 'Aren't you going to let us in? Where are

201

you?' – and his familiar footsteps running along the passage. He burst in with arms outstretched, crying: 'Peter! It's good to see you again! All our personal stuff is in a couple of tongas outside. We're on our way to the dâk bungalow, but we had to drop in to tell you we're here. Emily!'

'Hullo, Walsh,' Peter was saying. 'And you must be Lyon? I'm Savage.'

Harry Walsh introduced the two big, quiet men in the background, one blue-eyed and blond, one dark and short. 'Fernand Lapeyrol – and I think you met Oliver Cadez in Chamonix?'

'Yes. *Tout va bien?*'

'*Fait chaud, monsieur. Enchanté, madame.*'

The time of peace was past now, and only the mountain mattered. Gerry kissed her cheek. Peter was telling the bearer to bring the decanters and the soda bottles off the ice in the godown. The two guides stood nervously, rolling their tweed caps in their hands, sweating like bulls in their heavy wool-suits. The whisky gurgled out; bottles and glasses clinked – Meru! The summit! Victory! Conquest!

'Let's have a look at the map,' Peter said.

Harry Walsh said: 'It's pretty late, isn't it? Besides, we've been studying it on the ship, you know.'

'Ah, that's the Survey of India map,' Peter said. 'This is my working map, an enlargement I had made and have been filling in with information from all sources since nineteen-seven. I'll go and get it.'

'Really, I think–' Harry began.

'You must eat here – except probably Lapeyrol

202

and Cadez would be happier in the dâk bungalow. They can take the kit over. The chuprassi will show them the way and see that they get a decent meal. Emily?'

'Of course you must eat here,' she said.

Harry Walsh did not look happy, for it was past midnight, but such irruptions were not uncommon in India, and everyone was prepared for them. 'It's quite all right,' she said.

Harry said doubtfully: 'Are you sure?'

'Quite,' she said, smiling. Peter had gone to get the map, and Gerry must have gone with him. The two guides had left, with undisguised relief. The young man Lyon was tall and rawboned and as dourly Scottish-looking as his name. Harry Walsh was on his guard. There were lines of experience in his strong face now. At thirty-five he was acknowledged to be the soundest and wisest as well as the most technically expert English climber of the day – and he was Peggy's husband.

'Quite all right,' she repeated as she went out to speak to the *khansamah*. She prayed that it would be.

CHAPTER 14

A few minutes after eleven o'clock at night the wind changed its note. For forty-eight hours it had been blowing a low, harsh chord among the guy ropes of the tents. During that time it had drowned all other sounds – except, when it slackened for a moment or changed its direction a fraction of a point, in the silence, Peter heard the moaning from the Rudwali porters' tents. There had been snow in the wind most of that time, but it did not lie.

When Peter noticed the change, and had waited half an hour to see if it was permanent or temporary, he struggled into his boots and coat and fur-lined Tibetan cap and went out of the tent. Some stars were dimly visible to the north. It was cold – howling, freezing cold – but nothing like the unspeakable cold of the first day of the blizzard. The weather was against him – as it had been all the way, since the torrential rain of the day they left Rudwal. That had raised all the mountain streams, and one of the porters was drowned well below the tree-line. They recovered the sack of flour he had been carrying, but most of it was ruined.

He went back inside the tent. Harry Walsh looked up quietly and asked him: 'What's it like?'

He had his boots off and was already snugged up inside the sleeping bag. 'Better,' he said. 'The wind's veering and there are some stars. We can push on tomorrow.'

He could just see the other man in some sky-glow reflected off the snow and through the tent walls, and Harry seemed about to say something. There were only the two of them in the tiny tent. Gerry and Lapeyrol were in another, pitched ten feet away, and the porters in two slightly larger ones close to Gerry's.

Peter waited. Harry at last said: 'Good night, then.'

It was going to be bad tomorrow. He knew that, without Harry Walsh's looking queerly at him and pretending to be too much of a loyal follower to speak. But only a fool would expect to conquer Meru, 27,141 feet – nearly 4,000 feet higher than anything yet climbed – without running into bad conditions and hard days. If Harry didn't like what he was being asked to do he had only to say no, and walk back down this gigantic south-east ridge. There was no squad of soldiers waiting at the bottom to haul him off to be court martialled and shot for cowardice in the face of the enemy. Only the Alpine Club – and they'd be happier to believe Walsh than himself. He went to sleep.

In the morning he aroused everyone before dawn so that they would be ready to move on as soon as the sun came up. It was a brilliant day, the sun so clear and pure on the new snow that his eyes ached for a while, even through the dark goggles. The porters were standing in a miserable silent cluster outside their tents with Naik Harkabir, the Gurkha corporal, fuming around them, trying to curse them into a better mood.

205

Lapeyrol and Lyon were looking up at the mountain in front of them: Harry and Gerry were staring back down the ridge towards Juniper Camp, 3,000 feet lower, where Cadez and the rest of the porters were.

Juniper Camp, at about 16,770 feet, was the base. One stunted tree stood there, and a trickle of water flowed by in the barren landscape, starting under the snout of one of the short, thick glaciers which ran down between all the Meru ridges, and disappearing a few miles off into the loess of the Parasian plateau. The camp they were now at was Camp I, at 19,700 feet. This was as high as he and Gerry had gone on their reconnaissance in 1911. About 4,000 feet farther up, say at 23,600, the ridge, which looked easy enough up there, was blocked by a rank of huge rock needles, standing in single file, one behind the other, up the ridge crest. There were four large ones, two small, and, at the back, one particularly thin and spire-like, which he had named Cleopatra's Needle. Once they had got over them, or round them, they would be at about 24,600 feet.

It had been obvious that they must establish a camp, Camp II, at the foot of the Needles, and by now this should have been done. The blizzard had deranged that plan, because during it they had eaten most of the supplies that should have been used to stock Camp II. So now they would have to start again – the porters going down to Juniper, loading, returning here to Camp I today; tomorrow on to Camp II, dump loads, and go right down to Juniper, or perhaps stop over here on their way down. There was a long haul between camps – too long. He had over-estimated the porters' stamina. They would have to be driven hard.

However, the two days need not be completely wasted. Today four climbers could get to the Needles, make a preliminary examination, and return here to Camp I. Tomorrow they could do the same, but would not have to return so far, as by that afternoon Camp II should have been set up.

He had decided to take Lapeyrol, Gerry, and Harry Walsh with him, leaving Lyon and Cadez in charge of the movement of the tents and stores. These last two were both hard men in their way, with plenty of driving power. They would need to be. The porters were men from the Northern Tehsils of the Rudwal district, and they were not used to carrying loads at these heights. The cold and the wind, on top of the long, hard approach march and the death of their companion in the river, had made them dis-pirited and at times surly.

They were like that now, standing like sullen, hunched cattle, while Harkabir barked and yapped. Well, he'd have to trust to Cadez and Lyon to see that the job was done.

It was time to go. He formed the climbing party into two cordées of two each, Lapeyrol and him-self as the leaders, and set off.

They climbed steadily. The ridge was never less than twenty feet wide and usually much more. Mostly the surface was thin snow, ending in an overhanging cornice on the right, but in many places the black rock stuck through where the wind had blown away the snow. Ahead the Needles waited like a row of soldiers, the sun full on the face of the front one, behind it the shadows, light violet on the green, black, and honey-coloured rock. The summit cone of the mountain, which had been clearly visible from Camp I, slowly sank behind the upper névé above the Needles as they climbed, so that Cleopatra's now seemed to be the final peak.

Getting to that summit, even to the névé would be very hard. On the left a snow slope curved away from the Needles like the inside of a cup, very steep at the top, moderating farther down as it ran into the South Glacier; but the glacier was a vertical mile down. This tremendous bowl they had named just that – the Bowl. To the right of the Needles, and hence of this south-east ridge which they were climbing and on which the Needles stood, the mountain fell into the huge trench leading on down to the Great Chimney Glacier. The Great Chimney, a nearly continuous series of cracks, channels, and faults, led up from the glacier to about 23,600 feet at the head of this trench-cirque between the south-east ridge and the one that fell towards the north-east and was called the Yangpa, after an ancient chorten some thirty miles out in the plateau from its foot.

If only the Great Chimney had continued another thousand feet it might have presented a possible route to the upper névé. But it didn't. It ended below the face of a vertical black cliff, five hundred feet high, half a mile wide, and so smooth that it had been named the Mirror Wall.

This strange formation, which would have been eerie enough on Cader Brith, and here aroused feelings of near-terror from its actual vastness and its apparent smallness on the sublimely vaster mountain, was flanked on the left by the Needles and on the right, short of the root of the Yangpa Ridge, by slopes of rock and ice, swept by avalanches and ice falls.

So, although the south-east ridge was not altogether easy even without the Needles, and with them was extremely severe, it was nevertheless the least difficult of all the approaches.

Peter thought back grimly to the reconnaissance of 1911. Without that he could not have believed – as Walsh and the rest hardly did now – that the other approaches were considerably worse: bitter cold ice walls, vertical ridges three thousand feet high, gullies where huge rocks bounded down in the glare of sun and powder snow, fluted cliffs topped by snow cornices with fifty feet of overhang and a hundred feet of depth, ice falls fissured by immense crevasses. By God, the south-east ridge *had* to go.

They did the 3,900 feet to the base of Needle One in just under five hours, starting fast and going noticeably slower as the altitude affected them. All the same, good enough. Eleven-twenty a.m. The Bowl stretched away to the left, the Mirror Wall to the right. He could see a hundred miles across the Parasian plateau to the south. Down there the earth was a pale gold, and a salt lake nearly seventy miles away was as blue and deep as when they had swum in it on the approach march.

Eleven-twenty, and dark at seven. Three hours to get down the ridge. They should start back from here not later than four. Say four hours of exploration. He would take Gerry and look at the Bowl. Harry and Lapeyrol could go to the Mirror Wall. The Needles themselves were obviously a last resort, to be examined in detail only if no way could be found round them.

They re-roped. Gerry waved his axe and shouted at Harry: 'Bet you your sugar ration that *we* find a way.'

'Nothing doing,' Harry answered briefly. He had been a good second-in-command, and there had not been as many differences of judgement as Peter had expected. The two parties moved off slowly in opposite directions.

The slope began to steepen as the ridge merged into the Bowl. The snow was fresh and true and Peter, leading, could cut steps quickly. He felt a little light-headed, with a touch of migraine. This was probably going to be it, if there was any route at all on this face.

The farther they went away from the Needles, the more the slope sharpened. Soon he saw that in less than a quarter of a mile, if they worked on diagonally up and round the inside of the Bowl, it would be all but vertical. They might have to try that later, though it would be very dangerous. The combination of its angle and the fact that it directly faced the midday sun would probably cause it to melt a little every day at this season, and freeze again every night. He could not tell how thick the snow was there, nor what held it against the steepness of the slope, except that the

210

constant freezing and melting might have made it into a sort of granulated ice. In the afternoon, when the sun dropped below the south-west ridge, this whole Bowl would fall into a deep indigo shadow – a great shield of darkness high on the mountain. They had seen it for days on the approach.

He decided to go straight up the slope from where they then were, instead of continuing the traverse. This route would take them towards the foot of Cleopatra's Needle.

At first the snow was still firm; later, as the slope steepened, it seemed to change almost imperceptibly to ice. Step-cutting became a slow, dangerous business. The head of the South Glacier was 6,000 feet below and behind him. The breath came short into his lungs, and it was hard to hold the rhythm of the axe blows. As he climbed he felt that it was ice, not air, that he breathed. The Needles, on the right, did not look quite so impossible in profile as when seen from directly below. Remember that. That was how the Hörnli was seen to be possible: look at it from the side.

They had made four hundred feet and were almost level with the top of Needle Three when the texture of the ice began to change. Steps cut in this stuff would not hold. It was half-past two.

He changed direction again, traversing the slope towards the Needles. After half an hour's hard and dangerous work he could see that there was a deep bergschrund between the Needles and the Bowl. The lip of this bergschrund, running up like an irregular rim of the white

Bowl, and falling vertically on the other side into the black trench of the bergschrund itself, might be the only possible way up this side of the mountain. It would be very delicate work, but it was possible – not now, though.

The wind was rising. He turned to Gerry, who had been covering well, and motioned to him to head back down to the ridge. Gerry kept staring up past him at the steepening slope. Peter looked up and saw wraiths of snow devils dancing along the sky-line. Gerry's goggles shone in the glare-back from the snow so that Peter could not see his eyes.

'Let's go on up,' Gerry bawled finally. 'Up – to the top.'

Peter thought: He's lost his judgement – through some effect of the altitude, probably, for he had been going very strongly. He motioned sharply down with his axe, and after a time Gerry slowly turned and led on down.

The next was a tense half-hour, since he was looking straight down into the South Glacier a mile below, and he did not know how badly Gerry's normal habits had been upset. He kept the rope tighter than he would usually have done, trying to give the impression that it was a kind of banister rail, but still Gerry went much too carelessly, and it was only a question of time before he would miss a step and go down the Bowl, probably jerking Peter with him.

Then he had an idea and made Gerry understand, by yelling into the wind until the roof of his mouth froze, that he was feeling groggy. Gerry stopped and seemed to collect himself, and went on down beautifully from that moment, treating him as a novice who'd suddenly got vertigo.

At the bottom, when they were again standing on the ridge – it felt as broad and safe as Piccadilly now, though it was steep and badly tilted there – Gerry said: 'I felt damned queer up there. Didn't want to stop. Couldn't see any reason to. You're all right really, aren't you?'

He nodded wearily. Suddenly he felt appallingly tired. Gerry's face twisted into a distorted, high-altitude grin; the cold seemed to freeze the exposed muscles so that no one had proper control over his lower jaw and the skin of the face.

They'd been up to about 24,200 feet, nearly a thousand feet higher than the summit of any mountain yet climbed. That meant nothing, but he would have given a lot to know more about what had happened to Gerry's mind. If Gerry's judgement had gone, had his own? The summit was another 3,000 feet higher again. What might happen to a man's brain up there? To his body, his heart, his lungs?

He saw that Gerry had a touch of frostbite on the nose and cheeks, and Gerry shouted with a disproportionate, unlikely glee that he was in the same boat himself; so they rubbed snow into each other, and then went on down the ridge to Camp I. He was very, very tired; Gerry still going like a chamois.

Harry and Lapeyrol were already back. They'd got cocoa and hot jam mixed into a delicious stew. Damn it, Harry ought to have had the self-control to keep a really good meal like that for Camp II, or higher. One of the porters' tents had been taken down the ridge, one was standing. They'd have to crowd into that for a time. There was no other place where they could talk. The four of them were alone on the ridge now, and it was dark, and the wind blew in long, fitful gusts.

Hunched round the lantern, he told them first what he and Gerry had done and seen. He gave them his opinion – that the only possible way up the left side of the ridge was via the rim of the bergschrund. He added that if the ascent were made during the two or three hours astride dawn the hanging ice in the upper centre of the Bowl might be firm enough to take steps; and that would therefore be another possibility.

Then he said: 'But before we commit ourselves to either of those, the Needles will have to be looked at properly. The others – the Bowl before dawn, and the rim of the bergschrund – are going to be pretty desperate.'

'I would say they were out of the question,' Harry said, mildly enough.

'Possibly,' Peter said. 'You might be able to see for yourself tomorrow. What about your side?'

'The Mirror Wall is impossible. Unthinkable,' Harry said at once. 'It's – well, it's a mirror. It's covered in verglas now, ninety degrees, five hundred feet.' He closed his fist with a jerk.

Lapeyrol, who understood English well enough, said in French that the Mirror Wall was the worst-looking piece of mountain he'd ever seen. 'It's in the shade – always, always – and the dim light crawls in it as though there are snakes under the ice, imprisoned between the rock and the verglas.'

Harry said: 'But between the Needles and the Mirror Wall proper there is a kind of fault – you remember that split in this ridge, about half-way up? I think it's a continuation of that. Or the Great Chimney fault, laterally displaced by the Mirror. It might go. We went about two hundred feet up it. It's a hair-raising proposition, and it looks as though it might widen higher up, which would make it impossible. But we can't tell until we try properly. From the east, the Needles look impossible.'

'Absolutely?' Peter asked sharply. 'Do you mean that? If you do, you're saying it's got to be this fault or nothing.'

Harry glanced at him and, when he answered, spoke deliberately. 'Perhaps I shouldn't have said impossible. From what Lapeyrol and I saw – the east side only, remember – I would say that they might be climbed by a pair of extremely good rock men, in the pink of condition, climbing at under twelve thousand feet. As it is, the only man who'd attempt them is someone who has lost his judgement – either through altitude or for some other reason – and thinks more about getting to the top than about his own life or anyone else's – or the elementary principles of mountaineering.'

Gerry said sharply: 'Peter will decide that–' But Peter waved to him to be quiet.

He lay back, thinking. If they were allotting marks to these routes, and ten was the highest level of difficulty or danger that could be accepted, even in perfect weather, then the rim and the Bowl were ten each; the left side of the Needles and Walsh's Fault – probably nine each; anything else, eleven or more.

He made up his mind. He said: 'Tomorrow, Harry, you and Lapeyrol have a real go at your fault. Gerry and I will try the left, west side of the Needles. Let's get off by five, now that we know the ridge.'

The others agreed, and after a few more moments of idle talk, mostly about new combinations of food, they separated to their own tents. Lying there, six inches from Harry Walsh, Peter thought: He seemed surprised that those last orders were the only sensible ones in the circumstances; he still thinks I am merely rash and dictatorial. If it had not been for Gerry he would probably not have accepted the invitation to join the expedition, much as he must have wanted to take part in the climbing of Meru. There was more than just the different views they had on mountaineering to explain his latent hostility, though those differences had been plain enough even when they last met, in Zermatt in '09, just after Peter and Emily became engaged. No, the thing to remember was that this was Peggy's husband. Peggy must be full of bitterness – a depth of it far greater than Peter would have thought it possible for her to contain. He had been wrong in his estimate of her character, and she had been pouring that bitterness into Harry's ear for three years now. He went to sleep.

The next day was as clear and harshly brilliant as the one before, but by the time he and Gerry came off the Needles at half-past four in the afternoon clouds were blowing about the upper cone of the mountain and a light snow was drifting across the great south-east ridge below, obscuring all downward visibility. Cadez had come up, Camp II was established, Harry and Lapeyrol were here, and everything was in order.

Lapeyrol seemed to be affected by the height, so Peter decided to send him down at once to join Lyon in Camp I, while Cadez stayed up here at Camp II. The same mixture of cocoa and jam was ready, but today it didn't taste good, and before they began the conference the four of them, now jammed into one of the tiny huts, had a brief, heated exchange of words about that. Couldn't someone think of something new for a change? Then, wearily, feeling that he was having to whip himself even to take the trouble to find out what had happened, Peter asked Harry to give his account of the day's work.

Harry said that he and Lapeyrol had taken four hours to get four hundred feet up Walsh's Fault, and had then been defeated. 'There's a section there, near the top,' he said, 'where all hand- and foot-holds simply vanish. The side walls spread back to twelve feet – too far for chimneying, and the fault itself actually overhangs. I mean the whole cliff leans out, and the fault in it, for fifty feet.'

Lapeyrol had said the same thing before he started down the ridge. *'Ne va pas, monsieur. Absolument – ne va point!'* He was dead beat, and his and Harry's clothes in tatters. It was obvious that they had pushed themselves to the limit – *their* limit.

Peter followed with his own story. He and Gerry had spent the day on the Needles. The climbing consisted in getting up each Needle in turn until a point was reached where there was some chance of making a traverse round it. They had got past two– One (which was large), and Two (which was small – comparatively). On Two they had had to go over the top, but on One had found a traverse, about a hundred and eighty feet up. It had taken them five hours to achieve an advance in height of some two hundred and fifty feet (from the top of Needle One to the foot of Needle Three), and three hours to get down again. Three more large Needles, one small, and Cleopatra's, remained. They hadn't found more than a dozen good holds in all. The rock was rotten, and at one point on Two, after a really severe climb, they had had to put in fifty feet of fixed rope, anchored to rocks, in order to get down again. They had spent those eight hours hanging by fingertips and tricounis over the Bowl, and he had not been able to stop his muscles trembling for over an hour after reaching camp.

Gerry had gone magnificently again, but his eyes were unnaturally bright, and at a couple of places his judgement had been at fault, though not seriously. They both had violent headaches all day, and considerable signs of nausea. Harry was the same; only Cadez, just up from Juniper, seemed in anything like good shape.

They crouched in a despondent, wordless huddle for a time when Peter had finished speaking. Peter thought any moment now they'd all agree to go down the mountain... By God, someone must keep on at the Needles; but at the present rate of progress Cleopatra's would not be surmounted for two more days, and the weather showed signs of breaking again.

He must see for himself whether the fault was impossible. He said: 'Cadez and I will try the fault tomorrow. Harry – I want you and Gerry to keep on at the Needles.'

There was silence for a moment. Cadez looked at him. Peter remembered that he and Lapeyrol had been talking before Lapeyrol went on down to Camp I. Obviously Lapeyrol had been giving an account of the horrors of Walsh's Fault. Harry began to speak; he was trying to control himself, but he had as bad a headache as the rest of them, and his voice shook. He said: 'The fault's impossible, Peter. Do you think Lapeyrol and I didn't try?'

'No,' he said, 'but I must see for myself.'

'Just see?' Harry said. 'You're not going to "see," you're going to go all out to *make* it go, and I tell you it won't! Didn't you hear me tell you – it widens, it's too wide for chimneying. When the sun's up, though the fault's always in shadow, stones and pieces of rock begin to fall down it. Twice small avalanches swept it from top to bottom, and we only managed to hang on because we were in good places each time – places that had three-inch foot-holds, I mean!' He stopped, panting. After a while he said: 'It's murder to take anyone up the fault, now that we've told you what it's like. It's suicide to go alone.'

'Do you think it's any better than the Needles?' Gerry suddenly blazed out. 'Good God, Harry, are we climbing Meru or going on a picnic up Monte Rosa?'

Harry turned slowly and stared as though Gerry had suddenly turned into a rhinoceros.

This wouldn't do.

Peter said to Cadez: 'Do you want to come with me tomorrow, or would you prefer to go with Mr Walsh?'

Harry said shortly: 'Cadez must go with you. I've got to have Gerry to show me the way up what you've already done on the Needles.'

Cadez was much the same build as Harry, strong and square, but darker. His brown eyes glittered, and he said: 'I will come with you, *mon général!* Doubtless you will make provisions for my children in the usual way.' Then he crawled out of the tent, quaking with fury. Peter caught Gerry's eye, and Gerry shrugged.

Peter did not go to sleep. The time had come to show these people what was meant by the phrase, 'at all costs.' In an unlabelled sack among the pile outside there were a hundred very large flat-sided nails, or steel pegs. They were about six inches long. Some of the German climbers had been using them for a year or so. You drove them into the rock with a special small hammer you carried with you when you were expecting to use them. When you got to a bad place you hammered one into a cleft or fissure of the rock as high or as far as you could conveniently reach. Then you slung the rope over it, or even used the protruding end as a hold for the hands or feet. So placed, you could hammer in another peg; and so on across traverses and down holdless pitches that would otherwise have been impossible. They were apparently usually used for difficult descents, but why should you not go up with, or on, or by them?

The English gentlemen-climbers would have nothing to do with them. But they wore boots, didn't they? It was no use talking logic to people like that. He had been sure that neither Walsh nor Lyon, nor any other English mountaineer, would come with the expedition if he had known that pegs would be used. He himself would have preferred not to use them, but – 'at all costs.' He at least knew what he meant when he said that. He had had the pegs and a pair of wrist-thonged hammers sent privately from Munich. That was where some of Emily's money had gone.

So in the morning he waited, delaying his preparations, until Harry and Gerry had set off. Then he turned to Cadez and said: 'We are going to take pegs. And the camera, to prove to the world that there was need for pegs.'

Cadez was a guide, a professional, and he had no particular love for English gentlemanliness as such. He made his living by climbing mountains, and he also liked to do it. The sight of the bright steel pegs and the two hammers in the sack did not shock him as much as it would have shocked Harry or Gerry. His expression altered all right, and he showed strong emotion, but it wasn't because the use of pegs basically shocked him; it was because it ought to shock Peter. He realized in that moment that Peter had secretly obtained them, secretly had them transported up the mountain, and meant to use them, in spite of the well-known aversion of the English milords to them. Peter was suddenly revealed to him as a new kind of animal altogether, a dangerous one.

Cadez, with that name, probably had Gascon blood in him. For a moment the revelation frightened him, and then anger brought out the Gascon fire. They set off, reached the foot of Walsh's fault in forty-five minutes and, without a pause for breath, set to work.

The fault gave them all that Harry and Lapeyrol had promised, and more. Cadez led most of the time, working like a madman, taking risks he would never have countenanced in the Alps. The sun shone eerily through the cornice of snow that vaulted out over the top of the fault, and every now and then stones and spears of ice bombarded them. They surmounted the over-hanging fifty feet which had stopped Harry and Lapeyrol, by hammering the pegs into the rotten rock and looping the rope over them, or by walking up the pegs themselves – like flies on a steep-pitched, crumbly ceiling.

Surely it was beaten now? But above the overhang the fault narrowed again until it was less than half an inch wide – no room for Cadez's gloved fingers, and he could not take off the gloves without getting frostbite.

Peter took the lead. To the right the verglas glittered evilly on the Mirror Wall. To the left – an ice wall, then the Needles. Standing on a peg, six thousand feet above the Great Chimney Glacier, the wind shrieking at him and the light failing as the sun sank behind the other side of the mountain, he took a last look upward, searching with a sudden enormous anger for some smallest break in the rock where he could hammer in another peg. There was none.

But there must be! His arms burned like fire, and he knew he could not hold his position for long. A thin trail of powder snow began to trickle down from the vaulted underside of the cornice far above. It increased quickly in volume. For a few moments the wind blew it away across the Mirror Wall to his right, but soon its weight would send it cascading straight down on to his head. He stepped down quickly and jammed himself above Cadez into a wider part of the fault. The avalanche fell on and over them for a minute and a half, and when it had finished a single stone hit him on the forehead. For a time he was semi-conscious, held there only by the pressure of Cadez's shoulders under his boots and an instinctive pushing outward of his own arms and back.

'Are you sure it won't go?' Cadez whispered venomously when he came to.

He ground his teeth together and looked up again. Cadez said: 'Now would you like me to take a picture?'

The avalanche had gone; but the fault would not go, not by any means. Not only was there no hold for a peg within close reach, there was none within twenty-five feet. He pointed down, and slowly they began the descent, at his insistence hammering out and taking back with them all the pegs they had so carefully, so breathtakingly hammered in. He would be using them again.

Lyon was at Camp II when they got there. He had come up from Camp I to get orders and report, curtly, that the porters down at Juniper were bordering on open mutiny. Harkabir was having a hard time preventing them from setting out at once for Rudwal – three weeks' march across deserts and mountains inhabited only by a few Tibetan bandits and vast herds of kiang.

After a moment's silent thought, while Lyon waited in the same hostile silence, Peter told him to go on down to Juniper himself and use any necessary means to keep the porters at their work. He might remind them that Savage Sahib was the Deputy Commissioner and District Magistrate of the area where their homes were. Their families in the Northern Tehsils were at his mercy. Lyon looked at him strangely but Peter felt no need to tell him whether he would or would not carry out his implied threats, and merely urged him to get a move on, as it was late, and to tell Lapeyrol to come up the following day. Lyon set off down the ridge. Peter thought, as he had done before, that the day wireless sets were made portable half the difficulties of 'big' mountaineering would be over.

Gerry and Harry returned at dark. After a cheery greeting Gerry crawled straight into his tent, humming. Peter looked after him in surprise: you didn't hear much humming, or cheeriness, at 23,600 feet. He was about to follow when Harry Walsh touched his arm. 'There's something wrong with Gerry.'

Peter asked: 'Did he fail?'

Walsh said: 'Just the opposite. He's tireless – but I don't like the look of him. Can you try and give him a day's rest? Or send him down to Juniper and bring up Lapeyrol or Lyon?'

Peter thought; that would be difficult. He shook his head non-committally. Walsh said: 'Go in and talk to him. You'll see.'

He knew what Walsh meant as soon as he got inside the tent and saw Gerry's face in the yellow glow of the lantern. It showed no trace of strain, yet Gerry had done more, perhaps, than any of them. His eyes were rather too bright, and of course he had a scruffy beard, like the rest – but, apart from that, he might have been sprawling on Cader Brith under a harvest moon, after a four-hour walk up from Llyn Gared.

Peter stared at him in perplexity. It was damned strange. But he would have to decide about Gerry later. First he must get the latest information.

So, when Harry had eaten – Gerry said happily that he wasn't hungry – the conference began.

Harry said briefly that he and Gerry had surmounted the next three Needles – two large and one small – so that now only one large and Cleopatra's remained; but it was not feasible to continue on that route. The difficulties already overcome were of such severity that the slightest change in the weather, when climbers were already on the Needles, would bring disaster.

Peter waited for the effect to sink in, and then pulled a peg from the place in the corner of the tent where he had hidden it and said: 'We got over the overhang. With these.'

There was a silence. Peter could have gone straight on to tell them that, in spite of the pegs, Walsh's Fault wouldn't go. But it was necessary to bring this particular matter to a head first. So he held the now battered peg in his hand and said: 'I take it you don't disapprove, then?'

After a time Walsh said: 'They must be very useful. Wouldn't it have been a good idea to tell us that you intended to bring some?'

He said: 'Would you have come?'

Walsh said: 'No.'

'Why not?'

Walsh shrugged. 'If you don't know, I can't explain. You got over the overhang? With them?'

Peter nodded. He said: 'It would have been impossible without them. Wouldn't it, Cadez?'

Cadez nodded.

Peter said: 'Will you agree to use them now?' He kept his eyes remorselessly on Walsh's. Walsh was in a turmoil, or as much as anyone could be when his reactions and thoughts were as sluggish as they are after a day or two at such a height. He said slowly: 'I think – on Meru – perhaps, if there is no other way – to get down.'

'To get up, too? If there's no other way to get to the top?' Peter said with brutal insistence. 'Even to make a dangerous but possible pitch less dangerous?'

At last Walsh nodded.

Peter turned his head. Walsh was broken. There had been no need to use the other arguments, and there were many. Meru spoke for itself.

He began to tell them about his day with Cadez on the fault. When he had finished he said care-

226

fully: 'Tomorrow I would like Cadez and Gerry to finish the Needles, if Cadez thinks he can be of use, while Harry and I rest here for an attempt on the summit the day after.'

Cadez was staring at him with the same kind of look, mixed of hatred and awe, that had turned Christian Holz from a guide into a man; but Cadez was much younger, about Peter's own age – thirty-two – and there was that Gascon blood to be put to use. Peter's plan succeeded.

Cadez said viciously: *'Bien, bien alors!'* and turned over to lie on his back and stare at the flapping, jerking canvas a few inches above his head. The wind droned, and from out in the pit to right or left, they heard the roar of an avalanche.

After a long silence Harry said: 'I don't think we ought to keep on at the Needles. There's one particular thing against it – it's worse coming down, when you're dead beat, than it is going up, in spite of everything we've done.'

Peter said: 'They'll have pegs tomorrow.'

Harry said: 'They'll help. Not enough to make it possible.'

'Have you got any other suggestions?' Peter asked, and added: 'That will take us towards the summit?'

'No,' Harry said slowly. Then, with a weary but growing emphasis: 'I think we ought to go down and give up for this season. We've done marvels. You and Cadez must have done the finest climbing of the century when you got up that fifty-foot overhang in the fault, pegs or not. But we've got to give up and try another approach

227

another year. This one will not go.'

'I can't accept that until we are actually stopped,' Peter said.

After a while Harry said: 'I thought you'd say that. Then let me go on the Needles with Cadez tomorrow. Gerry needs a rest. Perhaps you and he, or you and Lapeyrol, can try for the top the next day, if we do manage to get over Six and Cleopatra.'

Gerry had been lying on his side, half dozing, between them. Now he said, very clearly: 'I'd better go, Peter.'

His meaning was obvious, and Harry Walsh understood it at once – that they could not really believe negative reports unless they were made by himself or Peter. Harry was looking at Peter without saying anything, but his expression spoke for him... See? That's not Gerry Wilcot speaking. When did anyone ever hear Gerry speak as insultingly as that? He's not himself.

All the same, what Gerry had said was true, Peter thought remorselessly. If Harry and Cadez went out on the Needles the next day, and reported that the route was finally impassable, he would have to take someone the day after and see for himself – and that would be the last day they could stay here at Camp II. The rations would be finished by then. They had already been five days over 23,000 feet and no one, except Gerry, was as good a man as he had been at lower levels. There would, in fact, be no attempt made for the summit.

Peter said: 'I think Gerry had better go.'

After a moment Harry crawled out of the tent,

without another word.

The next morning when Peter awoke it was bitter cold and the wind howled and it was dark, utter dark, not even the snow reflecting any glimmer, for there was no light in the sky. Peering at his luminous watch, he saw that it was half-past six. He struggled into his frozen boots and staggered across and into Gerry's tent.

'Wake up!' he screamed. 'Half-past six.'

Gerry awoke with a low moaning shout, with words embedded in it. 'Yes!... Hold, hold... Eh, wha'?'

'Half-past six,' Peter repeated. 'Get Cadez up. I'll try and get something hot.'

The Primus would not start, and everything was clogged by the cold, and the pair were not ready until eight. There was an evil light over the world by then and the Needles stood like black sentries directly over the little tents, their heads hidden in drifting snow. Walsh had protested twice that the weather was not good enough for any work on the Needles today, but Gerry said, 'Nonsense,' cheerfully, and Cadez said nothing. At last they roped up and clumped slowly away up the snow-bank towards the foot of Needle One.

Peter followed Harry back into the tent, crawled into his bag, and tried to get some more sleep. It was not a luxurious place, Camp II. The tents were perched on a tiny ledge, sloping sharply to the south, a little below the crest of the ridge and perhaps one hundred yards from the base of Needle One. Their breath had been freezing on the inside of the canvas all these days and now there was a kind of congealed greasy scum there, and the tent was permeated with the smells of kerosene and sweat and woollen socks. The wind shrieked all day so that they had to shout when they wanted to say anything. It had seemed to drop a bit most evenings, but even so he realized that all their conferences and conversations had been carried on at the tops of their voices; each one had been as tiring as an average day's low-altitude climbing. Their headaches were now permanent.

He had nothing to say to Harry Walsh, and Harry had nothing to say to him. There had been a definite break between them, no less definite for being unspoken. Harry would obey him as the leader of this expedition until they got back to Rudwal; but he would never climb with him again. It was a pity, though expected. Only Gerry could be trusted, because only Gerry trusted him.

At eleven o'clock he finally dozed off. At one, Lapeyrol, grim and short-spoken, crawled into the tent to report that the porters were in hand and that he had six of them down at Camp I, and what were the gentleman's orders?

It might be a good idea to send Harry down to Camp I and keep Lapeyrol here for the attempt on the summit tomorrow. But Lapeyrol had shown quite clearly that he did not want to climb with Peter again; so he had better go back down with orders to bring the porters up here the following day, with sufficient tentage. The day after that they would all go down to Juniper by convenient stages. Lapeyrol said: *'Oui, monsieur,'* and eased out of the tent, and they were alone again.

Two o'clock. Three o'clock. Four o'clock. No sign of Gerry and Cadez. They scrambled out of the tent, stood in the wind, beat their hands and arms. Back into the tent. Half-past five. The light was beginning to fade. Heavy clouds overhead. They went out again.

At six o'clock Harry said: 'There they are.' They were the first words he had spoken since Lapeyrol left.

Peter scanned Needle One and with difficulty made out a figure near the top, coming down slowly – very slowly, because he was alone. Harry saw at the same time that there was only one climber. They grabbed ropes and ice-axes and hurried up the ridge.

Who was lost – Gerry or Cadez? His best friend or the paid guide? Peter hoped it would be the guide. Gerry was worth three of Cadez – more; there could be no comparison of their values, to himself and to mankind. But neither was it right that a man should be killed like this while earning money. Peter promised himself then and there that he would never again take guides on a big climb.

It was Gerry whose arms they grasped as he swung down off the lowest rocks of Needle One. 'Cadez is dead,' he said at once. One end of the rope coiled round his waist was broken.

'Later,' Peter said, for Gerry had stopped and was looking miserably at him. 'Come on down.'

Then Gerry went with them, and they hurried to the tent. By then it was full dark. They lit the

Primus and melted snow and rubbed Gerry's face with snow, and he began to speak. They were jammed together like sardines.

'I led to the foot of Six. As far as we'd gone yesterday. Three hours. Cadez took over. Peter, it was hard! Inch by inch, searching, hammering in pegs, stretching the rope, moving on. The weather changed – we got sudden blasts of wind that shook the mountain, Peter! They roared like explosions, only they lasted a minute – two minutes – each, and we clung to the side of the Needle. Then it blew from all points, with snow. *"Ne va pas"* Cadez said at last. That was on Cleopatra's, low down. He'd been going like a god, Peter, like you – standing on one foot, on holds less than a quarter of an inch wide, hammering at full stretch of his arm in front of him. *"Ne va pas,"* he said again. "We've done our best, monsieur. More, more!" He was right, Peter. His best and mine, but not yours. I said: "I'll lead!" I've got five, six inches longer reach than Cadez. We were in cloud. Lit by flashes of something – lightning? Green, yellow, black light. So much noise that it was really silent except for the booming of the wind. "I'll lead," I said again, screaming in his ear. "Suicide," Cadez shrieked. I shook my head. "Murder, then," Cadez screamed. "Murder!" I began to untie the rope, but I was slow. My fingers cold, thick, fumbling. Cadez snatched it from me and tightened the knots. He said: "It is not you who are the murderer, milord. Go on!" What did he mean?'

He looked from Peter to Harry, and Harry looked at Peter, and Peter said: 'Go on.'

'Cadez led on. Fifteen minutes in one place – one hold, I mean. Rock broke. I fell. Cadez held me. We got over Six, Cleopatra's. It's all done, Peter.'

Peter patted his shoulder. Gerry was calming down and spoke – shouted – more rationally now. 'On the way back, Cadez as Number Two, he fell. Wind blew him off. Or he was using a peg – stepping down on to it. He wasn't used to them. Or he was trying not to use them, he didn't trust them. I don't know – I had a good belay, good anchor. But it was on Three, you know, Harry, the place where there's a runout of nearly forty feet. No belay will hold the leader going up, or the Number Two coming down, if he falls there. The anchor held. The rope broke. He disappeared into the Bowl. I saw him for about two hundred, three hundred feet. Arms and legs out, stiff, flat, like a black cross, whirling, I'm sorry, Peter.'

Oh God, this was a time when Gerry should have been a woman, so that he could take him in his arms and comfort him as one could a woman. He gave Gerry ten aspirins and lay quiet, patting his hands. It was bitterly, furiously cold.

His body was growing numb from the cramped position he was in. What fantastic power of fear or remorse had got Gerry down the Needles alone after the accident? What he and Cadez had done on the fault was nothing compared to that.

After a long time, when Gerry sounded as though he were asleep, Harry Walsh said: 'And tomorrow?'

Peter said: 'Are you going to come with me?'

Walsh said: 'No. And Gerry obviously can't. So we'll go down. We ought to look for Cadez's body – though it's hopeless. All you have to say is that it was your decision to turn down. I'll back you to the hilt, here and at home.'

Peter said: 'Good night,' and left the tent.

CHAPTER 15

He did not get to sleep for a long time. Cadez was dead. He had chosen his way of life, and must have been prepared for such a manner of death. All the same it was sad that he had died, sadder still that in the moment of his falling he had not thought of the greatness of the endeavour, but of Peter, and with hate.

Harry had refused to climb tomorrow. He had reached his limit. Lyon had never been really fit – not because of the altitude, but because the food and water and the general conditions of Indian travel had started to upset his disciplined Scottish stomach the moment he landed at Bombay. Besides, he was at Juniper; and, if asked, he would follow Harry's lead and refuse to come. Lapeyrol would refuse.

No one, including Peter himself, now knew the whole route up the Needles, except Gerry.

Gerry was still going strongly. Something had changed in his ego and his personality – but not, apparently, his climbing nerve. He was the only man Peter could trust to the end; and he was the only one who would come with him; and he was here.

He, Peter, might go alone.

He thought about that for a time and soon dismissed it as folly. There were places, Harry had said, where one man literally could not pass without help from above or below. The chances would be at least even that he would fall; then nothing could prevent Gerry from coming to find him, not even a direct order from himself before he set out.

Gerry would expect to come with him as soon as he learned that Harry would not. This was the mountain, this the effort, towards which they had been pointing their mountaineering selves for six years – longer, perhaps, without knowing the exact place. They had talked bravely about how nothing could stop them. Now, here, was the opportunity to put that philosophy into practice and seal their lives to each other.

All the same, it was hard. He was afraid of the mountain by now. As he lay there he could feel the fear creeping along his veins, and crawling in the muscles of his thighs. Gerry was doing superhumanly well; but how much longer could he keep it up? When would something break? What would it be? What harm might it do to both of them? Suddenly he was again clinging to the highest pitch on the fault, and vertigo pounced on him so that he had to press down with both hands against the ground to control himself.

Down, down, then! Turn away from the mountain, his own mountain, for this time. They had done all and more than all that men could do. Harry would support him. Cadez's death would be told to the world in different words. Harry himself would probably relent, for he was not a vindictive person, and might even again climb with him. Emily would not reproach him over Cadez – or Gerry. He himself would live to fight another day, on another ridge of Meru. Lapeyrol, Lyon, the porters, everyone would be happy. All he had to do was give the word – down!

Very well, then. They would go up, to the summit. Gerry and he. Who else? Nothing would stop them. Harry and Lyon and Lapeyrol would stir the climbing world against him; and their tale would react in other quarters as well. Those people who called him the Duke of Rudwal would call him the Butcher of Meru. And if they failed, Gerry and he, then it would be worse.

So be it.

He kept thinking of Emily. He wanted to explain to her why he must go on, but she was not there with him. She was asleep in their big bed in the big bungalow, tranquil and strong. How could she be so strong and not need to lead? Would she understand if he came back tomorrow, and not Gerry?

He started violently, as from one of those muscular and nervous contractions which often made him jerk, like a dying fish, when he was near sleep. Whatever happened, that must not. If anyone was to come back alone tomorrow, it must be Gerry. He could not face Emily if it were not, because she loved Gerry. Not as she loved *him,* not in any way that could make a man jealous of his sexual rights, his private possession of her body; hardly even as a brother or a son. She loved him for the same causes that he, Peter, did – as an ideal, a personification of decency and unselfishness. 'Sir Galahad,' she had once called him; but if she had spoken her inmost thoughts, and his own, she would have said

'Christ,' a twentieth-century Christ, born in the unlikely mould of an English earl.

But if that was the truth, or near the truth, what, who, was *he?*

No, not Christ. Gerry did not have the strength. One of those wounded Italian saints, with blood streaming from life-like arrows implanted in his body, and a beatific smile on the gentle face and an iridescent halo held by waiting angels above his head.

Peter could pursue his thoughts no further, though he tried. He could only fall asleep.

He awoke at five o'clock and aroused Gerry. 'Wake up, old man. We're going to the top.' It was impossible to tell what had happened to the weather, except that it was not snowing. The wind blew a gentler note and the air, though cold, had lost its bitter point.

Harry Walsh sat up, fully awake on the instant, and said fiercely: 'You're coming down with me, Gerry! I told him last night I wouldn't go with him.'

Gerry was not fully awake, though he was already half into one boot. 'Eh?' he mumbled. 'Are we going down?' The tent seemed to have shrunk. There was hardly room to move, and they were all shouting.

'Yes,' Harry said. 'If you refuse, he can't go by himself. *You'll save his life, Gerry.*'

Gerry seemed to grasp what was happening. 'Are we going up, Peter, you and I?' he asked simply.

Peter said: 'Yes.'

Gerry nodded and kept working at his boots.

Harry turned on Peter. 'You can't take Gerry! By God, Savage, you're the biggest swine I've ever met!' He mouthed almost incoherent words of loathing. Then he said: 'I thought even you must see that Gerry's not fit to climb.'

'Of course I'm fit, Harry,' Gerry said reasonably.

Harry went on as though Gerry had not spoken. 'Cadez didn't matter a damn to you, I know – but Gerry!'

Peter said nothing. Harry said at last, after a violent, single oath: 'I'll come. Forget what I said last night.'

Peter had been expecting this, and had decided on the right response. He said: 'I'm sorry, Harry. I have no confidence in your guts.'

Harry tried to hit him then, but the blow glanced harmlessly off his shoulder, and Gerry said calmly: 'There's no need to get excited, Harry. Peter won't hold anything against you.'

Harry groaned and put his head in his hands. Gerry busied himself with the Primus and then went outside for a moment.

Harry began again, speaking with desperate reasonableness. 'Listen,' he said, 'the Matterhorn didn't fall at the first attempt. Nor did the Eiger or the Jungfrau–'

'Trisul did,' Peter said.

Harry shook his head. 'That was different. Give it up,' he said. 'I swear that I'll say nothing about anything that's happened here. I'll keep Lapeyrol's mouth shut. I – I promise I'll come with you on your next expedition to Meru. I promise I won't form one of my own before you

239

can get back here. I'll use all my influence to see that no one else does. I'll–'

Peter said flatly: 'We came here to climb Meru. I expected you as deputy leader, to see that the attempt was forced home if I were killed or injured. I was mistaken. You're a great climber, Harry, but you're not fit to lead on Meru – or even to follow. Now, listen. If Gerry and I are not back by nightfall you are to go on down to Juniper first thing tomorrow morning. Lapeyrol and some porters will be here by this afternoon. Take them down with you, but leave this tent with a little food, all that you can spare, in case we have to spend the night out on the Needles or higher. I doubt if we'd survive, but we might, and if we did we'd need to find the tent and food here. Do you understand?'

Harry said: 'Yes, but–'

Peter went on. 'Lapeyrol and Lyon are to spend one more night – tomorrow night – at Camp I, and then join you at Juniper. After that you will be in command. Harkabir will help you get everyone back to Rudwal. One more thing. No attempt is to be made by anyone to look for us if we do not come back. No one, under any circumstances, is to go beyond the base of Needle One. Do you understand?'

'That's against all the traditions of mountaineering,' Harry said hoarsely.

'I know,' he said. 'Meru is not a traditional mountain.'

Harry said: 'But... Look, what can I say, what can any of us say, if you and Gerry don't come down, and I do? How can I explain that I didn't

240

make any attempt to find you or rescue you? Lapeyrol will never be employed again. You might be dead – or you might only have sprained an ankle on the other side of Needle One.'

Peter fumbled in the small leather box where he kept his diary, in which he recorded all that happened, for the sake of the articles he would later write about the expedition. He took off his gloves, tore out a sheet of paper, found his pencil, and wrote slowly: 'Harry– Under no circumstances is any attempt to be made to rescue or search for Gerry and myself if we do not return to Camp II as planned – P Savage, Camp II, July 19, 1913.'

He handed it to Harry. Harry glanced at it and cried: 'This won't help, and you know it. You can't bind me once I'm the leader. And I tell you that if you don't come back I'm coming to look for you, with Lapeyrol.'

'Please yourself,' Peter said. 'There are your orders. Gerry, are you ready?'

The tent leaned gently this way and that in the slow air, and the first touch of light glinted on the peaks of the Needles.

'Good luck,' Harry said to Gerry.

Gerry said: 'Thanks, old boy.'

They roped up. Gerry's eyes glowed like fires; then they put on their goggles and started up the ridge.

As the light strengthened, Peter saw that a heavy storm was brewing somewhere to the south-west. Above the mountain lay a crochet-work coverlet of high, pale clouds, closely knit, and becoming more solid to the south-west.

There the clouds swirled down in heavy, dark spirals towards India over the Parasian plain. There was no sun, only different shades of black and grey and, close at hand, bluish snow and the lifeless rock. They climbed fairly quickly as far as Peter had been, and after that what little energy he had left was expended in admiring the work that Gerry, Harry, and Cadez had done on the route. It was fantastic.

On Three, at the long lead, Gerry pointed down, and they paused a moment. It was difficult to tell anything about a man's face in that light, under the dirty beard, but Peter thought Gerry had lost all colour and was perhaps far away in his mind. Time and again Peter wished that he also could be far away from here, as one vertical pitch succeeded another and he felt his will to go on being pulled tauter and tauter, and each moment the fraying at it continued, step after step, reach after reach.

At the hour when the sun struck the cloud-banks above, and some of its heat filtered through the heavy air, rocks began to break loose from the Needles. The climbers moved steadily on under a fire like small arms, the stones falling silently or whining past or hitting the cliff like pistol bullets, then leaping out over the Bowl, where Cadez had gone.

At ten o'clock they came down the north side of Cleopatra's and stood at the foot of the sloping nevé, perhaps a thousand feet high. They were at about 24,600 feet. Above the nevé there must be another 1,500 feet. Gerry turned to him and thrust out his gloved hand.

'We've done it!'

Peter wanted desperately to believe it, but it was not true. The far clouds had come perceptibly nearer. He took over the lead, and they went on.

As soon as he began to break the clean snow he knew that he had, so far, been working at only half-throttle. He had done his best all the time, but that best was nothing to what he could do now. His headache faded; new strength came to his legs. He could not see the summit, but it was there, and now nothing, nothing could stop him.

They went up the névé at a good speed, reaching the rolling crest at about noon. Ahead lay a new ridge, and Peter's breath was coming very short. He felt good, but the weakness of human physique laid heavy hands on him and dragged him back. An easy step became a long reach – place the foot down, struggle against the thing that was trying to prevent him from breathing, wait for the congealed lead that had risen to the thigh to sink back to the calves; another step; reach up, the fingers like woollen bales – on. He realized slowly that the wind had stopped. They were high, high – 26,300, perhaps. Half-past one. Couldn't go on after two, two-thirty.

The wind began to whistle a slow tune, almost like a love song, across the face of the rock. The great clouds had come, and towered above him now. The snow scurried across the steep slope to the right of the ridge. Far above he could see the projecting sharp edge of a big rock – the top itself. Or the end of this ridge and the beginning of the summit dome.

He reached across and up a steep, warped rock. The snow lying on its upper edge ten feet above him trickled down in a stream into his eyes. He struggled up, waited to catch his breath, anchored, belayed. Gerry did not move.

He beckoned with his hand. Gerry was standing like a sack of potatoes under the left side of the knife-ridge, twenty feet behind and ten or twelve feet down. Between them lay a slope of snow with a step cut in it, a good foothold on rock, a hand-hold, two flat steps on sloping ice, two holds on the rock – and the rope.

Gerry let go his hold and cupped his hands, the ice-axe swinging loosely across the front of his body by its thong. His voice came very loud and clear. 'I can't cross that, Peter.'

Peter felt that he was praying... Not here, not now, please! Controlling his voice, he shouted back, though the sound came out as a feeble croak: 'Come on – nothing difficult. Rock firm.'

Gerry shook his head and bawled with that unnatural strength: 'I can't cross that, Peter. Out of the question.'

The wind was bitter as salt and strong as hammers in his face now. He could tell Gerry to sit down where he was, while he, Peter, went on to the top. He could do it. He opened his mouth – Gerry would understand.

Suddenly Gerry began to shiver and shake. The ice-axe began to swing, like a loose anchor at the bow of a rolling tramp ship. It swung wider and wider, a pendulum in Gerry's hand, and his wrist was out of the thong. Then deliberately he cast it away. It swung out, the adze blade flashing momentarily in the thick sky, and vanished. Thin snowflakes lashed Peter's face, and Gerry cried: 'You're right. Easy. I don't need it,' and stepped out towards him, swaying, stumbling, his eyes looking at nothing but Peter's face. Peter whipped off his goggles and held Gerry's eyes and kept the rope taut between them. It was no use telling him to look for his holds, no use to do anything but imprison his eyes and *will* him across – so, step by step, lurching, shaking, Gerry came on. At the foot of the rock where Peter was, when he could almost have touched Peter's hands, he stepped off over the cliff.

Peter held him. Then, with the rope on its anchor, he went down to him. Gerry was lying on his front in the steep snow, looking down into the whirling blizzard that hid the ridge, the névé, the Needles, the Bowl, the South Glacier. He was crying, his mouth full of snow.

'No good. Failed.'

Peter leaned down and slapped him as hard as he could across the side of his face with a gloved hand. He gave Gerry his own ice-axe and told him angrily to get up to the rock. Gerry dragged himself up, the tears running down under his goggles and freezing in long icicles on his cheek and in the matted hair of his beard.

Peter rejoined him, using neither rope nor axe, and patted his shoulder. 'Time to go down now, Gerry. We can't reach it. Another year, eh?'

They went down, not as slowly as he had expected. Harry and Lapeyrol and six porters were at Camp II, and it was seven o'clock. Harry gave him one glance and then put his arms around Gerry's shoulders and helped him into his tent. Peter followed. Gerry did not speak until he had drunk some cocoa. Then he said: 'Peter saved my life again. And I lost my nerve. If it hadn't been for me, we would have climbed Meru today. Now he'll have to go again.' His eyes widened. 'Again,' he stammered, 'ag-gain. He'll have to go again!'

Peter saw that Harry was glaring at him with open hatred. He said: 'Gerry, if it hadn't been for you we wouldn't have got past Needle Three. Now we know the way. The only reason we failed today was because we didn't have enough time. When we come again–'

'No,' Harry shouted, the wind suddenly roaring against him. 'Neither of you are coming again.'

'Of course we are,' Gerry said. 'Aren't we, Peter?'

Peter said: 'I don't know about me, Gerry. I won't be able to leave Rudwal again for a few years. Harry will come, though, I'm sure, and he can climb Meru, now that we've made the trail for him.' He spoke bitterly, because that was what was going to happen, and he could not bear to think of Harry Walsh's conquering this mountain. Harry would call him a sadistic swine before the world, but that would not prevent him from using the route *he,* Peter, had launched them on, and held them to, while they, like curs, tried to get away from the lash. But on Meru, and in the world, if you were going to the top you had to take the lash, stand up to it, go forward against it, break it, and break the will of

246

the gods or men wielding it.

A blizzard snarled around the ridge and the porters in the other tent were moaning like lost men, and Lapeyrol was yelling at them in French to hold their tongues.

After all, he had failed. That was the fact that mattered; that was what remained after all the heroics and the hysterics. Gerry was ill – mentally, and now, Peter thought, physically as well, for he had begun to spit a little blood and he was very pale. They would go home to Rudwal, and Emily would make Gerry well again.

Then – another year, Meru again. One failure was not going to stop him any more than one obstacle, one cliff could.

CHAPTER 16

Emily noticed that it was ten o'clock; time to go back to the bungalow. The new baby did not kick so violently as Rodney had, but at six months it was an uncomfortable burden enough. So, when Gerry had asked one more question of Dr Parkash, she interrupted smoothly to say that they would be back tomorrow at eight, or perhaps in the early afternoon, to continue their discussion.

Dr Parkash said: 'Certainly, madame, very good – ah, no.' He raised one big brown hand in a theatrical gesture and boomed: 'Not tomorrow in the afternoon, madame – in the morning, or in the evening. Tomorrow afternoon, March twenty-eighth, at three p.m, is the appointed hour for the small riot. It will take place near here. Your husband will not wish you to come, especially in your condition, and I myself will be busy stitching up heads and setting broken bones.'

'What riot?' she asked, mildly interested. She could not, offhand, think of any religious occasion due so soon after the Hindu Holi, just finished, which might lead to any 'small riot.'

Dr Parkash said: 'The Committee for Good Government has voted, late last night, to hold a procession of protest against the impending execution of that assassin in Dacca, Bengal. The vote was four for the protest procession and three against. There is much astonishment that the chairman, Mr Adam Afzal Khan, cast his vote *for* the protest. So, the procession is likely to proceed.'

Dr Parkash was a big, full-natured buffalo of a man, who looked as if he should have been a wrestler. Peter had found him working with venomous gusto at a rejuvenation and venereal practice in Lahore two or three years ago, and persuaded him to come to the wilds of Rudwal to take charge of this tiny dispensary, whose façade was hardly long enough to support the name hand-painted in blue letters on a red board across the front of the veranda – THE MARCHIONESS OF CURZON AND KEDLES-TON MEMORIAL HOSPITAL. Dr Parkash had hated his Lahore patients and had plunged into the work here with an enormous enthusiasm that had seemed to grow rather than diminish. Peter had also persuaded the hospital's board of trustees, headed by the Old Captain (who had given the money to build the hut, in Philipson's time), to accept Parkash, a Bengali Hindu, as doctor in charge of a hospital whose patients were equally divided among Punjabi Moslems and hill Dogras, with a few Sikhs, and a few Buddhists from the Northern Tehsils.

Gerry said: 'Adam Khan voted in favour of a protest? Against the punishment of a murderer? The man who shot the judge's wife?'

'Oh, yes, milord,' Dr Parkash shouted genially. He had somewhere picked up a manner of saying 'milord' which would have done credit to the cockaded doormen at Claridge's. 'Mr Adam Khan is becoming quite a revolutionary fellow.'

'But what is going to cause the riot?' Gerry insisted anxiously.

'Ah! I can explain.' He raised his voice a few decibels. 'The District Magistrate – madame's husband – has forbidden *all* processions, or any procession, to use Akbar Street. The Committee for Good Government will not want to proceed in seclusion, obviously, skulking down back alleys and so forth. They will march down Akbar Street. The police will stop them. The bad hats – and, great Scott, we have plenty – will throw stones. A riot. A *small* riot. But it would be a big riot if Mr Harnarayan had his way. He is a *very* revolutionary fellow.'

Emily said thoughtfully: 'Tomorrow afternoon. Mr Savage is going on tour this evening, you know, to look at the co-operative breeding station. He confirmed it this morning.'

Dr Parkash lowered his voice until it was almost normal, and a somewhat guilty expression settled on his large face. He said: 'There is *also* a rumour that there will be no procession. And one that the C.G.G has been dissolved. But it is best to play safe, what? Now, my God, it is ten-fifteen and I am due to operate at ten-thirty – poor woman from Bhasoli, carcinoma of the left breast. Not a job for amateurs, milord, I fear. Good day, madame, good day, milord – tomorrow, but not in the afternoon, eh, just in case?'

She raised her parasol and stepped out into the sun. It seemed cooler there than in the stuffy little room with its smells of ether and its resigned, disease-eroded faces, like a frieze, around the walls.

'I hope no one gets hurt – not even Mr Harnarayan,' Gerry said with an attempt at a laugh; but she saw that the doctor's tale had disturbed him. Any kind of intrigue, violence, or political dissension disturbed him. He didn't want to know about it and had confided to her that he positively dreaded to think of the time when he would be governor of a vast province, and such matters would be his daily bread. His mind returned, as she knew it would, to the hospital. He began to talk of Dr Parkash's problems, and she answered when necessary.

Whenever, now, something approached that Gerry had grown to fear he would turn his mind away and think of the hospital, almost as though he were taking refuge, as a patient, inside it. She had known the old Gerry well, of course, but since his return from Meru she had had an opportunity to see into a new Gerry, the one that her husband was moulding. This new Gerry she now understood as well as she had the old, for his had been a long convalescence, and it was the hospital – the Marchioness of Curzon and Kedleston Memorial Hospital, and the plans for the new, bigger one – that had done the most to lift him out of the strange world of physical sickness and mental inertia wherein he had lived for the first four months after they had come back – Harry, Lapeyrol, and young Mr Lyon silent in one group; Peter and Gerry silent in another. The new Gerry was conceived, for her, that moment when she first saw them; and the new baby in her flesh that night, when Peter had come to her like a tiger, but there too had failed, again, to pass over the known boundaries.

She had thought at first that there was something unhealthy in Gerry's persistent desire to visit the hospital – to sit there for hours at a time while Dr Parkash dealt with cuts, glaucoma, dysentery, tuberculosis, leopard slashes, hookworm. He had even watched operations with awed attention, and learned enough about operating-room procedures to be more than a little help to the doctor in those primitive circumstances where, as Dr Parkash bellowed: 'We do our best, milord! If I waited for you to get the proper degree, I'd have to wait a long, long time, and *no one* would get their bloody leg cut off, eh?'

Then she noticed something. One evening Gerry upheld Dr Parkash's opinion, in some administrative matter, against Peter's. She didn't think Peter had noticed; he was not a vain man and really believed that Gerry agreed with him from conviction, not from absorption; but she noticed. From then on she made no attempt to discourage Gerry's interest in the hospital – rather the opposite. Most English women went down to Lahore, where there were English doctors (Irish and Scottish, really), for whatever pre-natal examinations were considered necessary; but she went to Dr Parkash; and she made other opportunities to accompany Gerry as often as she could.

Dr Parkash had become something of a hero to Gerry – a worthy one, she thought, though he was probably not a very learned doctor. From

watching the work of healing, Gerry had progressed to administration. He wanted to know
what hospitals cost to build and run; how nurses
were trained, and by whom; where the medicines
and the instruments and the beds came from
(there were eight beds in the Lady Curzon, and
the nurses were really midwives and nothing
else). But, whatever the subject of his interest, he
came to it with a new sense of personally chosen
commitment. And the foundation of his interest
and concern was always in the individual man or
woman. When he talked about scalpels, it was not
only of the shining blades that he thought, and of
their cost, but of what they could do of good or
bad to human flesh. Pillows and sheets interested
him because they affected the patient. Every sick
man became Gerry's personal concern. He
thought like a doctor.

Peter had noticed that, of course, and suggested that Gerry might do some work for the
new Hospital Committee while he was here –
investigate different plans, talk to the architects
in Lahore, in general help to make the decisions
that would be put into effect as soon as an
additional lakh of rupees was raised.

Gerry had agreed eagerly, and this latest visit
was one of several they had made to Dr Parkash
to talk over with him his ideas on what was
needed.

She glanced at Gerry as they turned into the
crowded main street of the bazaar. 'Of course it'll
be better,' he was saying – he was talking about
the new hospital – 'but will it be enough? Look!
Look!' He pointed out the hobbling man, the girl

with the streaming eyes. 'What can be done for them?' His voice was compounded of concern and guilt.

She said: 'We do our best. If we wait for everything to become perfect – "no one will get their bloody leg cut off."' He laughed then, and she squeezed his arm gently.

The people made way for them, many salaaming, for they were both well known in the city, especially in this street. The clamour of the bazaar surrounded them, but they were alone, as alone and together as they had been through a hundred evenings, while she read and Gerry sat in the chair opposite her, a book in his hands; and his eyes, dull and deep, would suddenly focus, but not on the book, or anywhere in the room; and Peter worked in his study, and they could hear the low voices of the visitors at the side door, and the pad-pad of bare feet as the chuprassi led them along the passage; the opening and gentle closing of a door; sometimes Peter's sharp, tireless voice.

Gerry was physically well now, though his face was thin, his eyes sunk a little deeper in his head, the structure of his bones clearer under the fair skin, the skin itself more deeply grooved. Well, he was thirty-three, and she herself, twenty-nine. There had been so many things wrong with him when he came back from Meru, none of them ordinary, few nameable. He did not have frostbite, though he had come near it; no bones were broken, though he was marked by many deep bruises, and he had suffered those not on Meru but on the way back – he had fallen on

254

paths flat and six feet wide, on stones, in streams, down a gentle grassy bank. He did not have malaria, cholera, or dysentery – none of the symptoms of the people waiting patiently back there at the Lady Curzon; yet he had been sicker than most of them – temperatures and fevers for days on end, delirium, vomiting fits, headaches, diarrhœa.

They had taken him to Lahore soon after he came back, and there the doctors had kept him in the military hospital for a week, then sent him away because he was fretting to be in Rudwal with Peter. The doctors strongly recommended that he return to England as soon as possible; but Gerry seemed to shrink inside his clothes, the thin cold-weather tweeds he had bought in Lahore, and said, joking (only who laughed? not he, or she), 'England at this time of year? Fog, rain, cold – not on your life, old girl.'

He wanted to be here, and she knew that he also feared to go back because of Harry Walsh and Meru.

The strain had exhausted her. She had thought more than once that she could not stand another moment – the long hours in the drawing-room, his eyes on the book but not in it; hearing him pace the floor of his bedroom at night. The first time she had heard that she whispered to Peter beside her: 'Gerry's walking – up, down. What time is it?'

Peter was awake silently, on the instant. 'Half-past two,' he said. 'I'll go and chat with him.'

Their door was open, a thin curtain hung across it to give them privacy and let in the night's freshness. The sound from the next room had changed. Now it was rhythmic and slow, like something dragging in slow time across the floor.

It was Peter whom Gerry would be hoping to see. After a talk with Peter he would go to sleep. However tired he was, however high his temperature, he could not rest at night until Peter had finished his work and joined them – or gone to Gerry's room, if he was confined to bed. Then Gerry's eyes would light, and he would talk of old times, of Zermatt and Llyn Gared and King's, until he was at ease. Then his eyelids would droop and he'd go to sleep. He was like a woman waiting for a lover or husband – for a part of her flesh that she knew was missing. Emily understood, because then, at that hour, she herself needed Peter in the same whole way, the physical and spiritual needs being inseparable.

She had whispered: 'I'll go to him. You've got to work tomorrow – today.'

Peter said: 'All right.' She slipped into a dressing-gown and left the room. No thought of impropriety would cross Peter's mind. She was his wife, and Gerry his – what? Slave? No, something deeper, and greater, and worse.

Gerry was sitting on the edge of his bed in the half-dark, rhythmically scraping his bare feet across the floor, one after the other, like a man shuffling on a long journey, but staying in the same place. He did not seem surprised to see her, asked only in a low whisper if he had disturbed Peter, and she told him the lie. 'No, he's fast asleep.'

This had happened many times, while the child

grew in her and the effort of getting out of bed grew greater; but now he was better. She remembered the smell of the August broom on Cader Brith, and the hissing gas mantle in the playroom on winter evenings, and the expression on his face the time she had first, secret and daring, used some of Mally's perfume. The man who walked beside her through the Rudwal bazaar remembered those things too, but that was all. The rest of him had been burned out by an electric arc, and where his personality had been there was nothing, except in Peter's presence; then something glowed again, and brightly in the void, but with an induced current only. But there was something else now, something growing slowly, something pushing as cautiously from the soil as snowdrops through the last snow, and this was her own creation, as though from her loins, with Dr Parkash the sunny, unknowing father. Gerry had been a young gentleman, and he was an earl, but he would be a physician.

Now, nearing the bungalow, Gerry said suddenly: 'Peter agrees that I ought to go back to England soon. That under-secretaryship is waiting for me – and they'll have to give it to someone else if I don't turn up in the next two or three months.'

She said, to gain a minute: 'Are you sure you're fit enough?' There was a time, soon after the return from Meru, when she would have been delighted to hear that Gerry was going to tear himself away; but the new plant needed more strength in its roots. She said: 'And what about the hospital? Haven't you got a lot of work to do there?'

Gerry shook his head. 'Nearly all done,' he said. 'In a month I can give Peter a full report and push off.' He spoke without any emphasis.

The baby was unbearably heavy, and she knew that her face was haggard and her lips were bloodless. Should she speak now? Or wait till there was more time, an opportunity not only to say out loud what she had to say but to strengthen Gerry's own desires? But such a time might not come till too late, till some arrangement had been made, something done or said, that Gerry would regard as binding him irrevocably to return to the India Office and the course that had been marked out for him. She was weak and tired but she could feel a surge of that special kind of strength, in relation to Gerry, which his illness and her role of nurse had given her.

They were outside the low wall of the bungalow, standing beside the pillars guarding the entrance to the drive. She stopped and looked back over the city, so that Gerry stopped and turned with her. She said: 'Don't go back to the India Office, Gerry. You're not cut out to be a governor – are you?'

Gerry laughed uneasily. 'I don't think so myself, but I expect I could do as good a job as most.'

'Is that enough?' she asked, pressing him. She nerved herself. 'Are you sure you might not – find it too much? At a time when a lot depended on it?'

Gerry was white now, the blood gone from his face, and he stood as brittle as a dead tree beside her. Her heart ached, because she knew the knife had struck home. She did not have to mention Peter's name. This was Gerry's secret terror, that he would fail his friend again, in his career as he had on his mountain.

She went on. '*There* are the people you – no one – can fail, as long as you do your best, because that's all they ask. People who need you, Gerry.' She pointed out over the jumbled roofs of the city. 'All the sick people here.'

She would have preferred to give him the vision of the sick and needy in England, but that would be too much to expect at one time – that he would doubly desert Peter. Here he might be persuaded, for were not the building of the new hospital and with it the nurses' school, and a ferocious assault on a people's way of living in order to improve their health, some of Peter's most urgent ambitions in Rudwal?

'You should be a doctor,' she said at last. 'Here, in Rudwal, in the new hospital with Dr Parkash. You should give Peter the rest of the money he needs – the money you've been saving to cover the expenses of being governor of a Presidency.'

'You know, I've thought of it,' Gerry whispered breathlessly. 'I diagnose every illness I see in the dispensary, to myself, and then listen to Parkash to find out whether I'm right. Only it seemed so impossible.'

'It's not impossible at all. You could study in England, and come back when you have your degree.'

259

Perhaps he wouldn't come back. That was why the idea of becoming a doctor was so peculiarly right for Gerry. A doctor, in the process of acquiring his skill, also acquired a personal integrity and self-dependence and entered into a new relationship with all men who were not physicians. Only a physician could tell his friend that he was drinking too much; only a physician *had* to tell him, in obedience to a law stronger than any friendship.

Gerry said: 'It was just daydreaming... I thought I'd go to England later. I thought it would be better to get my first M.B in Lahore. If I was going to work in India I should at least do some of my studying in Indian conditions.'

'That sounds sensible,' she said. It was hard to control the jubilation that was filling her. Gerry had gone to the trouble of finding out what steps were necessary for him to become a doctor! He did want to do this! She had been afraid of forcing him, of taking Peter's place, instead of letting Gerry stand alone.

'The only thing is, it'll take so long,' Gerry said. 'Five or six years – and I'm thirty-three.'

'What does that matter?' she said. 'This is what you want to do. You don't let delays put you off on Meru, do you? It's been seven years since Peter told you about it, and you won't – I mean, it won't be climbed till – I don't know when, now.'

'Nineteen-sixteen, Peter's going again,' Gerry said. 'He'd need me.'

She hesitated. She was sure that Gerry must not go again to that terrible mountain, at least not with Peter; but it was better to say nothing about it now. Two years of medical school would do more than she could. 'That's a long way off,' she said in the end. 'You can cross that bridge when you come to it. Let's go in. It's terribly hot out here. Don't say anything about the plan just yet. Let me tell Peter, eh? He'll understand.'

'Of course,' Gerry said. 'He'll agree right away. Only I wish I didn't feel I was letting him down, somehow.'

'You're not,' she said gently. 'Do you think Peter can't make his own way?'

'Of course not,' Gerry said, and then they entered the bungalow, and the bearer was waiting inside the door with a message. 'There is a lady to see you, memsahib.'

CHAPTER 17

'Who?' Emily asked, putting her parasol carefully into the rack.

'It is the wife of Adam Afzal Khan,' the bearer said. 'She is waiting in the drawing-room. She is a purdah lady,' he added meaningly with a glance at Gerry.

She walked along the passage, wondering.

'I'll go to my room,' Gerry said. 'See you at lunch.'

The woman waiting in the drawing-room, huddled uncomfortably in the corner of the sofa, was covered from head to foot in a white burqa, only her dark, wet eyes showing through the netting in front of the face. Emily greeted her in her careful Punjabi and sat down beside her. She had met the woman twice before, but in the Old Captain's house, when Peter had been there. Adam's wife had worn a burqa both times, and Emily had no idea what she looked like in face or figure.

The woman seemed tongue-tied, and Emily said: 'Won't you take off your burqa? It is very hot in here. I can lock the door.'

The woman nodded, and when Emily turned from the door the burqa had been thrown back over her visitor's head, and she was facing a woman of about her own age, the skin a pale wheat colour and the dark eyes, kohl-rimmed, large as a doe's in a round, ageless, but childish face.

The woman had been crying. She said: 'I am happy that you are going to have a baby. The little boy is beautiful. I see him in the Lawrence Park sometimes, when the ayah takes him there. Your time is near?'

'Three months,' Emily said. 'At the end of June. I hope it is a girl this time.' She smiled encouragingly.

The woman was picking nervously at the pleats in the top of her wide white pyjamas. 'I am going to lose my child,' she said suddenly.

'I didn't know–' Emily began. The woman did not look pregnant, and the son, Baber, was nearly fifteen now.

'It is Baber I mean,' she said. 'Our father, the Old Captain, has told us to leave his house – but he is keeping Baber. Baber – Baber wants to stay with him.' Now the tears were trickling down her face, and Emily found it difficult to understand the sobbed, slurred Punjabi.

'I'll do anything I can,' she said. 'But–'

'It is politics,' the woman cried. 'Men's cursed politics! The man of my house voted last night for the protest, and his father became very angry. This was the end of his patience, he said, that his son should march in the streets to prevent the hanging of an assassin, a dirty, idolatrous, snivelling Bengali, at that. He raged up and down like a bull. He told me to go – my husband was not there. He laid hands on me and pushed me out, at midnight, and his servants put all our belongings into three bullock carts, and–'

Emily's head ached quietly, in a rhythm that kept time with the clock on the mantelpiece. She said: 'But where did you go? Where are you living?'

'At the house of Harnarayan, in the city,' the woman said. 'But my son – I shall never see him again! He hates his father and loves his grandfather. It is the Old Captain who has taught him to ride and hawk and shoot and fish, while the man of my house has been to meetings, talking, talking. Who is right, I don't know. But it is *he*, my husband, who has lost our son for us! The Old Captain is of the old school, like *my* father. *He* knew it. Why did he have to go to meetings and talk treason with those lawyers?'

'Would it do any good if I spoke to my husband about it?' Emily asked. She wanted to pat the woman's arm, where the two gold bangles chinked heavily together as she wiped her eyes.

She is like me, Emily thought. We live in and are bounded by woman's unavoidable practicalness while our husbands, whom we love, are for ever fashioning crystal wings to fly to the rainbow's end. How deeply, really, had Peter's apocalyptic visions touched her, Emily? What did Meru really mean to her, though she had loved mountains all her life for the way the air slanted sharp across them and the sunshine made shadows that strode down the valleys? She had gone with Peter up the Zmutt ridge of the Matterhorn, but what had she discovered, except Peter?

The woman beside her said: '*He* says it was because the Deputy Commissioner Sahib wanted it that he made his vote the way he did. So if the Deputy Commissioner Sahib can tell the Old Captain that it is so, that it was for his sake, then the Old Captain will–'

Emily came abruptly back from her wanderings. 'What? My husband wanted him – your husband – to vote for the protest?'

The woman stirred uneasily, for Emily was staring at her as though she did not believe her. In truth it was her ears, or her knowledge of Punjab, that she did not trust.

'That is what *he* said,' the woman muttered doggedly, 'when I met him in the city and told him what had happened. I was very angry with him. He may have said it to make me hold my tongue.'

There was a knock on the door, and Peter's voice – 'Emily?' The woman gave a little gasp and grabbed for her burqa. 'The door is locked,' Emily assured her, 'but perhaps – I will ask my husband now.'

'Oh, no,' the woman said. 'Later, when I have gone.' She was struggling to pull the garment back on her head, and speaking rapidly at the same time. 'This is man's business. I should not have told anyone – *he* made me promise. Let me go out – that way.' Emily opened the French windows for her, assuring her that she would do what she could. The woman grabbed her hands, squeezed them, and left. Emily went over and unlocked the door, and Peter came in.

'Ahwaz told me Roshani was here – Adam Khan's wife. What did she want? Tiffin's ready.'

She said: 'Peter, is it true that Adam Khan

265

voted for the protest in the C.G.G because you wanted him to?'

'I advised it,' he said. 'Did Roshani tell you?'

She said: 'Yes. I didn't believe her.'

Peter said: 'Adam should not have told her, or anyone else.'

She felt her voice rising. 'The Old Captain's thrown them out of the house because of it! Adam Khan had to tell someone. He couldn't stand any more. Why did you advise him to vote for the protest? What is the Commissioner going to think when he hears of it?'

It was a very hot day, and Peter's shirt was black with sweat and his face pale and damp. He had spent the morning at a meeting of the District Board and was probably hungry, thirsty, and on edge. When he sat down and answered her quietly she remembered that she loved him, and that for all his faults he was a greater man than any of them, including Gerry and Adam Khan.

He said: 'The C.G.G is divided, four to three, in just about everything they do – three who want to tear down, and four who want to build. The three wreckers – two of them really are scoundrels, only Harnarayan is an honest man – have been sheltering behind the four builders. They have been using their position inside the C.G.G to get kudos, but at the same time they have been preventing the C.G.G from doing all kinds of things which would help the district. They're against the new hospital, for instance. They say that it's a devious scheme whereby only the rich landowners and the British will benefit –

but in fact they don't want it because the more misery there is, the more readily the people will accept extreme remedies. This group forced a vote on the question of a protest on behalf of that Bengali murderer. They expected to be voted down, three to four, so that they could keep out of trouble but at the same time let it be known that they are for *all* Indians against all British, regardless of law and order. There's some sympathy for that point of view, both in and out of the criminal classes. In fact one of the objects of these revolutionary groups is to cause such an increase in crime – by giving support, shelter, and legal aid to anyone who commits a crime, as long as he's Indian – that the administration of justice will break down and the police be strained to breaking point. But Adam Khan voted for the protest, so it was four to three–'

'On your orders?'

'My recommendation. I can't give Adam Khan orders. Then the other three good men – one of them is the most pompous ass in the Punjab, but he does mean well – said that they would not join such a procession, whatever the vote was. Adam Khan promptly moved that the C.G.G be dissolved, and it would have been, but the three extremists, by desperate use of parliamentary hocus pocus – they're great on procedures down there, as long as it's to prevent anything being done – put off the vote until tomorrow. They also somehow moved that the vote on the protest procession was out of order – so there won't be any protest, unless Harnarayan leads one himself – and tomorrow the C.G.G will be dissolved, and

267

those three will be smoked out into the open. A few days later Adam Khan will form a new C.G.G under another name, so organized that they won't be able to get in. They'll have to start a new organization of their own, under their true colours. Let's go and have tiffin.'

She sat thinking. It was wrong that bad men should shelter behind good men; worse that they should use their position to prevent things being done to improve the people's condition. The results of Peter's Machiavellian plan would probably be good – but the means? And the people? Adam Khan must be in a terrible state, having been made to put the knife, for however good a cause, to the throat of his own child; for that was what the C.G.G was – his, and secretly, Peter's. What about Roshani, floundering about in a trap set for other game altogether? And Baber? And even Harnarayan the idealist who disagreed with, but loved, Adam Khan?

She said heavily: 'I don't think it's right.'

'I know,' Peter said. 'I'm sorry.' She looked at him miserably, near tears, and put out her hand, trying to show him that though she could not approve, and would always try to prevent him from doing things like this, yet she loved him.

The bearer came in, his usually impassive face quite charged with excitement. 'The Old Captain prays permission to see you – also, his son.'

Peter stood up, glancing at his wrist-watch. 'I'll see them here,' he said, 'and tell the khansamah to keep tiffin for us till two. Tell Lord Wilcot not to wait.'

Emily got up to go. Peter said: 'Stay here, unless

268

you're too tired.' She sat down again.

The Old Captain strode in, the huge sabre in its scabbard held loosely across his waist. His feet were bare, for he always took off his shoes on entering any house. Adam Khan followed a little behind his father. After greeting Peter, the Old Captain looked at Emily and said: 'It is man's business that brings me here, sahib.'

'Let her stay, sahib,' Peter replied. 'Roshani has told her of your affairs.'

The old man looked disapprovingly at her for a moment and then plunged into his story. It was a brief summary of all that had happened since Adam Khan came back from Cambridge, culminating in the news he had heard last night, that Adam had voted for a protest in favour of some Bengali murderer. Now he heard that the protest was not going to take place after all, but that made no difference – though it was typical of the lily-livered rascals who were his son's boon companions that, once they had made up their footling minds to protest, they couldn't even go ahead and do it. For his part, he had had enough. He had dismissed his son from his house, with the woman. He was keeping his grandson, and would continue to raise him as he had been doing, as a Punjabi gentleman. He had sent for Adam Khan and brought him here in order that the Deputy Commissioner Sahib might be a witness to the justness of his decision. Also because his miserable son, a friend of lawyers and tradesmen and snivelling agitators, had threatened the law on him to have his son back. 'But the boy does not want to go, sahib, and rather than let him go, whatever the courts say, I will send him down to my relatives in Montgomery. I have finished.' He folded his arms, the sword sticking up across his left shoulder.

Peter said: 'Sahib, you should know that it was at my suggestion that Adam Khan voted for the protest.'

He began to explain what he had just told Emily. She was watching Adam Khan. He had been taut and nervous when he came in, but as his father's recital had proceeded he had calmed down, and now he listened with an almost detached air while the Old Captain, at first frankly incredulous, gradually came to understand what had been and was being achieved through Adam Khan's position in the C.G.G. The old man was delighted, and once or twice laughed so that his jaw waggled and his big dyed beard shook and the sword rattled in its scabbard.

At last he clapped Adam Khan on the shoulder and cried: 'Excellent, my son, excellent! Though I can see it was the Deputy Commissioner Sahib's brain that thought of this plan, and not yours. But why did you not tell me? Am I not to be trusted? Am I a babbler?'

He was, of course, and probably would have been even more delighted if Adam had said so. But Adam kept that look of sombre detachment and now spoke for the first time since entering the room. 'I did not tell you, Father, because Peter, the Deputy Commissioner Sahib, told me to tell no one. I agreed with him. For that reason I have not seen him, who was my closest friend and the man I most admired in the world, for nearly seven years, except in hurried midnight visits, or in assignations at far places. I was going to vote against the protest until he showed me what we could achieve if I voted the other way. I thought nothing could make me break our agreement of secrecy but when Roshani came to me in tears, and I knew I had lost my son too, it was like the breaking of a stick – a weak stick, Peter, not a treacherous one, only human and weak. All night I thought of what I had done. I knew that I had come to love my companions in the C.G.G as I came to understand them. Even the weak, the foolish, the wrong-headed ones – they more than the rest, even.'

The Old Captain was stirring uneasily, his prominent eyes fixed with growing hostility on his son. Adam Khan turned suddenly to Emily, and, though he wore his usual Punjabi clothes, they two were back at Cambridge, or in the cirque below Cader Brith. He said: 'Emily, I saw that if I am to live I must break away. I am miserable at the thought, but I must. Tell Gerry – make him understand.' He swung round on Peter. 'When I come to see you again, Peter, I'm coming on my own terms.'

'That has always been so,' Peter said coldly.

'Yes – but now I am myself, Adam Afzal Khan, a muddle-headed Indian with a B.A from Cambridge, nothing more. Tomorrow, when the vote on the dissolution of the C.G.G comes up, I am going to vote to keep it in being, just as it is. I know some of the group are dangerous – but this is the only way. It doesn't matter what the end is, how important, how great. The means must be this – people like us struggling and talking among ourselves.'

Peter said: 'It's more comfortable in a crowd.'

The Old Captain cried: 'Traitor!' in a loud voice.

Adam went on. 'I'm going to do more. I'm going to approach the Indian National Congress, and try to affiliate the C.G.G with them in some way, or join them as a group if necessary.'

'That would effectively save you from having to make any decisions,' Peter said.

Adam flushed and said, his voice rising: 'We will have a voice in a council representing all India.'

'Most of political India,' Peter amended, 'about three per cent of the country, perhaps, not including your father, or your son.'

'I have heard enough,' the Old Captain said harshly. 'Congress! Now it is proved that I am right to keep my grandson. If you try to bring lawyers to get him back, the Deputy Commissioner Sahib will send you to jail.'

'No, I won't, sahib,' Peter interrupted sharply. 'Adam, do you want Baber?'

Adam hesitated. 'Of course I want him, Peter. I love him. But you are quite right – I am cutting myself off from the India that my father belongs to, and the one you love. The kind of life I lead – and it will get worse – is no life for a boy to grow up in. We snap and snarl like rats, and I sometimes think that when we become free we shall be so warped that we are not Indian. Let Baber stay with my father – especially as he would run back to him if I took him away. Then there'll be real

272

Indians to use the freedom, with generosity, that we will have given up our good tempers to earn for them. But I must be able to see him when I want to.'

'I'll see to that,' Peter said. 'Also that he's free to come to you if he changes his mind.' He sounded quite normal, as though nothing that had been said or done in the burning room, full of anger and sadness, had affected him closely, though Adam Khan had stabbed him under the heart. Emily thought of Gerry, and the long dagger ready in her own hand, concealed behind her back, which she intended to place beside the other in Peter's spirit.

Adam Khan looked at Peter for a long time and said gently: 'Of course. I'd trust you before anyone else in the world.'

Peter turned to the Old Captain and said: 'Let it be so. It is just... There is permission.'

The Old Captain began to speak, even after those last words of abrupt dismissal; but though he was not a sensitive man he saw something in Peter's face that even she could not see – she supposed it was because they had both hoped for so much from Adam Khan – and he held out the sword hilt for Peter to touch, and there were tears in his eyes.

When they were gone Peter said: 'Has Gerry finished his report on the new hospital? This morning I was promised the rest of the money we need to get started. It won't be as big as it should be, but we can at least make a beginning.'

She was weak from hunger, and it was past two. Gerry made a point of keeping out of their way before tiffin time, though he usually ate with them. By now he would have finished and be back in his room. Now was the time.

She said: 'Gerry's going to give you the money to build the hospital the right size, and he's going to work in it as a doctor.'

Peter said: 'Is he?' He looked fully at her, his eyes bitter cold.

She jumped up and clung to him and could not speak properly, only sobbed, but forced the words out somehow so that they should be said before she lost the will to say them. 'He can't be a politician,' she cried. 'He can't. It'll break him and no one, not even you, can stand over him all the time and make all his decisions for him. He doesn't want to rule people, only to heal them. He lies awake, thinking of being a governor, or the Viceroy, of having to order this and suppress that, sacrifice people like Mr Philipson or people like Adam Khan. It's worse than a nightmare. Let him go, Peter – please, please, darling, let him go!'

Peter said abruptly: 'There was so much we would have done. A doctor in a miserable little hospital! If it was research, I could understand it – to find the causes of disease, and wipe them out at the root, for the whole world. But this – it's like painting a house over and over again, and still it cracks and peels. Parkash is the man for that. Dr Tanner at Llyn Gared. Thousands of them. Gerry's too good. He can do more. Why have you put this idea into his head?' He looked at her with a kind of sadness that she had seen seldom – and no one else, perhaps, ever.

'It was not my idea, it was his,' she said. 'Peter, you haven't done anything wrong. You showed Gerry that a man must live for something, but what you wanted him to live for was not right for him. That's all. You brought him to India to show him one thing, power – but what he saw was people ill, and poor. He wants to work in the new hospital all his life.'

'He won't if you can help it,' he said, unsmiling. 'You want him to go to England. But suppose he does stay? Am I to spend the rest of my life here too? Am I to follow Gerry, instead of the other way round?'

It was all coming out, and now of all times was the time to speak the truth and go on speaking it until all was said. She said: 'Yes. Yes! You know Rudwal, and the people know you. No one who's ever been here has used it as a stepping stone. They've made it their home, as I have. I don't want to leave Rudwal.'

Again it was near, the thing that she had been trying for so long to put in Peter's mind instead of, or alongside of, to give balance to, his drive towards the peaks. It was a vision, perhaps too female for him to see without difficulty, of achieving happiness and knowing fulfilment by staying, not by moving; by being, not by working. It was the ideal of the flower; and his, of the towering clouds – the lotus and the wind. She held out the budding flower to him now and she thought the lineaments of it were beginning to show themselves to him because he was very tired and bled in secret places from two wounds. He wanted to believe her, and, most desperately,

275

he wanted rest and shelter such as she promised. Like a brave soldier, gravely hurt, he wanted to believe that it would not be cowardly of him now if he let her take him back and show him peace. She thought she was winning, that his indomitable, almost insane urge to fight on and up had been beaten to its knees, perhaps mortally stricken – when Gerry came in.

He rushed in, the newspaper in his hand. 'Peter,' he cried, 'have you seen this? Look.'

She read over Peter's shoulder. There was a small item low down on the front page: ANOTHER ATTEMPT TO BE MADE ON MERU. She read on: an expedition had been formed in England, under the auspices of the Alpine Club, to make a second attempt on Meru. The leader of the expedition was Mr Henry Walsh, the well-known mountaineer, who had been deputy to Mr Peter Savage, I.C.S, on the previous attempt. The other members of the expedition were to be... Three names were listed. The attempt would take place this year, 1914. The party was due to sail for India late in April. The permission of the Government of India had been obtained.

She looked at Peter. It was all gone, all the peace, and the wind was rising, strong, and edged now with a bitter edge.

'Haven't they asked you?' Gerry asked.

'No,' Peter said. 'For one thing, Harry knows I can't get away. For another, he wouldn't ask me. The Government of India haven't asked me either, as D.C of Rudwal. I shall get a note from the Chief Secretary in Lahore soon, letting me know that the Alpine Club asked to go through into Parasia and that he wired permission because he knew I'd have nothing against it. The Chief Secretary doesn't like me.'

'Harry ought to have asked you to join the expedition,' Gerry said.

'Or you,' Peter said.

'I wouldn't like to go without you,' Gerry said. 'Not to Meru.'

'Why not?' Peter said. 'You don't have to worry about me. If Harry Walsh is going to walk up Meru by the route we discovered, why shouldn't you go with him, and share the glory?'

She knew, because of what had been passing between them before Gerry came in, that he spoke with a lightly controlled sarcasm. Gerry did not know and did not guess, particularly because sarcasm was foreign to Peter's nature and he very rarely employed it.

'Anyway, he hasn't asked me,' Gerry said. 'If he did, I'd have a damn good mind to go so that I could plant a flag on the top, labelled "By Courtesy of Savage and Wilcot."'

Peter said: 'I'm going to have tiffin,' and left the room. Before following him, Emily said: 'Gerry, I've told him about your wanting to be a doctor – and that you're going to give money to the fund for the new hospital.'

'What did he say?' Gerry asked anxiously.

'Nothing,' she said. 'But he understands. Why don't you go down to Lahore tomorrow and make arrangements to study for your – whatever it was?'

'That's a good idea,' he said. 'Peter's leaving for an inspection of the breeding station, isn't he?'

'This evening,' she said, and kept her face calm until he had closed the door behind him. Then she stumbled to the bedroom and lay down slowly, her eyes closed, feeling like a murderess.

CHAPTER 18

She was at the hospital again, but now it was near the end of May of that year, 1914, and now, however hot the inside of the dispensary might seem, it was hotter outside. She almost dreaded the moment when Gerry would finish checking blueprints out there with the master builder, for then she would have to put up her parasol and go out into the leaden furnace of May, when the sun had turned to dull copper, and the eyes hurt so that they could not distinguish sunlight from shade, and the heat struck like hammers across the forehead.

Dr Parkash had been called away before they came – to the dâk bungalow, where the members of the expedition to Meru were staying – but no one knew why. It might be that one of the climbers – Mr Lyon, probably – had an upset stomach; or it might be that the watchman's wife was at last giving birth to the twins, already a month late, who had been causing her so much illness. Emily stirred uncomfortably in the rickety chair. Five weeks to go. Lord, nine months was a long time.

Gerry came in, taking off his topee and mopping his brow. 'Parkash not back yet? I wonder... Perhaps we should go by the dâk bungalow and find out?'

She shook her head. 'Harry will let us know if

it's anything serious.' Besides, she added privately, I can't face the detour, even in the carriage. I want to go home.

The syce brought the carriage out from under the feeble shade of a tree, and they got in. 'Is everything going well?' she asked Gerry when the slight wind of their movement had begun to cool her face.

'Fine,' Gerry said enthusiastically. 'Of course, there's not much to see yet. They're still digging the foundations – but it's coming along.'

She agreed and thought: So is Gerry. The university authorities had kept him a week at Lahore, somewhat at a loss as to what to do with a Cambridge B.A who wanted to do work that medical students should have completed before joining the university; and finally sent him back to Rudwal with a trunk full of books and old examination papers, and a suggestion that if he really wanted to continue on the strange course he had outlined he should read them and report to the university in the first week of September. They would then decide whether to enrol him as a second- or third-year student.

So he had been working late each night on the books of chemistry and biology, and, when he went to bed, sleeping properly. There had been no more walkings and shufflings in the night, and even when Peter was away he slept soundly. That was as well, for fate seemed to have been conspiring with her to keep Gerry clear of Peter's influence, at least from the direct rays of his personal presence, ever since she had told him of Gerry's wish to become a doctor. One thing after another had required the Deputy Commissioner Sahib's presence – at the other end of the district, in the Northern Tehsils, at Lahore to attend an emergency conference of D.Cs – and finally, during the last two weeks, a sudden threat of famine in a small but backward area farther down the Maghra.

On the rare occasions when Peter had been at home she tried to be doubly affectionate towards him, but he was in a strange, sombre mood, and not easy to approach. He was working with the same tireless efficiency, and approached each new crisis with the same awesome incisiveness, like a circular saw, but she had begun to wonder whether this was not mere habit. One stifling night, when nothing could bring sleep, the thought had come to her that Peter was lost; that the defection of Gerry and Adam had drained away his heroic will to do. Had he then been driving himself for their sakes? Did he need them as much as – more than – they had thought they needed him? If so, she had truly done a terrible thing to him – but what else could she have done? And how much was actually her doing, and how much the will to self-preservation in Gerry and Adam, which must warn even the most loyal of men that they are heading for destruction?

The carriage halted in front of the bungalow. She went directly to the bedroom and lay down. When she awoke the heat of the day was past and she felt better. She spent an hour with her son, had a bath, and began to dress.

Peter had been away for nearly a week. He had left Rudwal the morning after the expedition arrived; so he had just seen them, wished them good weather and good luck, and gone. He was not due back for another four days – the day after they were due to set off. She remembered that he had not expressed a hope that they climb the mountain. He meant exactly what he said, no more, no less! That they should have good luck and good weather – and still fail. She did not know what to hope for. Well, all their arrangements were made, and perhaps the large contingent of Dhoital coolies they had imported from Garhwal would serve them better on the mountain than the Rudwalis had – though Peter doubted it.

The day after they marched off, the two expedition wives now staying at the dâk bungalow – Mrs Ewell and Peggy Walsh – would go up to the hill station of Manali to wait there until the party returned.

Peggy had changed – outwardly, little, except in a fining-down of her face and a hardening of her expression; inwardly, a great deal. She was a secretive woman now, giving the impression that she had some deep but shocking source of pleasure concealed about her person, like a child who intends, at the right moment, to give her grandmother a long-dead frog. Emily had not spoken to Peggy of the past – there was no purpose in it – but had tried to show by her manner, and in the genuine love she felt for her, that they could make a new affection in the present. Peggy smiled carefully and moved more gracefully about her life, and hugged the unseen thing.

Emily was in the drawing-room, talking to Gerry, when the bearer announced the arrival of Walsh Sahib and Memsahib.

Gerry sprang to his feet. 'Someone's ill?' Then Harry and Peggy came in, and Emily saw at once that, while Harry was worried, Peggy was doubly wrapped up in expectations.

Gerry said anxiously: 'What is it, Harry? What's the matter?'

Harry said: 'Ewell broke his ankle this afternoon.'

'No!' Gerry cried. 'How?'

'He slipped on that board you have in the bathrooms out here.'

Peggy said: 'Isn't it an *awful* place for a thing like that to happen to a mountaineer?' She looked at Emily with an unhappy, sympathetic shake of her head, her eyes bright.

'The doctor came up,' Harry said, 'and told us there's no chance of it healing in time to let him climb this year. Is he any good, Gerry? I mean Parkash? I must say I'm a little dubious of these brown chaps with a degree from heaven knows where.'

'Parkash is an excellent doctor,' Gerry said indignantly. 'Why, he–'

Harry went on. 'It doesn't much matter, because it's obvious the ankle's broken – his foot was twisted right round. So he's going home, and spending his furlough there instead of with us. It's hard luck. He was very keen.' He twisted the whisky glass Emily had signalled the bearer to give him, and spoke slowly, as much to Emily as Gerry. 'The point is that he was the only Urdu speaker on the expedition. He was going to look after the porters and the administration, though he'd have been available for climbing too. You remember, Gerry, when we were coming down last year, Peter said that the whole administrative side would have to be more carefully organized – and now Ewell can't come.'

Peggy was looking at her brother with alert eyes, her second drink steady in her hand, though the rest of them had hardly touched their first.

Harry went on, 'That's bad enough, but the actual climbing problems are worse. If there are only three of us we'll have to try to be in two places at once. We'll have to do more than it is really sound to ask anyone to do.'

'Oh, don't get so tired that there's an accident,' Peggy said loudly. Gerry's shoulders hunched a little, as though something cold had touched the back of his neck.

'It reduces our chances almost to vanishing point,' Harry said, 'but I can't give up without even trying. And there's one more thing. Ever since we came back last year I've been trying desperately to find some faint hope that we would be able to approach the mountain from some other angle. We're going to look at the Yangpa ridge first – but the more I remember of what I saw of it–'

'It's out of the question,' Gerry said. 'Peter said so.'

'I'm beginning to be afraid so. I was just mentally trying to get away from the certainty that we will have to tackle the Needles again. Gerry, you've learned Urdu pretty well. You

284

know the mountain – and you know the whole of the Needles. Will you please come with us?'

Emily had seen it coming and grown cold, but Gerry had not, or had hidden the certainty from himself. 'Me?' he muttered. He stared at Harry; then his eyes wandered to Emily, as though for help. He said: 'Meru. When do you expect to be back?'

Emily watched him, and the room was silent. She saw that the first emotion to come to Gerry was fear, fear that sprang on him so powerfully and from so deep in his being that he could not prevent it from flashing momentarily in his eyes and at the corners of his mouth. Then his courage beat it down and conquered it. He would be afraid, but that alone should not prevent him. But ... his medical studies?

Harry said: 'The end of August, without fail.'

Gerry was due at the university by the first week in September. As to the work he was supposed to do before then, he had already done it.

'Are you sure he's fit enough?' Emily asked. Meru was towering over them again, and Peter was not here. Perhaps Gerry should go – to purge himself of that, at least.

Harry said: 'Yes. That's really why I was asking what sort of a doctor Parkash was – because I asked him today about Gerry. He said he had examined him a couple of times recently and thought he was thoroughly fit, physically.' He went on quickly. 'I know you're fit enough in every other way, Gerry. There's not another man in the world I'd rather be with, on any mountain, at any time.'

Gerry nodded abstractedly. He said: 'I'd want to have an equal chance at being chosen for the summit party, Harry... Because of Peter. He can't come, I know, but I could sort of represent him, couldn't I?'

Harry hesitated for a perceptible moment. Then he said: 'I was hoping to rely on you to establish a new camp above the Needles, if that's the route we have to use. But – all right. An equal chance, depending on what happens – how we all go.' Emily knew that he would have liked to keep Gerry off the heights, because of what had happened last time. But the Needles still stood, and this time Peter would not be there. If Gerry was himself – his old superb but normal self – Harry would give him a chance at the summit, even at the cost of his own place.

Gerry still stood thinking, a whisky glass in his hand.

He turned to Emily. 'Do you think Peter will–?' She braced herself to lie.

'Gerry, Harry needs you,' Peggy broke in gently.

Gerry made up his mind. 'I'll come,' he said. 'Yes, I'll come.' He put out his hand.

Harry jumped up. 'Wonderful!' They clasped hands.

Gerry said: 'All my things are here. And you're not off for a couple of days. Wish I had time to go and say good-bye to Peter. I'll send him a note. Get it off first thing in the morning.'

Emily saw Peggy make a small, happy movement. Dear God, what would Peter say? He would never believe that Gerry had not appreciated his bitter sarcasm when they had talked about this very thing as an impossibility two months ago. He would see it as a deliberate action to wound him, on Gerry's part. Perhaps it would lead to a final break between the two of them, and Gerry would go back to England to be a doctor. That would hurt, too, but it might be best in the long run.

Gerry said suddenly: 'Peter's the best climber in the world. It's a damn shame. But his work's important too. I never realized how important until this year.'

Peggy said eagerly: 'Of course!' Harry nodded without speaking. Harry had been very careful to say nothing during his week here that might even hint of any adverse opinion he held of Peter. When he could praise, he did; when he did not wish to, he was silent.

A thought suddenly struck Emily. She said: 'Peggy, Mrs Ewell must be going home with her husband?'

'Oh, yes,' Peggy said brightly. 'She is going to look after him, and has made all the arrangements. She's very efficient. They're going to start out the day after tomorrow. Dr Parkash has set his foot in plaster of Paris, and they'll have it looked at in Lahore and then go on.'

'What will you do? You were going to stay with Mrs Ewell in Manali. You'll be alone.' Emily knew what she must do – what it could be best to do, in spite of the obvious disadvantages.

'Yes,' Peggy said.

Emily said: 'You must stay with us here.'

'Of course, you'll be alone too, most of the time,' Peggy said. 'I never thought of that – with Gerry gone.' There was the secret self-hugging again, and Emily waited; but that was all. Peggy said: 'Are you sure I won't be in the way? It seems such an awful imposition to have someone settle on you for three months.'

'It isn't as though we were strangers,' Emily said evenly, looking directly at her girlhood friend, trying to make her come to the point, to say something that would clear the air and dispel the metallic shimmering of the atmosphere around them.

'Of *course* not,' Peggy said. 'I'd love to. And I can help with the baby. *I* don't seem able to have one. It'll be quite like old times, won't it?'

No, it won't, Emily thought, not a bit; not until you come out and scratch my face, and we argue and fight and cry and know what has happened to each other. It would be difficult, especially at first. Having the baby would help her over that time. Later, surely, they would be able to find each other again?

'That's wonderful,' she said. 'You can have Gerry's room.'

'We'd better get back to the dâk bungalow,' Harry said. 'Goodwin and Lyon will be delighted to hear you're coming, Gerry. Really overjoyed. Ewell too, poor devil. What stinking luck!'

Emily, smiling, full of unease, saw them to the outer door.

CHAPTER 19

She looked around the table carefully, the bearer at her side. Harry on her right; Gerry sitting as host with Peggy on his right; Mr Lyon; Mr Goodwin. It was a pity that the Ewells had had to go, as that left herself and Peggy as the only women. Flowers. Everything in place. The menu rechecked and the khansamah busy in his kitchen.

They'd be off at ten tomorrow morning. 'Never like to make a long stage the first day, or try to get away too early,' Harry had said. Gerry was over there at the dâk bungalow, trying to get the others to admit that pegs were permissible aids on Meru. A refusal on their part would imply that they thought Peter had been wrong to use them in '13. She thought that they would accept the pegs, with private reservations, as much for Gerry's sake as because even Harry seemed to think the Needles would be impossible without them. She had taken it on herself to offer them the pegs brought down from last year, though each one would have to be carefully examined before use.

The time passed; Gerry returned; the guests arrived; and slowly the evening began to take shape. It was a time such as she had often watched from the outside, or from the shadowed edge, at Llyn Gared while she was growing up, but had seldom fully been a part of herself. The men were all of the same metal, though formed into different shapes. Gerry was at ease, happy and excited as he used to be in the untroubled days. He and Lyon were going to climb as a pair as much as possible, because Lyon knew nothing about pegs and didn't like them. He explained that he would trust Gerry, not only to show him their uses but to find the balance of justification, so that they would not be used needlessly but would not be shunned when they might make for greater safety.

Even Peggy had relaxed something of her disquietingly eager manner. After all, Emily thought, Gerry *is* going tomorrow, and, whatever Gerry thinks, Peggy is quite well aware that Peter would have preferred him not to go. And Peggy's feelings towards Peter were – strange.

The warmth of friendship and common endeavour wrapped them all through the meal and after, when the men stayed in the dining-room and she talked with Peggy in the drawing-room, discussing a few details of the life they would share here until the end of August; and after again, when the men joined them.

They were still talking about the mountain, and as she listened she thought that in some odd way, without detracting from Harry's leadership, Gerry had become the focus of the expedition. She had not seen the places they talked of, though they were as real in her mind as the room wherein she was sitting, but she thought that the others felt that Gerry knew more about Meru than any of them, even felt perhaps that he had some indirectly acquired communion with the mountain which they would never have. Of course it was a fact that he had been higher than any of them. Perhaps that explained it. Or perhaps the secret was that Peter was not coming this time, and Gerry felt that he must in himself represent as much of that daemon power as he could; and it was there, certainly, but transmuted by his character into a firm, steady desire to help them all to do well what they had come so far to do. Harry, the wise leader, sat a little back and left the spirits of his companions to gather inspiration and strength where they would.

Gerry said: 'Look, Harry, I've got an idea about Needle Five—'

'*If* we find the Yangpa won't go,' Harry said with a smile.

'Yes. Em, can I have six pepper-pots?'

'Six!' she cried. 'Well, I'll see.' She got up to call the bearer.

He entered the room before she had reached the door. He was smiling. He said: '*Sahib a-gya.*'

She gasped. 'What! Oh, no!'

Peggy said urgently: 'What's the matter?'

'Peter's back.'

'Peter!' Gerry cried.

'How wonderful! He'll be able to see them off in the morning after all.' Peggy's voice was suddenly full of suppressed excitement.

Emily asked the bearer: 'Where is he?'

'In the study, memsahib.' He salaamed and went out.

She said: 'I must go. I'll be back in a minute. Gerry, do the honours, please.'

'We'll be all right,' Peggy said happily.

Emily hurried along the passage, her mind racing. She found Peter at his desk, scribbling notes with one hand, mopping his forehead with the other. He was covered with dust, and outside she saw the syce leading away his horse.

He got up and kissed her quickly as she came in, and asked, 'How's the baby?' His icy eyes were rimmed with red, and yellow dust lay like a hood under his brows and in the corners of his nose. He began scribbling again while he talked. 'We've broken it – the famine,' he said. 'I forced the speculators down there to put their stocks on the market. I'm on my way to Lahore to make a special report to the Lieutenant-Governor. I have to catch the midnight train. You've had dinner?'

'Yes–'

'Good. I've told the khansamah to make me some scrambled eggs. Harry's expedition's off to-morrow?'

'Yes–'

'I'll come in and wish them luck before I change. Though they won't climb it.' He laid down his pen – 'There' – and stood up.

She said: 'I've asked Peggy to stay with us while the expedition's away. Did Gerry tell you in his note?' She had to find out whether he had received the note, or whether he had come back now, two days early, only because his work was done.

He looked at her, his brows bent, and said: 'Why did you do that? You can't re-create Llyn Gared in Rudwal. We'd have had a better time as we are, the three of us – you, me, and Gerry.'

292

'Then you didn't get Gerry's note.'

'Yes, I did,' he said quietly, still holding her eyes on his.

She said: 'Then you know Gerry's going with them – but you just said, "the three of us." Peter, what–?'

His left hand rested on the table-top, the long fingers taut under the bright glare of the pressure lamp. The fizzing light fell on white papers; red tape binding the files; gleaming black-japanned metal of two boxes; red ink, blue ink in glass pots. His face was in shadow, and behind him on the walls the pictures of mountains.

'Do you think Gerry really believed I wanted him to go?' he said at last. Again she had to forget some of the urgency of her emotion in admiration of his perspicacity and of his self-control.

'Yes,' she said, 'of course! That was why he accepted.'

Peter said: 'I think I'd like to tell him the truth.'

She lurched in front of him as he made to pass her. She caught hold of the lapels of his thin, stained coat and whispered fiercely: 'Listen, Peter! You've *got* to let him go, because he's promised. If you make him break his promise... Oh, God, it's awful to think that you might be able to. Before he met you no one, nothing, could have made him break a promise. If you do he'll have nothing left in the world except you, no place to go, no one who will speak to him, accept him – only you.'

'And his patients,' Peter said. 'Does he want anything else?'

Gently he put her hands away and went out.

She followed him heavily along the passage. At the drawing-room he opened the door for her, so that she might precede him into the room.

The four men were on their feet. Peter went past them to take Peggy's hand. He said: 'Hello, Peggy. I hear you're staying with us while the expedition's away.'

Gerry said: 'Peter, did you get my note?'

Peter, facing Harry Walsh, ignored him. Peggy was looking up at Emily, smiling, almost leering. Peter said: 'Harry, why didn't you ask me to join your expedition?'

Emily realized that they were all holding their breaths, and the room was silent, so that the words went home like unexpected swords. Oh, damn him! she whispered to herself, he won't play the rules as Harry and poor Gerry know them; he won't pass it off; he won't fence with buttons on the points; the boat race is beginning again.

Harry flushed and said: 'I knew the I.C.S wouldn't release you again this year.'

'That's not true,' Peter said, smiling, the cold grin widely white in his mouth amid the dust. 'I mean, it isn't the reason.'

'I didn't think you would take to being a member under my leadership,' Harry said, the flush dying away as he found his balance.

'Go on.'

Harry looked at him. 'Isn't that enough?'

'No, the whole truth is better, so that Gerry can understand. All right. I'm not going to Lahore tonight. I'm resigning, here and now. I'm available. I'm willing to serve under you in any capacity that you order. I hereby apply to join you. Will you take me?'

This time the silence was short, because Harry had regained his footing and remembered that this was Peter Savage and not Gerry, not a mountaineering gentleman, not a decent member of the Alpine Club, with whom he was dealing. He said: 'You know quite well that I am never going to climb with you again.'

Emily caught Peter's arm and cried: 'Must we say this now? Here? You aren't going to resign, so you can't go. Why can't we leave it at that?' But she knew, and Harry knew, that Peter would resign if necessary. There was nothing he would not do, and that was the secret, all the way up and down.

'I'm afraid I can't leave it,' Peter said. 'Sit down, Emily. You're looking very tired... Why aren't you going to climb with me again Harry?'

Emily stole a look at Gerry's face. Gerry's mouth was open, his eyes wide in growing horror.

Harry said: 'Because you're not a mountaineer and never will be. You're a climber, in every sense of the word – a conqueror. A selfish, cruel swine. And a murderer.'

Peter said: 'I'm going to have a bath, Gerry.' He turned and walked out, and in the creaking silence, with a night bird hooting across the hot lawns, they heard him call, 'Bearer! *Ghusl tayyar karna, ek dam.*'

Sweat stood out in jewelled beads on Gerry's forehead, and now his cheeks were tight as a corpse's. 'Harry,' he said in a choked voice,

'Harry, you've got to apologize.'

'I can't,' Harry said gruffly. 'It's the truth. Everyone knows it but you. I'm sorry, Emily but–'

'Peter can speak for himself,' she said wearily. She had no wish to defend Peter. What Harry said was true as far as the rest of the world could understand. Only she and Peter himself and Gerry – yes, Gerry above all – could tell them that it wasn't the whole truth.

Gerry said: 'You're not fit to clean his shoes, Harry.' His voice shook. 'I never guessed – I never dreamed you wouldn't have asked him if you thought he could come. So you sneaked in and organized this party to the mountain that *he* discovered, *he* worked on, *he* showed you everything you know about–'

'Oh, God,' Peggy said, and now the brittle expectation had broken and her face was twisted in ugliness. 'How long did Peter rehearse him?'

'He doesn't have to,' Emily said, all sensation slowly freezing as she watched Gerry, heard the words come out of his mouth, saw his blazing eyes. Lyon and Goodwin, on either side of him, were full of a furious, helpless anger.

'I can't come with you,' Gerry said.

'I'm sorry,' Harry said at last. 'I understand. Don't worry about it. Peg, we'd better go back to the dâk bungalow. I hope you'll excuse us, Emily.'

'Of course.'

Peggy said: 'I suppose you'd rather I didn't come to stay, after this?'

Emily felt that, in spite of the words, Peggy did want to stay, even that there had been in them a faint, miserable reawakening of that air of expectancy.

She said: 'No – I'd like you to, if you want to. There's another room. Peter won't be unpleasant, if that's what you mean.' She tried to keep her eyes and mind off Gerry, standing aside, set, looking away from them all, out of the window on to the garden. 'He only made Harry say what we all know that he feels. Nothing's really changed.'

'No, it hasn't,' Peggy said. 'That's what's so wonderful about Peter... Yes, I'll be back... No, we'll walk... Good night. Good night, Gerry.'

The other men muttered their curt good-byes, and Emily forced herself to accompany them to the front door. As soon as they had gone down the front steps she hurried back to the drawing-room, her skirts hissing like vipers along the stone floor. 'Gerry,' she cried. 'Gerry!'

He was sitting on the sofa, staring straight ahead, an unlit cigarette between his lips, a box of matches shaking in his hand – but he never smoked. She sank awkwardly to her knees beside him. 'Gerry! You haven't done anything wrong. Nor has Harry. He's just – people.'

He said: 'They can't touch Peter. They're like mice, nibbling at his feet. "Murderer!" He saved Harry once, me twice–'

She stroked his hand and spoke urgently. 'It doesn't matter, Gerry. It's done, finished with. Forget it happened. Peter has.'

When Gerry spoke again his voice was very low, so that she could hear only by straining forward. 'I cursed Harry just now,' he said. 'But I'm as bad. I've been weak and selfish, thinking only of myself, of being a doctor – leaving Peter in the lurch after he's trusted me all these years, and he's never said a word.'

She raised herself slowly and sat down beside him on the sofa. Looking at his face, incredibly handsome as it had always been and now with an added strength of suffering, a grimness of self-discovery, she recognized as clearly as though she had read it in a book that Gerry now, in this shape, meant more than anything else in the world to her. For his sake she would sacrifice herself and her hopes of happiness; the child in her womb; the sharp-eyed, electrically capable boy of two who slept in his cot in the quiet nursery; Peter, whom she loved, but who was so much a law to himself that she could not understand how she had ever thought to guide him one inch off the path which that law ruled he must follow. She loved Gerry as a brother and as a son, and now, in this livid silence, as a lover. Her flesh yearned after him, that they could comfort each other in love. Her hand, still stroking his, passed a new message to her brain and to the pit of her stomach and to the small of her back.

She knew, as from a flash of lightning, what secret it was that Peggy hugged so jealously to her breast. Peggy's jealousy of her had seen the physical aspect of this love in her before she herself was aware of it.

She stood up finally. There was still a chance. That chance lay in keeping Gerry to the only course which would free him from Peter, and so free her from her compulsion to protect him at all costs. She said: 'Now, Gerry, the reason Peter has never said a word is that he does *not* think you have left him in the lurch. Surely we saw tonight, if we didn't know already, that Peter is not afraid to speak his mind?'

Gerry nodded.

'You're doing the only thing that is right for you to do. After all these years you discovered it – through Peter, indirectly – and you know it, and he knows it. But I still think you'd do better to study in England.'

Gerry stood up and took her hands in his. She held them tightly, recognized the involuntary spasm of love that had made her do so, and then relaxed her grip. 'I suppose you're right, old girl – but I don't want to go back to England. Can't you see the headlines? EARL CUTS FIRST CORPSE! Not so many distractions in Lahore... My gosh, what a night! Think I'll wander along to my room and turn in. Good night.'

She heard him go down the passage and shout through the door of Peter's bathroom: 'Good night. Feeling awfully tired. When will you be back?'

Peter's voice was faint. 'Next week, Gerry. Anything I can get for you in Lahore?'

'No. Anything you want seen to here? Well, good night.'

Ten minutes later Peter joined her in the living-room, and the bearer laid the occasional table for his supper. She waited, collecting her thoughts into orderly sentences, until they were alone, and then said: 'I'll never forgive you for what you did

tonight, Peter. Now I want you to know something else. If you stop Gerry from becoming a
doctor, for any reason whatever, I'll leave you.'

'To look after Gerry?' Peter asked.

'Gerry won't be alive for long to need looking
after if you do that,' she said. 'Good night.'

He stood up to kiss her, but she leaned away
from him. 'I don't want to kiss you now. I'm
sorry.'

He sat down again and said matter-of-factly:
'So am I. Just remember that you're the only
person I love – you and Gerry.'

She walked heavily along to the nursery. The
ayah was fast asleep on her *charpoy* at the foot of
Rodney's cot. The little boy's hair was thick and
straight and the colour of tarnished gold. He had
the edge of the single sheet that covered him
grasped firmly in his thin, strong hand. She
leaned down, almost unwillingly, to kiss him,
while the ayah's rasping snores shook the room.
He was his father's son and she found it difficult,
tonight, not to fear him.

CHAPTER 20

They were in the drawing-room, on a day early in August, the afternoon heavy with the close, wet air that swirled in mist about the town as though round some high Alpine mountain. Rainwater lay in puddles across the lawn and the carriage wheels had left narrow curving canals and the horses' hoofs crescent-shaped lakes in the gravel of the drive. The leaves of the walnut tree hung dark over the grass, and beyond the wall the city might not have existed, for the mist hid it.

The telegraph lines had been down for forty-eight hours, somewhere between Rudwal and Lahore. Before they broke they had been bringing every day an increasingly loud clamour from Europe. Nations were at war, peoples were mobilizing, statesmen sending ultimatums. Now, lost in the mist, the wires down, there was silence; like the city, the crisis might not have existed; only, like the city, it did.

Rodney was playing on the floor, piling bricks one on top of another, then neatly destroying his creations. Elizabeth, five weeks old today, lay at the far end of the sofa, wrapped in swaddling clothes, looking mistily at the ceiling. Gerry was in his room, working. Peggy had gone out for a walk; she liked walking in the rain.

Peter sat in his chair, a heavy report in his hand. He was nearing the end of it, and Emily could tell by the way he flicked over the pages that, though he was absorbing all it had to tell him, he was not interested in it. Her feeling that Peter had at least temporarily disengaged himself from commitment to his work had strengthened during the two and a half months that had passed since the expedition left. There had been an armed caution between them since that day; she showing her affection for him, but on her guard to withdraw it and attack him tooth and nail if he made a move to exert his power over Gerry; he carrying out his duties, solicitous of her through the time of Elizabeth's birth, never coming so far forward that she would have a chance to rebuff him. He had seemed to be waiting; she thought at first that it was for word from Meru. Perhaps it had been, but then, in July, the news from Europe began to come like the hammer blows, daily gaining in strength, of crazed giants smashing away at the foundations of their existence, at everything that held up the world they knew – Meru, Peter's ambitions, Gerry's new career, the lives of the babies. Whatever the cause of his brooding had been before, now it was this – war, world war, for he had already told them that that was what it would be. 'A war of peoples,' he'd said, and his eyes he had veiled, hiding their intensity while he waited.

Gerry had returned to his books and the building of the new hospital almost as though nothing had happened, and she had marvelled at the power of this new love that could enable him to take such a night in his stride. Once or twice she had caught Peter looking at him with the same astonishment; but Peter had said nothing. And, as far as Peter had stepped back and left Gerry to follow his own path, that far she found that her physical love for Gerry had lessened. It was still there, close beneath the surface of sisterhood, but she had no difficulty in keeping it there, where it did no harm but lay like a battle fleet at anchor, ready to sail out and alter the balance of destiny. *'Ultima ratio regis!* – the last resort of a king,' they often used to engrave round the muzzles of great guns; but what was the last resort of a queen?

In another month Gerry would be at the university and irrevocably launched on his career. Then, she thought, this waiting love would wait no more but would vanish and be remembered only as were those week-long lusts of adolescence, when she had prayed – and feared – that the butcher's boy in Llyn Gared would take her behind the hedge and kiss her and put his hand on her breast.

She looked down at Rodney and smiled at him, for he was smiling up at her, a crooked, reasonless grin. All would yet be well.

'Adam Afzal Khan is here, huzoor, and his son, Baber.'

She let her knitting fall into her lap. All might be well, but not yet. The city and the war would not be hidden for ever by the mist, and here was Adam Khan standing in the door, the chuprassi holding it open for him, and Baber, the tall youth, upright at his father's side.

Peter said: 'Come in.' He rose and motioned Adam Khan to a chair. 'Baber, I'm glad to see you.' He shook hands with the boy, who then joined his palms in a graceful old-time gesture that held courtesy and no hint of servility in it. Adam watched with a peculiar, wry smile as his son sat down in a hard chair beside him. 'Baber has been well taught, hasn't he?'

'By my grandfather,' the boy said in stiff English. 'He gave me a gun today. A four-ten single-barrelled gun by Purdy.'

'I asked the boy to come with me today because I want him to hear what I have to say to you,' Adam Khan began. 'Also because he wanted to see you. He says he is going to be a mountaineer when he grows up. He says he will learn to climb from the English sahibs, and then climb with them – and then climb higher than they.'

'Good,' Peter said. 'When you're eighteen, Baber, I'll take you into the Northern Tehsils – if I'm still here.'

'Your children are beautiful, Emily,' Adam murmured. He brushed his hand lightly through Rodney's hair. Rodney ignored him and crawled over to sit at Baber's feet, staring intently into his face, while the boy smiled and held down a finger for him to play with.

'*Maila!*' Rodney said, pointing at the mud on Baber's light trousers.

'Well,' Peter said, 'is it peace or war that brings you here?'

Adam Khan said: 'Peace or war. That's it. Is there any news from Europe?'

Peter said: 'I heard a rumour that the Germans had invaded Belgium.'

Adam said: 'And our – the British – ultimatum?'

'I don't know. The telegraph's down.'

Adam was leaning forward, his thin hands clasped together so tightly that Emily thought the knuckles would crack. He said: 'This war will be a terrible thing, Peter – perhaps the most terrible that has ever come to civilization.'

Peter said: 'A lot of people don't think so. The general opinion among the soldiers in Manali seems to be that the French will beat them in six weeks, without us. They're fed up because they don't see any chance of getting into it.'

'And taking their Indian soldiers with them.'

'Gurkhas.'

Adam jerked his hands free. 'There will be Indians too.' Emily saw that the boy Baber was listening intently now, his eyes sparkling. 'Peter, I can't stand aside from this war, if it comes – India can't – but it is very important that we should come in the right way. The Viceroy must not declare war as though we were chattels. He must ask the leaders of Indian opinion.'

'Such as who?' Peter asked. 'Your South African lawyer, Gandhi? The Maharajah of Bikaner? Rabindranath Tagore?'

'It doesn't matter who,' Adam said strongly, 'but ask someone. I came here because I want you to know that I, personally, perhaps because of Cambridge, believe that India ought to be in this war if England is. I am going to try and persuade our leaders that it would be short-sighted and – well, mean, un-Indian – to use England's involvement to increase our demands. But you must understand that we have pride. There will be tragic consequences if you don't make some gesture to India before declaring war on our behalf.'

'That was what you were going to do, wasn't it – after you and I had decided what was best? You were going to consult, explain – remember?' Peter said, the corners of his mouth hard set. Adam flushed slightly. Peter went on. 'Even as things are, I agree. But I don't think any such gesture will be made. We are not strong on imagination, especially in the councils of the Great Ornamental. They will decide, quite correctly as far as facts go, that people like you don't stand for much in India besides yourselves, yet.'

The boy Baber said: 'Of course we must fight. Anyone who does not think so is a coward.' He met his father's eyes defiantly.

Emily listened closely, her head bent over her knitting, now and again stealing a glance at Elizabeth or at Adam Khan's intent, sad face. Adam had gained a lot of stature since he had made the great effort and freed himself to stand alone, for better or for worse, in the turgid whirlpools of Indian politics.

Now Adam had turned away from his son's hostile stare and said: 'He's right, Peter. There are more who think as he does than as I do – and I wouldn't really have it otherwise; but to *us* it's frightening, it's absolutely appalling, to think that our fate is going to be settled six thousand miles away and without our having a word to say in it. We could finish up as a colony of Germany!'

Peter said: 'Would you prefer that? It's not our fault that it's the truth. It's yours, for being such

306

a mess of corruption and civil war a hundred and fifty years ago. If it wasn't us dragging you around at the wheels of our chariot it would be the French or the Russians. What the devil do you want? To be left on the sidelines as a kind of trophy to be picked up by the winner? If you'd prefer the Germans, make trouble for us here. If you don't, put your pride in your pocket and come and fight. I can assure you that we won't be starting this war, and certainly not with the express purpose of insulting Indians, as I expect Harnarayan has already decided.'

Adam Khan said slowly: 'You are trying to annoy me, Peter.'

Peter said: 'No, I'm not. I just want to make it quite clear that your fate *and mine* are going to move out of our hands if this war begins. Soldiers in Europe and sailors in the Atlantic are going to settle it.'

'That is wrong,' Adam said heavily.

'But true,' Peter said, showing his teeth.

The boy Baber said: 'Do not care what my father says, sahib. With him it is–' He broke into rapid, clean Punjabi. 'We have been hearing for weeks about the war that might come. Grandfather says the armies used to invade us from Burma, Persia, Afghanistan, China, Nepal. Where is our Peacock Throne? In Teheran! Carried off by the son of an Afghan pastry cook! But for a hundred years we have been marching out upon *them,* to chastise them. We can hold up our heads anywhere, not because of what my father says, but because of what he, my grandfather, *did...*'

Emily covertly eyed Adam and saw him gazing at his son with that same wry admiration; his eyes met Peter's with an obvious message: You see? This is what we must not lose while we worry about freedom. The boy surged on, standing up now, for he was full of passion, and Rodney had stood up too and was clutching at the skirt of Baber's beautifully cut black achkan.

'Grandfather says when we can beat anyone in the world, as the English are teaching us; when there is no need to send English soldiers with us to see that we do not become frightened at strange new things; when we can build bridges and roads, and give judgement by what is right, not by what will please our friends; when the King Emperor can say to us: "Do this," and we can do it – then we *shall* be free, whoever sits in your seat, sahib, whatever anyone writes on any piece of paper, whoever is Viceroy, even if there is no Viceroy. If we cannot do these things, Grandfather says, we shall be free as we were after the time of the Emperor Aurangzeb – free, and slaves to fear.'

He stopped and sat down slowly. 'I am sorry, sahib. I spoke because I wanted you to know that *Indians have pride.*' He turned away from his father.

'Well spoken, my son,' Adam said softly. 'Well spoken indeed. When you are a man, after this war is over – for I feel in my bones that it is coming – you will know that I too have spoken well. Also the Deputy Commissioner Sahib. And my father. That is our tragedy.'

The youth closed his handsome face in

disbelief. Adam turned to Peter. 'I hope that's what happens, that we all fight together and that India does more than her share, because then, afterwards, everything will have to be different. Then, when we will have helped to win the war, we cannot be treated as a trophy but as an ally, an equal.'

Peter was silent, and Emily saw that he was looking sombrely at Adam Khan. At length... 'Perhaps,' he said. 'But nothing will be settled in India. *That's* our tragedy.'

Adam Khan stood up, and Baber automatically with him. 'That's all I had to say, Peter. I'm going to call a meeting of the local branch of Congress as soon as we hear any definite news. I'll let you know about any resolutions we pass.'

'Thanks,' Peter said.

'And another thing,' Adam added with a half-smile. 'Everyone in Rudwal hopes Harry Walsh breaks his neck on Meru – some because they think you are their father and mother, almost God; others because they think you're the devil, but our own personal Rudwal devil. Give my regards to Gerry. Did you tell him I'd finally persuaded our anti-British wing to join us in giving our blessing to the hospital?'

'Yes. He was delighted. Parkash wanted to go and bash your heads in for being so long about it. "Don't the bloody British have dysentery too?" he bawled. Good-bye, Adam. I hope I'm not putting you in jail next time I see you – I or whoever occupies my chair. If there is a war we shall have to take the gloves off.'

Adam Khan nodded, hesitated as though about

to speak, and then turned and left with his son.

Peter returned to his chair. The heavy report lay on the floor, where Rodney began to tear pages out of it. 'No, Rodney,' Emily cried, and stooped to take it from him.

'Let him,' Peter said. 'That's all it's good for.' He stared out of the windows, where a driving grey rain was dispelling the mist.

The chuprassi was at the door. *'Huzoor sahib – tar a-gya.'*

Peter put his hand back over his shoulder, while looking at her. 'The wires are up again, then,' he said softly. He tore open the envelope, and read aloud: 'HARKAMU AUGUST 4 BY GALLOPERS FROM JUNIPER JULY 26 LAST ATTEMPTS MERU FAILED JULY 22 23 24 REGRET REPORT JAMES LYON KILLED JULY 24 ALL OTHER MEMBERS OF EXPEDITION SAFE RETURN-ING AT ONCE DUE RUDWAL APPROX AUGUST 29 WALSH.'

'Mr Lyon,' she whispered. 'The one who was going to be Gerry's partner.'

'Don't remind him of that,' Peter said sharply. 'We'd better tell him, though.'

'Now?' she said doubtfully.

'Yes. Otherwise he'll hear rumours first. Do you think the telegraph operator hasn't told all his friends already?' He got up and left the room with the telegram in his hand.

He did not return for ten minutes, and then Gerry was with him. Gerry was trembling, hardly so much that you could notice it, but definitely, a light, continuous shivering of the skin, and his face was pale. 'I wonder how it happened,' he muttered. 'How did it happen?' – over and over.

'You mustn't worry about it, Gerry,' she said quietly.

Peter said: 'Isn't it time ayah took the children?' She glanced up in surprise, for usually he liked to play with Rodney till late on such afternoons as this, when he was in the bungalow; but she saw the child staring at Gerry with absorbed interest and she moved at once to pick them both up and carry them off, and call to the ayah to come and take charge of them.

When she returned to the drawing-room Peter said: 'Now I want to show you something else. This came five days ago.' He pulled a sheet of white paper from a pocket and began to read aloud.

The letter was from the Chief Secretary to the Government of the Punjab. It contained a copy of an informal note from the Home Member of the Government of India to the Lieutenant-Governor of the Punjab, informing the latter that Mr Peter Savage, I.C.S, at present serving in the Punjab Commission, was being considered for the post of Deputy Secretary of the Home Department of the Government of India. The step would be a most unusual one, but Mr Savage seemed brilliantly qualified for the appointment. However, before it was made he, the Home Member, would be glad if, according to the normal custom of the service, the gentleman was consulted. The Chief Secretary now informed his 'Dear Peter' that H.E would like to know as soon as convenient what he was to reply to the Home Member.

Peter returned the letter to his pocket.

He said: 'That wire from Harry came from the north. Nothing's been wrong with the telegraph in that direction – but they'll have the wire through to Lahore any moment now. But – suppose they were never going to; suppose this is all we have to go on – this letter from the Chief Secretary, the telegram from Harry – now what?'

Emily had put down her knitting while he read. Gerry's trembling had stopped, but he was even paler than before.

'What do you mean?' Gerry asked at last.

'I mean – what am I to do? We were going to do great things, starting from here, weren't we? You and Adam and I. But you both turned back into Rudwal. Adam is going to stay as chief of the local Congress. You're going to stay as a doctor. Now I've forced open the gate that lets me get out and on, and I'm ready to go. Am I to turn back too?'

His voice was quite normal, as was his manner, but his words were so unlike him that the total impression was as though he were playing a part. Watching him carefully, on her guard, Emily thought that that was what he was doing; he was pretending that there would be no telegram from Europe. But partly the questions were genuine: *if* that overriding message were not waiting somewhere between Rudwal and Lahore, then all this would have been of the greatest importance, because he really wanted to know.

Gerry said anxiously: 'What do you want to do, Peter? If you go to Calcutta I don't think anything can stop you from becoming Viceroy, whatever the policy may have been. Where's the present Secretary going?'

'Lieutenant-governor of a province,' Peter said. 'It's Mainwaring – he's forty-eight. A coming young fellow!'

Gerry said: 'And you're – thirty-three. You'll go on to be a lieutenant-governor before you're thirty-eight. That's what you want, isn't it?'

'Is it?' Peter asked, and he turned to her with the same dark smile he had held through the reading of the letter and his questioning of Gerry.

Was he playing with her? When had Peter not known exactly what he wanted? But he wasn't. He wanted her to interpret him to himself so that he might understand the strange forces that had been pulling him this way and that since Adam and Gerry left him climbing alone.

She said: 'I think you want to stay here, Peter. With Gerry and Adam. I know that I–' She hesitated, wondering whether she dared push him at all in any direction, knowing his old instinct to go then in another because it would be harder.

'Go on,' he said.

'I want you to stay here. Everyone knows you here, and you know so many. You've done wonderful things for Rudwal – really done them, so that you can see them and feel them and live with them. Remember what Adam said. You – you're the people's father and mother, or a devil, but *their* devil.' She laughed awkwardly, for Peter was watching her like a cat.

He said: 'Savage of Rudwal – whose *shauq* was building hospitals and climbing some mountain over *there*. "He was a great man, my son. They are not the same nowadays. There is his grave, under that peepul tree, where he used to sit in judgement." One's stature grows several inches every year, and Baber's grandson will be told that I was a hundred feet high, ate a whole bullock for breakfast every morning, and knew how often each man in the district lay with his wife. I'll be immortal. There's an old beggar beyond Dagoh who calls me Auchterlony Sahib. Says I haven't changed a bit. Is that what you want?'

She said: 'Yes. So do you.'

She wanted to say more: that the hurtful thing which Peter felt so uncomfortable within him was the burgeoning capacity to love. She wanted to tell him that, in him, the enemy of the ability to love was the power to lead; that he wanted instinctively to stay here, because once he left there would have to be more leading than loving; that his instinct was reinforced by the fact of his strong ties to Adam and Gerry.

All this and more she would have liked to say, and would have said, with Gerry standing concerned at her side – only, this was the day of the telegrams. The chuprassi was at the door, and for the third time she knew that she had been near, but would not yet win him over.

Peter took the telegram. Footsteps rushed down the passage, and Peggy burst in, water dripping from her cape and oilskin hat. 'War!' she cried. 'We're at war.'

Emily stood up suddenly, her eyes tingling. After all, after waiting and knowing for half a week that it would come, and refusing to face it –

still it struck like a gust of bitter smoke, swirling round the room, making the eyes smart and the breath come choking out of her lungs.

'War–' Gerry gasped and sat down suddenly on the sofa.

'War,' Peter said, glancing at the telegram.

Peggy had torn off her cape and hat, and the bearer had mysteriously appeared to take them away. Puddles of water stained the carpet. Peggy was so moved that she had almost reverted to her old simplicity of manner, and Emily found that they were holding hands and crying.

'There will be a call for volunteers,' Peter said. 'The plans already made here are to be put into effect. In other words, war – in Europe.'

'But India must be in it?' Peggy cried.

'Yes,' Peter said with a strange look at her. 'India is in. *Now* what?'

Emily said urgently: 'It makes no difference, Peter! Stay here. You can look after Rudwal as no one else can. There'll be all sorts of trouble. Remember what Adam said! And thousands of our people going into the Army. Men short for the crops everywhere – food shortages–'

'Don't be silly, Emily,' her husband said softly. 'If I stay here I'll be like a man busily sweeping the galley floor while the ship goes down. Remember something else Adam said– "Our fate is going to be settled six thousand miles away." I said it too. It isn't only Rudwal's – it's India's. Rodney's. Elizabeth's. England's. Yours. Any way you look, to the bigger or smaller things, you get the same answer.'

His eyes were brilliant now, and his voice as

young and sharp and harshly decisive as when she had first seen the power and the longing in him, not at the boat race but under the fluted challenge of King's College Chapel.

'War,' Peter said. 'World war, and they'll be asking for volunteers.' He turned suddenly on Gerry. 'What are you going to do?'

Gerry's mouth shut with a snap. 'There's no choice. I must go and fight.'

'No,' she cried.

'Yes,' Peter said fiercely. 'Do you want to put a knife in his back as well as mine?' Peggy listened, alert, waiting again, fallen away from Emily in expectancy. 'How can he live with himself if he skulks here while the fate of the world's being settled in Europe? What's going to happen to the hospital if the Germans win?'

'He can still work in it. There'll still be sick Indians,' Emily said miserably. It was true, though it sounded almost traitorous to say it, and no man, least of all Gerry, could accept it, certainly not at this moment in history.

'I am sure Harry will be volunteering,' Peggy said smoothly.

Emily stared at her with cold hatred. These two and a half months had caused no rebirth of any love from the past, only an understanding that the wound she and Peter had inflicted on Peggy was not healed, was in fact still festering and would continue to do so until some great cauterization burned away all evil – and perhaps all good too.

Peter said: 'And I'm going too. My duty is supposed to be to stay here, but I'm not going to.

Gerry, I'll wire Cox's at once, to get passage for you and Emily and the kids as soon as possible.'

'Yes,' Peggy said, 'Gerry can look after you on the journey.'

Peter went on: 'I'll leave for Manali tonight, see Forsythe, and arrange to get into the Thirteenth Gurkhas. Grandfather raised them, and my father served in them till he disappeared. That's the first step. Once I'm in uniform I'll get to Europe quick enough.'

'The I.C.S won't release you,' Emily said.

'Yes, they will. The Chief Secretary will be delighted to smooth my path on what he will see as a greatly mistaken course.'

'So it is,' Emily said, 'but not for that reason. Your job, your life, is here.'

'I'm sorry,' Peter said. 'It might have been.'

He went out quickly. After a moment's staring at the brother and sister standing with such different expressions in the drawing-room, Emily hurried after him. She found him in his study and closed the door behind her.

'I warned you,' she said breathlessly. 'I warned you.'

He looked up from his writing. 'About Gerry? If you want to hold me responsible for starting the war, I can't prevent you – but it's not reasonable.'

'If you'd stay here, he'd stay. If you'd say it was the right thing to do, he wouldn't care who else was going to sneer. Why should he? After you made him let Harry down, his reputation's gone. How was Mr Lyon killed? I know, and you know! Because they were tired – three men doing the work of four! That'll be on Gerry's head too. He only had your opinion left to care about – and you say he's got to volunteer.'

Peter put down his pencil and began folding the telegram into an envelope. He said: 'If there hadn't been this war, things might have been different. You were right. I wanted to stay. I was ready to give up everything else.'

He was walking slowly up and down the big study, facing her, turning his back, the envelope in his hand, his face keen but not hostile, turned inward as he tried to explain to her something he hardly understood. He said: 'Now – I can't. How can *I* stay here and let my fate, and yours, be decided by other people? Besides, I have always been ready for something like this to happen. I told you about Grandfather, and the Mutiny changing his world, the conditions of life, all his ambitions, overnight. I have always expected something of the same sort to happen – you dying, something like this – God lying in wait to catch us out. Well. He didn't catch me! I'm ready. Emily, I can be a better soldier than ever I was a District Officer. A soldier doesn't have to ask – he commands. From now on, until the war's over, it's the soldiers who are going to decide what happens.'

'And you – as a second lieutenant?' she said bitterly.

'The war's going to last a long time,' he said. 'Higher up, war and policy go hand in hand.'

'And afterwards?' she asked. 'After you've won?'

'I don't know. Back here, perhaps, to be the

D.C and climb Meru. That'll be it, darling! After the war we'll all come back and stay.'

Just this once, he seemed to be saying, just this one more time, let me go out and guide and conquer and lead men breathless in my wake – then I'll come back, and we'll live in peace and grow love like a flower garden...

She turned away. After a moment he said harshly: 'I should be in London by the middle of next year. Omar! Take this to the telegraph office.'

She went out and stood a moment in the passage. It was unfair to blame Peter. There would be thousands of other men doing this same thing – how few with his burning desire to do it, his driving certainty that he could succeed at it! – thousands of other wives as stricken as she. There was a war. Perhaps the soldiers in Manali were right, and it would be over in a few weeks. She could only pray that it would be so – for the sake of the men who would die, for her own sake, for Gerry's and for Peter's. It was an act of God that war, so perfectly suited to Peter's temperament, should have come to relight the fires that she had almost stifled in him. Now he would be on his own, and she had Gerry to look after, who was not going to be a doctor after all, because of the war and because of Peter. She must go to Gerry, and comfort him. Yes, now, now! Send Peggy away and take Gerry into her arms and scream in his ear, I'm yours, I love you... And then, of course, he'd go away for ever.

She went to her room to compose herself before entering the drawing-room. There was no need to get hysterical. There was a definite need to keep tight hold of herself, for nothing irrevocable had happened yet. Peter would eventually come back to Rudwal; Gerry would not – because he would be killed the first time he went into action. The bullets would seek him out, recognizing gold, and shatter him. So he must not be allowed to volunteer – or, if he did, only for the Medical Corps. Gerry must not be allowed to come near glory. She would have allies – people had talked, garbled rumours flown about. He was supposed to be a coward now because he had refused to go to Meru. Good.

Oh, Peter, Peter, the dagger is always ready in my hand, but I love you too; I love you.

CHAPTER 21

June 12, 1915. London. Yesterday morning she had been thinking that this was 'the middle of next year' and Peter would be due at any moment if he were to keep up with his forecast, insolently careless in the face of this terrible war. This morning the telegram had come. Sent from Cairo five days earlier, it told her that he was on his way, should arrive about June 16, had won a D.S.O, sent her his love.

But where would he have won a D.S.O? In the East? Mesopotamia? East Africa? It didn't matter. He was on his way, rushing towards London with the speed of the fastest liners and express trains.

Alice should have brought in that telegram, murmuring, *'Tar a-gya,'* like the chuprassi on that dreadful day in Rudwal – the Day of the Telegrams, as she remembered it. Those oblong slips of buff paper carried messages from the gods, and there ought to be a familiar messenger to bring them in, lay them before the human beings whose lives were to be turned about by them, and say: 'What answer?'

But it was Alice's day off today, when she would take her elderly angularity out into the streets and be winked and whistled at by hundreds of soldiers, and return hot with lust and scorn– 'Men, ma'am!' The war was a great thing for her, but Emily was sure she had kept and would keep her militant Welsh virginity through all temptations and corruptions.

Rodney and Elizabeth were asleep, the house on Minden Square warm with the scent of London in June, the windows open to the blossoms of night, and the pale sky powdered with silver stars.

What answer?

The answer was the old one, of love and reluctant pride in his exploits – and a warning bell. Gerry was living here with her in her father's house. The Wilcot town house had been commandeered by the Admiralty for the duration, and she would not allow him to try and find other accommodation. There had probably been some gossip about it, but she did not care, and her father, rather to her surprise, had supported her. He had spent a week with them soon after they reached Tilbury, late in October 1914. At the end of the week he had returned to Llyn Gared and his increasingly numbed studies of the casualty lists. Peggy also had been firm against worrying about possible scandal. She had been very helpful on the journey back to England and if it had not been for her rather obvious tact in leaving Emily alone with Gerry whenever possible Emily might have thought that the roots of the old Llyn Gared relationships had been refound. Now Peggy was living in Mayfair, and they saw her about once a week at one house or the other. Harry was a lieutenant in France, with a battalion of infantry.

Peter's telegram she had burned in the empty

fireplace. She stared, unseeing, at the grey ashes and thought, as dispassionately as she could, of Gerry.

He too was in uniform – Lieutenant the Earl of Wilcot, Royal South Wiltshire Yeomanry. He had not been sent to France after training at Salisbury, though his regiment had gone in November of '14. They had instead posted him to the War Office, where his main task seemed to be to have lunch at the Savoy with American journalists and occasionally take them in large automobiles to training establishments outside, but not too far outside, London. She had kept him at his medical books, and he had made contacts with a senior member of the medical school at Edinburgh University. He had not been able to bring himself, yet, to apply to resign his commission, in spite of the already evident and rapidly growing shortage of doctors for the armies abroad and the people at home. He was not happy as a soldier, especially not in the gilded role they had given him, and she had felt for some weeks that only some small incident, one extra push, was needed to make him take the step and go to Edinburgh.

There had been progress in another, more dangerous direction. The relationship between them had become so obviously different from the old brother-sister comradeship that Gerry had been forced to recognize it. He said nothing, but she knew he admitted to himself that he loved her. There was nothing more, nothing at all, for both of them had been rigorously trained in self-control, and Emily, for her part, had lived long enough with the knowledge so that she was able to control its effect to an exact degree. She wondered whether Gerry was happier with the love and the acknowledgement of it – but there was no answer to that. She had thought of interesting him in other women, and had tried to do so, in spite of an unwilling jealousy; but Gerry remained polite, friendly, and untouched.

She had used the intimacy with delicate ruthlessness to plant in Gerry's mind the seed of a critical awareness of Peter. It had been most subtly done, with so sure a hand (did anyone know Gerry, or Peter, as she did?) that although Gerry had lost none of his admiration of Peter's tremendous qualities he had admitted to himself, in the same loyal secrecy with his admission of his love for her, that Peter Savage was a leader and not a guide; that, knowing Peter's ability to force a path up any cliff, yet a man must decide for himself whether he needed and wanted to go up that particular cliff to that particular summit. This she had done without Gerry's knowing where the seed had come from, and without changing anything of her attitude towards either man. Only one doubt fretted in her mind. Had she really done it only for Gerry's sake? Or was it also jealousy that had lent her such cunning? If so, of whom was she jealous?

To these questions, too, there was no answer.

Now Peter was on his way, and again: 'What answer?' the voices asked, and this time there must be one. It would have to depend, but certainly she must arise at once, now, from the relaxed lethargy which had been her prevailing mood, tinged with energy where Gerry's future was concerned, since their return from India.

She went to her room, made up her face lightly, kissed the children in their cots, said good night to Nanny, who was reading a shilling shocker in her room, and went downstairs.

Gerry came in. She gauged his expression carefully. There might be a sign there. He would have heard, perhaps, if not of the return, then of the D.S.O, since he worked in the War Office. Because he was Gerry Wilcot his uniform fitted him with casual perfection, as though he had never worn anything else.

'Dinner with four journalists,' he said wearily when they were in the drawing-room. 'At the Cecil this time. And they were Swedes.'

He was pale, and the hand he had brushed across her bare arm when he came in was as cold as a fish.

'What's the matter with you?' she said, smiling. 'You feel as though you've just come from the North Pole, and it's a warm night. Are you sickening for something?'

'Good heavens, no, old girl. Fit as a fiddle. I'm going to have a peg. I feel a little tired, that's all.'

She said calmly: 'That's not all, Gerry. What's happened?'

'Oh, nothing.' He glanced up, met her eyes, and looked down into the big glass full and dark with whisky in his hand. 'I tried to get to France again. Got turned down again. They said they couldn't spare me. I suppose it's partly my title. They think I'm just the man to impress the Americans – though I think it would be better if those chaps went to France and saw a few earls being killed.'

'Is that all? I know you think you *ought* to go to the front, Gerry, but you don't want to, do you? You want to go to Edinburgh. I certainly don't think you ought to go to France, whatever I'm supposed to think. We must be honest with ourselves.'

He glanced up with a vaguely warning look. No, she thought, we had better not be too honest.

'Well, there was something else,' he said, gulping down his drink. 'I met Mrs Lyon in Whitehall today. Lunch-time. Her brother's dead now, died of wounds yesterday. Been in hospital since Neuve Chapelle.'

She said nothing. Lyon had fallen from Needle Five, and they'd recovered his mangled body.

He said: 'Mrs Lyon had a big bonnet on with a kind of sweeping feather – white. There were a lot of silly flappers there, giving feathers to men in mufti. *She* ripped the feather out of her hat and gave it to me. The flappers started to call her names – I was in uniform, of course – but she said: "He knows," and walked off.' He un-buttoned his tunic pocket and drew out the crumpled feather and looked at it.

'Throw it away,' she said angrily. 'Here.' She snatched it from his hand and threw it out of the window.

'But she's right, in a way,' Gerry said wearily. 'Lyon was killed because of me. It's not the only reason no one'll have me in a regiment in France, but it's one of them.'

She sat still, watching him, thinking. The

authorities had thought they could pick and choose their officers until Neuve Chapelle. Now that was changing as the war opened its mouth wider and wider, and the people began to have a terrified feeling that there would be no limit to it, that it would gape larger and hungrier until it swallowed everything.

She said: 'This settles it, Gerry. You must see that. You've got to resign your commission at once and go to Edinburgh. Could you do it?'

He said: 'Oh, yes. To become a doctor. They'd let me go, anyway. House of Lords… And no one being very anxious to have me in their uniform. Didn't Peter say he'd be back about now?'

She nodded and said steadily: 'I haven't had any news.'

'Not much point in waiting for him then, I suppose. I'd have liked to see him before I threw my hand in. Tell him about it.'

'Yes.'

He sat with his hands in his lap, staring into the empty fireplace. 'It hasn't worked out the way we thought it was going to, has it? My going to fight for King and Country. No one wants me to. They will next year. Then I'd be able to – show them.'

'Show them what?' she said sharply. She felt a tinge of exasperation at all the race of men. 'Prove to people you don't care for that you can do something you don't want to? If you want to show real courage to people who do care, and who do mean something to you – Peter and me, for instance – you'll send in your papers tomorrow.'

Gerry nodded. 'I'm going to,' he said. 'There's

nothing else for it.'

She said: '*Tomorrow*. And leave London the next day. There's not a day to waste. The hospital's finished and waiting for you.'

Gerry got up. 'I know,' he said, his voice firmer. 'I keep thinking about it. Parkash writes to me every week. There's a man called Wibley officiating as D.C. No one likes him. I'm off to bed.'

She held up her mouth, and after a brief pause he kissed her gently on the lips. 'There's no one like you in the world, Emily,' he said gravely. 'I suppose you know that's what I feel.'

She nodded.

'I'll hurry up and get myself to Edinburgh,' he said. 'Then one day we'll all be together in Rudwal again, and it'll be different. I'll find a pretty nurse up there in Scotland and take her out to India.' He laughed quite naturally, and she thought: He really might; peace is settling on him, and he really might; he's got enough love, and to spare, for it to come out right.

Then he left her, and, after an hour alone, she went to bed.

But Gerry had not gone to Edinburgh by the fifteenth, for there was a scornful delay in releasing him from the War Office, and that afternoon a telegram arrived from Peter, in Dover, presaging his arrival at the house at six o'clock, and at six o'clock a taxi wheezed up to the door and Peter stepped lightly out. Knowing that there were still needs for caution and alertness, still she could not stop herself from running out and down the steps and into his

328

arms while he was in the act of paying the taxi driver.

'Peter, Peter,' she cried. 'You're back – a day early.' His brief kiss tingled electrically on her mouth.

'Flew from Marseilles to Paris in a French Army bombing aeroplane,' he said, smiling down at her.

When they were inside – he carried nothing but a small, dusty valise – she looked at him more closely. Uniform patched, clean, not too well-fitting; blue and red ribbon on his left breast; captain's rank badges on his sleeve; cap soft, racy-looking, black belt and shoulder straps polished like glass – he must have been working at them on the train from Dover – white teeth flashing in a face tanned deep golden brown; eyes like points of ice under a gay sun; his movements lithe and flowing – a blue, puckered scar on his wrist.

'What's that?' she asked quickly.

'Bullet wound,' he said. 'I had a bad time for a week. Where are the children?'

'Upstairs, having their supper. We'll go up in a moment. But where have you been? How did you become a captain so quickly?' For the moment nothing mattered except the blaze of his eager personality in the room.

'I'll be a major tomorrow,' he said, 'and a lieutenant-colonel by autumn. Where's Gerry? I've got to see him urgently.'

She sat back slowly, and the warmth from the blaze drained away. She said: 'Gerry's at the War Office. Today's his last day there. Do you want to see him about anything special?'

Peter nodded.

'Tell me – quick,' she said, her voice straining. 'Before he comes in.'

Peter looked at her for a time and then said: 'This is secret, and I'm not supposed to tell anyone not already in it, but I can see you think you've got to know, so I'll tell you.'

She heard the front door open and close, and Gerry's step in the passage. A moment later he came into the room and stopped dead as he saw Peter by the window.

Peter stepped forward, his hand jumping out. 'Gerry! Just the man I'm looking for! You're a bit pale. Are you all right otherwise? Are you fit?'

Their hands were still clasped. Astonishment, delight, anxiety, and enquiry had chased themselves across Gerry's face. Now he said: 'Fit enough. They've got a gym at one of my clubs.'

Peter said: 'Good. I was just going to tell Emily. This is very hush-hush, Gerry. I'm going on a secret reconnaissance to the Italian front, starting next week. I've asked for you to come with me.'

'You're going away again in a week!' she cried.

Peter said: 'This is war. There are plenty of men who haven't seen their families since August, and plenty who never will... It's in the mountains, Gerry. That's why I wanted to know if you were fit.'

'He's not,' Emily said.

'Yes, I am,' Gerry said.

She said: 'Do you remember me telling you this was Gerry's last day at the War Office, Peter? That's because he has sent in his papers and is going to Edinburgh to the medical school.'

'After the white feather that woman gave you the other day in Whitehall?' Peter said keenly. 'That's guts, Gerry. Yes, I heard about it – in Paris. Battle intelligence doesn't travel half as fast as gossip. You can go to Edinburgh when we've done this.'

'I can't, Peter,' Gerry said in anguish. 'They're expecting me the day after tomorrow. I've promised.'

Peter said forcefully: 'Edinburgh University is not going to care one small damn whether one middle-aged medical student arrives the day after tomorrow or two months hence. It's only two months, Emily... I can just about guarantee you an M.C out of it, Gerry – not because I have strings to pull, but because I know you and because you're going to earn it.'

So Gerry would have the purple and white ribbon, which could be earned only by gallantry in the face of the enemy, to wear on his breast, and the letters to put after his name, to stop any other foolish woman from giving him a white feather, any other stupid man from whispering that 'Wilcot's got a streak.' It was all beautifully thought out, for Gerry's good. Only, at any cost, it must not happen.

She said quite calmly: 'Gerry is not going with you, Peter. It's disgraceful of you to ask him when you know he's trying to become a doctor, and you know how much that means to him. You agreed once in Rudwal that that is what he ought to do, and we've found since we came home that it's the only life left for him. Now please don't

331

speak of your expedition again.'

Peter said fiercely: 'There's a war on. I've got a very important job to do for England. I don't know how many lives might be saved or lost through our information. A hundred thousand, perhaps – Harry Walsh's life, my own, those men walking into the pub on the corner. If we risk our lives to climb Meru, how much more should we risk them for England – for India, Gerry; for Rudwal, and the hospital you're going back to?'

Gerry had been standing, stiffer and stiffer, his head going back and his jaw coming up under the vicious, accurate thrusts.

'I'll come, Peter,' Gerry said. 'Of course I'll come.'

Peter shook his hand again, and Emily thought the bright eyes were almost damp – but that was impossible.

'Now let's go and see the children,' Peter said. 'Good heavens, they must think you're their father by now, Gerry.'

He ran up the stairs, two at a time. Gerry followed more slowly behind; Emily came last. 'Oh – I forgot to tell you, Emily,' he called down. 'I'm going to G.H.Q in France tomorrow – back two days later.'

She said nothing.

Peter left the house at eight the next morning, debonair in his battle-worn khaki, so that the nursemaid on the corner gazed at him with open adoration, and the sun made gold the commonplace houses of Minden Square.

Emily took the children to Regent's Park in the

332

afternoon, and in the evening sat in the chair in her bedroom, polishing her nails, brushing her auburn hair, looking at her grey eyes in the mirror, and wondering what lay beyond the sunset. She and Peter had come to each other with a peculiar passion last night in this room. There should have been nothing strange about that, since the embrace of her flesh had the power to charge him with a frenzied, seeking energy, and he had been nearly ten months away from her. The strangeness lay more in herself. She had made up her mind that she must stay aloof from his ecstasies since she hated him, and would be served coldly as a duty and nothing more. Usually when she was at all withdrawn from him he knew at once and either went directly to sleep or did what he did with brief precision and a short word of thanks. Last night he had seen her coldness, had heard her say: 'Please make sure I do not become pregnant, Peter,' and had yet come forward.

And now she was here, making herself more desirable than Helen, with her eyes deep with love and pain, and her bosom swelling under the dull green velvet of an old, loved dress, her movements softened with the voluptuous lassitude her daemon husband had implanted in her, hair curving as a sea wave over her forehead and a single diamond – her mother's – on a pendant in the valley of her breasts.

She heard Gerry come into the house while she stayed in her room, wondering at her own image in the mirror. While he bathed and changed she went to her children, who stared at her with big eyes, and she played with them and at last swept slowly down to the drawing-room. Nothing was formed in her mind. Looking at herself, she had thought: That woman is too beautiful to have a mind; what she causes she must cause by instinct, surely, or by mere being – as Helen, only being beautiful and desired, launched a thousand ships.

They ate in the dining-room, which looked out across the small green square of summer, and the syringa spread flowering arms against the farther wall. This they had done a hundred times – and more before, when they were young. Gerry had stopped short when he came into the drawing-room before dinner, with something of the same fearful wonder that Peter's arrival had caused. Almost the same emotions had moved, like a stirring on the surface of deep water, across his face, but at the end there was not even the vague disquiet of enquiry left there. Everything is settled, he seemed to be saying, and I cannot allow myself to be moved by this beauty – or by my longings to be a doctor; they are both dreams, foolish and perhaps wicked.

During dinner, and in the drawing-room afterwards, while Gerry played Bach – why did he choose those records from the stacks under the gramophone table? – she became weak with love for him, for the strained, fine thread of his character, that made him so wonderful and desirable to Peter. It was an unusual love that she felt, impossible to classify as 'affection,' or 'pity,' or in any other single category. He was a young man, found dying in the street, and no one else was there – only he, and she holding him tight and whispering: What can I do? What can I give?

The hours ticked by, and at last he would hear no more music. 'Bedtime,' he muttered, half looking at her. She lay back in the corner of the sofa, the single light behind her head and in her hair. When he stood up and moved towards her to kiss her good night she moved her thighs gracefully, for there was warmth flowing between them. A violent tremor of lasciviousness sent her arms out, crawling up and round his neck as he stooped over her – and somewhere, now smooth as polished silver in her right hand, now floating like the vision of it before Macbeth, the half of a dagger, and Peter. The eyes above her had dulled, man's eyes, and swayed from side to side, and there was a pulling-away inside the circle of her arms. She dragged her arms down and to her, dragging him into her open mouth and where the velvet curved close to the inside of her spread thighs. She was soft and strong, and suddenly the gold thread broke. She closed her eyes and moved, and held. The dagger in her hand thrust into flesh. She guided it, forced it deep home, and it was done.

CHAPTER 22

'Faster!' she cried into the speaking tube. 'We've *got* to catch that train.'

'I'm going as fast as I can, mum,' the old man in the driving seat threw over his shoulder.

It was two days later – and two nights full of making love, on her part with affection but no more pleasure, only an urgent desire that he should go, because it was done.

'I've got to go,' Gerry had muttered a hundred times, and she had answered sadly: 'Yes. We must never see each other again.' It was all true, the sadness and the joy that it was done, and the joy that Gerry was going, and the sadness that she would never see him again.

'I've got to go. I can't face him after this.'

'Yes. You must go.' But a hundred unexpected things had cropped up, and only now was he on his way.

'Will you come with me?' he'd asked passionately, knowing before she answered that she could not.

Now he was going – eleven-thirty p.m from King's Cross, and it was eleven-twenty now. The taxi lurched round another corner, headed down another long street between two rows of darkened houses. Pencils of light wandered round the sky. They were there.

'Platform Ten, sir!... Sorry, no porters at this

time of night. There's a war on' – and a cold glance at the blue civilian suit. She hurried him on towards the barrier, the collector waiting under the shaded lights.

'Don't come any farther, darling.' He lowered his suitcase to the stone and swung round, his arms open.

'Oh, quick, quick, Gerry!' She gasped. 'There are only two minutes left, and *you've got to go.*' He was kissing her, and the tears were wet on his face – she dry-eyed, full of frenzy that he should go and it be altogether done.

'Good-bye. Oh darling – I can't leave you.'

'Go!' She pushed him frantically towards the barrier and the man, his back sympathetically turned.

'Hi – Gerry! Emily!'

The clear, high voice rang under the vast arch from far away. The ticket collector turned quickly; a woman hurrying to catch the train stopped and looked; two sailors turned – all lingering a moment as Peter, the man in faded khaki, his belt supernaturally, brilliantly black, and the single ribbon on his breast, ran soundlessly across the stone towards them.

'Where are you off to, Gerry?'

Gerry said: 'Edinburgh – Edinburgh. I promised – to see, visit McVeigh even if I couldn't start now. I'll be back – the day after tomorrow – I promise.'

Peter said: 'Well, it's lucky I caught you. *We're* off tomorrow. The operation's been put forward a week.'

'Where have you been?' she asked listlessly,

because it didn't matter. She felt that all she had done had been doomed to uselessness before she ever dreamed of doing it. It was a wild coincidence – an act of God – that Peter should be here at this time, and yet it wasn't. If he hadn't been here he'd have been at Edinburgh, or would have gone there. 'Weren't you going to G.H.Q in France?' she said.

'That was a lie,' Peter said. 'I went north on other business altogether.'

The whistles shrilled. 'Better hurry, sir,' the man at the gate said.

'He's not going,' Peter said. Slowly Gerry turned away. The red tail-light slid into motion; the shining rails unwound in broad steel ribbons behind it.

Peter said: 'It's time we got away alone, Gerry. We've got a lot to tell each other, haven't we? I'll want to know how you've been looking after Emily, for one thing, since I seem fated not to be able to do it myself.'

She glanced at him with near-fear. Did he know already? Had he not gone to G.H.Q, or 'north,' but stayed in London, spying on them? It was unthinkable, and, scanning his face, she was certain that he did not know.

Her eyes fell on Gerry, and now she really was afraid. Gerry was certain that Peter did know. He thought Peter's quick, careless words presaged a time when he would be taxed with his crime and punished for it. He was grey with misery, hiding it as he spoke. Now nothing on earth could stop him from going with Peter, because he knew that he had deserved punishment and must face it.

338

CHAPTER 23

While Peter listened to the Italian major he was thinking about meeting Gerry and Emily at King's Cross. It was puzzling. Gerry, of course, had been running away to Edinburgh. It was sad that he should have felt he needed to lie about it – but Peter could not then, nor now, understand what he hoped to achieve by it.

Gerry was going to be a doctor. Emily, and some kinship with the sick that he had discovered in himself, had persuaded him that that was his only hope of happiness. So be it. But he was also coming back to Rudwal and Parkash – or *going* back, for Peter could no longer be so sure of himself; he was finding the military life so full of rewards and summits, in wartime at any rate. But how could Gerry hope to work with him, Peter, in any relationship, if he ran away from a job that only he could do – and he knowing it? And also knowing the importance of this mission?

Emily, being a woman and loving Gerry as she might a brother or an only son, thought Peter could get someone else instead of Gerry. There were aspects that Emily didn't understand. Suppose, for instance, that he, Peter, went out to do this job with some incompetent or fearful companion, and was killed – what would Gerry do then? He might shoot himself. What would Gerry have thought, how would he have felt, if he had learned that Peter was hunting round for a mountaineer to accompany him and had not come to him first? The mountaineering fraternity, these same people Peter would be asking amongst to find a companion, had turned their backs on Gerry because of what he had done, for Peter's sake, to Harry Walsh. Peter could not also turn his back. Besides, there was the fact that the mountaineering Brahmins would have had nothing to do with him. There was no one left for him but Gerry; and for Gerry no one but him. There was nothing bad about that. Rudwal waited for them – the sound and the sick. Meru waited for them. They had a place, they two and Emily; and Adam belonged there, and Dr Parkash, and young Baber.

He realized, vaguely annoyed, that Emily's promised land, the flowered Canaan he could never see very clearly, was still in his mind. He tried to smother the lure of its lotus promises. He was not born to lie among lotus flowers. Gerry had been trying to get away; and it was not clear how or why he had brought himself to the point of forgetting everything else to do it. Emily must have practically dragged him to the station.

Peter turned his whole attention to the Italian major. The man spoke very good English, and, looking at him more closely, Peter knew that he had seen him before, or pictures of him. He was called Gabriele Cammarota and had done a couple of spectacular ascents with Di Cella, about 1910. Therefore he must know about Meru and Peter Savage. But he had made no sign of recognition and no mention of ever having heard of Peter or Gerry. He was a tall man, angular, blue-eyed, as unlike the conventional picture of an Italian as could be. They were sitting opposite each other in the back room of an inn twelve miles behind the Italian front in the Alps.

The rest of the reconnaissance party, which would set out tomorrow, were hunched over the table to right and left. There was a dark young lieutenant, Count Fraschelli, who showed little stomach for the job ahead; Gerry; and two men in the uniform of Italian corporals, but the uniform sat tight on their broad shoulders, they were considerably older than most corporals, and they spoke very politely in deep voices. There was no doubt what their peace-time occupation was – mountain guiding. They were Italians from this region, who had lived all their lives as part of the Austro-Hungarian Empire. Staldi and Carana were their names.

Cammarota was explaining the operation again to the two guides. There was no need. They might not know much about drill or warfare but they knew the lie of the land and could use their eyes a deal better than the next man. Besides, their task was really to act as close escort, riflemen of great accuracy and cross-country ability, to protect the core of the party – Cammarota and Peter himself – on their reconnaissance. Peter needed Gerry as a reliable second in all things, and as witness and corroboration for his eventual report. The Italians had then sent Count Fraschelli too, ostensibly to act as commanding officer over the two corporals; but it would probably end up the other way round, they looking after Fraschelli. Peter decided that Fraschelli had probably been sent in order that the Italians should not be socially out-ranked by the English milord.

The mission itself was not complicated. The front line lay twelve miles ahead – though the words 'front line' conveyed a false impression. In fact the leading Italian troops lived in houses and cowsheds two or three miles back from and three thousand feet below the severe crest line of the mountain ridges that separated this valley, the Paola, from the next one to the north, the Saraco. Nor were the Austrians occupying the crest. It was far too bleak and unpleasant, and the difficulties of supply would have been too great from either side. Like the Italians, the Austrians lived in bivouacs and billets on their side of the crest, as near as they could comfortably get to the top. Both sides maintained sentry posts just below the main pass, the Saraco Pass, which was surmounted, from one valley to the other, by a precipitous cart track. Both sides sent patrols scouting along the ridges in the hours of darkness, and both had posts on the mountains to each flank, linked by field telephone to head-quarters and gun positions in the valleys below, so that if either decided to begin an offensive the other would be able to rush up troops and, far more important, bring down heavy artillery fire on the pass and on the approaches to it.

On the north, the enemy side of the pass, the cart track wound down into the head of the Saraco Valley; became a road that could, with little work, be used by heavy trucks, guns, and supply wagons; and went on towards upper Austria. Twelve miles to the west, along the same ridge, there was another pass, the Julio. The ridge between the Saraco and the Julio passes was big country indeed, containing three different mountains of over 11,000 feet. The Julio was a high pass, not easy for men on foot and impossible for carts or wheeled transport of any kind. Five miles west again, over the huge single block of Monte Michele, was the third and last pass – the Michele Pass. Neither it nor the Julio led directly to the Saraco Valley and its motor road, but from the Julio at least it would probably be possible, without too much trouble, to build or develop roads into the Saraco Valley.

War had not been declared between Austria and Italy until May 24, 1915 – just over a month ago. The easiest way for the Italians to invade Austria was along the Adriatic eastward from Venice; but the lines of communication supporting such an advance would be threatened from the beginning by the Austrian positions along the Alpine ranges forming Italy's northern border, and every mile of farther advance would be still further threatened. The Italians would be like a diver walking out of one door of a room, trailing his air hose behind him, while his enemy, at the side door, could with progressive ease rush in and cut it. It was therefore certainly necessary to guard that side door – the northern Alps and the passes over them – and it might even be desirable to make the main offensive over it, if only to cause the Austrians to weaken the Adriatic front before a further and major offensive was launched in that direction.

Years before the outbreak of war, of course, the Italian General Staff had worked out such a plan in some detail. Having interior lines – that is, being in the middle of the room, while the Austrians were forced to rush round the outside – the Italians could shift reserves more easily than the latter, and therefore did not need to be so rigid in their planning. They could launch an offensive and see what happened, being ready to reinforce or switch troops according to their success and the nature of the Austrian reactions.

In the first stages of this plan a feint would be made at the Saraco Pass but the main effort, at least by the infantry in the early days, would be over the Julio. These troops would then swing right to take in rear and flank the Austrian defences of the Saraco. A sufficiency of light-armed men would take a slightly wider swing from the Julio and cut the Saraco road, isolating the defenders of the pass from help. The way would then be opened for a large-scale advance towards Austria; the Austrians would throw in more troops from other fronts, and the Italians could act accordingly.

When this had first been explained to Peter he had at once asked about the Michele Pass, farther to the west, and had been assured that no kind of major operation could be launched over it, owing to the extremely difficult nature of the approaches on the Italian side. A flank attack over the Julio was as wide a 'hook' as they could manage.

The plans that had been worked out showed that the proposed coup could not be effectively exploited by the Italian Army in its then circumstances. If, however, the British or French cared to help – not to undertake the actual operation, but to supply reinforcements to exploit success once success had been achieved – then all would be well. The French weren't interested; the British were. But the British General Staff wanted to see with its own eyes, not through the eyes of its allies. It was not that they mistrusted their Italian friends, but... Well, the English could not climb like the Italians, et cetera, et cetera.

'Mind, we want an honest report, Savage. The wops seem very excited about it, but – *verb. sap.* – the C-in-C is not going to favour any diversions from France, however favourable this operation may look at first sight.' So, with a wink and a nod, the War Office major-general who spoke to Peter in Cairo had outlined the mission, also mentioning medals and promotions for him, in a gentlemanly manner, to make sure he got the idea.

If they thought they had bribed him, they were mistaken. The politicians probably hoped the operation was feasible, so that they could get some troops away from the Western Front butchery and also keep the Italians in good humour. The generals were against it. They wanted him to report that the operation was impracticable. They would then say to the politicians: 'This man Savage, who made this report, isn't even one of us, a soldier; he's a civil servant, and he has a reputation for boldness amounting to rashness. If he says it's no go, you'll have to believe him.'

But Peter had an open mind, and he knew that in an operation this size his report could not by itself be the deciding factor. All the same, nothing was going to stop him from finding out the truth. The generals had forgotten that through Gerry and the Viceroy and the Secretary of State several members of the cabinet knew a lot about him. He could get a hearing from the Prime Minister any time he wanted to.

He had a feeling that the operation might be a good one. He would not be surprised to find himself back here early the following year with considerably higher rank, acting as watchdog and galvanizer to the general who would be put in command of the British part of the operation. In the meantime, when this reconnaissance was finished, he was going on a mission to the Turkish Eastern Front, in Kurdistan. He had pointed out to an influential M.P some facts of geography, strategy, and politics in connection with Kurdistan, Azerbaijan, and the area on the southern flank of the Russian advance against Erzerum. That mission was being studied in secret on a geopolitical level. The generals would be told about it later.

Gerry ought to come with him, at least on the Kurdistan trip, if this present one gave him a taste for the work. The possibilities ahead were stupendous. The Indian Expeditionary Force in Mesopotamia could join hands with the Russians somewhere in southern Turkey; the Arabs in the desert and the Kurds in the mountains could be led to revolt simultaneously – Turkey forced out of the war by the end of 1916; this Alpine operation driving into southern Germany, where there were few troops, at the same time; the war over by the end of 1917. And then...

Peter did not attempt to think further, for no one could know the conditions so far ahead. But Germany must be conquered quickly. Empires, powers, whole ways of life were at stake – all this he saw, and Gerry saw a woman with a boil on the back of her neck! Before God, *he* knew the woman was there and that someone must look after her; but it was a criminal waste for Gerry to devote himself to her when he could do so much, at Peter's side, to stir the generals to grasp new ideas, fire the politicians to forget votes and think of the fate of mankind.

'We will start at ten o'clock tomorrow, Major Savage,' Cammarota said at last in English, turning to Peter. 'A supply convoy will carry us to the headquarters of the Fifty-sixth Bersaglieri, and from there we will walk. We must practice our walking.' He smiled, but not warmly.

Peter said to himself: You don't like me, Major Gabriele Cammarota, and you don't like my being here; you think we ought to trust you to your judgement, but I think you will be well advised to speak your mind with me.

'Come on, Gerry,' he said. 'Let's go to bed.'

That was a Monday night. On the Tuesday they reached the Bersaglieri early in the afternoon and in the evening moved up to their forward listening-post, some trenches dug and well sheltered beside a rough stone hut on the slope of rock and snow to the west side of the Saraco Pass. Scattered shots echoed among the mountains as two patrols engaged each other with rifle fire, somewhere the other side of the saddle. A minute later half a dozen shells from each side rumbled up like carts from the valley and dumped explosive on the crest of the pass itself, throwing up tons of earth and rock splinters.

Peter asked Cammarota whether anything special was going on. The major said: 'There's never anyone on the pass. The artillery on both sides know it. They drop a few shells there to let the other side know they are still awake and could do worse if they wanted to.'

They moved on in the first dusk, not over the pass but along the steep valley that led west towards the Julio under the lee of the three big peaks. After travelling all night on goat tracks parallel with the 'front,' they reached a cirque a couple of miles below the Julio. It was nearly dawn, and Cammarota said: 'We bivouac here.'

Peter said: 'All right.'

Count Fraschelli said: 'The enemy may send patrols this far over the side of the mountain.' He and Cammarota always spoke in English, perhaps to reassure Peter that they had no secrets from him.

Cammarota looked contemptuously at Fraschelli in the starlight and answered politely: 'Certainly, Lieutenant, but they will not harm us, I am sure. We too have patrols. A sergeant from the detachment at the pass should make touch with us during the day.'

They found places to lie down, curled up in blankets they carried rolled over their shoulders, and tried to get to sleep. Peter was amused to see that each of the two corporal-guides had chosen a pair of them – Gerry and he had Staldi – and were unofficiously looking after them just as though they were *signores* of a peace-time climbing expedition. The light came up then, and he had a look at the steep slopes that hid the pass. It was harsh country, and if they ran into any trouble they would have to do some severe mountaineering to get back to the Italian side.

About two in the afternoon the sergeant came from the platoon that watched the pass and conferred an hour with Cammarota. When he had finished Cammarota strolled over with Fraschelli to where Gerry and Peter lay sprawled with their backs to rocks in the warm sun, smoking.

'It is clear as we can hope,' the major said. 'An Austrian post of about a platoon lives in a forester's hut the other side of the pass, but they seldom keep more than four men actually on the top. The sergeant thinks it will not be difficult to keep those four busy for an hour while our party traverses the mountain a few hundred feet higher up, and drops in again behind them. The main difficulty will be to avoid stumbling on the forester's hut in the dark. But Carana was here twenty years ago with a party of climbers who were doing Monte Michele from the Austrian side. He thinks he remembers exactly where the hut is – unless it has burned down and been rebuilt in another place. That happens.'

He smiled his mirthless smile, and Peter asked: 'When shall we move off, then?'

'I thought at dark – or perhaps two hours later? That should put us near the crest by eleven. Allowing an hour for the diversion to take effect, we should be over, down, and in shelter in the woods well before dawn. You agree?'

Peter agreed and began to eat some Italian bread and sausage from his pack. 'Oh, by the way,' Cammarota said, 'we pick up four days' rations each at the platoon post when we pass through.'

Peter nodded, finished eating, and tried to get back to sleep. The rocks were hard, and the sun had gone behind clouds. They were high, and a cold wind blew up the valley, and he did not feel sleepy. The Julio Pass lay round the corner there, and, beyond that, in the dark of night, the enemy and action and a hundred quick decisions.

War was good. In peace-time, except on the worst places of the hardest mountains, people needed to be persuaded to do what must be done. They had to be overcome, urged, driven, shamed, shown the way forward. In war it was different. He had found that most men knew then that something *had* to be done, and most had tightened themselves to a higher pitch than they found comfortable in peace, but few knew *what* to do, and fewer still how to do it. There was a look in men's eyes that he had not known before. We've got to do something tremendous, it said; but for God's sake, who knows what, who will lead the way?... And, after the war, what then?... After Meru, what then?

But now he had to go to sleep, because there would be little sleep in the next few days. He rolled over one last time, settling himself, and saw that Gerry's eyes were wide open and he was staring at the windy, wraith-blown sky racing past to the east over the crests of the mountains behind them.

Peter said suddenly: 'Penny for your thoughts, Gerry.'

Gerry started and turned his face slowly. 'What? Oh, nothing,' he said. 'I was trying to get to sleep.'

'And I disturbed you? You won't get to sleep very quickly with your eyes open. I wonder what Emily's doing now.'

He didn't know why he said that except that the thought of her came suddenly into his mind and gave him a twinge of homesickness.

Gerry said: 'She doesn't go out much.'

Peter knew that. She had looked quite drawn from worrying about Gerry. On the way out to Italy he had teasingly told Gerry he'd been neglecting his duty to Emily. If he didn't want to take her out himself he should have found some nice safe man for her – a captain, R.N, with a wooden leg, perhaps. It was not a good idea for her and Gerry to shut themselves up in the house all the time.

Now– 'Emily's a–' Peter began, but stopped. He wanted to tell Gerry that few such women as Emily existed, or had ever existed, in the world. She had the power to be exciting and serene at the same time, and to put a tarnish, while he was in her presence, on any dreams of high adventure and universal victory. He felt a little of the same now, partly because he was thinking of Emily and partly because there was always a dulling of the vision when dreams had to be reduced to the scale of people. What was there of the giant in Cammarota, the stiff mountaineer who didn't like him; or Fraschelli, who would have given a thousand lire to be back in his natural habitat, pinching the behinds of the pretty tourists as they leaned over the wall of the Colosseum; or the guides, with their air of patient responsibility?

He began again: 'Emily is a–' And again he stopped. How could he find words to tell Gerry what kind of woman she was, when Gerry could never exactly understand? To him she would always be a different woman. She would never show her strength to Gerry, for instance; or if she did, Gerry would not know that she had.

Gerry said: 'Peter – I–'

Peter said: 'To hell with her. I don't want to think about her. Let's get to sleep.'

Gerry was going to try and say something personal, probably about that time six years ago when he had lost Emily. He would have told how it had wounded him then, but how he came to feel that the best man ought to win, that it was best for all of them that it should have turned out this way. It would have hurt and embarrassed him to say it, so Peter prevented him. It did not need saying, anyway.

He rolled over again, turning his back to Gerry, and went to sleep.

They moved off as soon as the dusk had settled to a point where Cammarota was sure any

Austrian standing patrol, hidden on the slopes, spending the daytime watching and listening, could not see them. The passage of the Julio went as planned. At quarter to eleven the Italian platoon crossed the pass, creeping forward in faint moonlight on a wide front, the centre in the neck of the pass, the wings well up to the slopes on each side. Soon after eleven they made contact with the Austrians sitting in their positions a little way down the northern slope. The Italians had been making plenty of noise, and the Austrians greeted them with an indignant volley of rifle shots. The Italians replied in kind. Someone on the Austrian side was cursing in Italian. Cammarota whispered that the man had not been hit; he was furious at the irruption into the calm. The Italians played their part well and moved forward, edging away to the left, advancing slowly and firing busily while Cammarota led the reconnaissance party high up the right-hand slope.

Soon, going fast over rock and scattered snow and at last a thousand feet of slaty shale, they reached the forests on the Austrian side. The firing on the pass had grown desultory by then. When they stopped, grouped under a heavy pine, Cammarota whispered: 'Now the rest of the Austrians from this side will be going up to see what is happening. Some of them may come this way to get behind our people. I am going to move north-east for an hour to make sure we do not run into them.'

They set off again. The going became harder as they traversed diagonally along the mountains for an hour, then plunged straight down into the narrow valley, at that point almost a gorge. This was one of the valleys, leading down from a subsidiary pass to the north of the main chain, which linked the Saraco with the Julio and Michele Passes. They crossed it, and Cammarota led on north at a good pace. At dawn they were in tangled mountains, not very high, far from any track or trail, seven miles beyond the 'front line.' They ate, rested for two hours, and pushed on again. Late in the afternoon they stood on the ridge line of rolling hills, which could hardly be called mountains here, overlooking the Saraco Valley from the west.

A mile below them a small village, about a dozen houses, was tucked into the head of a hanging alp, with cows grazing in the low sun and a pair of old women watching them. Staldi said it was an Italian-speaking village, like most in this area. A thin haze of smoke or dust hung over the main valley and even more obviously over a side valley directly opposite, on the east side of the Saraco. Peter raised his binoculars.

The forests ran down to within two or three hundred yards of the motor road on that opposite side. A small, widely-spaced string of trucks was moving up the road, heading south, each vehicle trailing a low, long-lived plume of dust. Opposite the watchers they turned left on to some side road which could not be seen, since a wall hid it, and climbed towards the forested side valley. It was a stiff gradient, apparently. In the still air he could hear the growl and whine of the engines as they changed gear and moved slowly away from him to disappear into the trees. Over the trees the dust hung.

This was interesting, and might be vital. Aerial reconnaissance was extremely hazardous in this mountain area, and what little the Italians had carried out had not brought any reports of large troop movements in the Saraco, or of major improvements to the road. But there was obviously a dump of some kind being stocked – or emptied – in the forests over there; and the road had obviously been improved from the cart road the Italians knew of, or it could not have stood heavy-truck traffic at the pace he could see the vehicles were moving. Armies did not build dumps for fun. They did it to place in a convenient position a stock of ammunition, rations, and so forth, sufficient to carry out some operation that was going to make extraordinary demands on those commodities. Since one man could eat only one ration a day, the existence of extra rations pointed to the expected arrival of extra men – that is, reinforcements – or to an expectation that the daily supply route might be cut off for some period of time by enemy action. Piled stacks of ammunition, on a front where so little was normally used, would point to the expectation of using more ammunition – such as in an attack, or a defence against an enemy attack.

No one could read a whole battle plan into a few dust trails. They must go and see. Even then they would not learn much more, probably. But already they knew that the Austrians were expecting something. Peter's guess was that they

355

were expecting an attack such as his party was now making the reconnaissance for.

He turned to Cammarota and told him that they must cross the valley and find out what was in the forests on the other side. Cammarota was looking worried. He knew perfectly well that he ought to do what was suggested; but it was outside the scope of his orders, which were to examine the topography of the possible routes from the Julio over into the Saraco that would have to be used by the light-armed troops making the 'hook.' However, he agreed at last, and they decided to sleep where they were until midnight.

Before they settled down Cammarota emphasized that his worry was lest the Austrians see the party, or, worse still, capture Gerry or Peter. It was of the first importance not to let the Austrians know that any patrol had been reconnoitring as deep as this into the Saraco Valley; vital not to let them get an inkling that officers as high-ranking as majors were with the patrol; and supreme that the presence of British officers should not be suspected, for that could mean only that the British were thinking of reinforcing the Italians in this theatre. (Peter and Gerry were wearing Italian mountain uniform, complete with rope and ice axe; but that disguise would not last a moment if they were captured.)

Peter recognized the importance of these considerations. But in the last resort they were here to find out whether this operation of war was or was not feasible. They had to press the reconnaissance home at all costs. He was not going to go back to London and tell them he *thought* it was possible. He was going to *know;* and he did not intend that Gerry or he should be captured. He lay down and went to sleep.

At midnight they moved off once more, crossed the valley without trouble, and entered the eastern forests. They moved with great caution and were not challenged, though in the momentary flash of a truck's headlights they twice saw Austrian sentries, rifles on their arms, a short distance below them through the woods.

An hour before dawn Cammarota whispered: 'I think this will be a good place to lie up, Major, at least till dawn, when we can see where we are. Lieutenant Fraschelli, you and Staldi stand sentry for the first hour.'

During the day they saw what they wanted to see. It was a widely scattered ammunition dump, piles of shells stacked under the trees, and rough roads winding in all directions. They worked in pairs, with one man always guarding the base. Peter returned there finally with Carana shortly after dark, and they all held a brief conference. There was no doubt that the Austrians were ready for something big. In the twilight Peter had slouched up to one pile of shells and identified them as twelve-inch howitzer.

'Interesting,' Cammarota muttered worriedly. 'No twelve-inch shell has yet been fired on this front... There will be ration dumps too, I suppose, but we do not have time to find those. Nor is that our task. We can return across the valley.'

They began to work down through the forest.

357

All went well until they reached the main road. Fraschelli and Staldi were in the lead, Gerry and Peter ten paces back, and Cammarota and Carana bringing up the rear. It was very dark, and Peter thought it would rain during the night, but the road showed as a dim white streak ahead. Staldi was stepping up on to it when a nervous voice challenged in German– *'Wer da?'*– and the beam of a torch illuminated the corrugated metalling of the road and the crouching figures of Fraschelli and Staldi, the former with his hands thrown up in front of his face as though to protect himself from a cuff.

Peter had carried an Italian carbine through-out, and fired at once at the torch. The light went out, and a man screamed. Peter charged forward with Gerry at his side. Down the road to the right the headlights of another convoy flared up, and the only sounds were the high whining of the gears and the man screaming. Then there was a face under Peter's, and he fired again. Cammarota was there, and strangers were among them, and the two guides were plunging into action as though this were their normal trade. Gerry was there, his face suddenly lit, livid and taut, by the rifle flashes. Peter could feel the skin drawn back over his own teeth in a snarl.

Everything was quiet. The trucks had stopped moving. 'Did we get them all?' Peter asked.

Major Cammarota said: 'Yes. Five. I didn't see anyone get away.' He stood up from the dead man he had been kneeling over. 'It was a party of criminals being taken back under escort.'

Peter bent down and saw that three of the men were chained together, their hands locked. Cammarota said bitterly: 'They were probably Italians, conscripted and trying to desert over to us. Well, they would have died anyway.'

Gerry muttered: 'Oh, God–'

Peter dismissed it from his mind. It was an accident of war, but it had happened and the men were dead, guards and prisoners alike. He turned urgently to Cammarota. 'Quick! What would partisans do if they had done this?'

Cammarota said: 'They would take the rifles and ammunition off the guards. But–'

Peter could hear shouting from the woods this side of the road leading to the ammunition dump. The headquarters of the dump were in an old farmhouse there, about half a mile away. An enemy patrol would take ten minutes to reach them if it hurried. But it wouldn't. He said: 'Well, we must take these, then.'

'Is it necessary?' Cammarota asked in a low voice.

'Of course it is,' Peter said. 'If we don't, the Austrians will suspect that a patrol has been over as deep as this.'

'Does it matter?' Cammarota asked. 'They can't move the dump.'

'No, but they can send out a few hundred Jaegers to prevent us getting back. You've insisted a dozen times that our presence must not be suspected. For Christ's sake, get a move on!'

Gerry said: 'Peter, the Austrians will think the villagers up there have done it.'

'That's exactly what they must think,' he

snapped. 'Otherwise we'll never get back.'

Damn them for a pack of treacle-witted cowards! He knew perfectly well what was on their minds. The wretched villagers were going to be descended on, tortured, a few shot. He knew that, had faced it, and decided what mattered most. Did the lives of those villagers matter more than the lives of the soldiers who would be killed – or saved – through what they discovered? Were the soldiers any less innocent of starting the war?

Cammarota said: 'Take their rifles. Empty their cartridge pouches.'

It was done, and they moved off. The investigating patrol was some distance off, firing at shadows. Cammarota shot Peter one look of pure hatred. Peter thought: That will show you, you miserable bastard. The major had learned that he wasn't as brave as he thought he was, and that the stories about Peter Savage were truer than he'd believed. He'd thought Peter was all bombast, and that his reconnaissance would have him eating out of his hand before it was done. Well, he'd learned differently.

They marched all night, heading along footpaths and occasional cart tracks and over open meadows, towards the Julio Pass. They spoke only four times, when Cammarota pointed out various places where the advancing Italians would have some small difficulties. Otherwise it was a good route: quite passable for troops with pack transport, and that was all that was needed.

At last they stopped, when the sun was rising over the mountains. It had rained twice during the night, but now the clouds were gone and it was a glorious, fresh July day. They lay down, and the birds began to sing, and the flowers smelled sweet where Peter's body crushed them.

They were to move on again early in the afternoon, so that they should reach the northern approaches to the Julio Pass by dusk. Peter awoke at noon and saw that Gerry was already awake, lying there a few feet away, his pistol in his hand, looking at him.

Gerry said quickly: 'I'm just cleaning it.'

For a few minutes before Peter awoke he had been in that half-land between sleep and waking, and had been reaching a decision. In the moment of awakening the decision became as hard and inescapable as the bulk of Monte Michele towering up to the south-west over intervening ridges. He said: 'We must have a look at the Michele Pass, Gerry.'

Gerry turned the pistol over slowly in his hands. Peter saw that it was loaded. A thought, sudden and ugly as the act itself, darkened his mind – that Gerry had been going to use the pistol. On himself – who else?

Gerry's eyes were red-rimmed, and his face had a dull, greenish pallor. It was the prisoners he had killed, and the thought of what must happen to the villagers back there, that had driven him to the cracking point. Being Gerry, he felt these things more acutely than many who talked and wept about them; perhaps even as much as Peter himself did, but without Peter's defences of reason and ultimate end.

The only thing to do was to pretend that he had noticed nothing. He could not, in enemy territory, tell Gerry to unload his pistol. So he merely told him of his decision, that they must cross back to the Italian side via the Michele Pass and have a good look at the approaches on the Austrian side while they were at it.

Gerry put the pistol slowly back to its holster. He said: 'Didn't you mention that to Cammarota once before, and he said we couldn't?'

The guides were up, building a tiny fire to make coffee. The two Italian officers lay at the far side of the clearing and seemed to be still asleep.

Peter said: 'Yes. But now we must. The operation across the Saraco and Julio Passes probably is not now feasible, because the Austrians seem to be ready for it. But supposing we could cross the Michele. It would be a wider, deeper hook, and it would cut off still more of the Austrian Army up the Saraco. Suppose they're proposing to attack *us* over the Michele. Either way, we can't go back without finding out.'

He got up, fastened his buttons, and walked over to Cammarota. The major awoke as soon as Peter's shadow passed over him. Peter said at once, sitting down beside him: 'I think we must return over the Michele.' He repeated the reasons he had just given to Gerry.

Cammarota was no fool. He was wideawake in an instant. Perhaps he had been expecting this. Fraschelli was sitting up in his blanket, his eyes heavy with sleep, looking now, unshaven for four days, extraordinarily like a nervous weasel. Cammarota decided to try irony. 'Ah, you are a fire-eater, Major Savage,' he said, smiling thinly. 'But I think we discussed this before. Our orders are to return when we have completed this mission. They are definite.' That was true.

Peter said: 'We must disobey the orders.'

Cammarota said: 'Agents can get any necessary information about the Michele more easily than we can, though, as you were assured by our General Staff, it is not worth while. The approaches to it on our side – which means the exits from it if the Austrians decide to attack – are absolutely impossible for the support of any major advance.' He was on his feet now, and they were facing each other at the edge of the clearing, Fraschelli behind Cammarota and Gerry behind Peter, and the two guides quietly cooking, a dozen yards off, and the high sun beating down on the forests and the mountains and the glaring ice of Monte Michele.

Peter said: 'Agents are not soldiers – certainly not British officers. What is called impossible at one time may have to be made possible at another. You're a mountaineer. You know that.'

Cammarota said: 'And some places cannot be made possible, Major Savage. Any attempts to do so only result in needless loss of life. *You* know that. At all events I must assure you that it is out of the question. You will recall how you insisted that the partisans be made to suffer for our actions last night in order that we should be able to get back with our information. That is the vital point, I agree. Hence, I cannot agree to the great risk of returning by this long circuit.'

'A day,' Peter interrupted.

'In country about which we know little, and of the enemy – nothing.'

'Then you refuse to take the patrol back over the Michele Pass?' Peter asked politely. This felt better. Cammarota's eyes were beginning to blur and he was finding it harder every moment to retain his mask of good breeding and military impersonality.

Cammarota said: 'I regret it, Major Savage. Yes, I refuse.'

Peter said: 'Will you allow me to ask Staldi and Carana if one of them will volunteer to come with me?' He was cold as ice then, and quite ready to shoot Cammarota and take command of the party if necessary.

Cammarota said: 'I regret it, Major Savage. No. I will not.' Obviously he thought that Peter must give in then, because anyone could see that Gerry was near the end of his tether. Apart from the nervous tension and the tragedy of the prisoners, he could not have been physically as fit as he thought he was before they started, and there had been strain in London – about the white feather, wanting to be a doctor, and Emily's pushing him. Cammarota also knew Peter could not go by himself because what he saw might not be given full credence, and because problems of moun-taineering and minor tactics would require at least two men. He had a grin hidden just behind his big, hard face.

Peter said: 'Then Lieutenant Lord Wilcot and I will go by ourselves.'

Cammarota stiffened. He said: 'Lord Wilcot? In the state he is in?'

Peter said: 'Yes.'

Cammarota said: 'You will disobey me? I am

the commander of this patrol, Major Savage, including you and Lord Wilcot.' His voice was choked with fury and disbelief.

Peter said: 'I hereby remove myself and Lord Wilcot from under your command. We will move off as soon as we have eaten.'

Cammarota snapped: 'I will prevent you. I will–'

'Shoot us?' Peter said. 'I do not think that will be a good way to get British reinforcements to this front.'

He waited a moment to give the major time to realize that he must now either carry out his threat, which *he* couldn't, or shut up. Then he said: 'I expect to cross the Michele Pass during tomorrow night. Please have word sent to the local commander.'

Cammarota got a grip on himself, managed a stiff bow, and turned his back. He still could not trust himself to speak.

Peter walked back to his own side of the clearing. Gerry said: 'We're going alone, then – you and I.'

He said: 'Yes,' rather curtly. It was a scandal that Cammarota should have forced him to take Gerry, when Staldi or Carana would have come willingly and been twice as useful. But he had, and when a man has to drive himself beyond what he believes to be his limit it is a help to know that collapse will not elicit any sympathy. It has something of the same effect that knowledge of the sea's impartiality has on a drowning man – because he knows he will get no help from it if he gives up, he does not give up. All the same, it hurt to do it, because Gerry was looking so strange.

Peter said, still curt: 'Come on. We've got no time to waste.'

They began eating. Staldi brought coffee and then returned to Carana. They were looking worried and muttering to each other. They knew what had happened, and Staldi could not bring himself to think that it was right, under any circumstances, to desert his *signores*. He went finally to speak to Cammarota and got snapped at.

Peter said: 'Eat up, Gerry. Who knows when you'll get another square meal.' He unslung his carbine and checked it briefly.

'I'm not hungry,' Gerry muttered.

Peter made him keep his scraps, which he had been about to throw away. Then they got up.

'We're going now,' Peter said to Cammarota as they passed by him.

'Good fortune,' Cammarota said coldly. 'I am sure you will get another medal.'

CHAPTER 24

'Alone again, at last,' Peter said after they had been going for an hour and the woods had long since swallowed up all trace of the Italians. He felt eager and full of a kind of febrile energy.

'Yes,' Gerry said. They were walking in single file, heading fast across the grain of the ridges to drop into the narrow valley that ran down from the Michele Pass to the Saraco, joining the latter about ten miles behind them.

When Peter glanced round he saw that Gerry was walking along with his hand on the butt of his pistol. He said: 'You needn't hang so tight on to the revolver yet, Gerry. There won't be any enemy until we get down into the valley, if then.' Gerry's nerves must be jangling like broken piano strings. Peter turned his back on him and marched on.

He breasted a rolling crest and stopped. He knew from his map that the Michele Valley lay below him. The trees obstructed the view but he could see, far down, touches of pale green, which must mean grass or crops. The map showed no road in this valley, only a cattle-path by which the villagers from the Middle Saraco would take their flocks and herds up to the high pastures under Monte Michele in late spring, and down again in early autumn.

He led on down. If the Austrians had any hopes

or fears of the Michele Pass, the signs of it would be here.

When they reached the valley it was nearly dark, and he decided to rest under cover for at least the first part of the night. The next day they would reconnoitre up the valley towards the pass and, if conditions were suitable, cross over either late in the evening or during the hours of darkness. They moved back a hundred yards into the heavy forests and lay down under a tree, without eating, and went to sleep.

They slept late. The morning broke in dull and cold for the season. The wind sang uneasy songs in the tree-tops, the great branches of the oaks thrashed around, and the limbs creaked. It was going to rain again soon. That would probably mean snow on the Michele Pass. It was going to be a miserable day, for they had no shelter and no adequate waterproof clothing; but the same conditions would serve to keep in their huts or tents any soldiers who might be here, and make it easier to wander about unobserved. They set out and began to walk south towards the pass, keeping in the edge of the forests, just above the narrow, level floor of the valley.

Towards midday the rain began. By then Peter thought the head of the valley could not be more than two miles away, and he knew that something was – or had been – going on here. Twice in the lowering banks of grey cloud that swept up the valley they waded the little torrent and crossed over to the other side. The cattle-path had been worked on so that it would take carts now, and there were wheel tracks and the hoofprints of shod horses and mules, and a single telegraph line. It seemed impossible that the track could ever be improved enough to take motor traffic, nor was there any sign that this had been attempted, but something had been done. Once they followed a short spur which led from the path into a clearing among the dripping woods. There they saw a pile of road metalling and a small wooden shelter with smoke curling from its chimney. There were a few small stacks of something, covered by tarpaulins, but Peter decided it was not worth the risk of being discovered to go forward and find out what was hidden there – probably nothing more exciting than fodder for the transport animals, some of which would obviously have to be based up here.

A little later, sheltering beneath a streaming pine – they were climbing all the time – while the rain hissed in the tree-tops a hundred feet above and the clouds swirled in the trough of the valley and water ran in a stream down the back of his neck, he tried to make out what the Austrians could be doing here. The cow-path had been improved – but that had involved so little work that it would have been worth while to do it if nothing more than a company was kept at the head of the valley, and the purpose might only be to ease the problems of maintaining the soldiers there. The dumps – very small. Signs of troops: empty tins of jam and sausage, toilet paper, empty cartridge cases – blanks. Blanks meant training, not operations.

'There's someone coming down the path,' Gerry muttered.

Peter moved quickly round the trees and dropped slowly to one knee. You could not see more than two hundred yards at the best today, seldom that much. There were three men, carrying rifles – no, two with rifles and one apparently unarmed. Probably had a pistol. Couldn't tell their rank. They were huddled in big army capes, high shako-type hats bowed forward, not looking where they were going, just longing to be back in shelter. One of those things was not a rifle, though. It was – a surveyor's tripod, legs closed, carried over the shoulder. They were fifty yards away now. A surveyor. He had to have that man's papers. Blame the partisans again.

'You take the front one,' he whispered.

'But–' Gerry said.

'Don't argue, man.' He crept ahead, so that Gerry and he would be separated by a few steps and the firing would come from both sides of the men, who trudged on. There was hardly any need to hide, for their faces were bent down. The unarmed man had a theodolite slung in a heavy case over his shoulder. Now they were level. Peter shot the last man dead, the one with the rifle. Before the smell of cordite had drifted into his nostrils he fired again and shot the second man, the one carrying the theodolite, dead. 'Fire!' he yelled at Gerry and ran forward. Gerry was standing there, his pistol raised, staring at the man with the tripod. Peter fired, but the man was already running, and he missed. Gerry fired and missed. Peter stopped, fired carefully. The man jerked his hand. Again – but he was behind a tree

370

now. Gerry fired twice. Peter began to run after the man. He'd thrown his tripod away. No chance. The man would be a fast runner at the best of times, and explosive fear had given him the speed and sure-footedness of Mercury. Peter felt very tired. In a few seconds the gleam of the wet cape fluttering and flickering among the dark trunks of the trees had gone.

Peter returned and bent over the body of the man with the theodolite, searching quickly through his pockets and his rough haversack. He was furious with Gerry, because the man with the tripod had seen them and soon the Austrians would be out looking for them. The man would insist that it was not partisans who had ambushed him. The only thing to do was hope that he would not be believed, and steal whatever was of value off the corpses – and the rifle, of course – to make his tale seem still less likely.

Gerry was staring at Peter, the pistol swinging in his hand. He said: 'I couldn't shoot him. I thought I was ready to kill after last night, night before – but I can't.'

'Put that thing away or you'll shoot me,' Peter said shortly. The surveyor had some maps and a blueprint trace. Peter took the other's rifle and cartridges, both men's watches, a pair of rings, some money.

'Come on,' he said.

Now it was south, fast, on the east side of the valley, the side away from the cart-road. Soon he hid the loot from the dead Austrians. He had not had time to study the surveyor's papers, and knew that he must find time, and quickly, to look at them and explain to Gerry what they told. Otherwise, if he was killed, they would have thrown away their luck in getting them. He stopped and decided to look at them immediately.

Nothing much. The cart-track was being improved only to the foot of the pass. Some houses or huts shown in that area. The blue trace was of a hut; it looked very simple and could hold about twenty men – a barrack, then. A company was a lot of men to put in this remote place – but not earth-shaking. Why the blank cartridges?

He told Gerry, and Gerry said yes, he understood. They went on.

Peter struck up diagonally left-handed into the forest, climbing away from the valley floor. Round the next corner, or the next, if they had stayed down there, they would have run into the huts, or soldier-defaulters laying white stones along the edges of the path, guarded by a glum armed sentry. Sooner or later, this hour or next, the man whom Gerry had let live would reach a post and tell what he had seen. Peter decided then and there that any dreams he had had of carrying Gerry to military glory must be abandoned. Gerry would have to be a doctor, though Peter could not help wondering what he would do if he had to kill a baby to save its mother, or vice versa. Still, if the worst came to the worst, Emily or he could decide for him, and bear the moral weight. Besides, Gerry would probably have so concentrated his mind on the saving part that he could face the killing. Back there with the Austrians he saw only the killing because the saving was not actual and present, being concerned with soldiers miles away and still alive, and boys not yet out of school.

He had forgotten something. 'Wait here,' he flung over his shoulder. 'I'm going down to cut the telegraph line.'

He hurried back down the three hundred feet or so that they had climbed, sliding and stumbling on the carpet of wet pine needles, and reached the valley. The telegraph poles were low – not more than twelve feet high, most of them, and not many even that. For the most part the line was strung along between pine trees at the edge of the forest. He found a good place, dragged down the wire, used his carbine as a lever to break the cable, and then carefully fastened the ends together in a narrow knot and tied that against a tree. Now only men following the wire in a good light would see where the break was. He trudged back up the hill, his head swimming and the trees beginning to sway in their places.

He had left Gerry there, by that fir with the fork near the ground and a big grey rock on its right. He wasn't there. Peter moved behind another tree, restlessly searching all around, up the streaming hill, down to the streaming valley floor, along to right and left. If Gerry had gone, something must have made him – something, someone he had seen. But there was no one. He was suddenly sure that there *was* no one else on that dripping mountainside at that time. Then Gerry had imagined he'd seen someone. Or he had suddenly decided he must move on, the same as he had decided he could not shoot when he had the man with the tripod, unsuspecting, over the barrel of his pistol. Perhaps a blind panic had fallen on him and he'd begun to run. Gerry was not a coward as people use the word, as Count Fraschelli was, but he was near his limit. He had a map, but he would not stand much chance of getting back alone. Nor would he himself.

Where would he have gone? Not back, surely? He wasn't mad. On then, probably on the line they had been following when he remembered the telegraph wires. He stumbled up the hill.

After ten minutes he had seen no sign of Gerry. He reached a place where a step in the sweep-down of the mountain offered alternative paths, on up towards the crest, or along, on the level. Which way would he have gone? He must be running like a stag that has seen the hunters. Put himself in Gerry's place – he would have gone up. But Gerry?

Peter turned right and ran along the side of the hill. Five minutes later he saw the shadow rushing through the pine trees ahead. He could make him hear now if he called loud enough, but that would be dangerous. He held his pace and saw that he was gaining. Gerry never looked over his shoulder. Then, when he was no more than ten yards behind and Gerry must have heard the crunch and thud of his boots, he called softly: 'Gerry!'

Gerry drew up slowly and at last turned. Peter was up to him then, his arm out to grip his shoulder. 'It's you,' Gerry said. 'I – I–' His eyes were big, with the same large, excited look Peter had seen once before, on the Needles of Meru, two years ago.

'I heard a shot and saw men moving through the forest,' Gerry said. 'I thought they'd got you.'

That was a palpable lie. Gerry would never have left him if he believed he was in trouble. Peter said: 'I'm all right. They didn't get me. Where's your pistol?'

'I don't know – I must have lost it somewhere. I had it.'

Peter said: 'It doesn't matter. Well, what about pushing on?'

Gerry nodded. He had collected himself: he too was going to pretend that what had happened had not. 'Yes,' he said. 'Lead on.'

'...Macduff,' Peter prompted. That was an old catch-phrase of theirs from Cambridge days. He hadn't thought it very funny at the time. Now Gerry didn't. He only groaned and prepared to follow.

Peter swung into the lead and did not look round, though he listened all the time to be sure that the footsteps were at his heels. Now – they should be on the side of the hill above the head of the valley. If they went down a few hundred paces to the right they should be looking down into the cirque or alp or moraine or whatever there was under the north slope of the Michele Pass. That much more they must do at all costs.

He turned down and went more cautiously, peering through the trunks of the trees ahead until they fell away, and then crept on very carefully to the lip of a last sharp slope. The rain still fell; clouds blew about the face of Monte Michele and its summit was completely shrouded in them; but in the gaps of the clouds, looking down, he could see. He told Gerry to go back a bit and keep a lookout to the rear. Then he leaned against the trunk of a tree and began to examine what he saw.

There were the huts shown on the surveyor's blueprint. Three extra ones – no, four. Not marked, probably because they weren't the surveyor's responsibility. A row of eight target frames on the hill-side not far below him. Firing points built out from the hill at one, two, three hundred metres, and probably more. Something in the trees, hard to make out – a log cabin – two. Something reminiscent about the neatness of the whole – jogging at his memory.

Manali. Lower Manali. The 13th Gurkhas' permanent manœuvre camp... This was a training camp. This was where the Austrians trained their men in mountain warfare. It was rather close to the battlefront for a training area, but on the other hand the troops here would also serve as an adequate protection against any light raid over the Michele – if they were not raw recruits. An N.C.O's training camp, probably.

A hot anticipation burned away his fatigue. Suppose it was not a light raid that came over the Michele Pass, but an attack by two or three battalions of Bersaglieri supported by mountain artillery on pack mules? The road to the rear, to the Saraco, had been improved. Such a force could do a far more decisive job in cutting off the whole Upper Saraco than the proposed shallow 'hook' over the Julio. Cammarota said that the approaches on the Italian side were impossible. They must be bad, or the Austrians would never allow men to wander around here with blank ammunition, carrying out manœuvres... Then those approaches would have to be made possible. This way the attack could succeed.

It had to be done. Men, thousands of labourers working at night to gouge out a path, hiding by day in the forests... Speed, secrecy, then – drive over the Michele, overwhelm these Austrians in the night, under a moon, and then burst down into the Saraco!

He had to get back into Italy at once.

No sign of activity down there. One sentry standing under a neat shelter outside one of the log cabins. Peter looked hard but could not see the pass. It was certain, though, that it would be guarded – lightly, but lightly was too much for him and Gerry. Nor could they move back, cross the valley, and try to enter Italy through the jagged tangle of mountains beyond the pass. For one thing, they were off his map; for another, the distance was too great.

It had to be Monte Michele itself, looming up there right ahead. So be it. He glanced at his watch. Half-past four in the afternoon. July, but it would soon be dark enough, in this weather, to risk moving up the bare ridge which led from where he stood towards the north wall of Monte Michele.

He swung round. Gerry was crouched, pointing back along the hill. He seemed almost glad; there was no sign of alarm or despair on his face. There were men moving in the forest back there, back the way they had come – five or six. The men had not seen them. They might not even be looking for them.

He beckoned to Gerry, and they dropped over the lip of that last slope, where the convexity prevented the men from seeing them, and hurried southward towards Monte Michele. Now they were in full view from the encampment, and would be for several minutes – it was hard to guess for exactly how long in this murk and driving mist.

After half an hour, without being shot at, they reached the shelter of tumbled piles of rock at the foot of Monte Michele's gigantic north face. Peter sank down, dragging Gerry with him. Gerry was looking back almost longingly.

The next problem began to pound away at him. The crossing of Monte Michele was going to be a difficult feat of mountaineering, because of the weather and their fatigue. From the climbing point of view it would be best to start now and climb as fast and as far as they could while the dim light lasted. The rock was wet here; above, there would be new, wet snow. A few yards up there began two hundred feet of steep cliff. As far up as he could see it offered small but adequate holds – an hour's hard work, probably the hardest technical piece of climbing on the mountain. By night it would take three, four hours, and possibly failure or a fall. But in daylight, during the hour on the cliff, they would be completely at the mercy of anyone who came along under the cliff to look for them.

It wouldn't do. They'd have to go over by night, all the way. He got out the map and began to study it with a concentration that amounted to frenzy.

'Aren't you cold or wet, Peter?' Gerry asked him. Gerry was sitting down beside him, watching as he worked with mind at full stretch to correlate the map with what he saw and what little he had ever heard about Monte Michele.

Gerry spoke so softly – tenderly, almost – that the curt answer died away in Peter's mouth. He said: 'Of course I am,' and gave Gerry a smile, only it probably looked more like a snarl, he was so clenched and cold. But looking at Gerry warmed him again and gave him his second wind – fifth or sixth, by then. Whatever he had done before in the way of lifting men above themselves was going to be nothing to what he must do if he was to get Gerry over Monte Michele tonight, and that he was going to do. The power to do it flowed into him as the darkness fell. He had not brought Gerry to this point through any selfish motives. He would have done it again – but now he must and he would lead Gerry over the mountain and into a safe and happy place. He would himself take him to Edinburgh and tell Dr McVeigh that Gerry could be a great physician – a surgeon, perhaps; a leader of the profession, a – humble doctor in a small Punjab town.

It didn't matter. Gerry wanted it. So be it. He'd go back too, when the war was over. He couldn't live without Gerry.

He heard the distant echo of a voice, answered by another. There were men on the ridge, then.

379

Nothing to do. Gerry was keeping a look-out.

From here, five thousand feet to the crest, three thousand if they crossed the shoulders. But the easiest – least hard – way was straight up. There was no 'official' route up this face. Hadn't Staldi said someone had done it in '06? The 'proper' approach was from the Michele Pass, 'an easy climb for a lady.' This was rather more than that, but nothing extreme – a good day's climb for a good man. They ought to come back here after the war, he and Gerry, and do it properly. Christ.

It was almost dark. Visibility, not more than fifty yards. 'Rope up.'

Thirty.

Twenty yards. 'Unroll the blankets. Leave them.' Like sodden corpses, they looked.

Ten. Good enough.

They faced the cliff.

The black rocks among which they had been sheltering, four and eight and ten feet high, had become blurs that might have been men. To right and left they seemed to move, though Peter knew it was the mist and the night that flowed past them, while the rocks stood silent, like rocks in a river.

He led. He took the first pitch at a steady pace, weaving across the face of the cliff to find easy holds, and making each run-out small so that Gerry never had to stand long alone before coming up to him. This was climbing, he thought with a grim lift of the spirit, such as no climber could face without a feeling that madness was in the air that it should have to be done. It was climbing, war, and rescue, all together.

In darkness, on an unknown mountain, he had to force into existence and instantly bring to full flower capabilities and knowledge that he had not possessed. He found that it was not his brain that guided him up the cliff as much as some inwardly felt knowledge of and communion with mountains. He had spent a large part of his energy and will-power, carefully concentrated for the purpose, on conquering mountains. Except for Meru, he had conquered them. Now he reached out in the flowing blackness and found a rugosity under his hand, just where it should have been. He felt a non-material contact with the rock, an actual spurt of friendship, as though it were human and gave him now the touch of a friend and passed him a word of greeting because he came to it in the night. It was a friend and had put a lamp in the window for him.

Feeling this for the first time, he knew that he had hated the mountains while he conquered them. Why, then, were they responding to his need tonight? Was it for Gerry's sake?

He searched left and right, like a hound on the trail. He walked, quick and light, across the face of the rock, hardly touching it. He guided Gerry up with voice and rope, and love and curses and sheer strength. When Gerry stood spreadeagled against the slope, shaking, half unconscious, he told him he'd shoot him. When Gerry groaned up to a finger-hold he told him Emily was waiting for them with tea and crumpets, on top. For forty feet, on an easier stretch, he dragged him.

At last there was no further way up but by chimneying. A vertical fissure began in the rock level with his waist, to the right, and led up into the dark beyond the farthest reach of his fingers. It was about the right width, a little narrow at first. When Gerry joined him on the shelf where he stood, he said: 'We're going up this crack here. Here, feel it.' He took Gerry's hand and made him gauge its width.

Gerry said: 'It's narrower than King's Chapel, Peter.'

Peter went up. Gerry followed, but his muscles failed when he was half-way up, and Peter brought him the rest of the way on the rope. Then Peter fainted, and when he came round it was eleven-twenty and they had surmounted the cliff, and Gerry was in a kind of delirium but fully conscious. They rested another hour, ate a scrap of bread, roped up. He led on.

Four hours of agonizing step-by-step slogging – shale – smooth rock – snow and rock – one or other or both of them falling down every few moments. The rain turned to sleet and then snow. At two o'clock, at the foot of the final rampart of nevé, and nothing but lead and pain in him, he stopped and lay down again. 'Wrong, wrong,' he whispered. 'We should go on.' He couldn't.

He awoke at five, feeling worse. He began to cut steps. The wind was dying down, and he could see a jumping, swaying line, white below and grey-green above – the summit slope.

The clouds still eddied about them. He was thankful, remembering the men with rifles. An hour later, full light but no sun, and they stood among clutching tendrils of cloud, cloud low overhead, snow beneath their feet.

'We've done it,' Gerry croaked. His eyes shone, almost as of old. 'We're there, Peter.'

'Got to get down first,' he said. 'Not done till then.'

Over to the right, beyond Gerry, there was something, half-man, half-cloud, snow and light and moving shadow. Peter unslung his carbine; he couldn't speak. Gerry had turned but saw nothing where he was looking, down into Italy; Peter couldn't, daren't shout. His hands were bitter cold, and snow clogged the bolt. The cloud slid back from a soldier, the soldier saw Gerry, his rifle was ready in his hand. A hard, blue-eyed mountain man he was, a guide, corporal, like Carana, but enemy. He fired at Gerry, and Peter fired at him.

Gerry swung round to Peter. The thin smoke still twisted from the muzzle of Peter's carbine.

Peter fired again; Gerry's blank eyes were on him, the face deep-cut and falling away, his eyes filling, swaying. 'Peter,' he said. 'Oh, Peter.' He fell. Behind him the mountain guide with the corporal's badges fell on his face. Behind again there was shouting, muffled and from everywhere in the cloud. No one else had seen Peter. Even then he could think of that, while Gerry lay on his side, unarmed, the tears frozen in their course, his lips apart.

Peter fired twice more, low over the snow, so that they should not come. He dragged Gerry by his feet to the edge of the drop – dead – and pushed him over, not knowing what lay below, only that it was steep and snow-covered, and

383

jumped after him. Gerry rode faster than he, flat at first, then rolling, jumping, jerking, swirling, and soon disappeared; while for Peter the snow hissed like a wave around him and he went down in the long glissade, the muzzle of his carbine supporting him, as he had practised a hundred times with the ice-axe, until the snow fell away and he was riding out over a gulf, deep blue snow and cloud waiting for him, and Gerry gone for ever.

CHAPTER 25

The smoke hung thick in Victoria Station and set Peter to coughing. There had been a big change, even in the last three months. The slaughter on the Western Front dragged on and on. They were still fighting at Loos, and the casualty lists staggered the imagination. For most it was the sheer numbers that caused the shock. For him, a dull realization that each one of those names had been someone's 'Gerry.'

He had to get to Emily. The moted beams filtered down from a weak October sun. It was khaki, khaki everywhere, and the trudge of khaki men; the women's dresses dull because it was October, only here and there a brave daub of crimson or green, a feather waving above a big blue bonnet. That was a different war they were fighting in France. You could see it in the hunched shoulders and clay-coloured faces. No one waiting for those trains was having any fun. The yellow smoke swirled high among the girders; out over the Thames a tug tooted; an engine whistled. The women edged closer, a throbbing frieze along the side of the train. The engine whistled again, and slowly the train began to move out. He turned away.

'Taxi!'

He'd have to tell Peggy the details. She was alone, Harry in France – a major by now, he'd heard. He himself was a lieutenant-colonel, as they'd promised. But first he had to get to Emily.

'Twenty-seven Minden Square.'

'Right-ho, guv'nor.'

He sank back, his hands clasped across his knees. The taxi driver was wrapped in several mufflers and wore a big moustache, and the air was grey-gold of October, the late sun slanting across the façade of Buckingham Palace. Gerry was dead.

Peter had been in Italian military hospitals for ten weeks with various bones broken, pneumonia, and – sickness. The Italians had been firm about the impossibility of building a route to the Michele, and he, lying in hospital, had not found the energy to make them see that it must be done. The War Office sent a brigadier-general to talk to him, and the influential M.P came, and both went away as unsure of what to do as before they came. He could not care. The Kurdistan project was held up, and nothing would come of it unless he went and relighted the fires of enthusiasm he had kindled in the first place. He could not care. The objects which had seemed so bright and worthy of any effort had become dull and grey – still large, but uninteresting.

Perhaps it was his physical weakness, he told himself. He would go home to Emily, with a month's sick leave, and get back all his strength. Other men had died. Why had Gerry's death cut all the sinews of desire? Emily could make him strong again.

''Ere y'are, guv'nor.'

He got out, tipped the man carefully, and

walked slowly up the steps to the front door. He found he did everything cautiously now. Harvey, Mr Fenton's valet, opened the door. Of course – he was too old for military service. That must mean Mr Fenton was here.

'Hello, Harvey,' Peter said.

'Mr Peter!' Harvey began, his eyes lighting up. Then he remembered some message he had been given and said: 'We were expecting you, sir. Mr Fenton is in the drawing-room.'

Peter went in slowly.

Mr Fenton had *The Times* in his hands, opened at the page where the casualty lists were. He had aged considerably. Good God, he must sit here all day, every day, reading the roll of the dead, of his friends and the sons of his friends, of his world slowly bleeding to death while daily the light grew dimmer behind the curtains and, without a trace, he too bled.

He looked up slowly and said: 'Peter...'

There was no sign of children, and no smell of a woman, no extra hats or coats on the rack in the hall. Peter felt suddenly afraid.

'What's the matter?' he cried urgently, grabbing the sleeve of his father-in-law's coat. 'Is anything the matter?'

'Sit down, Peter,' Mr Fenton said. He folded the paper carefully and laid it on the occasional table beside his chair.

'Emily's gone away,' he said at last.

'Where? Gone away? What do you mean, sir?' Peter cried.

Mr Fenton spoke coldly. 'She's gone away. That's all I can tell you. She's left a letter for you.

There, in the top left-hand drawer of the writing desk.'

Peter found the letter and gazed at it for a moment before opening it. It was addressed to 'Major Peter Savage, D.S.O.' This was like the first quiet hiss of powder snow, when the mountain spoke in a quiet voice, and the sky was blue overhead, and the ice-axe had a good grip in the slope, and the rope was taut and well anchored and the climbers all in harmony and climbing with the rhythm of success. That was when the mountain spoke, not to be argued with – the little hiss that would grow and become a surge like the surf, and then the grumble of the deep snow underneath as it moved, and then the avalanche, sweeping away shining axe and rough rope and brave climbers and all. He opened the letter.

Dear Peter,

I am going away, with the children, because I cannot bear to see you or speak to you again. As long as you make no attempt to find me, or see the children, ever, I will say nothing. If you do, I will publish everything, and though I am sure you can never be punished there will be a scandal which even you will not be able to surmount.

Emily

Dated August second. That would be a week or so after the War Office heard of Gerry's death. He had wondered vaguely why he had not received any letters, but the mails to Italy were very bad, and they had moved him from one

388

hospital to another. It had all seemed quite reasonable. Nothing could happen to Emily, because he loved her, and he had been absorbed in such lassitude that he had hardly noticed the absence of news from her.

He turned to Mr Fenton. He found he could speak gently because a kind of strength was coming back to him. Whatever had to be done to find Emily, that he would be able to do. Nothing else mattered.

'You know where she is,' he said.

Mr Fenton said: 'Yes. I know.'

'Will you tell me, sir?'

'No, Peter. I'm sorry.'

Peter said: 'I am going to find her, sir, whether you help me or not – if necessary, through the police.' He meant it. Nothing was going to stop him... Oh, God, it was true again, already!

'Don't do that, it's no use.' Mr Fenton got up, clutching the paper, as though its freight of dead names was the only reality to him now.

But Peter said: 'Good-bye, sir,' picked up his bag, which Harvey had left in the hall, and went out into the street. He stood awhile on the corner, slowly drawing out a cigar and lighting it. Where to now? D.S.O and bar. Hero of the Kingdom and Empire. Appointment with the King at Buckingham Palace next week. Gerry dead. Emily... Oh, Emily! The hiss of the snow grew louder in his ears, but for the moment he had not lost control.

A taxi cruised by. 'Two ninety-three Nashe Street, Kensington,' he said.

'I know it, sir.'

That was his grandfather's house. He didn't know why he was going there or what he would say when he arrived. Perhaps Grandfather was dead too.

He arrived, and the taxi puttered off along the darkening street. The door was unlocked, and he let himself in and walked slowly up the stairs. Ashraf creaked out on to the landing just before he reached it and peered down at him under the high, round globe of the gas light. 'Peter sahib,' he whispered, stooping, putting out both hands.

Peter touched them. *'General sahib gol-kamra men hai,'* the bearer said.

'So-raha?' Peter asked.

'Nahin, huzoor.' Ashraf opened the door into the drawing-room and walked with painful slowness ahead of him into the room, so that Peter saw his bent back and, beyond, his grandfather in a high chair, *The Times* fallen on his lap, opened at those same stark columns. For a moment the two old men – eighty-nine and eighty-four – were close together; then Ashraf stood aside, his hand indicating Peter. Then he went out.

Grandfather said: 'I'm a little deaf now, Peter. Speak clearly and close to my ear. It doesn't matter which ear.'

He left the paper in his lap. Of course it was not his friends or the sons of his friends who gave those lists their mass. The names could have been little more than names to him, reminding him of events long past. He was thinner, and the veins stood out with the thin blueness of tattooed snakes against the parchment brown of his long

390

eagle-talon hands. His eyes were clear under the bushy white eyebrows and the Regency whiskers, white as snow now, curled down his hollow cheeks.

'Another D.S.O,' he said. 'There's nothing wrong with my eyes, thank God. Where did you get that?'

'The Italian Alps, Grandfather,' he said. 'Emily's left me.' He shouted that very loud, because he didn't want to repeat it.

'I know,' the old man said, looking at him suddenly with such keenness that all the marks of age ceased to have any importance. 'Will you have some whisky?'

'Yes, please,' he said. He went to the sideboard in the dining-room next door, opened it, and brought back two bottles, two glasses, and the soda siphon on a tray. Grandfather had always drunk brandy.

When he had poured out drinks for both of them, he asked his grandfather why he hadn't written to tell him about Emily. The general had lighted a vile black Trichinopoly cheroot, though the doctors had told him in '06 that he must give them up. He said: 'Emily brought the children here on July twenty-ninth and told me she was leaving you. She did not say why. She obtained my promise not to tell you. I gave it, since it had only been a courteous gesture that had sent her to me at all. She knew I would like to see the children again before I die.'

Peter said: 'I think she holds me responsible for Gerry's death. I can't think of anything else.'

'She gave me no reason,' the general said, 'and

I did not ask her for one.'

Peter thought desperately. *Had* he killed Gerry? Gerry would not have been on Monte Michele if it had not been for him; he would have been safe in Edinburgh. He, Peter, had taken him to Italy – so he had killed him. But the same could be said of hundreds of thousands of men. Everyone from lance-corporal up could be held responsible, as murderer, for the death of men he had ordered on some particular duty, doing his own duty. Many a man had had to send his friend to death. Did Emily think he had enjoyed doing it?

'You tried Gerry high,' his grandfather said suddenly.

Yes, he had done that. He knew it, and Gerry had known and accepted it. But this last time? No. Gerry had been different.

The old general said: 'Your father – my son – left your mother.' Peter knew that, of course, and had always held it bitterly against his father. No one had ever talked much about it. His mother had died when he was ten.

His grandfather said: 'It was not because he did not love your mother, Peter. It was because he had to go. It was not he, but she, who explained it to me later. He said nothing to me. He had never liked me because he blamed me for the death of his mother in the Mutiny, and because I married again... Your father left because he found that he could not accept the ties of marriage.'

'He'd have done better to find that out before he married Mummy and had two children,' Peter said shortly. The other child was his twin sister.

They kept in desultory touch but meant nothing to each other and never had.

His grandfather said: 'Your father felt that the ordinary human ties that most of us welcome would suffocate him. His actual body could not be tied – he had to explore, to go to the lonely places of the earth, alone. But he had to walk alone in the mind and spirit too. He was looking for God.' Peter glanced up, but his grandfather did not elaborate. 'It was your mother who married him, knowing what kind of man he was but believing she could forge some way of life that would give her the ordinary love she wanted, as a woman and a wife and a mother – and allow him to go free as the wind.'

It was strange to hear his father and mother discussed like this, as though they were living neighbours whose strange problems had become a source of common wonder. His grandfather said: 'She thought love would find a way. It didn't, though the love was deep on both sides. He disappeared one night in Peshawar. He had to go.'

His voice had been fading, and Peter stood up. 'He had to go.' Why had his grandfather talked about his missing, disappeared father? It had not had the air of a senile anecdote, without point. Did he imply that Emily also felt she had to go? Peter didn't think so. It was himself who had been 'going' in that sense – on and up and out, impatient of ties, except those with people whom he needed or who would go as fast and as far as he. Then – was the old man asking: 'Do you have to go on the way you have been going?' Was he pointing out that he had reached the place his father reached that night in Peshawar? That here he must make up his mind whether his superiority to ordinary men or his kinship with them mattered more to him?

Peter kissed his grandfather on the cheek. When you had done something like that since you were two, it didn't come easily to change the habit. The old man said: 'I think you'd better go and find her, Peter.'

Peter told Ashraf not to come down the stairs, and let himself out into the street. It was dark, and it took a long time to find a taxi. When he found one: 'Green Mansion Hotel,' he said.

The driver looked round at him with a wink. 'That's the stuff, mister, after what you been through – a little fling, eh?' Peter remembered that the G.M had quite a sordid reputation, but no other name came into his mind.

They looked grave at first when he asked for a room, but then the girl glanced at his ribbon and rosette and smiled, and it was all right. He went up, bathed, changed into a clean tunic, and rang for the waiter to bring him up a bottle of whisky and some soda. It was stuffy in there, the air-raid curtains drawn and the traffic in Piccadilly a dull roar, throbbing through his head.

What next? Was he to go round London, asking: 'Has anyone seen my wife?' Should he go to the police at once? Or try and forget about her and plunge back into the big plans that were waiting for him, confident that one day she would regain her sense of proportion?

The last he dismissed at once. He didn't have

the desire to take great affairs into his hands.

Everything came back to Emily, and her anger at him was hardly relevant, a little misunderstanding that could be brushed aside in a moment's reasoned talk. The formless weariness of the Italian hospitals had taken shape, and the shape was a need for Emily.

The whisky swirled in his glass. Peggy, he thought. Lady Margaret Walsh.

He gulped the rest of the whisky and hurried downstairs. The telephone booth was in the lobby. The telephone girl gave him Peggy's number, and soon he heard the ring-ring at the other end of the line.

She answered the call herself. 'Who's there, please?'

'Peter Savage,' he said.

There was a short pause, then: 'Peter? How nice to know you're back safe.' He gritted his teeth. Then she said what he had been hoping for. 'How's Emily?'

He sighed with relief. Peggy had watched Emily like a hawk all the time she was staying in Rudwal during Harry's 1914 expedition to Meru. She hated Emily, and himself perhaps a little bit more. He was certain that she would have known about it the moment anything untoward happened to either of them, or to their marriage. He had a strong feeling that Peggy would also have found out where Emily had gone. She'd had time.

He said: 'Emily isn't here. Do you know where she is?'

'Not there? What do you mean? Oh, what's the

matter, Peter? Don't say something's happened to her too.'

He fumbled for a cigar and began to light it. Her voice sounded tinny, brittle, and over-solicitous. He said: 'I'm desperate. Please come round.' He wasn't desperate yet but he knew that was the surest way to bring her, offering her the prospect of gloating over his wretchedness. 'I'm at the Green Mansion,' he said.

'Do you think it's all right? I mean, will they let me in?' she asked girlishly. 'I mean, the G.M, and war, and a lone woman, and all that.'

'I'll be standing outside the Albemarle Street entrance,' he said. 'How long will you be?'

'Not more than ten minutes. I'm only just round the corner.'

'I'll be waiting,' he said and hung the receiver carefully on the hook.

Peggy knew. He did not believe Emily had told her. She had taken pains to find out. July 29 was a long time ago now. Today was October 10. The question was, would she tell him, or would she hug her secret through two or three more meetings? He walked out of the main entrance and stood leaning against the wall in the darkness, his cigar burning fitfully.

A bull's-eye of light flashed on him, wandered down his tunic. 'I should keep that cigar low if I was you, sir. In case the sergeant comes round.'

'Thanks, officer, I will,' he said.

The measured footsteps faded. Girls passed, bright eyes closing to his own. He shook his head, and they passed on with a suspicion of a smile. 'Waiting for someone, dearie?' He nodded.

After half an hour Peggy came. He stubbed out the cigar against the wall and threw it in the gutter. She came through the pale fog under a wide hat with a sweeping ostrich feather curled round the brim, and her eyes searching the street, eager for this first triumph of seeing him waiting for her, and Emily gone. He stepped forward and took her arm, and she gave a little scream before she recognized him. 'Oh – Peter, it's you. You gave me such a fright.'

He led her into the lounge. The fog had seeped in there from many openings and closings of the door. Groups of officers, alone and with women, sat drinking in as many small, hazy worlds, and ancient waiters shuffled about with drinks on trays, and Kitchener pointed from the wall: 'Your King and Country need YOU.' She was eyeing him openly as she slowly pulled off her gloves and raised her veil.

'Another D.S.O,' she said. 'How wonderful for you. And we're all so proud of you. You don't look very well, though.'

'Whisky?' he asked abruptly. She nodded.

In the old days a lady would never have drunk whisky in public, and seldom in private, but this was 1915. The old days had gone, crept between the pages of *The Times* and hidden there forever under the casualty lists. Also, Peggy was drinking. She had been for a good many years; not too heavily, but it was beginning to show in her face.

'I saw Uncle George this evening,' she said at last. 'Just after you'd left the house.'

He said: 'Then you knew that Emily had gone.

Why did you pretend to be surprised she wasn't with me?'

She took up her whisky and drank deeply. 'I knew she'd left the house,' she said. 'I thought she might have quarrelled with Uncle George – wanted to be alone. I didn't know what had happened.'

He said: 'For God's sake, Peggy, tell me where she is.'

'Harry's in hospital in Brighton,' she said suddenly. 'A flesh wound, in the leg – shrapnel. Nothing serious, he says. Only he didn't get a medal. He hasn't got any medals yet, though he's been wounded twice and has been out since before Neuve Chapelle.'

'Where has Emily gone?' he cut in harshly. He didn't have to pretend so much now, for he was becoming truly desperate.

Peggy said: 'Emily? Poor Emily. She missed you so much – before you came back in June, I mean. Gerry tried to comfort her while he was in London, but then you came back and took him away. Emily was so afraid for both of you – really for Gerry more than you, I think sometimes. Because she knew you'd come out all right. I knew that. Everyone knew that. Even Gerry knew, at the end, didn't he?' She drank again, and he signalled to the waiter to refill her glass. This would be her third, and her tight control was going.

He said: 'You know what Gerry meant to me.'

'Oh yes, yes,' she said. 'That's what makes it all so awful, for everyone.'

'Where's Emily?'

'Lonely,' Peggy said. 'I'm sure she's lonely, whatever she said. Did she tell you she didn't want to see you ever again?'

'Where is she?'

'And that it was no use your trying to find her? It isn't, either, even if you use the police, because those Welsh people are so devoted, and they wouldn't give her away to the police or anyone else if she asked them not to.'

He kept silent until, from waiting for him to renew his pleading, she realized that he wasn't going to. Her eyes came slowly round, and he held them. He got them tight and leaned forward, as he had a hundred times before in the old days when he was going to do something and wanted to let them all know that nothing would stop him.

He said: 'Peggy, if you don't tell me where Emily is I am going to walk out of this hotel, now, and report to the War Office. By tomorrow night I'll be out of the country. You won't ever see me again. There'll be no more gloating, because I won't make any other attempt to find Emily. It will all be over. You don't want that.'

He didn't mean what he said, but this was perhaps the first time in Peggy's experience that that had been so. She believed him. Simultaneously, her concentration dispersed by the whisky, she realized what had happened to her, that his last statement should be true. She didn't want his and Emily's unhappiness to be resolved, because her hatred of them meant more to her than any love. This she realized, and of this she realized the bitter ugliness. Her puffy face dissolved, and she stood up suddenly. 'Did Gerry die quickly?'

He stood up with her, facing her across the glass-cluttered table. 'Instantly,' he said.

'Was he happy? He should have been. *"Dulce et decorum est–"* And Gerry was a gentleman, you know.'

He said: 'No. He wasn't happy.'

'Why?'

'I don't know.'

She lowered her veil and said: 'Perhaps he had learned he had an incurable disease. Perhaps Emily found she was going to get it – or the children – if she didn't run away. Peter Savageitis.'

He said: 'Good-bye, Peggy.'

She said: 'Wait. She's at Gaerwen cottage. It's in Merionethshire, at the head of Cwm Bychan' – she pulled on her gloves – 'but I'm sure you'd do better to go to the War Office.'

CHAPTER 26

In the train he had studied the map and found the lane marked on it. There were two ways to it: up from Llanbedr or Harlech, on a country road which would take wheeled traffic as far as the farm below Cwm Bychan; or by a footpath from Trawsfynydd, over the mountains to the east, and then down on the cottage by the old Roman Steps. He had decided to come this latter way, fearing that word would be sent ahead of him if he came through Llanbedr.

The journey from London to Trawsfynydd was long and slow, but once he got out of the train and could stretch his legs some of his morbid anticipation fell away. The Welsh hills rolled higher around him, and on the eastern slope it was a fresh October day. On the tops ahead the rain-clouds hung low, and only a shepherd and his sheep were there, huddled together under a wall. Peter climbed steadily up the old footpath, treading in the footsteps of Druids and Roman soldiers and English bowmen.

At the top the path entered a defile, so sharp that it appeared to be man-made between the rocks, and then swung down the hill among bracken and heather and the twisted roots of small trees and slabs of stone lying every way on the hill-side. Here there were paving stones set on the mountain, some broken, some still dovetailed as closely together as when the Druids had put them there, the outer edges now worn smooth and the centres hollowed and shallow with rain.

After three hours he came to the valley floor of Cwm Bychan, passed the old farmhouse at the head, and swung down the road. Now it was close. The road ran between a low rise of rock and a black lake. The map showed that the cottage lay behind the rise, and a short lane led to it from this narrow road, a hundred yards farther on. A mist from the sea swirled in irregular patches about the valley and over the lake, and suddenly he came upon her – walking towards him, a basket over her arm.

She stopped and stepped back. He went forward slowly, his hands out. She clasped her hands behind her back, and he felt his face hardening and determination welling up. He *would* take her back – but that was the voice of the Peter Savage she was running away from.

He said: 'Emily.'

'Why do you have to be so dramatic?' she cried. 'Striding out of the mountains with mist all over your clothes, looking like the devil?'

'I thought you would be told if I came from Llanbedr,' he said. 'I came from Trawsfynydd.'

'That's a long way. Who told you I was here? Daddy? Your grandfather? No, he wouldn't.'

'Peggy.'

She said: 'Yes, she would. You are as clever as you used to be. Now go back the way you came.'

'I'm not going back till I know what's happened,' he said.

'What has happened?' she said slowly. 'Nothing's *happened*. I just found out that you're a murderer, a real cold murderer. I've always known you would lead men to their deaths for something you thought worth while. I didn't like it, but it was a part of you. I was fool enough to think I could have the excitement and hold that in check, that we'd perhaps find some way of life together that would replace it, or turn it to good use. But – a murderer–'

The water of the lake hung suspended, like a wavering curtain of slate and ebony, on his left hand. The little hill rose steeply in broken rock and tufted grass on his right. The soft Welsh wind blew the mist about them so that they were in a private place, there in the middle of the road.

He said: 'I – I didn't mean to harm Gerry.'

She said: 'A liar, too? Did you tell him before you shot him? Or did you shoot him in the back? You kept him waiting till the very last possible moment, though, didn't you? Wouldn't it have been more efficient, more typical, to have pushed him off the Channel steamer the night you left England? Weren't you afraid, at all, that he might shoot *you*? I suppose he must have carried a loaded pistol all the time – but you would be sure he wouldn't do that. *You* hadn't done anything a gentleman must expect to be punished for.'

He sat down slowly on a rock, because his legs were weak. This was the avalanche that had presaged its coming as soon as Harvey opened the front door of 27 Minden Square to him two days ago.

For a moment Emily's terrible certainty, the

403

sheer loathing in her face, made him believe that he had actually shot Gerry. It must have been Gerry's chest that he had centred in the sights of the carbine that dawn on Monte Michele. He had been so exhausted, his eyes so blurred, that it was possible.

With a tremendous effort he forced that picture out of his mind. It was the Austrian corporal he had shot. He said: 'I didn't kill Gerry, Emily. I didn't shoot him,' he added, because he knew that in another sense he had broken and then killed Gerry. This, he realized, was the cause of his desperate need to find Emily. He had to ask her to shrive him, so that they could start again – this time he following her, to find the place of peace that she had often tried to tell him about.

She was looking into his face with a new anxiety, for he had never lied to her. She said suddenly: 'Tell me.'

He told her, only of those last seconds on Monte Michele. When he had finished, and after she had held her hand to her eyes for a little while, she said: 'I had made sure you had shot Gerry. I *knew* it.' She spoke wearily, and quietly, as though to herself.

'*Why* should you think so?' he burst out passionately. 'By God, what have I done to you that you should jump to that conclusion?'

She looked at him carefully. 'I suppose I wanted to,' she said at last. 'It was nothing that you had done. But it doesn't matter now. I believe you, but I don't need to think you're a common murderer to get the strength to tell you to go. Now go, go, for God's *sake* go, Peter!'

'Why should you not believe me?' he cried. 'Why should you believe, without even asking me, without waiting to speak to me, that I would kill my best friend deliberately, by shooting him in the back?'

She grabbed his arm. 'You know, damn you! Do you think I'm going to believe Peggy didn't tell you?'

He said: 'Emily, I don't know what you are talking about.'

She looked at him again, that look of careful study. But still it was true – he had never lied to her. She unfastened the cloak that had been billowing and flapping about her, and he saw that she was newly pregnant. She said: 'Gerry's.'

He held his breath. This was the full force of the avalanche. He was under it, and also above it, watching himself go down and round and over and over inside the snow, now coming up to catch air, now being struck by the rocks and trees embedded in the falling snow. He thought: Any man must feel some jealousy when he learns that his wife has lain with another man. Any man must suffer a wound to his pride. He felt the jealousy and the wound, but they were smothered in the enormity of realizing, feeling in himself, what pressure must have made Gerry and Emily do it. As soon as the opened cloak revealed the swelling of her body and she said 'Gerry's,' he knew why she had done it.

Emily said: 'So *I* killed him, really, didn't I? Trying to save him.'

Peter shook his head. 'Will you take me back?' he asked her humbly.

She hesitated a fraction of a second before answering: 'No. I'm afraid of you now, Peter. Because of you I did this. Do you think I don't feel soiled and ashamed all the time? What might you make me do next? Will I find myself one night, at midnight, bending over Rodney's bed to kill him because I have seen that he is going to be his father's son?'

He stood looking into the lake. The mist was rolling back, and it was an October evening. His eyes were dim with tears for the first time he could remember. His wife stood before him, and he loved her. But the avalanche had at last come to rest, and there he lay, revealed for what he was. Whatever he loved, he must conquer. Whoever followed him, he destroyed. Grandfather's warning came to him. *Do you have to go?*

No, he didn't, but he had discovered it too late, when he had already succeeded, by unparalleled strength and daemonic courage, in shattering the only people who could have led him towards peace.

The ruins stretched as far as his eye could see in every direction. His children? – he dared not go near them for what he might influence them to become. Emily? – he had made her an adulteress and self-accused accomplice in murder. Rudwal? – every action he took there would lead to glory for him and bitter despair for others.

'What are you going to do?' Emily asked almost conversationally.

He thought as matter-of-factly of that problem. Suicide was no sort of answer to this. Even in

death he'd fill the headlines, sadden Grandfather's quiet dusk, leave a stain of rumour on his
own children and the one yet to be born. By
God, by the steely lake there he could at last
smell what must have been stinking in their
nostrils for years past, the odour of death that
hung around him.

'Let me see the children,' he said.

They walked together down the road, turned
up the lane, and came to the cottage. An angular
middle-aged woman opened the door and stared
grimly at him. He recognized her as Alice.

Rodney was playing on the floor, an oil lamp on
the table above him – and outside the dusk
falling fast across the tarn of Cwm Bychan. The
boy recognized him and jumped up with a shout.
'Daddy, Da-a-a-addy!' Peter kissed him once and
then put him down, for fear. Elizabeth came out
of the tiny kitchen and ran to her mother, eyeing
him with distrust. Rodney wanted to know where
he had been, and how many men he had killed.
Elizabeth came to him slowly, of her own accord,
and he held her at his knee for a time and then
got up.

It was time to go. He said: 'Have you got any
men's clothes here that would fit me?'

'Yes,' she said, 'a suitcase of yours. I didn't
mean to bring it. It came by mistake. What are
you going to do?'

'It doesn't matter. Only if anyone comes
looking for me, don't tell them about the clothes.
Where's the suitcase?'

'Upstairs. I'll show you.' He followed her to the
narrow bedroom at the head of the stairs. He

opened the case and found, among other things, an old tweed suit he had worn a lot in Zermatt in '09. Emily went downstairs, and he changed quickly. Emily's wounds were so deep that he wondered whether she would ever recover from them, even if she never thought of him again. All the quickness and warmth of her response to life had gone. He carried his uniform downstairs. She was sitting in an old kitchen chair by the fire. He began to throw the uniform on the fire, piece by piece. 'Take the buttons and metal bits out and bury them tomorrow,' he said.

She said she would.

'What are you going to do?' he asked her when he was ready.

'Stay here till the baby is born. After that – I don't know.'

That was the cruellest moment. He knew that he could keep her. He could take her round the waist, and his arms were strong. He could say: 'It's all right. I love you. I loved Gerry and I'll love his baby. We'll start again.'

But he was not David, but Cain.

He stood away, when he had got control of himself, and said: 'I won't tell you where I'm going, in case you change your mind. Good-bye, darling.'

He swung quickly out of the door before the need to throw himself into her arms overcame him. He ran for a mile down the Llanbedr road and then, his breath still coming easily, settled down to a driving, punishing walking pace that would leave him thoroughly exhausted by the time he reached the village and the railway.

He knew what he was going to do. He was going to join the New Armies as a private soldier of infantry. It was as deep, as anonymous a place as he could think of, and no one would think to look for him there. There, in the universal slime of the trenches, he would be made to feel kinship and renounce leadership. There he would be helpless in the power of others, as so many had been helpless in his. He would learn what Emily and Gerry had learned, and suffer as they had suffered in learning it. Above all, he would never influence a soul again, for good or evil.

CHAPTER 27

There was a rat. It moved slowly through the deep shadows of the corner of the barn where he lay. They were used to the darkness in there now, after a day of waiting, no one knew why, so that the single strong bar of July sunlight pouring through a wall where a shell had torn a long, narrow hole hurt his eyes. The rat was not afraid of any of them. It seemed to know that they were in no mood to hurt it now, and if they tried it could easily escape through the missing lath or under the pile of sour straw. The guns were shouting and booming all the time, but the men hardly heard them.

On the other side, near the place where the door of the barn had been, a dozen men of the platoon lay in a circle and played cards. Their rifles and bulging packs were stacked in a rough row along the wall there – entrenching tools, water-bottles, grenades in festoons hanging on to the dust-soiled equipment, ammunition pouches bulging square and hard-edged with the fullness of the sharp-pointed brass cartridge cases and nickel-nosed bullets inside, rolled blankets, greatcoats. When they put all that on they lost resemblance to human beings. They would do that soon, and crawl east along the wide, empty road, past the rubbled houses and the inn sign where no inn stood. The eyes would flicker under the steel bowls of the helmets – eyes of automata, men with no reality and no difference between them, in spite of the identity discs round each neck; 10948475 Smith, W, C of E, the one they had allotted him said.

It was July 1916, and he had been William Smith for eight months. It was a name, but he had prevented it from becoming clothed in any personality. The recruiting officer looked sharply at him when he reached the barracks with the rest of them picked up there in Birmingham, but he asked no questions. There was a war on.

'Fall in for inspection!' The platoon sergeant was at the door of the barn, his rifle on his shoulder.

'What's the matter, Sar'nt? We going, Sar'nt? We going up now?'

'How the 'ell do I know? Field Marshal 'Aig forgot to tell me. Get fell in. You too, Smith. No packs or equipment, just rifles. You, Williams, stand sentry over the kit.'

They fell in, blinking in the strong sunlight. The sergeant checked them with his platoon roll and stood aside as Second Lieutenant Hardcastle came down the street from the officers' mess, swinging his swagger stick.

He inspected them briefly, making no comments except to compliment Private Freeth on the cleanliness of his rifle, and to berate Private Smith, W, on the dirtiness of his clothes and person. 'Filthy fingernails, Smith. You're the dirtiest man in the platoon. See that they're clean next time I inspect.'

'Yessir,' Peter said automatically.

411

The officer walked out in front of them. 'Stand easy. We're going up the line at dusk to relieve the Lancashires in front of Thiepval. That's over there.' He waved his cane vaguely to the east, where a part of the living earth hovered above the rest in a permanent dark haze. A medium battery behind the village began to fire steadily. The air heaved; the ground shook from the sound of guns north and south down the line. The German guns awoke, and from there too the clamour began, and from far and high steel birds whistled in the blue sky and the starlings rose spiralling from the ragged cornfields and the shattered trees.

'The offensive has been going on for three weeks now,' the officer said, 'and the Huns have had about enough. The general expects them to break any time now – somewhere. We are attacking all the time. *We* shall attack the day after we get into the line, the whole division. Let's see that the Huns break opposite us. Platoon guide to company headquarters at six, Sergeant. Evening meal at five. Platoon, stand at ease! Platoon, 'shun. Slope – arms! Dismiss!'

He returned their salute and walked away. They shuffled back into the barn, leaned their rifles against the wall where they had been, and in a minute there was no difference between this scene and the earlier, except that Freeth was standing beside him in the shadows near the far corner.

'What do you want to be so dirty for, chum?' Freeth said, sitting down. 'Have a fag. I got a packet this morning. Won it off Lofty... It only gets the officer down on you.'

'I haven't noticed you caring much what the officer says or thinks,' Peter said, lighting the cigarette and leaning back against the wall of the barn. Freeth was about five foot four inches high, lean and wiry, about forty years of age. However much they were in the sun, he never sunburned, because his skin was a kind of pale yellow-grey, like parchment, bloodless, the muscles at either side of his neck sticking out in thin cords. He had twenty-two years' service in the regulars, mostly in India.

Freeth said: 'That's different. When you been in the Shiny as long as I have, you know you've got to keep clean if you're going to keep well.' The platoon called him Shiny Freeth because most of his sentences began and ended with India, which he always called the Shiny. He kept himself to himself almost as much as Peter did, and he was the best shot in the platoon. 'Ought to be,' he'd muttered, 'seeing I fired seventeen annual practices in the Shiny and was a marksman every time. Christ, I fired more rounds, snap, from the kneel, than you buggers ever fired in your lives, including Second Ypres.'

'You got to be what you are,' he said now to Peter. 'That's the difference. Hardcastle and Old Taylor, everybody, even that dim corporal, know what *I* am. They all know what you are too, same as you and I do. That's why you can't do the same things the rest of us do.'

'I'm the same as anyone else,' Peter said.

'You're an officer,' Freeth said. 'We don't know what you did, but you're a gent. Maybe you been

413

to jail. Most of the fellows think so, but I don't…
No, I don't want to know, one way or t'other, see?
I'm just telling you what everyone thinks. *I* don't
think you've been to the Moor or the Villa or any
other civvy glass-house. But you been to the
Shiny, eh?'

Peter said: 'Have it your own way.'

Freeth said: 'You was a young officer, and you
did something, so they court martialled you, eh?
It doesn't matter. What does matter is you aren't
being what you are. You been with us four
months now. Look at you, always sitting back in
the dark corners with the rats. It's no good trying
to hide, because you stick out more. See? If you
want to be let be, act more natural, see?'

He got up and wandered off to the card-
players, his stub of cigarette hanging from his
lower lip, his steel helmet on the back of his head,
and his shirt unbuttoned to the navel; but his
puttees lay in tight, neat spirals round his legs, his
boots shone, and the rifle against the wall was
bright-clean and slightly-oiled.

Peter lit another cigarette. He didn't like them,
but of course he couldn't smoke cigars. Freeth
didn't understand. If he acted naturally, someone
would suffer. The officers knew there was something strange about him, for sure, but he wasn't
the only one, even in this battalion of the New
Armies. There was Henderson in B Company, a
professor if ever he saw one; and Maurice, also in
B, who raved in his sleep of Sandhurst, so they
said; but they were not dangerous, except to
themselves.

The sun sank lower, the glorious July day wore

414

to its end. The cigarette smoke faded as the evening light turned to an equivalent blue, and a bugle sounded from the far end of the village street. The war began to stir its limbs. In the woods behind the village big trucks came slowly to life with a roar of engines. Horses went down to the filthy stream to be watered. Ten shells burst in a field a quarter of a mile away. More and more men, loaded with the full accoutrements of war, trudged up the road, always on the verge, as far as they could get from the middle, where the dead horses lay with legs up. Motor cycles blared westward, and there were two pigeons making love in the dust.

It was dark, and they had eaten and were moving up in fours on the road – a long, slow step at first, no sound in the ranks but the creak of the equipment, the slung rifles swinging and they breathing hard, the road soft as powder under the nailed boots. No one sang, because they were going into the Battle of the Somme, and they knew what they were going towards. They had been there before, except for the new drafts from England. Peter had been there. It was unbelievable, worse than anything the mind could conjure up. The dead lay not in drifts, not in piles, but in acres like wheat. The earth was not torn but dug down to its foundations, thrown into the sky and allowed to fall, all of it, with the men underneath and the birds under the men, and, lowest of all, trees; on top, worms and steel which should have lived deep but now glittered in the surface water. Yes, they'd dug up water in a dry place with their shells and made stinking ponds in the desert. None of that was the worst. The worst was what he had come to seek, and had found – utter helplessness. There was no room for thoughts of gallantry, fear, or cowardice, because no man had any room for choice. There was no leadership, because everyone had to go. No place to say, I will do this, not that; only the parapet, and beyond it the crawling earth, the rusty jungles of wire that ran across France. There was no room to deviate an inch to right or left, forward or back. The orders came, and they went or stayed. The machine-gun sang in the night, and where it stopped on a swinging traverse, and whether it swung to the right or the left, no man knew – or could avoid it if he did know.

This was the war Harry Walsh had been in for nearly eighteen months now. How could he stand it? Harry was a brave man, and in his own way a leader, but this must be more harrowing to him even than Peter's old kind of leadership had been. How could Harry reconcile this with his care 'for the safety of all concerned'? No one had imagined anything like this – not even he, Peter, when he talked of 'at all costs.' A man would have to be very low-keyed to be able to come out of this as he went in, and Harry was not low-keyed. He had control, that was all; but how long could a man hold control of himself in this? It was something Peter waited, still numb, to find out about himself.

He acknowledged with a small burst of pleasure that he was frightened. The steel was frightening, and the night's silence under the artillery, and the men marching silent up the road, the slow river of men moving up like rats to the trenches ahead. They stood bowed in the ditch, bowed under great weight, as another river passed by the other way – men on stretchers here, hundreds of them, on carts, on their feet, the bandages dim in that gloom, universal groaning while the night birds flew on muffled wings overhead and the steel sang higher in the sky and the fitful bursts of the shells ahead came closer while they watched and waited.

'It'll all be the same in a 'undred years,' the platoon funny man muttered.

'I wish it was a hundred years now, then,' someone else answered.

'Quiet there,' the officer whispered furiously.

Oh, this was anonymity! Darkness, and the men moving, waiting, moving, strong and helpless as the tide. They moved on and came close.

Bang! – then the short sharp bang-bang-bang and the whining of the steel birds. '****, they got me. I got it, Gerry.' No, another Gerry. 'In the leg – oh, ****, ****!'

'Keep moving' – the officer's voice. 'It's only harassing fire.'

Only harassing fire. That was it. German whizzbangs firing from somewhere behind the enemy support line, less than a mile and a half from here. No, they'd seen nothing, but they knew that this was the last stretch of road before the communication trenches began. They were ranged in on it, and let off at intervals during the night, any night – *bang-bang-bang*.

'I don't like this.'

'Keep your **** head down,' Freeth muttered. 'Keep moving. I don't want to stand here and get my balls shot off.'

They fell into the communication trench and shuffled on in single file. The sky was lazy with the curve of star shells; the artillery grumbled around them now, for there were guns ahead and guns behind, but it was a peaceful night in France until the machine-guns opened up, and then the bullets rattled harshly with a personal hate overhead. 'Over,' Freeth muttered.

They reached the front line at last, and the Lancashires stood back. ''Ere y'ar, choom, there's your 'ole. You'll find it a little wet in t'rain, but us can't hov fairy queens for fourpence, can us?' He was gone, and Freeth muttering: 'All very well for him to be hearty, he's going **** back.'

'Smith 'seventy-five, Freeth, sentry till eleven. Here's the chart. Left front, a shell hole, twenty yards beyond the wire. There's a dead German in it, his legs sticking up like a semaphore, and some silly **** put one of our steel helmets on it, so every sniper down the line likes to see if he can make the **** ring. Another hole fifty yards out, half-right, that's empty except for some gas shells that didn't explode and of course about a hundred corpses of fellows who jumped in when machine-guns opened on them and didn't know Jerry has a mortar ranged so **** well on it that the first bomb falls right in the **** eye of the silly **** sheltering in there.'

'*Thik hai*, Corpril.'

The platoon lay down in the foot of the trench, on the fire-step, in the holes scooped out of the

418

back wall. Peter leaned against the front wall, looking at the night. Boots and arms stuck out of the earth beside him. The whole trench was dug out of bodies, and riveted with bodies.

'This ain't war,' Freeth muttered. 'This is ★★★★ madness. It's not right. Twenty-two years' service I got, and look.' He lifted his foot, and, looking down in the dim moonlight, Peter saw that he was standing on a platform of bodies, mixed British and German. 'This is to keep my feet out of the mud,' Freeth said. 'It ain't right.'

No, it wasn't right. Against all the traditions of war – and of mountaineering.

The night passed. The day began, silent, with summer rain slanting down on the trenches and occasionally gleaming on a German helmet as a man moved along the trench opposite, the other side of the tangled thickets of wire. The attack was postponed twenty-four hours. At two o'clock the next morning the bombardment began, designed to cut the enemy wire. That lasted three hours – three hours more than the month it had already lasted. At four o'clock the engineers went out to cut and mark the gaps in their own wire for the British to go through.

Peter slept fitfully, thinking of Emily and of Gerry, until they awakened and gave him hot cocoa and a double tot of rum and a pair of hard biscuits. C Company came up to relieve the sentry posts. The wire snipped and the guns deafened and the earth roared and flashed, and down in the mud the men were playing cards, drinking rum, begging for another tot. Thunder-thunder-thunder the war shouted in his ear, but still impersonally. Second Lieutenant Hardcastle's face was anxious. He was sharp-nosed and eager, a good young man. The whistle was in his mouth; the voice of the guns became a shriek as they propped the ladders in place and climbed up and over.

Instantly, though nothing was silent, only the machine-guns had a voice for Peter. The field guns lifted and yet made as much noise as ever; the heavy guns were firing on the support trenches not two hundred yards ahead; the German guns opened up, and a fury of shells burst above the front line and among them, but in his ears only the enemy spoke, and the enemy was the machine-guns. He forced through the wire, moved five paces to his left, and began to advance slowly, his rifle held across his body and the bayonet fixed. The scythe of a machine-gun to the left reached out towards him and swung back. Hardcastle was dead, or gone, already. He walked slowly on.

He wanted to run. Now was the worst time. Now was the time to break into a run and bear down on them over there, screaming, the bayonet low and long and searching in front. Now one man could lift a hundred beyond fear and fatigue, so that they'd forget the leaden feet and the machine-gun.

But no, now, deep in the tide of death, he would flow with it, no faster, no slower. A man to his right pitched forward silently.

The sergeant beyond him was shouting, but no one could hear. The sergeant fell flat on his belly. Dead too? No, he'd found that the German wire was uncut. The Germans were twenty yards away, helmets and faces peering over the wire. Peter fumbled for grenades and began to throw carefully while the sergeant tried to cut the wire. The Germans shot him, and the long wire-cutters in his hand fell down in the noise, and Peter could not see them. The machine-gun scythes hissed back and forth, like slowly torn canvas.

He found the wire-cutters, ran back, and jumped into a shell hole, falling in sideways as two machine-gun arcs from opposite directions met overhead. There were twelve men in the shell hole already, besides the uncountable dead who lay among the rotting seed potatoes and rusted steel. The attack had died away, and no one was moving. Smoke drifted across the crater, obscuring the pale sky, and a lance corporal said: 'That's to let us get back. Quick, for Christ's sake! Up and run for it, while the smoke's here.'

'I'll shoot you if you do,' a lieutenant said. He was from another regiment altogether, and Peter didn't know how he'd got there with them. 'That's for the support waves to get over the top and cut the wire,' the lieutenant said angrily. 'Stay here until they get this far, and then up and join them.'

The shelling increased, and every now and then a shell or a mortar bomb dropped into the crater, usually killing or wounding someone among them. As though to replenish the stock, half a dozen more men fell in on them from the second wave of the assault, most of them Bristols. Now they had two corporals and a sergeant, but the lieutenant had been hit on the helmet and was singing and muttering to himself as he lay on his side in the bottom of the crater. It was about six o'clock in the morning.

Helplessly pinned down in a hole in the ground with ten frightened strangers, Peter thought. This was what he'd been looking for.

Every now and then during the following hours he crawled up the side of the crater and peered over the top. The German wire was about thirty yards away, lying in mountainous coils, torn and piled so that it was impossible to tell where or whether there was a gap. Smoke drifted across the churned soil, yellow from cordite, black, grey, green, a thin multi-coloured pall. There were no men in sight, nothing moving as, in this billionth year since the slime, man knew movement – only a crawling here and there where maimed things raised an arm; or a headless, legless, armless trunk rolled down a slope to the near burst of a shell. The sun wheeled across the sky, the guns crashed, and the sky held curious streaks and bars of colour and single points of light. When all other sounds hushed for a moment, the master devils of both sides sat back above the thick barrels, and the machine-guns recited long monologues over the dead and the dying.

Yet, in the wire, every time he looked, he thought there might be a place, directly in front, where a man could get through. He'd wait. If they were to advance again in the night, that was the place to head for. One of the corporals was dragging himself round telling them to get ready to go back as soon as it was dusk. The lieutenant nodded vaguely and pointed to the Germans.

'Back,' he said. 'Yes, we've got to go back.' The corporal could not make him understand that that was not back but forward, and after a time gave up because the lieutenant began to abuse him.

Night dropped slowly on them, and with it the light grew stronger, for now more flashes prickled along the low horizons and the guns on both sides were firing star shells. When it was full dark a sergeant said: 'Go back now, in twos and threes.'

'What's the password?' somebody mumbled.

'I don't know. It was "Piccadilly" yesterday.'

A salvo of German mortar bombs burst a few yards outside the lip of the crater. The lieutenant said: 'Ready, everyone, time to go back,' and climbed the opposite lip, towards the Germans.

'Not that way, sir! Stop him, someone, for Christ's sake. You!' The sergeant pointed at Peter. 'Pull him back. Hit him.'

A wall of men loomed up from the direction of the British trenches. The German machine-guns opened up all along the line; for miles to north and south the long golden streams of machine-gun bullets howled and screamed across the earth.

'Jesus Christ,' the corporal muttered. 'What the hell's going on now?'

Three men dropped into the crater. 'Get moving,' one shouted. 'Get on, we're attacking.'

'Again?' the sergeant yelled. 'We've been here all day without food or water.'

'Get moving,' the man screamed, pushing his rifle forward.

'That's it, back,' the lieutenant said, and scrambled out towards the Germans.

A shell burst in the crater, and Peter seemed to be the only man left unwounded.

Peering out to right and left, he saw the dim shapes of the infantry crawling forward like prehistoric animals, lit by the stuttering flash of the star shells. The machine-guns scythed them down, and even as he watched he saw the attack grinding to a standstill as so many had before. It was like a tide creeping up a beach, fated to get only so far and then to recede, leaving a rotting mess at the farthest point. He felt physically sick at the sight of the slaughter. He could not bear to watch, for there was nothing he could do.

But there was that gap in the German wire directly in front of him and only thirty yards away. More men were jumping into the crater as the new attack died away. He couldn't tell how many there were – ten, fifteen, perhaps, with rifles and bombs and bayonets ready.

Something *could* be done, and he could do it. The taste of hunger and thirst was sour in his mouth, and the smell of death clung to his clothes. The lieutenant with concussion had come back, from God knew where.

Peter grabbed his arm and shouted: 'There's a gap in our wire that way, sir, that way.' The poor devil was off his head, but for the moment Peter had to have his rank to get the rest of the men moving. The lieutenant whipped round on the rest of them and shouted: 'Come on!'

'Come on!' Peter yelled, and started up the side of the crater after the lieutenant. He'd go on by himself, if need be. But they'd follow. They were only stunned and frightened and could be lifted out of it, turned into demons. He shouted once more, and then he was over the lip of the crater and running towards the orange-tendrilled jungle of wire ahead. He glanced once over his shoulder and saw that two, three men were following him, and another head had appeared, lividly pale, startled by its own temerity in the burst of a star shell. He turned and saw an astonished German sentry and shot him dead. The lieutenant was dead in his path. Peter threw himself down, the wire-cutters in his hand. Men were beside and behind him. 'You,' he shouted. 'Keep their heads down with grenades. Slow! Right into the trench! You, you, shoot at anything that moves. Keep their heads down. I don't need more than a minute.'

They began firing and throwing, while in Peter's hands the wire-cutters snipped and the wire sprang back and he crawled on towards the enemy.

CHAPTER 28

Almost at once it began to rain. In the Alps, in Asia, the rain would have meant protection for fighting men who walked on silent feet with the long knives to kill in their hands, but here on the Western Front silence had gone, like the birds and the girls from the fields, and the rain meant only misery. The long handles of the wire-cutters kicked sharply once in his hands, and he knew that they had been hit in the dark by a bullet or splinter of steel. But he was untouched, and behind him the rain shone on the steel helmets.

The last strands of wire sprang apart with a humming of violin purity. He jumped to his feet, shouting: 'Follow me, lads!' The bayonet ran like an oriflamme in front of him, and his lungs were full of shrieking power. He came to the parapet of the enemy's trench and went eight feet straight down, the bayonet point leading, down through a man's neck just below the curved rim of his helmet, and out under the opposite armpit.

But he was not fighting mad, and it was a deliberate stroke. At any other time it would have been wasteful – three inches was enough – but *now* was different, with the eyes of a half-dozen men in field grey hypnotized on to him. *They* weren't wounded. Nothing of the weeks-long bombardment had harmed them, and if he was to go forward now he had first to break their will.

He stared at them while he lifted the corpse on his bayonet and with a short jerk threw it off at their feet. They raised their hands slowly, never taking their eyes off him.

A rifle cracked in his ear, and one of the surrendered Germans fell, shrieking, his hands to his stomach. Peter wheeled round and slammed the butt of his rifle into Freeth's jaw. 'Do you want all the **** to fight for their lives?' he screamed. 'Get on round the corner. No, that way, bombs first.'

Freeth scrambled to his feet, mouthing: 'Yes, sir,' and spitting teeth into the mud. Peter didn't know where he'd come from. A soldier dragged the pin from a grenade with his teeth and drooped it over the traverse. Freeth shouted: 'One, two, three, *four.*' They charged round the traverse as the grenade exploded. More British soldiers tumbled into the trench. Peter stood upright under the rain. Fierce stars gleamed over the battlefield, glaring, falling, dying in the rain. 'This way, that way, this way, that way,' he shouted, and sent the men running out from him to left and right. To the left the bombs receded along the trench. To the right, where Freeth had gone, they stayed close. Three traverses they'd made, no more. There was no way of telling in which direction lay the nearest communication trench leading to the rear. He grabbed a man's shoulder and bellowed: 'Stay here. Send everyone who comes left, that way!'

'Yazzur,' the man bellowed, and touched his finger to the rim of his gleaming helmet in a farmer's-boy gesture. He had a red farmer's-boy

427

face, and rain and blood streaming down his scratched cheeks.

Peter ran right, found Freeth, and told him to keep trying but he'd get no reinforcements. 'Yessir,' Freeth said.

Peter ran back, past the farmer's boy, and on. Steadily in front of him the bombing receded – *crash!* One, two, three, four, *crash* cra-cra-cra-sh! a series of vivid half-subterranean orange flashes, then the yells and screams. He came up with the front of the rush. They were flowing on like a white-hot river, there were dead men and wet, torn faces underfoot, and Germans staring dully, hands up, at the khaki running, shouldering past.

A trench passage opened up in the right-hand wall. This was it, the communication trench for this sector. The river stopped, eddied, wondering what to do. 'Grenades!' Peter yelled. 'Give me grenades, for *** sake!' Hands pressed three into his hands. He put two in his pocket, wrenched the pin out of the third, and lobbed it over the first traverse in the communication trench. Count four – follow the explosion, bayonet first, and everyone pushing and running behind him. Faster they went, and filled with a kind of ecstasy because they had made a revolution and overthrown the sovereigns of the battlefield, for the machine-guns were quiet on the parapet, and the gunners had become mortal, throats gashed behind the guns, or slumped over them, or fallen half-way back, faces staring at the rain, or standing, like ordinary men, their hands raised.

They cleared the communication trench and burst into the support trench. Peter stood aside to let the flood pass. They were going strong now, with pressure behind. It was safer in the maze of trenches than out on the swept battlefield where the shells still thundered without cease. From the point of his original entry a maelstrom of men was pouring into the German trenches, fanning out both ways, down the communication trench, right and left along the support trench.

They had momentum for a few minutes. He must think. What next? Where now to direct this torrent of confused courage, and its bombs and bayonets? There'd be another support trench ahead, a reserve line; and a communication trench leading to it. But on the right, where Freeth was, they were held up in the front line. If this were an organized battle, like the ones they'd taught him at Manali, he'd do better to lead on, knifing deeper in a straight line, as far as the mortar positions certainly, perhaps to the field guns. Then reserves would pour through behind him, and the Germans on the flanks would be shot up from the rear and both sides. They'd pull back, the British eating away the sides of the breach as the sea eats sand. But it wasn't like that. Perhaps no battle was like that. At any moment the Germans might pinch shut that gap behind him, by counter-attacking inward along the front-line trench.

He decided to feint forward, to keep the enemy reserves engaged, but to press his own attack sideways. He would roll the Germans back along the trenches so that the gap would be wide but not deep. It would be easier to reinforce and hold if no preparations had been made for a big advance. There were a dozen men round him now, and in the light of a star shell he saw a sergeant's stripes.

'Six Platoon, Forty-third Kents, sir,' the sergeant shouted.

Peter told him to push on, not more than two hundred yards, keep the enemy busy, and prevent reinforcements from coming forward. 'Right, sir!' The sergeant scrambled up the back of the trench, followed by his men, and they all vanished into the rain. More men appeared. He saw a single cloth star and a young, eager face.

'Second Lieutenant Gale,' the man said. 'F.O.O with the Fusiliers, sir. I've lost them. I'd better stick with you.' The young man was peering at his shoulders, puzzled at finding no rank badges, because Peter was obviously in command here.

F.O.O. That meant Forward Observation Officer. These were the young men who had wires to the guns. Yes, there was a signaller beside him, and the wire trailing back along the trench. 'Did you hear what I told that sergeant of the Kents to do?' Peter said.

'Yes, sir.'

'Be ready to support him on front and flanks.'

'Yes, sir.'

Freeth was there, his jaw sagging where the rifle butt had hit him, and a sly grin on his twisted face. 'We're all here, Major Smith, sir,' he said. 'I handed over that front trench to some fellows in the Kents.'

Peter collected them, found a lieutenant, and sent them along the trench to the right. They ran into a pocket of undemoralized Germans on the other side of the second traverse, and he went to get them started. For a few seconds grenades fell like rain, and everyone in the leading bay was wounded, including himself. A splinter took a piece out of his cheek, and he bled heavily. Then they were through, and all the Germans dead, and he left the lieutenant in command and returned to his post, where the communication trench led from the front to the support trench.

The hours passed like grenades, whirling through the night, falling leaden as mortar shells from the sky, dying in the aftermath of the endless explosions. Twelve o'clock, one o'clock, two o'clock, three... He led half a dozen attacks, pushed back half a dozen German counter-attacks. The artillery subaltern was like a faithful sheep-dog at his heels. That was a capable, brave young man, risking his life all the time, quick and accurate with his orders, skilled and unhurried. Every time trouble threatened, within seconds shells began to burst – crump, crump, boom – all along the place where the counter-attack was forming or among the Germans advancing from their reserve lines.

In the captured trenches there were the beginnings of order and shape. Men stumbled up and down, calling for the Kents, the Fusiliers, the Staffords. God knows how many men were in the captured lines – perhaps a hundred and fifty, and Peter had several sergeants and at least three infantry officers among them, and Freeth calling him Major and muttering: 'Did you ever see British trenches as good made as these bastards?'

An hour before first light a lieutenant-colonel and a captain appeared, looking fairly fresh, followed by a lot of soldiers loaded down with bright new grenades and full ammunition pouches.

'I'm Jennings, commanding the Second Glasgow Rifles,' the colonel said. 'And this is Taliaferro, the battery commander supporting me. I have orders from division to take over this sector and consolidate. You're in command here, aren't you, er–?'

'Smith, sir,' Peter said. He leaned back against the wall of the trench and fumbled for his water-bottle. All the fatigue he hadn't felt during the night now reached him.

The young artillery officer said: 'Yes, sir, Major Smith's in command.'

The Glasgow colonel said: 'No one seems to know what's been happening up here. Your fellows seem to have put up a good show.' He peered at Peter, worried, like young Gale, because he couldn't see any rank badges.

'Thanks,' Peter said. 'Freeth, tell everyone to get back to our front line, quick. It'll be dawn in less than an hour, and then–'

Freeth said: 'Yessir,' saluted smartly, and ran off along the trench.

'You're dead beat, sir,' the young gunner said, catching his arm. Peter found he was swaying, and had to let the young man help him. He'd lost a lot of blood.

They stumbled back along the trenches. The young man pushed and heaved him up what had been the front wall of the German front-line trench, and they were in No Man's Land. They passed the crater, and later he remembered mumbling, 'Spent yesterday there. Nice place.'

Then on, past the legs and heads. His old sergeant was there, smiling in the moonlight. Down into their old trench, and he saw faces there, and military police.

'What regiment?' they asked him.

'Birmingham,' he muttered.

'Straight back. They're shelling the reserve lines. Better hurry, mate. It's getting light.'

'Call an officer "sir,"' Gale said furiously, but he was too tired to pursue the matter. 'Where's Two-sixty-seven Field Battery?' he asked.

The M.P peered at a paper by the light of a torch. 'Same position, as far as I know, sir.'

They moved on. They tramped down endless trenches to the rear, among stretcher-bearers and carrying parties and walking wounded. They got out into the open shortly after first light and trudged along the sides of the road among the skeletal poplars.

The young officer said: 'I'm going to make a report, of course, sir, and I dare say it's none of my business, but – I've been out for seven months now, and I've never seen anything like the way you got that mess organized. Or anyone so – well – brave, sir.' He said the word awkwardly, as though mentioning something indecent.

'Thank you,' Peter said. The daylight streamed

in long, flat bars across the earth, and the rain was stopping.

'Jolly good idea not even to wear cloth badges,' the young man said. 'The snipers have been learning to pick them up.'

Peter said: 'I am a private.'

The young man chuckled appreciatively, but he was tired, and he said: 'Major Smith, Birmingham Regiment, isn't it, sir? I have to know for my report – and if I and your Private Freeth have anything to do with it, sir, you'll get a V.C.'

'Anything you like,' Peter said. 'Call me Wilcot, South Wiltshire Yeomanry – or Walsh, Rifle Brigade. It doesn't matter.' His head was spinning, and he really felt that he might be Harry or Gerry just as easily as Smith or Savage.

The young man stopped anxiously. 'Are you sure you're all right, sir?' He looked up and down the road, but there was no one near them just then.

'Quite all right,' Peter said. 'You're a good boy. Don't believe in anyone, or you'll get into trouble.'

'I've got to go,' the young man said. 'My battery's behind the wood. Can't I get someone to look after you till you reach hospital, sir?'

'No,' Peter said. He grabbed the boy's hand, said, 'I'm sorry,' and walked on. The poor boy was staring at him, not knowing what to do.

But everyone on that road was near the end of his tether and when Peter glanced back, a hundred yards farther on, the young man had given up and was stumbling slowly across a muddy field towards his battery. The German

434

heavy artillery from five or six miles behind the front line was ranged in, and every now and then huge, dull explosions tore up the fields or crashed on the road. Peter kept trudging back and back, and gradually men caught up with him so that again he was in a tide, but now he was of it also, and it had no leadership and no will, just the power of automatic movement. If he had stood up there and raised his hand, or even taken each paste-skinned sleepwalker and turned him round, they would all have walked the other way with as little knowledge or care.

He had done it again, and even in his extreme exhaustion he could feel a thin tightening of hatred and fear of himself. Glory, glory trailed about him, and the young man would remember him all his life – the brave hero he had met in the trenches before Thiepval.

If he had not led through the gap in the wire, they would all have stayed in the crater. The attack would have wholly failed, as it was destined to do. He had torn a gap in the German wire and launched men against grenades and bayonets until they had wrenched victory and glory from defeat. Tonight the Germans would mount a full-scale counter-attack and, since they could fire into the gap from three sides, they would succeed, and more men would die, and afterwards all would be as it had been before.

Worse than any thoughts of the men he had killed was the realization that he had no real power of self-control. In spite of his vows to be among people instead of in front of them, he had fallen to the first serious temptation.

He trudged ever more slowly, because some day this road that stretched on and on in front of him would come to an end, and he did not know what he was going to do when he got there. If he had lost control over himself, where else could he turn?

There was a sign at the edge of a little farm – BIRMINGHAMS – and a couple of soldiers. But that wasn't his place any more, with so many men lying dead in the German trenches because of him, and the rest agog with the heroism of Private Smith. He couldn't face them, because he knew what they'd have waiting for him – a good big medal, the V.C or the D.C.M, and a commission. All their faces would be proud, as Gerry's used to be, as Adam Khan's used to be, as Emily's used to be, because the elemental shape of power had come among them and taken them to places where they would be glad, tomorrow, not to have been.

He saw other regimental and brigade signs. He threw his rifle into the ditch and walked on. Now a supply company, and division headquarters, and it was mid-morning. He smelled stables and saw horses and mules among trees. The sun was hot, and the rutted road nearly dry, and steam rising from the fields. His pack was heavy, and he slipped it off on to the road behind him, and his steel helmet was heavy, and he let it fall; it clanged once and again into the road. His haversack hurt his thigh; his bayonet flapped against his leg; his water-bottle was empty – all he let go, unbuckling them and letting them fall, because ahead he saw that the road was going to fork and he would have to choose, right or left, when he got to that place. He would not be able to, in fact he must not even dare to try to make that decision, but must sit down in the road, and wait. He unbuttoned his tunic.

'Halt,' a voice said.

He halted. They meant him. They must, because there was no one else in sight except the two military policemen with red caps and pistols standing beside a barn at the edge of the road.

They came forward to him, and, 'Where are you going, chum?' one of them asked.

He thought about it and said: 'I don't know.' He added: 'I won't fight any more.' He was happy that they had spoken to him, and wanted them to understand that whatever they decided, he would do it – except go back towards the fighting, where he'd get a medal.

The corporal's face hardened then, and the other said: 'Let's see your pay book, chum.'

He fumbled in his pocket, but he didn't have it. He remembered he had thrown it away.

'Where's your rifle, chum?' the corporal said. He had a notebook out and was writing in it with a stub of pencil.

'I threw it away,' he said.

'Threw – rifle – away. And your equipment, chum?'

'I threw it away.'

'Threw – equipment – away. Name, rank, number, and regiment or corps?'

He thought again and knew that he was not William Smith after all. Peter Savage the murderer was who he was, and must remain until it was all finished.

He said: 'Peter Savage, Lieutenant-Colonel, Thirteenth Gurkha Rifles.'

The corporal closed the book with a snap and looked at him almost pityingly.

'Come along,' he said.

CHAPTER 29

Emily heard the distant clang of the front doorbell, and, a time later, Alice's tapping steps along the stone floor of the hall. Her father awoke with a start and sat up, his knuckles tight on the arms of the big chair where he sat by the window, the inevitable newspaper across his knees, inevitably open at the casualty lists.

'That was the front door. It will be a telegram – from Charlie Moss. His son has been out eighteen months, and not touched yet. Or Peggy. Harry's been out since before Neuve Chapelle.'

'Now, Daddy, you mustn't worry yourself,' she said. All the same, it probably was a telegram, and telegrams usually meant death in the autumn of 1916.

Alice's steps approached, and she came in, holding out the envelope with gloomy relish. 'It was Jones the post, m'm. A telegraph letter, for you.'

'It won't be Moss,' her father said. 'It'll be Harry. Open it, Emily – open it!' But she had already opened it, and it was from Peggy: ARRIVING ON SEVEN-FORTY TRAIN AND ON IN STATION TRAP HOPE I CAN STAY THE NIGHT PEGGY.

She gave it to her father. He read it, and then again, as though he disbelieved it. 'No one killed,' he said. 'It's strange.' He handed it back to her, and slowly his head sank again on his chest.

Emily went out thoughtfully to speak to Alice and Bertha. The bed in the Sea Room would have to be made. Even if the train was on time, Peggy couldn't be here before nine. Daddy liked to eat at seven and went to his room immediately afterwards. It was better that way. She and Peggy would have supper alone.

It was six o'clock now. Peggy had sent the telegram from Birmingham. Strange. Stranger that she was coming at all. Strangest to be walking alone in this great house, with all the voices stilled or gone – Gerry dead at the foot of an Italian mountain; Mally dead, lying in the churchyard in the valley; Daddy, here but gone; Peter, gone; only the children made loud sounds here now, and it was impossible to remember back so far, to the time when she had been as young and had filled this house with those shouts and laughs. It was October, and the wind blew through the great house as though the stone walls had ceased to exist. But it had been warm with voices and lights and quarrels. What had happened?

She spoke to Bertha, helped Alice make the bed, and went upstairs to give the children their supper.

Peggy was coming to Llyn Gared. As though she had already heard the whistle of the train, she began to gather her emotions together to meet the assault – for that it would certainly be. The power to feel, dried for a year, welled up slowly in warm spurts as she watched Rodney and Elizabeth dip greedily into their bowls of bread and milk. The knowledge of hate, dead for a year, came again to life in her as she held the baby to her breast. It was a year since Peter came to Gaerwen cottage by Cwm Bychan, and went away. Now, soon, Peggy would be driving in the dark along the mountain road, which was heavy in this unaccustomed drought with the same dust that had heralded the coming of the young men from Cambridge. She and Peggy had been so young then, stirred by feelings that were no more than ripples over the surface of a little pond, yet seeing those ripples as great waves of passion and themselves as parts of the single storm-tossed ocean of womanhood. Now in the years it had come true. It would be no light ripple that stirred Peggy to come now, without explanation or warning.

The baby was light in her arms and light on her breast. He was not a Savage. He was not greedy as babies should be, as her others were, but took his nourishment almost politely, with his blue-wash eyes gentle on her and ready at a sign to turn away. He seemed humbly eager to make sure he did not hurt her. She pressed his head softly closer so that he could not see her face, could only feel the nipple in his mouth and the breast clutched in his hands. Rodney had finished his supper and stood now a yard away, as he often did, watching, with arms folded. Rodney was not jealous; he was a strong little boy, over four now, and quick and accurate, but he did not seem to know what jealousy was. Elizabeth would take his toy while he was playing with it, and he only looked at her, turned away, and found another. Or he would begin a private game, and soon she would put down her newly-won toy and wait humbly till he asked her to join him, or pushed the new game towards her. Emily smiled to see him, a thin baby man, standing there with a censorious look while she bared her breast for Gerry; but he was not censorious, either. The terrible and wonderful truth was that he was waiting for Gerry to play with him. Gerry was six months old. Whenever she put him back in his cot Rodney went and stood there, leaning over, holding out his finger, and talking to the baby. Gerry loved him.

Peggy was coming with news of Peter. Emily felt strength running like wine into her veins.

There had never been any news at all. The police came once to the cottage and went away. Peter had not written, and she had not expected him to. In the first six months – longer, until after Gerry was born – she had not wanted him to. Then, gradually, the sense of death began to envelop her, the death of feeling and emotion. She had sent Peter away because he was a murderer. But life without him was a slow death of her own spirit, because somehow the rope had formed a permanent union and she, at least, could not survive alone. Could he? Peggy would tell her, tonight.

She tucked the children into bed, read a story to Rodney and Elizabeth, and went downstairs. Her father was finishing his lonely meal in the dining-room, and she sat with him until he rose, kissed her forehead, and went slowly up to bed, the newspaper in his hands. Then she waited.

At nine she heard wheels crunching on the gravel and went to the front door. Alice had just opened it, and the lamp in the *porte cochère* shone on the dusty wheels, on Jones-the-trap's long, cold nose, and on the smoothed, round beauty of Lady Margaret Walsh.

Peggy came forward quickly to embrace her. 'Emily! … You look well… It's lovely to be back at Llyn Gared. How are you, Alice?'

There wasn't a male servant in the house these days, for they had gone to war, or worked in ammunition factories. The three women struggled up the stairs with Peggy's heavy suitcase, and then Emily returned to the drawing-room. She was excited now, but knew she must control herself as fiercely as Peter did.

The fire burned quietly in the big fireplace. Alice came in and out, putting up an occasional table near the fire, spreading cloth and cutlery, bringing in the cold supper and the plates. 'Will that be all, m'm?' Emily thanked her, and she went. Emily waited by the fire.

Peggy had a menacing confidence about her. The long skirt, short fur-trimmed jacket, and dark blue travelling bonnet were in the height of inconspicuous fashion. Her face was made up, but you'd have to know her very well to know that it was. Her eyes were wide, frank, and watchful. Now it was she who carried a hidden dagger. Emily waited, holding more firmly with each minute on to one strength: she needed Peter.

At last Peggy came gliding into the room in a velvet dress that swept the floor, her head up and the gaslight flaring through her piled hair. She was a vision – not from the past, for never here at Llyn Gared had Emily seen her like this, but from another world, a strange world to Emily now, where people knew heights of love and depths of despair, jealousy, and malice.

'How nice,' Peggy said. 'Cold mutton. Where do you get it from, dear? Of course there are plenty of sheep on the hills still, aren't there? Do you think I could have a little wine?'

'I'll get it,' Emily said, and went out.

So Peggy would play a game with her, waiting, glowing with fashion and with the news she carried, and, below that, close to her heart, her feeling about the news – delight? triumph? vindication?

She'd find out; but she would not be the first to speak of it. She stopped suddenly, half-way up the cellar stairs, the dusty bottle of burgundy cold against her chest. Peter had been killed! Her heart sank, and her feet seemed to be losing their grip, the wide tread of the steps becoming a steeply tilted ramp. With an effort she recovered herself. It would not be that; that would be too simple, too final an end to bring Peggy here to watch it.

As she re-entered the drawing-room she found herself smiling as she said: 'A Nuits Saint George, nought-eight. It'll be too cold, of course, but that can't be helped.'

She could smile easily because there was a warmth in her feet, where she had felt the ground move, and in her heart, which rose now as the ground had sunk then, and was filling

444

with a wonderful anger.

For a few minutes they ate and talked lightly, Emily feeling better all the time. Then, the food only half finished on her plate, the glass empty at her right hand, Peggy wiped her lips delicately on the napkin and said: 'You must be wondering why I came down, Emily.'

'Not at all,' she said. 'Have some more wine.' She refilled the other's glass. 'You're always welcome here.'

Peggy's eyes flashed momentarily; then she said: 'There is a special reason, as a matter of fact. I've heard something. It may be just a rumour. You know how many rumours there are – the Russians coming through England with snow on their boots–'

'I've never heard that one,' Emily said. 'Tell me.'

Peggy's voice was a little sharper. 'I've heard something about Peter. It's incredible, I can't *believe* it, but I thought how awful it would be if you heard it from someone else, so I thought I'd come down.'

'He's not killed?' she asked steadily, looking straight at Peggy.

'Oh, you know he's in the Army then?' Peggy said.

'I know nothing at all.'

Peggy said: 'It's rather worse than being killed, in a way.' She drank again, making the movements last a long time, and again wiping her lips carefully, and delicately laying down the napkin on the tablecloth. 'He's supposed to have been arrested as a deserter.'

Emily kept her head up. This was really ludicrous. Peter? Deserting? 'In action?' she asked.

'That's what they are saying,' Peggy said.

Emily nodded slowly. It could not be true. But it *was* true; this one fact she must be really sure of and hold on to like a pillar – that whatever evil rumours Peggy brought her would be true. Peggy would have checked and double-checked them before she came here. What good news she brought, if any, would be rumours, later to collapse like the bright hopes they had raised.

Peggy was speaking. 'You know, dear, it was I who told Peter where you were hiding when he came back from the Italian front.'

'I know,' Emily said.

Peggy said: 'I knew you'd be angry with me – perhaps you still are – but I couldn't bear to think of you and Peter separating because of some misunderstanding when perhaps getting together again and having a chance to talk it out might have put everything right.'

Emily glanced up and saw that her torturer's eyes were bright and large, and her hands flat on the table, the forefinger and second finger of the right hand meeting and parting, like scissors, on the stem of the wineglass.

Peggy continued: 'Well, you were right, and I was wrong. When Peter left you he must have gone straight to join up in the infantry – as a private soldier, my dear, and under an assumed name – Smith, I heard. After a time they sent him out to France, and then in the big battles in the late summer – Harry was in them too – Peter ran

446

away. Just threw down his rifle and ran away.'

Emily held her head up. It was the truth and nothing but the truth, perhaps, but not the whole truth; there would be more, and worse. Worse? Was it really so bad that Peter should have run away from a fight? Such a thing could happen only if his whole outlook on life had changed. That might not be bad at all.

Peggy said: 'Harry is going to get a D.S.O... The military police caught Peter, of course, before he'd got very far. It's taken a long time to come out, because of course they don't publish that sort of thing in the papers, and then apparently they spent weeks trying to find out who he really was and why he'd been hiding under a false name, and it was all so complicated, because he'd deserted from the Gurkhas in a way, too, hadn't he? And no one would believe what anyone else said, and–'

'Where is he?' Emily interrupted harshly.

'He's supposed to be in London,' Peggy said, her confident expression of sympathy deepening.

Emily said: 'You *know* he's in London, don't you, Peggy? You've seen him, haven't you? Do you think I'd believe you'd come down here without making sure of every last detail that might hurt me? Hating us so much has made you more stupid than you used to be, Peggy.'

Peggy's fingers stiffened convulsively on the stem of the wineglass. Then she relaxed, and when she spoke her voice was commiserating. 'I'm sorry you should think that, Emily. Yes, I've seen him. I wanted to break it to you gently.'

'Yes,' Emily said. 'Go on.'

Peggy said – seeming to pick her words with care, but Emily knew she had rehearsed them – 'I came down, really, to tell you that you ought to think of taking the children out of the country – for a time, at any rate. Peter's changed out of all recognition. I don't think he's quite sane. He can't be, really, to do this – running away from a battle. *You* know how mad just *saying* it is in connection with him, but it's true.'

Peggy waited for Emily to deny it with fear and anger, but Emily only nodded. Perhaps Peter had been mad before and now he was sane, but she did not want to talk to Peggy about it.

Peggy said: 'He's – completely empty, Emily. He doesn't seem to care what he's done, or what's going to happen to him, or what he'll do next. There's no one looking after him or speaking to him. He has been in open arrest so he's been able to go about if he wanted to, but he didn't, much. But sooner or later he'll remember that you are rich – well, not so rich now, I suppose, like the rest of us – and then he'll come to you and you'll be left with him, and all the talk, for the rest of your life. Think of the children! Think of little Gerry. Honestly, Emily, you ought to go *now*. Go and stay with those friends of Mally's in Virginia for a few years. If you do that I think he'll disappear again and not bother you.'

Emily said: 'Don't be silly. I must go and see him.'

Peggy sat back slowly, and now the look of triumph was unmistakable. She had succeeded. Now the vision was coming true in front of her eyes, of Emily tied for the rest of her life to a trembling piece of flotsam – Emily, who had married him for his power, his destiny, his vivid awareness of living. That was why Peggy had savoured so lovingly the cold and echoing sadness of Llyn Gared when she came in, and looked so tenderly down the long, empty passages. These were the prospects of Emily's life, until death.

Emily could not keep her head up any longer, and it bowed slowly under the weight of Peggy's implacable joy. Yet, after a time, she thought she could bear it, and even move forward under it. This feeling of burden was nothing to that other, of the world slipping away from under her feet, when she had imagined Peter gone for ever. There was even a new hope, for Peggy's news made it certain that Peter would not reject her; he was not strong enough to reject anyone. She glanced up and saw a subsidiary gleam in Peggy's smooth, adult face. Peggy was not spent, as she ought to have been with the accomplishment of her purpose. It was better to go forward against her than to suffer the wounds to be made in Peggy's good time.

Emily said: 'You have seen him – often?'

Peggy nodded, and looked away. After a moment she refilled her glass. 'As a matter of fact, yes. I told you, I wanted to be sure. I didn't want to alarm you without good reason. He's living with his grandfather. No one seemed to want to go and see him, now that Gerry's dead, so I went. I got him to take me out two or three times, trying to cheer him up, you know – but it was no good.'

Emily sat up quietly. The burden was gone, or become so light she did not feel it, or love had given her strength to make its weight inconsequent. She was so full of pride and anger and her love for Peter that when she spoke her voice was thick and deep.

She said: 'You tried to get him to sleep with you, Peggy. And you succeeded.' Peggy's face was changing colour, a red coming into it, and the wine bottle was empty; she, Emily, had not finished her first glass. She went on: 'You are a bitch, Peggy. A rather stupid bitch now. Did you hope I'd go running round London, trying to find out about Peter, slowly learning that what you said was the truth? Did you want to see me making plans to get to America and then gradually realizing that I couldn't leave Peter? You are a fool, as well as a bitch and a whore. You know I will go to him, and you know why. Because I love him. Because he's my husband, Peggy. Husband. It's no pain, no dreadful thing that I'm going to face when I see him, only my husband, and my marriage.'

Peggy was sitting back, her face dull red and her lips white-clenched between her teeth and the napkin crushed between her fingers. Emily pushed back her chair with such force that it teetered a moment and then crashed to the floor.

'You hate me, don't you?' she said.

'Yes. Yes,' Peggy said suddenly. 'I hate you.'

'Because Peter married me instead of you?'

'Because you made love to him to get him. Oh, don't think it wasn't obvious in your eyes when you got down the Matterhorn that day – a cheap, dirty skivvy's trick, and you pretending to be so virginal, and my best friend. How often did you sleep with Gerry, too, in the old days, in Zermatt, in London?'

Emily said: 'I was your best friend, and I tried to be for years after – till you showed that all you could find to remember, out of everything we'd been to each other, was hate. Well, go on. You were saying that you'd persuaded my husband to take you out two or three times, and that you then seduced him because he's got shell shock. What did you expect to come of that? That Peter would run away from me, because he felt guilty, when I tried to find him? So that you would be able to hug yourself for ever while Peter and I spent our lives in fear and loathing of each other?'

'You haven't answered about Gerry,' Peggy said breathlessly. 'Who killed Gerry? Why did you get yourself a baby from him? Of course it's Gerry's. Why else did you run away? But why did you make him have you? I never understood. Just to make sure of his death, by suicide if not by Peter's bullet in the back?'

'No,' Emily said. 'No, Peter didn't!'

'Didn't he? You are the fool, to believe that. And you're wrong about another thing, too.' Peggy regained some part of her old manner and spoke with an attempt at nonchalance, though her heavy breathing raised her breasts in a slow, irregular rhythm. 'I did not seduce Peter. I tried, though. I thought I'd learn what were the secrets of your success. For the first time in my life I

451

went out to get a man. I thought I'd find out how skivvies act and feel, skivvies in rich clothes lying on the grass with their skirts up, with their best friend's man. I even thought I might get a baby, too. Harry doesn't seem to be able to give me one. But nothing happened, my dear. I tried *every* way. So did Peter. I'm afraid that, in that way, the same as in every other way, Peter is impotent.'

Inconsequent thoughts flowed through Emily's mind. She'd had trousers on that day, her skirt being under the bed in the Schönbühl hut. It must have made it more difficult, but she couldn't remember any mechanical details of love-making at all, only love. Tears were beginning to flow down her cheeks because the triumph in Peggy's face was unbearable. To realize that Peggy thought this was the ultimate blow, the last torturing wound – that Peggy believed their sexual union had been the only cause of their marriage, the only bond between them! And in a moment Peggy would learn that this whole journey of hate had been destined, even before she set out on it, only to breed more love in Emily for her husband.

'Peggy,' she said at last, drying her eyes, 'you'd better go to your room. Alice will give you breakfast, and I'll order the trap from the village in the morning, so that you can catch the first train. Thank you for coming down to tell me.'

The triumph dimmed and went out. Peggy's face set to stone, and without a word she turned on her heel and ran out of the room. Her running feet echoed in the empty passage and died.

Emily sat down in front of the dying fire. It was a shame that Peter should have this misfortune too, because in the physical acts of love she could have told him of love and trust in ways that no words can encompass. There, too, was an arena in which a man, shattered in everything else, could yet build a sort of confidence. Well, it didn't matter very much, and even if it turned out that it did – from Peter's point of view more, probably, than from hers – then it might not be permanent; it might not be even true, with her. She put it out of her mind.

The really important thing was to go to Peter, with the children, and start rebuilding. She would have to find out what had happened in France – not as others saw it, but as Peter saw it. It might have been not so much a separate incident as the culmination of his whole life to that point. It might have been the end of something that began with Gerry's death, or with her own rejection of him. At any rate, he was in London, and he needed her. She would make no more plans now, beyond going to her husband.

CHAPTER 30

There was a long wait after she had rung the bell at 293 Nashe Street, and then Peter opened the door. He showed no surprise at seeing her and neither stepped towards her nor recoiled away from her. She held herself in check, wanting to overwhelm him with knowledge of her love, and said only: 'Peter – I've come to see you.'

'Come in,' he said. She held up her cheek to be kissed, and after a hesitation he kissed her. She saw that he was wearing 13th Gurkhas uniform, but with no medal ribbons, and the rank badges were those of a lieutenant.

'Let's go upstairs,' she said, touching his arm. He nodded, and they went up the narrow stairs together, she a little in front. When she entered the drawing-room she went quickly to the window, stooped over the old general before he could get up, and kissed him.

'I thought you'd come,' he said. 'How are the children?'

'Very well, Grandfather,' she said. 'I left them at home – in Minden Square, I mean.'

The old man nodded. He rose slowly to his feet, the stick trembling under his veined hand. 'Now I will lie down,' he said.

She made a motion of dissent, but the blue eyes glittered sharply and he said: 'Do not be foolish, Emily. You have not come to talk about the weather? Also, I need to lie down. As I told your mother the first time you came here, I was born in the reign of King George the Fourth. There is very little I have not seen.' He walked slowly out of the room, his stick making a small feathery noise on the carpet.

She sat down on the ornately curved sofa and quietly pulled Peter down beside her. It was a strange feeling, indeed, to direct Peter where he should go, as though he were a child. Only no child that was not exhausted to the verge of sleep or delirium would follow so unresistingly every slightest indication of a wish.

He began to speak at once. She listened and watched.

He was not mad, certainly not in any way yet known to the doctors. He was not physically ill, as Gerry had been ill when they came back from Meru. He was not angry or depressed, or perhaps inhabited by any other emotion at all. He spoke in a perfectly natural voice, with enough emphasis in the right places and sufficient changes of tone and pitch to make his recital sound quite normal. There was nothing of the sleep-talking or the trance-like monotone about it. When he related something funny that had happened, he smiled; once he laughed lightly; a few times he told of resentment over trivial injustices; but humour and resentment were emotions that he described, not ones that he felt.

At the end, when he had talked for an hour and a half, she understood quite clearly that on the battlefields of the Somme the flames of his courage and his will had burst once more into a conflagration, after he had sworn to himself that they should never do so again. He had turned defeat into victory, but he saw only death.

Somehow, somewhere, he had disposed of his strength. She felt that since returning from the battlefield he had deliberately allowed himself to bleed into some kind of death of the personality. He had no strength left to make decisions of any kind. He was not trying to hide; that would have been a decision in itself, and he would know that as a result certain people – herself perhaps included – would come to look for him. He was not trying to decide what to do next; decision was an act that had become, for him, synonymous with murder, so he had made himself incapable of deciding.

He might have suffered greatly in these past months if he had been in any other state. She did not think he had, though, because he had merely lived and waited. It had taken the authorities a long time to find out who he was because, as Peggy had said, they hadn't believed him when he told them the truth. They'd kept him in a prison camp near Abbeville. At last the young gunner, Gale, had been sent for, and the colonel of the battalion Peter had been with, and there had been many interviews, ending with a very senior general at the War Office. She could hardly blame them for not knowing what to do, when one group of witnesses insisted that Private Smith be given the Victoria Cross and an immediate commission; a second that Private Smith be shot as a deserter; and a third, mainly politicians, urged that the whole affair must be part of some further super-secret exploit of the galvanic Colonel Savage.

In the end they had torn up the twelve recommendations for a V.C, stripped him of his acting rank, and sent him away to await shipment back to the 13th Gurkhas in Mesopotamia.

'What will you do?' she asked when he had finished.

'They're sending me back to the regiment,' he said.

'But I thought you didn't want to fight any more,' she said.

He said: 'I don't think I do. Just after the battle, on the Somme, I would have refused to go. I don't feel the same now. If that's what they think's right, I'll go. I'm not afraid.'

'No,' she said, almost absently, 'I know that.' He would accept another's decision, even to go back to the war, but would not decide himself, even to refuse.

They were silent for a long time. At length he said: 'Is the baby all right? Peggy said he was. I'm glad you called him Gerry.'

'Gerry's very well,' she said. 'He's a lovely baby.'

Peter said: 'Of course... That was my fault too – if you can call it a fault that you tried to help Gerry, my Gerry.'

'It wasn't your fault,' she said. 'It was mine.' The pressed-down emotion was beginning to hurt. She said: 'Have I had nothing to do with – all this? Do you think I've been a doll jerking about on the end of a string that you and only you held? You aren't responsible for everything that happens to everyone, you know.'

Peter shook his head quietly. Here was one point, at least, on which he could make a decision. It was something, she thought grimly.

He said: 'Would you have married Gerry if I hadn't killed him?'

She said: 'No. Not even if you were dead. Not even if you had killed him – and you didn't, not alone. All three of us did.' She gathered herself. 'Peter, do you remember what we were talking about the night the telegrams came, about the war, about Harry's failure on Meru?'

'Yes,' he said at once. 'About love. Peace. And then the telegrams came and I found that love wasn't enough for me. I had to win.'

'That couldn't happen again, could it?' she asked.

'I don't think so,' he said. 'I don't want to win, and I physically couldn't. What I touch, I destroy. I'm not going to touch anything.'

She said: 'That won't work either. You're alive, and it's no good trying to pretend you're dead. I want you to apply to be released from the Army and go back to Rudwal. We can arrange that, between us.'

'Perhaps I'd destroy Rudwal,' he said seriously. 'I – really, I wouldn't know what to do that was safe.'

'I'll help you,' she said.

The afternoon light shone thinly on his pale eyes. He said nothing.

She said: 'I and the children, Peter. You can't hurt us, because we love you.'

'That's when you can be hurt the most,' he said sadly.

'It isn't true,' she cried. 'You've got to forget and begin again, because you're not the same person any more, any more than I am, or Peggy is. Things have happened to us, Peter. We've got to begin again, seeing ourselves as we are, not as we were. We must go to Rudwal because there's a home and work there, and people who need you, the new you, more than they ever needed the old you.'

'All right,' he said. 'You'll bring Gerry?'

'*We* will *take* Gerry,' she said. 'And … Peter, I don't want to talk about this ever again, but you must not treat Gerry differently from the others. You mustn't try to make amends to him or shelter him or guide him, or anything. Only love him.'

'Yes,' he said, 'I'm sure you're right. I won't bother you – I mean physically. I can't. I tried to make love to Peggy, and–'

She interrupted quietly. 'Peggy told me. I'm not interested one way or the other – yet. From now on all we have to do is love each other. I suppose I have been trying to guide you, in my own way, as much as you were trying to lead me. But we'll stand together now, Peter, and I won't have you cowering before me or anyone else. Did they take your medals away?'

He shook his head.

She said: 'Well, put the ribbons back. You won't be in uniform long.' She stood up. 'Will you come home with me now?'

'If you want me to,' he said readily.

'No,' she answered, watching him as he rose to his feet, so that he stood a little taller than she. 'You must decide.'

There was no light now, not even the old glacial cold, in his eyes. After a time, the words coming slowly up from the depths, he said: 'Yes. I'd like to come – if you think it's best.'

'I do,' she said.

He said: 'I'll tell Grandfather. I suppose he'll be surprised.'

She said: 'I don't think so. He's lived a long time. Where are your clothes?'

CHAPTER 31

LETTERS FROM INDIA

D.C's BUNGALOW
RUDWAL, PUNJAB
May 2nd, 1917

Dear Grandfather,

It is a fortnight since we arrived back here, but we have been so busy settling in that I have had no time to write. I am sure you will understand. The children are still excited and a little overwrought by all the travelling, and they are finding India quite strange. Well, even Rodney was only two when we left in '14. They have had no actual illness, though, nor have Peter or I. It is just as well, as there is so much to do. All our old staff were waiting for us, except the masalchi, who had graduated to khansama with a family in Manali.

People were very good to us all the way up. Many who had known Peter in the old days went out of their way to be nice. I nearly cried once or twice, because I wasn't expecting it. When we got to Rudwal at last there was a tremendous to-do, with all sorts of people who had probably never spoken to each other for years getting together to make a big reception at the station, with a band and a ton of garlands. The Old Captain was there, in command so to speak, and

Adam Khan his son, and Dr Parkash, and Harnarayan the Congress leader, who was one of the firebrands of the old C.G.G but now seems to have turned into a politician. (I am sorry, I don't suppose Peter told you anything about the C.G.G. It was an organization to improve co-operation between the government and the people, but it finally broke up early in the war and most of its members, including Adam Khan, joined the Congress Party. Adam Khan was the local Congress leader until early this year, but at their last elections Harnarayan beat him.)

Now I suppose you are wondering why I know so much about the politics here! Well, I promised Peter before we left England that I would take more interest in his work, so that he could have someone to talk to about it instead of just having to brood by himself. I am sure it helps anyone a lot to be able to talk about problems. I found out all I could while we were in Lahore, and have been doing the same here.

To get back to the reception at the station – there were several speeches, ranging from Adam Khan's little Horatian gem to fifteen minutes of blood and thunder Punjabi from the Old Captain (delivered while glaring at his son and Harnarayan). Everyone seems overjoyed to have Peter back, even Harnarayan, although he did hint politely that his reason for being pleased was to find a foeman worthy of his steel holding the reins here. The hospital Peter was working so hard at has been built and the nurses' school started, in a small way. Dr Parkash's speech was very short. He just shouted: '*Now* we will get the girls coming in to the school, eh?' I do wish you could meet him.

The truth is that everyone is keyed up to do great things, now that Peter is back. The Congress people know they won't be able to get away with vague slogans any more, but will have to be precise and bold. The air is quite electric with readiness. It is wonderful – and terrifying. I am hoping against hope that it will rouse Peter to be what they all expect him to be.

Llyn Gared has not been sold yet. I have been tempted to take it off the market and keep it as a place we could go to if we had to… I mean, when Peter retires. But the truth is we are no longer rich. My shares have gone down a lot, and I simply don't think we are going to be able to afford a place like that as well as the London house, even in another year or two. Also, I think I would feel sad if we went back there and tried to live in that kind of isolation from the world, as squires of Llyn Gared. It's not possible any more, because of what has happened to us. Daddy didn't say anything about it in his will. I only hope that whoever buys it will love mountains and Wales as he and Mally did.

The war seems very far away here, but I think we will get a different impression when we go on tour into the villages. There has been very heavy enlistment from the district, and we have suffered a lot of casualties, particularly in Mesopotamia.

Peter and Rodney send their love. Rodney wants to know how you can possibly blow out ninety-one candles with one breath on your birthday cake.

Your affectionate granddaughter,
Emily

D.C's BUNGALOW
RUDWAL, PUNJAB
March 30th, 1918

Dear Grandfather,

The children continue to keep well, except that Elizabeth had whooping-cough last month and Gerry fell and cut his chin quite badly on the gravel yesterday morning. And of course they have had occasional upset stomachs like everyone else.

The news from France is so bad that one hesitates to open the paper, and I suppose even what we are being allowed to learn from the newspapers is not the whole truth. Sometimes I have nightmares that all this bloodshed will be in vain after all, and that the Germans are going to win – in France, at least. When I think of it, and read the newspapers and look at the casualty lists, I wonder whether it wouldn't have been better for England if our own worries had turned out differently. I mean, if Peter had gone on the way he was perhaps meant to, and become a general. Now he reads the paper and says: 'The Germans are attacking,' and that's all.

The honeymoon spirit that met Peter at the railway station last April, and the eagerness that I felt among the people, have nearly all evaporated by now. The usual problems come up all the time, of a thousand different kinds, and for the first five or six months they seemed to solve themselves with little trouble. Peter would call conferences and ask for advice from the D.S.P and Harnarayan and Adam Khan and Parkash, or whoever else was involved, and some solution would soon be put forward and happily accepted by everyone. He still holds the conferences, but solutions to problems are much harder to come by. Instead of trying to find a way to agree they seem intent on finding places where they can disagree. Partly this is because more deep-rooted problems are coming to the surface, but more than that it's because in the beginning they all *knew* that if they didn't find an answer in quick time Peter would give them one and see that it was put into effect. Now they are finding that this is not true after all.

I know what's happening because I have taken a correspondence course in Pitman's shorthand and usually sit as secretary at the conferences. Sometimes someone tries to force Peter into giving a decision, but he won't be forced. He says quietly: 'This is a problem affecting everyone, and you must find a solution and make a recommendation to me, and I will see that it is carried out.' The Congress people like this, of course, but it doesn't help when their opinion is directly contrary to someone else's.

Adam Khan has been in slightly better grace with his father since a man who is apparently becoming important, a lawyer named Gandhi, declared in Bombay a few weeks ago that every patriotic Indian should get into the Army and help us win the war. (Adam has felt this all the

465

way along.) Adam's son, Baber, has been talking for a year about going into the Army. He would go tomorrow if he could decide whether to enlist, as the Old Captain did, and start as a sowar in the Guides, or wait a bit and get a direct Viceroy's commission as jemadar, or wait still more and try to get to Sandhurst. As you will have heard, Indians are now going to be admitted there, and will get the King's Commission. I can't think why it wasn't done ages ago, when you think that Indians have been going into the I.C.S, which is supposed to be far more important than the Army, since 1860. The D.C of the district next to us is an Indian, by the way.

The Commissioner is coming next week to stay a few days, and there is a lot to do. A land dispute he said ought to have been dealt with six months ago has still not been decided, and I must rush, as I want to write out a solution which I think they will both accept, if only Peter will bark at them a little.

Llyn Gared was sold last month. Now I really feel as if I had no past, only the present. The future no one can know – luckily, perhaps.

Your affectionate granddaughter,
Emily

D.C's CAMP,
RUDWAL, PUNJAB
November 13th, 1918

Dear Grandfather,

I can hardly believe it's over. When we got the telegram I suddenly started crying. The immediate feeling was what I suppose one had expected, that a great load had been lifted, or a cloud gone away and the sun was shining again. But very soon afterwards it seemed that the light only enabled us to see better the ruins in which we are standing. For four and a quarter years everyone has been deliberately wearing blinkers, seeing only what had to be done at once and what was going on under his nose. Now we have to take the blinkers off and look around, and forward.

There are, or soon will be, a thousand problems to be settled, a thousand decisions to be made, even inside the family. I am thirty-three, but I feel about fifty, and sometimes look it, too! These past two years have been very wearing, somehow. Rodney is six, and in another two or three years he ought to be going home to prep school. I don't want to think of leaving Peter so soon, yet there's no one in England we could send Rodney to, even if we wanted to, except some distant cousins of mine.

There is already an air of expectancy in political circles here. It has been growing since it became obvious in the summer that Germany had shot her bolt. There is talk of every kind, ranging from suggestions that the District Board will be given authority over the police, to rumours (started by Harnarayan, I think) that India will be given complete self-government, like Canada. There is a truce between the politicians and the soldiers, because even people like Harnarayan can see that the latter (who are still just farmers in uniform, as they used to be in your day) have done more to put India on the map than any politician ever did. Everyone is in a good temper, the women thinking of their men returning, the harvest coming in well, the war won, the future looking so bright. A company of British soldiers marching through Rudwal on their way to manœuvres was cheered all the way, which is unusual.

When I think that Peter might have been coming back to India by express P & O, a general, world-famous, the darling of the government at home, I really believe he would have been made Viceroy to succeed Lord Chelmsford, and then what might not have happened! India would be the most exciting place in the world.

But it's no good thinking of what might have been.

I can't say Peter is as popular as he was with the people he has to deal with, or even among the peasants. Harnarayan and the rest of the Congress crowd are finding that it is all very well for the D.C to listen to all sides, but sooner or later someone has to give a decision. They say that all will be well when everything can be decided by a vote, but as a matter of fact they know that this is not true. It is impossible to take a vote on which of two stud bulls the breeding co-operative should buy, or whether the new road to Naughat should go east or west of Ghulam Hussain's field, because then there'd be no time to discuss really important things, like policies.

But all this is really in the background, at least for the moment. The end of the war is like a silence, so sudden and after so long a noise, that you can hear it. I find myself remembering people I have not seen since '07, and wondering what happened to them. Unless Harry Walsh was killed in the last few days, he will have escaped. It is a miracle, as I believe the average infantry officer's life-expectancy was two weeks, but I can't help wondering what effect it will have had on him. The death of Cadez on Meru in '13 affected him very much, I know, so the war must have been one long, mad nightmare to him – and he not able to show it, because that's the sort of man he is.

No more now. We are moving camp tomorrow. We had meant to cover the whole of the Southern Tehsils on this tour, but there have been so many complications and so many involved cases to listen to that we won't be able to do more than a third of the work before Peter has to get back to Rudwal.

Peter is writing separately about Ashraf, but I am sure you know how sorry I am too. He was always a dear to me. I hope the new man will look after you properly. If he served twenty-five years in India, you probably speak almost as much Hindustani to him as you did to Ashraf!

Your affectionate granddaughter,
Emily

D.C's BUNGALOW
RUDWAL, PUNJAB
September 12th, 1919

Dearest Grandfather,

Yes, I am afraid that affairs here are just as bad as the newspapers have painted them – worse in some ways. There was a little violence in Rudwal, but what is far worse is the change in atmosphere. After all the expectancy the actual reforms seemed rather ungracious, and a lot of Indians felt they hadn't been given enough. Then came the awful Dyer business in Amritsar in April, and, though the province is as quiet as a mouse again, it's a very different sort of quiet. Harnarayan and his group are now saying that they will never get justice from England, and that they must work for total independence. This is the first time such an idea has been heard of, and, though only the extremists talk like that now, it is an omen, or could be.

Harnarayan has tried to get Peter to say something in public to show that he disapproves of the way General Dyer kept on firing until all those people had been killed, and even more of his order that Indians had to crawl past the place where the missionary woman was killed earlier. For a time I thought Peter was going to, which would have got us into trouble in some quarters but would at least have been taking a stand. Then the Commissioner came here – he was with a general from Lahore – and Peter said nothing one way or the other. Harnarayan was angry with him, and so was the Old Captain (who has had a mild stroke since). *He* wanted to come out and say that anyone who tried to cause trouble here would get the same treatment General Dyer gave them in Amritsar. He said to Peter: 'There was an order that they should not gather in this Jallianwala Bagh. They disobeyed, and now it is said the general sahib was wrong to kill so many. *I* only know that if *I* were ruling the Punjab, and it was as full of Sikhs as it is now, I would not have stopped firing while even one of them was left alive. Then we would have peace for fifty years.' This is really what General Dyer is saying, without the bit about the Sikhs.

Dr Parkash is furious too because politics have crept into the hospital. He found that one of the new doctors was a fanatical Congress man and was using his position not only to convert the girls in the nurses' school to his views but to keep out any who were likely to be loyal to us. It would have been very effective if he had succeeded, because when the girls went to their homes and to the village dispensaries which we were getting started (before the trouble), they would have been very influential proselytizers. Dr Parkash dismissed the doctor, and now the Congress people are after him, and unless Peter uses the power and influence he's still got they'll be able to dismiss him, too, because of the strength they have on the Hospital Board.

You asked me to tell you honestly how Peter was. Well, Grandfather, that is difficult to answer, except to say that he is the same as when he was with you at Nashe Street after he came back from the Somme. He is so gentle and kind, but it is almost worse than brutality because I feel that it is not a gentleness of the strong, as it used to be. The Commissioner has been getting more and more outspoken, and has even warned me that the new Lieutenant-Governor is very dissatisfied with Peter – but you know what the I.C.S is. They had their chance to refuse to take him back in '17, but they couldn't believe he had changed so much (with little or nothing of it showing on the surface) so they took him, and now he would have to do something terrible, or *not* do something in a terrible situation, before they could get rid of him. The awful thing is that I feel more and more strongly, and more and more often, that this is just what will happen. Troubles are piling up like clouds. The harvest was not good in Rudwal this year, nor were the rains. There is a much stronger pressure behind situations than there has been since I knew India, probably since 1857, and when there is an explosion it might be a very bad one.

I don't know what to do, whether to go on here, trying and trying – and I have tried so hard to show Peter that I and other people trust him – or give up and go back to England. But what then? What are we going to do?

I have been thinking about your suggestion that Peter try his hand at mountaineering again and, though it might be dangerous, and it probably won't work, it seems the only thing left. So I am going to arrange for us all to spend a month in the Northern Tehsils next summer, if the situation will allow Peter to leave Rudwal. Perhaps the mountains will arouse him. They meant so much in the old days and caused him so much sadness and disillusion with himself – I suppose everything began with his climbing – that I felt at all costs he must never climb again. Now, thinking over what you said, I feel I may have made a mistake – or perhaps the passing of time and the complete change in him have altered the proportions of things. I think I would

472

die of happiness if I heard him say, the way he used to, 'I'm going to get to the top of that mountain, at all costs.'

Talking about mountains, you may not have heard that Harry Walsh is going to bring out another expedition to Meru next year. We saw a little snippet about it in the *C & M* – no other details.

Baber has made up his mind to take the Sandhurst exam – next year. Adam Khan was in favour of the idea, before the Amritsar massacre; now he is very strong against it and has been to see his father several times to try and persuade him that now even he must see it's no use kowtowing to us. The Old Captain no longer tells Peter what's happening, but I imagine he sent Adam Khan away without satisfaction. Those two will never see any problem in the same light.

I really should not have bothered you with such a long letter, but it is a great comfort and source of strength to me to be able to write to you, so forgive me.

Your loving granddaughter,
Emily

D.C's BUNGALOW
RUDWAL, PUNJAB
September 13th, 1920

Dearest Grandfather,

We only got back from the Northern Tehsils on the second, and since then the world seems to have been toppling about us. That is an exaggeration, and I know you don't like exaggeration, but it has been bad. The least of the worries has been the arrival of Harry Walsh's expedition, which began to gather a week ago. Harry and Peggy will be here this evening. Peggy wrote to me a few months ago, more or less making up a quarrel that had estranged us, so we will be seeing each other, but not, I fear, very cordially.

It really looks as if the mountain must be climbed this time. Besides Harry there are seven other climbers – all English – and a doctor. Everyone's new except Harry – Capt Ewell and Lapeyrol were both killed in '16, Capt Ewell at the Somme and Lapeyrol at Verdun. An enormous number of porters and pack animals have been hired for this expedition, and Sherpa porters brought from Nepal, so that the expedition's going to look like an army when it leaves here. There has been a lot of talk about Harry's idea in trying the mountain now, after the monsoon, instead of earlier. Peter thinks they have a good chance, though the monsoon hardly reaches up there anyway, and while we were in Harkamu he did what he could to ensure that the 'army's' procession through the Northern Tehsils would be as smooth as possible.

It is hot and muggy, as it usually is at this time of year, of course, but it seems worse this year, and everyone is in a bad temper, except Peter. The Old Captain won't speak to him at all because of something he did, or rather didn't do, in a criminal case a few months ago. Young Baber has been to see us to tell us that he passed the Sandhurst exam and is sailing after Christmas. For a time we thought he would be coming with us on our trek into the Northern Tehsils. Peter once had promised him, before the war, that he would take him into the mountains and teach him how to climb, but when Baber suddenly appeared after all these years and reminded him of the promise, Peter backed out. He told me afterwards he didn't want to take responsibility for Baber, who is a headstrong young man now. Peter didn't do any climbing while we were up there.

The harvest was not good, in spite of heavy rains. There is a good deal of sickness, and Dr Parkash has left, feeling rather bitter. They (the Congress people) forced him to resign.

Rodney is eight now and I have made up my mind that he must go home at the end of this cold weather. He is thin and quite sallow, in spite of a month in the mountains. Also he is getting to be a terror to the servants, none of whom correct him – how can they? – and so I will be writing soon to Cox's to book passages for myself and all the children in March. Peter has not made up his mind yet. He is eligible for furlough next year.

I feel very tired, so please excuse me,

Your loving granddaughter,
Emily

P.S – Peter will be coming home with us. He is going to resign from the service. I don't know what he will do.

CHAPTER 32

She dipped the pen in the ink and carefully wrote the address – Major-General R Savage, C.B, 293 Nashe Street, Kensington, London, England. As long as she could write that address and that name, and in her mind see the old man with the eagle's eyes, there was still something firm left in the world. He was ninety-four now, and he could not last much longer. She did not disguise from herself that a strong element in her decision to take the children back to England was her wish that he should see them again before he died – perhaps even more that young Rodney should see him, whose name he bore.

She found a stamp in her bureau drawer and put it on, and laid the envelope aside with the three other letters for the mail.

It was done.

She called for the bearer to light the lamps. It was only half-past five but the sky was overcast, and it was gloomy inside the drawing-room. Peter was in his study, at work on a report for the Commissioner. She ought to go and help him but she did not have the desire at this time, for the writing of the letter to his grandfather had emptied her.

The summer journey to the Northern Tehsils should have been an idyll of pleasure. They had met rather more rain than was usual on that side of the Himalaya, but there had still been plenty of perfect days. Nothing went amiss with the arrangements; no one got hurt or fell sick. Peter was calm, as usual, and apparently absorbed in making notes of the flowers and birds that they saw. He had told her once or twice, when she found him sitting in the garden here, staring seemingly at nothing, that he was watching the birds; and she knew that he had bought some ornithological books a year or two ago – but she had believed that it was an excuse to be alone with his thoughts, or even a shelter to conceal the fact that he was thinking of nothing at all. She now knew she had been wrong, for on the journey and in their camp twelve miles above Harkamu he had shown a deep understanding of the habits of birds and a wide knowledge of them in their species, sub-species, and families.

Ten, five years ago she would been delirious with joy to find Peter peacefully watching the lammergeier glide across the face of the precipice, to hear him answer: 'No, thank you, darling,' when she asked him whether he wanted to go climbing some high mountain. Now her memories of the journey were sad, because the quiescence which it had once been her aim to induce in him was his only state of mind, and it was a sad thing to see. He had walked up a few hills, but only as far as young Rodney could accompany him, and turned back when a point was reached where Rodney would have to use his hands. Rodney was disappointed then, and once, when Peter would not heed his eager requests that they go forward, called his father a *soor*, a pig. She had slapped him sharply, but Peter had said nothing.

She should be grateful that somewhere through the listless years Peter had found at least these resources of contemplation. He had never before seen any static beauty in mountains or in the shapes of rocks or in the run of water over stone; now he would stand for minutes on end drinking them in, pointing them out to her or the children with something approaching enthusiasm in his voice. She was grateful, but she could not accept this as an adequate answer to the problems of life and of living that had crowded her and now seemed to be gathering for a final catastrophe.

She did not think they would be able to afford to keep the children at expensive schools for the next fifteen years. Peter was going to resign and would not find other employment easy to come by. His class would reject him, for he had broken its rules. Librarian in a small provincial town seemed to be his mark now. Even if the money problem could be overcome, she could not raise the children to adulthood without a man. Peter was not a man. Indignantly she brushed aside her own reminder that he was indeed impotent. That did not matter except to remove from her reach a means which she sometimes thought God had specially provided to allow human beings to resolve, at least temporarily, and for the sake of a night's sleep, otherwise over-whelming tensions. No, he was not a man because he was hardly human. Somewhere in history, among the galley slaves perhaps, there may have been men with this quality of emptiness, as though all that made them human had been drained out and nothing put in its place; but she had never met one. Usually hate crept in to take the room of other emotions, or sometimes nostalgia, so that the victim's feelings were still bright and strong but enclosed in those past times. Peter was nothing – a mirror to reflect the good and bad of the day, a photographer's plate to record the beauty and sin of the world that passed before him; that was all.

For almost four years she had been fighting, fighting, fighting against a host of enemies, seen and unseen. She had used every particle of her energy and her will to make Peter feel; and then, when she knew that she did not have anything left, there was the house to run, and Rodney and Elizabeth to bring up in love and care, and the training of baby Gerry – but he was four now – and the protection of Peter's reputation. How many disputes had she solved in his name since that June night of 1917, when, feeling as though she were robbing the Bank of England, she had done it the first time? How many letters had she written and put to him for his signature – explaining, accepting, refusing; brusque, pliant, apologetic; whatever was needed to give him peace?

From the beginning she had felt that she was bleeding slowly to death. For a year she had known that the time approached when she must give up from sheer fatigue. She had put high hopes in the journey to the mountains, and as soon as they returned, the hopes unfulfilled, she knew that the time had come. For the sake of the children she must now leave him. Her mind trembled as an exhausted body trembles, and she could not find a way to care what he did. He must decide.

She had thought, that first week after their return from the north: Suppose he decides to come home with me? She would love him, because she couldn't help it, but she must not think first of him and his well-being, for both were beyond her help. She must not think of the children. She would have to be father and mother to them, and that would make her less of a mother and less of a woman. People would laugh at the matriarch, and the children would notice, but she could not help that. Gentleness at least they could learn from Peter – but they were too sharply intelligent for that; they knew perfectly well, especially Rodney, that their father's tenderness did not come from strength. Rodney took delight in showing that *he* could rage and command and fill even grown-ups with alarm at his anger.

It was the thought of Rodney that had made her break her own resolution not to answer Peter's problem for him (*he* did not know he had got one.) So she had gone in yesterday after tiffin, meaning to tell him that unless he had any good reason to the contrary she thought he'd better stay in the I.C.S and continue to earn its good salary as long as he could. But, when she was face to face with him and had looked into his eyes and seen the pale unshadowed depths of them, and taken note of the unlined face and the black hair, grey at the temples (the silver streaks in her own hair matched it), she had said instead: 'Come home with us, Peter.'

He had nodded, while she touched his cheek, and said: 'I will ask for my furlough.'

Peggy would be in Rudwal by now. The advance party of the expedition had put up a dozen tents in the grounds of the dâk bungalow, leaving one of the rooms empty for Harry and Peggy. The train would be in, and soon they would be here. Would Peggy be disappointed to find her too exhausted to feel the daggers of malicious triumph? Or would the sight of the exhaustion itself be an adequate reward for having made such a long journey? When Peggy wrote four months ago Emily had been in no doubt of her motive. There was an apology for things said and done; a statement that time had passed, and remorse and perhaps wisdom come; a wish to meet again and start again; and, between the lines, the unslaked lust of a *voyeur* of misery. Peggy needed to see with her own eyes what must by now have been spread in gossip through all interested circles of society – the sad end of Peter and Emily Savage.

PS meant *post scriptum*. There had been no need to put the news that Peter was resigning from the service in a postscript to the letter to Grandfather, because she had known it before she started to write. She had somehow hoped, though, while writing, that she would not have to say it this time; that she could wait another few weeks, and then write a special letter, clothing the announcement with a kind of furry importance, as the official communiqués padded their tales of the arrivals and departures of Viceroys, Proconsuls, and eminent politicians – not 'The Viceroy is ill and is going home,' but 'His Excellency the Most Honourable the Marquess of Kirkcudbright and Clackmannan, G.M.S.I, G.M.I.E, K.C.V.O, Viceroy and Governor-General of India, has intimated to His Majesty's Principal Secretary of State for India that in view of the state of his health he...'

But when she got to the end of the letter she knew that it could not wait and that it did not have the grandeur to support a bulk of circumstance.

Yesterday she had told Peter to come home with the rest of them. Peter had gone as far as the literal meaning of her words. He had said he would ask for furlough. At the end of the furlough he would have returned to Rudwal, or wherever the authorities posted him if they had had enough of him here, and she would have stayed in England. Until lunch-time today, that was what she had to tell his grandfather, and it could have waited.

But after lunch Baber came. In the letter she had told the old general that he came with the news of his success in the Sandhurst examination. That was true, but not the whole truth. Baber was six feet, two inches high now, fine-boned, handsome as a hawk, with wide-set velvet brown eyes. His teeth were very white, and his hands, clasped nervously together, were strong and sinewy. He told them he had passed into Sandhurst. Twenty, thirty years from now he would command the Guides. Baber was excited, thrilled – and desperate.

It was she who had to bring it out of him by a broad hint that if he had any questions to ask they would be glad to answer them. Then his hands unclasped slowly and fell to his sides, and he sat up straight and looked at her. He said: 'Mrs Savage – I think I am in love.'

She wanted to smile, feeling the old laugh of happiness to hear these simple words and see the young man so perturbed. But it was not a time to laugh, even with joy, for being in love was as terrible a state for the young man as it had become to her.

She said: 'And you want to get married?'

He said: 'Yes, Mrs Savage. Very much.'

Peter said: 'That's difficult, isn't it?'

The young man hardly glanced at him but kept watching Emily with that hungry, nervous look, his hands straight by his sides, his long body stiffly upright. She fenced for time and found out, though it made no difference, that the girl was a student at Punjab University in Lahore, nineteen, the daughter of a well-to-do and sophisticated Moslem family. There could be no objections to the match on any possible grounds, and the quality of Baber's love reminded her of her own feelings when she had first seen the soaring, ethereal beauty of King's College Chapel – she could hardly bear to go away from it.

She looked at Peter and prayed that he would say something. The boy would not be accepted for Sandhurst if he was married. He did not

483

know what to do. Love was so strange to him, and perhaps it felt like a new kind of suffocation, so that he could breathe only in his lady's presence.

Peter said: 'Which is the more important to you – the Guides or the young lady?'

Baber said: 'Both.'

Peter shook his head wonderingly. Watching the young man, she felt sure that he wanted an affirmation of his faith in service. His grandfather had brought him up to believe in duty, and his inclination also pointed that way. The army was a desire as strong and clear to him as love – much, much clearer, for he had lived with that desire for many years and knew its dimensions. Now this new thing had sprung upon him, and she thought he wanted strength to hold to his course.

She said: 'Well...'

But she must not say anything. She was a woman, and it would be cruel to give advice on a problem that was man's alone. How could she weigh the disruptive forces of marriage when for her marriage was itself a vocation, a need, and the fulfilment of the need? Besides, she had reached the end of her powers of decision. She could not face the responsibility of laying even the lightest of hands on Baber's destiny.

Peter said nothing more. Almost imperceptibly the young man's face hardened. He had expected counsel and was too young to understand why it was not given to him. After a few desultory platitudes, during which he sat farther and farther forward on the edge of his chair, he excused himself and went away.

A little later she had made what she knew must be her last decision, for she was spent. Peter had sat quiet for half an hour after the young man had gone. Then he said: 'I am no use to anyone.'

If he had spoken with the kind of theatrical despair the remark seemed to call for; if he had looked at her and demanded by the very excess of dejection in his tone and words that she deny his statement – she might have done so. But he spoke matter-of-factly, and the words only expressed something that he had believed since the Somme and that she had come painfully, bleedingly, strugglingly to this point of accepting.

She did not speak. The only word was 'Yes,' and there seemed no need to say anything so trite.

Very well, she had thought dispassionately. It is true. Then what is the point of his returning to India after a furlough in England? Was it not her duty to take him with her and look after him as best she could, always bearing in mind the predominant importance of the children? But – suppose she said nothing? Then he would return to India, and she would not see him more than once every four years. There would be excitement and movement again in her life. The children, with their careless power and short-lived enthusiasms and reckless doings and changings of mind, would make life new.

She found it hard to think. She was bogged in mud. She was on an unnatural mountain, where it was hard at the bottom and muddy at the top. She was tired and short of breath.

It would be easier to leave him behind, for he

485

made the mud muddier, the darkness darker. Then she looked at him, and for a moment the years dropped away, and he was the young man of ice and fire who had lifted her and Gerry, and even Peggy, and a thousand others, towards heights of emotion and passion they had not had the strength of will or the ordinary courage to face, sometimes not even the imagination to guess the existence of. In those times he would not have left one of *them*. He had spent his fire for them, and the ashes were cold, but she would remember. She would try to nourish in herself a little of the spark and pray it might rekindle in another generation.

She leaned forward, the tears slowly filling her eyes, until her head rested on his knees and her arms were thrown around his body. After a moment she felt his hand on her hair, quietly stroking it. She muttered: 'Don't come back to India, Peter. We'll find a way to live somehow.'

'All right,' he said after a while.

Now it was six o'clock. This was the day her war had ended. A war of attrition, they had called that other one in France, and at the end the fields lay shattered and bloodless under the watery November sun, and victory meant as little as defeat. She knew the truth of that because in this long struggle she had lost, and it was just the same. All was quiet, and her thoughts moved like sleepwalkers through the wreckage of dreams and hopes. The blood ran slow and tepid in her veins. There were weights on her legs and in her heart. The birds had gone from the garden, and the children were hushed at the other end of the big bungalow, and the footsteps in the passage were slow, quiet, and heavy. This was the place of abandonment, where she gave up.

CHAPTER 33

The footsteps came to the door and the chuprassi entered. He said: *'Sahib salaam bolta, daftar-men.'*

She got up. Peter would like her to come to the office. Her shorthand pad and pencils were already there. She followed the chuprassi along the passage and went into the office as he held the door open for her.

Adam Khan was there, sitting on the other side of the big table from Peter. The two men rose as she came in. She greeted Adam and sat down. Peter said: 'Take notes, will you, dear? Now, Adam...'

Adam Khan was wearing a long dark grey *achkan* and a lamb's-wool cap of the same colour. The only traces of age in his face were in the lines from his nose to the corners of his mouth, and in the network of fine wrinkles at the side of his eyes. He said: 'I was going to make some suggestions to Peter about the flood situation, and he thought you'd better be here. Peter, what are your reports?'

Peter said: 'About as usual. The Maghra is fourteen point three feet above mean level at Naughat, but–'

Adam said: 'And the danger level is nineteen?'

Peter nodded. Adam said: 'Have you had any reports from Manohar Singh about the situation up there?'

Emily jotted down: 'Manohar Singh, Chhandawal.' Manohar Singh was an amiable old Dogra gentleman who was *tehsildar* of Chhandawal, the easternmost of the Southern Tehsils. A tributary of the Maghra, called the Harab, rose there under the southern slope of the main chain of the Himalaya. It was a picturesque, dead-end region of huge peaks, hanging villages, and narrow footpaths, all looking down into the short steep torrent of the Harab.

Peter said: 'No... Wait a minute. Manohar Singh reported a week ago that the level of the Harab was normal for the time of year.'

Adam said: 'Manohar Singh has been sick for the last *two* weeks, Peter. Our man up there came down today and told us that the Harab is several feet *below* normal level.'

She said involuntarily: 'Below?'

Adam looked at her and said: 'Yes, Emily – below. He thinks there's been a landslide, and the main channel's blocked higher up.'

She said: 'And you're afraid that when the river comes over the top of the dam, or whatever's blocking it, there might be a flash flood?'

He said: 'Yes. There's not much danger up there in Chhandawal, because none of the villages are close to the river, but there would be danger here. The Maghra can't take it. It's rising an inch an hour here now, and all the sheepherders who've come down from the Lakho La and the Northern Tehsils say it was raining heavily up there when they came through.'

'I know,' Peter said. 'The D.S.P has been

bringing me reports every two days.'

Adam leaned forward. 'Peter, something's got to be done, now, to prepare Rudwal for a flood in case it comes – and to give us better warning.'

'I could send a telegram to Manohar Singh,' Peter said. 'He ought to send a man up to find if the Harab is blocked or not.'

Adam said forcefully: 'That's not enough!' He checked himself, and her heart twisted as she saw him gaining control over himself and forcing himself to speak gently. He was like a father, strong-willed and powerful, ready to lose patience with a feckless son, but for the sake of his love holding himself back with tenderness. He went on: 'We, the local Congress Committee, think you ought to put out a flood warning all along the lower Maghra, especially here in Rudwal. We suggest you call for volunteers to help the police watch the banks. There's a section below the Naughat road bridge where the bank needs strengthening – now!'

Peter nodded thoughtfully. 'You're right. I'll call a conference tomorrow. The D.S.P can give us the latest reports. You can send a man to it, and I'll have Mughrib representing the shop-keepers, and all the District Board members that I can get hold of, of course.'

Adam said carefully: 'That's a good idea, Peter, but tomorrow may be too late. The warnings ought to go out now – immediately.'

'That would mean closing a lot of the go-downs along River Street,' Peter said, 'and moving the people out of some of the houses, too.'

'Yes,' Adam said, 'it would.'

Peter said: 'That's going to cause a lot of disruption. I think we can leave it to the conference tomorrow to decide what should be done.'

Adam said: 'But–' With a superhuman effort he held down his impatience. 'Very well, Peter. Make it early, won't you? And you'll send that telegram right away?'

'I have it ready,' Emily broke in. 'Sign it here, will you, Peter.' He signed absently, and she called the chuprassi and told him to take the message to the telegraph office at once. She felt Adam Khan's eyes on her all the time.

Adam stood up. 'I must go, Peter. What about half-past eight?'

'For the conference?'

'Yes.'

She said: 'I'll see that everyone's notified.'

Adam had opened the door, and she followed him out, calling over her shoulder. 'I'll see Adam out, Peter.'

Then Adam closed the door gently and they walked down the passage side by side.

He said: 'I'm going to send out flood warnings right away, on behalf of the Congress Committee. Harnarayan's due back from Lahore this evening, but I don't know whether we dare wait even that long.'

They had stopped under the *porte cochère*. It was a heavy, dull evening, and behind her she could hear ayah singing to the children, and the splashings in the bathtub. Adam said: 'I think Harnarayan is going to come back with a new policy, not to co-operate with you at all – but I am afraid that nine-tenths of the people won't

491

believe us if we issue a flood warning on our own. They'll think it's some trick of politics. And of course we have no power to make them *do* anything. All the same, I'm afraid I'll have to do it.'

She said: 'Peter's going to retire early next year.'

He said nothing for a time, and when he spoke it was only to say: 'Gerry would have died twice rather than that this should happen.' They were silent together, standing on the top step. Adam said in a different tone of voice: 'I hear Baber came to see you this afternoon. It was about his young lady, I suppose? She is an excellent girl. What did you advise?'

She said: 'Nothing. I felt I couldn't.'

'That was wise of you. But you have always been wise. The poor boy is in such a turmoil that he is coming to see me tomorrow. I think, even, that he will take my advice.'

'What are you going to tell him?'

'After the Amritsar massacre, what can I say?' Adam said sadly. 'I will do all I can to prevent him joining your army. Perhaps he will come to us in the party yet. Good night.'

'Good night, Adam,' she said. 'I'll make sure everything's seen to right away.'

A tonga bell jangled cheerfully at the entrance to the drive, and she saw the tonga lights swing into view. Adam's face began to tilt sideways, and the sound of the tonga wheels on the gravel grew louder and louder. She was on her knees, her hands supporting her. Adam was rolling down the steps head over heels the lights swayed, swayed swung, a sound of rushing tearing grinding increased, a wind coming, from nowhere shrieked up and up in pitch till her eardrums would break I am dying, she thought I have had a heart attack, I am dying. Oh! The children's faces sprang into form, and she began, to crawl, towards them, calling, 'Peter! Darling!' But a huge formless weight pressed her into the gravel and Adam was there bleeding from a long cut, his trousers torn, and Peggy's voice rose in a shrill low sound like the howling of a dog – 'Harry! Harry! What's happened?' The wind! Ah, the wind had gone as suddenly as it came. She stood up, unsteadily, climbing, the steps to, get to Peter.

The side of the *porte cochère* had collapsed. The tonga lights had gone out, and the lights in the bungalow, and in the city. It was absolutely silent and there was glass under her feet. The bungalow still stood, but slowly chunks of noise roared like avalanches through the silence as a distant house fell, a block of plaster fell, a tower in the city fell. Then, rising like the wind that had accompanied the earthquake, she heard the slowly gathering sigh of men and women and children crying under the ruins.

Near at hand heavily shod feet pounded towards her – *crash, crash, crash.* Harry Walsh's voice was yelling: 'Steady! Steady!' He was beside her, his face a foot from hers. 'Are you hurt?' he said curtly. 'Good. Get the children, everyone, out of the building. It'll come again.' His voice was harsh, and she saw that he was trembling and shaking and visibly fighting to quiet the shrieking of his nerves. His eyes were never still and snapped from her to the dark garden, to Adam, to Peggy coming slowly forward behind him, to the sky. 'It's come again,' Harry said. 'It's just like the war – everything ruined, everything, everything everyone had made.' His voice rose in a yell. 'Look! Look!' He pointed at the city, where there was nothing to see and to hear, only the rising moan.

Peter came out, nursing his arm. 'No one is seriously hurt here,' he said. 'Now – what's the first thing to be done?'

CHAPTER 34

By nine o'clock the sense of a visitation from forces more powerful than any on earth had left her, slowly submerged under the lesser, because understood, realization of an appalling natural calamity – a violent earthquake. From eastern dark to western trees the night sky flared with the licking tongues of fires. Her children and household were safe. The bungalow had suffered no major damage though one end of the veranda had caved in, a beam fallen across Peter's study, and most of the glass shattered. There was no rain, though clouds hid the stars. A wind had been growing gradually for the past hour and a half as the heat of the fires in the city sucked in the cold air from the Maghra Valley. Occasionally the rumble of stone and brick, sounding like a train in a tunnel, came through the whipping curtains into the drawing-room.

Much had happened. Officials and private citizens had come, and gone or stayed. A dozen families had come to the compound, carrying a few bundles, their children clutched in their arms or running silent and frightened at their knees, and now squatted in huddled groups under the wall or along the veranda. She herself had just gone with the *bhisti* to make sure that the well was in working order, for the town mains had burst and there was no water in the taps.

Six people were gathered in the drawing-room – Peter; Adam Khan; his son Baber; Smythe, the District Superintendent of Police; Harry; and Peggy. It was not a formal conference, since these and others had been coming and going since the shock. All were filthy, and the carpet was stained and splotched with ash and cinders and powdered brick. Smythe's tunic was smeared with blood, but no one had time or interest to ask him whose blood it was.

Baber stood with legs apart and nostrils flared, tensed for action, and his young Arab stallion champed at its head-rope in the garden. 'I will bring in all the men from the villages to the west,' he said, 'with mattocks and spades. They will need crowbars too, sir. Can you provide them?'

Peter said: 'I think so... Yes... Emily, make a note to get Yar Khan back here... But, Baber, perhaps the villages have suffered as much as the city.'

'No, sir,' Baber cried energetically. 'I told you when I came in, there was little damage. The houses are not heavy. Can I go now?'

Peter said: 'Very well... I think that's best.'

Baber strode to the open French windows. 'I'll bring them to the octroi post on the Lahore road. The first ones should be in by midnight.' A moment later she heard the stallion's neigh, and then the crunch and gallop of its hoofs fading down the drive.

'Looting's going to be a problem later,' Smythe said. He was a short man with a cropped ginger moustache and ginger hair. 'My chaps have so much else to do. I'd like three or four hundred

Gurkhas from Manali to help with street cordons and the rest of it – more, if we can get them.'

'Have you been able to make any guess at the number of casualties yet?' Adam Khan asked. He was more composed than his son but there was the same excited sense of crisis there, softened in him by sadness at the human effects of the calamity.

'About ten thousand dead,' Smythe said bluntly, 'mostly in the Gujarabad sector. Everyone who can is running away from it now, but in the morning they'll start coming back to rescue Granny and dig up the gold *mohurs* from under the floor. We'll have to cordon the whole sector off while we search the ruins. We ought to ask for those soldiers at once, Peter. The telegraph's open to Manali. They know we've had a 'quake.'

'We're not through to Lahore, though?' Peter said.

'No,' Smythe said, impatiently brushing his hand up under his moustache. 'But we don't need to ask H.E's permission to call on the Army now. I'll sign the message if you like.' His look was openly contemptuous. Emily told herself that she hated him for his insensitiveness, his coarse skin and manner, and his taking advantage of Peter. But it was not true. She sympathized with him.

'Well, can I?' he repeated harshly.

'If you think you'll need them... Yes,' Peter said.

'Good. I'm going down to the kutcherry now. You'll find me there if you want me.' He walked out, swinging his swagger cape. At the window a

497

constable handed him a shotgun. He put it over his shoulder and disappeared. The two pairs of boots faded, crunch-crunch, down the drive.

Emily could not bear to look at Peter sitting there alone in the middle of the big sofa, and stole a glance at Harry and Peggy. Harry's face was without expression; only his eyes moved restlessly, like a bird's, fastening on to the face of each person who spoke and, when there was silence, turning to Peggy or looking out of the windows to catch something in the heaving sky. Peggy was beautiful, calm, smooth and rounded and lovely. Smythe had hardly taken his eyes off her; and Peggy had not taken her eyes off Peter. She sat on a high chair in sensuous, drowsy satisfaction, a woman fulfilled.

Now she spoke. 'Peter, why don't you get Harry to put each member of the Meru expedition in charge of a gang of volunteers and set them to rescue work? Most of them were officers in the war and have some sort of experience that would be useful.'

Peter nodded. 'That's a good idea, Peggy. What do you say, Harry?'

'Yes,' Harry said, the word tight and bitten off. 'I've been over there once. They're all working on a house that fell down right next to the dâk bungalow. Where shall I bring them?'

Peter appeared to be thinking. Emily said: 'The kutcherry would be best, Peter. It's on the edge of the Gujarabad sector.'

'And that young man, Baber, Adam's son, can be told to bring his men there, can't he?' Peggy said.

Peter said: 'All right. As soon as you can, Harry. Smythe will find something for you to do until the volunteers arrive.'

Harry and Peggy rose to their feet. Peggy came over to Emily. 'Can't we start a tea and soup kitchen or something, Emily, at the kutcherry? For the people who are working, I mean. We can't possibly feed the victims.'

'Yes,' she said. 'Speak to my cook, and get the khansamah down from the dâk bungalow with all the stores he has. There's a shop close to the kutcherry which we can raid, and get tea and sugar at least. I'll be down in an hour.' She knew she ought to go at once, not in an hour, but she dared not leave Peter; and Peggy, lazily competent, knew that.

Adam Khan said: 'We can help there, Peter. As Peggy said, we can't feed all the victims, but we can get an organization to do so started. I've sent messengers to get hold of the committee, telling them to meet at that shop Emily was talking about, next to the kutcherry. About an hour and a half from now I can get, say, two hundred people together to run a camp for refugees. You designate a place and give us authority to get supplies wherever we can find them.'

'I thought Harnarayan was away,' Peter said.

'He is,' Adam said impatiently. 'He was due back by bus this evening from Lahore, but we don't need to wait for him. I can vouch for the committee and the party. We'll do all we can now, and argue later. This is no time for politics.'

Peter said: 'I agree. Where do you suggest would be a good place for your camp?'

Adam said: 'We're going to need plenty of room – water – but not far out, because a lot of people aren't going to be able to walk very far.'

'The fields outside the River Gate?' Peter said enquiringly.

Adam shook his head. 'No. Don't forget the flood. Have you had any report on the river? That's still rising, as far as we know.'

Peter said: 'I suppose it is. Emily, we'll have to get Yar Khan to keep an eye on that too.'

'The old cavalry *maidan* and the fields beyond are the best area,' Adam said. 'I'll tell them that's the place.'

'All right,' Peter said. 'I don't think there's anything else we can do just now... I'll be going down to the kutcherry as soon as I've had something to eat.'

Now, at the heels of a distant rumble, Emily heard sandalled feet slapping down the veranda towards the windows. The three of them turned as a thin, tall man with an ascetic face entered the room. His eyes were black and luminous and his hair thick, luxuriant, and black above the tall, narrow forehead.

'Harnarayan!' Adam said. 'Thank heaven you got here.'

'We were only five miles out when the shock came,' the man said. 'The driver refused to go on, so I walked. Good evening, Mr Savage. Good evening, ma'am.'

'Can I give you something to eat?' Emily said. 'Some tea?' He looked tired and taut.

'No, thank you, ma'am, I came only to find Adam. I was told he was here. Will you come along now, Adam? We have something urgent to discuss.'

'I have called the committee to meet in the room above Gupta's store,' Adam said. 'We're going to organize a refugee camp on the old cavalry *maidan*.'

'I'm afraid that will be impossible,' Harnarayan said formally.

Adam said: 'It is not impossible. We can't do everything, but we can provide a framework. Otherwise there'd be no leaders, and everything would take much longer.'

'Exactly,' Harnarayan said harshly. 'Why should we get the British out of trouble? They suppress us, and then when they need us they think they can call on us and we'll help them.'

Peter said nothing. Emily blurted: 'Ten thousand people – Indians – are dead, Mr Harnarayan! More are dying every minute. Besides, isn't this a chance for you to show that you can organize help as well as resistance?'

Harnarayan said: 'Possibly, madam, but we prefer to let the people see for themselves how thoroughly bad and helpless your government is, even mechanically. That way they will realize their own strength. We must go, Adam.'

'Wait!' Adam said. 'I can't believe you mean what you say, Haru. Look!' He pointed out of the windows, where the sky hung like an embroidered curtain over the city and the low wailing faltered up and down the scale and in the foreground men and women trailed slowly across the lawns. 'Our people are dying, they're trapped in the houses! Those who got out have no food,

501

no shelter, no water!'

'Individually any member of the Congress may do what he wishes,' Harnarayan said. 'As a party we will not raise a finger to help the British.'

'You're wrong,' Adam said, and now he spoke as harshly as Harnarayan. 'You're wrong, even politically. Don't you realize that every man and woman we help will know it's the Congress that's helping him? We'll come out of this with the party stronger here than anywhere in India.'

'No,' Harnarayan said. 'There can be no compromise. We are not going to co-operate, in anything, at any time, with the British oppressors. This disaster will show a lot of things up in their true colours. All those who have accepted the sops the British throw to them will wait for the British to do something. And they can't. It's too big. They need everyone's help – but everyone's indifferent. "The English will rescue us," they say. Well, we're going to let them.'

Adam Khan turned back from the windows. He said quietly. 'No, we're not, Harnarayan. We're going to help. We have to. I gave my word to Peter, and even if I hadn't, I would say that we must.'

Emily thought: Peter ought to have Harnarayan arrested at once. That would leave Adam a free hand to persuade his committee to do what they should. She glanced outside, where a chuprassi and a policeman squatted, half dozing against a pillar of the veranda.

Adam saw her look, and must have guessed her thoughts, for he said: 'It won't do any good to arrest him – in the long run. This is something we must argue out among ourselves. Come on, Haru.'

'Very well,' Harnarayan said. 'But you will lose. The committee will do what I tell them.'

'We'll see,' Adam said. 'I'll meet you at the kutcherry in about an hour, Peter. Don't forget about the floods.' He followed Harnarayan out of the room, and she was alone with the man on the sofa, Mr Peter Savage, D.S.O, I.C.S, Deputy Commissioner and District Magistrate of the Rudwal District of the Punjab.

An hour later, with Emily riding at Peter's side, a groom running at their heels and the policeman and the chuprassi hurrying behind, they reached the kutcherry. It was an ugly quadrangle of buildings containing a small treasury, Peter's court, and a few offices, including Smythe's. A high wall surrounded it, and one entered through a tall arch set just back from the busy street. Now the arch had fallen in, and a few of the offices had crumbled, but as a whole the group still stood.

Emily saw at once that Gupta's shop was undamaged, and that there was a crowd outside it. The only light came from reflections in the low sky and from a house burning a hundred yards away down a side street. Peggy was there already, a tent set like an awning beside the fallen arch, the khansamah from the dâk bungalow lighting a fire, and nameless men running hither and thither with pots, pans, sacks, and buckets. Harry stood beside Peggy, staring at the rubble, at the burning house, at the sky. When Emily came close enough she saw that his face was set, emotionless, and deliberately unanxious. That look – she had watched it for an hour in the living-room – had worried her by calling up memories, and now she placed them. Gerry used to look like that when Peter was leading towards some height that Gerry feared he was incapable of surmounting. It was panic, transmuted by a lifetime of training into something that was the opposite of panic – a control so tight that a sudden, unexpected blow would shatter it.

After speaking to Peggy, she turned away. They needed more wood to keep the fire going. She would ask Peter... No, she would not. There was wood aplenty in the fallen offices. 'Burn the tables,' she said; and men hurried to obey her.

The minutes, and then the hours, passed unheeded; some order appeared at the kutcherry; there were always tea and chupattis, and tired men, and bandages. Smythe arrived to say that the police cordon was in place round the Gujarabad sector; but it was too weak to be of the slightest use by day, as most of his men were on rescue work. Peter went off with him to make a personal inspection. Baber came with a hundred men, armed with picks and mattocks and crowbars from the Public Works Department store. Yar Khan, the P.W.D overseer, was in tears because Baber had broken open the store and taken the articles without permission, and no one had signed a chit for them, or even counted what had been taken.

A nightwatchman came and reported that the Maghra was rising at the same rate; Emily sent him off to find Peter. The members of the Meru expedition took Baber's villagers, group by group, and disappeared into the smoking alleys of the city. The flames died here and rose there, but the smell of burning never left her nostrils – burning grain, old timber, prepared food, books, flesh. Sparks rose in towering pillars from afar; men and women walked past, hurrying, carrying beds on their heads... 'Where do we go, mem-sahib? Where do we go?'

'*Purana risala ki maidan*,' she repeated, over and over.

Adam Khan had emerged, tight-lipped, from Gupta's shop and told her that the Congress party was not going to run the camp; but he personally would – with volunteers, many of them Congress men.

Smythe returned and told her Peter was having a look at the river. After an hour Smythe muttered: 'He ought to be back by now. It's not my bloody job to make these decisions. I've got my own work to do.'

She said nothing; Peter *ought* to be back. Someone else made the decisions – either herself or Baber or Smythe or Harry, and, most of all, Peggy. Peggy was smooth and exultant. She took care of everything, thought of everything. She was tireless, heroic, competent and calm, and her every word and action gloated over Emily.

Harry returned, and Emily gave him hot tea in a tin bowl. He was dyed with soot now, and his hands when he showed them to her, had been badly scorched. He drank, looked at her, and said: 'I came to climb Meru – sun, snow, ice, nothing changed, not just since I saw it last, but ever. *This!* I told you, it's just like France.' He drank again. 'I've never seen a real city in rubble, though.'

Emily glanced at him wearily. It must be near dawn, for there were pale green and dove-grey banners in the sky, and a pallor shone in the eyes of the townspeople shuffling by and in the faces of the villagers wearily slumped over their mattocks. Fifty yards down the street corpses were piling high in an empty lot, and soon the sun would be up. Something would have to be done about them before the day was far advanced. She thought there must be six hundred bodies there already. Peggy had disappeared.

'That's the same too,' Harry said. 'Corpses, piled on each other, and men walking across them. I don't feel it any more, after France.'

You don't feel it, she thought. You're ready to scream with the horror of it. It is I who feel nothing, because I am thinking and feeling for one individual only – my husband.

Where was he? What was he doing, what was he feeling in this climactic moment when all his power should have been released in an explosion of will – the survivors of a city frantic to turn the will into action?

Poor Harry. There was no escape, as there had been none in France. The stifling heat pressed smoke and the smell of death into the nostrils; the houses enclosed the horizon, bringing closer the empty lot where mangled women lay, their red clothes crushed into the flesh, and men lay hooked round each other in broken swastikas of white sharp bone and pasty skin, and children lay face up, naked in the warmth of the night, unknowing, wide-eyed.

Baber and his men came, with Peggy. 'Lady Margaret is a hero,' Baber said. 'She went with us into a burning house to help a woman who was trapped under a beam – she was having a baby. We saved the baby.' Peggy had it in her arms, small, squalling – and Peggy's face alight with a different warmth under the elegant filth. Baber called to a villager. 'Ohé, take the child from the memsahib.'

Emily gave Peggy a bowl of tea. 'Baber's a hero too,' Peggy said. 'He worked for half an hour with a burning beam just above his back – and then half a wall fell on him. Where's Peter?'

'I don't know,' Emily said.

Everyone was a hero, except Peter, that night. But the dawn was up, and, as at the end of the war, she could see for the first time the extent of the destruction.

A villager ran up and spoke rapidly to Baber. Baber swung round. The villager pointed to a three-storey house only twenty yards down the street, on the opposite side.

Baber turned. 'That house settled forward just now, he says. It's creaking inside. He doesn't know whether there's anyone in it.' He shouted to the villagers. Half a dozen of them sprang forward. He cried: 'Bring them along, Mr Walsh – quickly!'

But Harry was already moving, the villagers hurrying after him. The sun was up now, and a tongue of flame licked out of the lower storey of the house. 'The fools!' Baber cried. 'They were cooking...' He ran after Harry, a crowbar in his hand. Emily realized that the street was full of people. They had been there all night, tucked into corners, waiting. Some were under the creaking house, some where the house would fall. She ran forward, screaming: 'Get out of the way! Hurry!'

Yar Khan panted up beside her as she stopped at the edge of the danger zone. 'The river is still rising, memsahib,' he said. 'I can't find the Deputy Commissioner Sahib anywhere. The Police Sahib says he can do nothing. There is nothing to do – but my go-down, with the accounts, is in danger. What shall we do?'

'Be quiet!' she screamed.

'Look at Harry!' Peggy cried, her voice exultant. 'Look at him!'

The men had run into the front door of the building and, a few seconds later, came tumbling out again as though they had met a tiger. A gout of fire and a torrent of black smoke followed them out, and no further explanation was needed. It was an old house, heavily ornamented in the Hindu style, and already Harry was going up the façade, his feet bare and a rope trailing from his waist.

'Look at Harry,' Peggy said. 'Look at him, Emily.'

Up he went, easily and quickly, and into a second-storey window. A moment later she saw him again as he helped an old man to get a grip on the rope. The old man slid down, Baber caught him at the bottom, and the old man danced about shrieking and holding his burned hands. A wailing woman followed. Finally Harry scrambled out and began to slide down, using one hand and his legs on the rope and holding a large shapeless bundle over his shoulder with his free hand. The building swayed slowly forward.

Peggy screamed: 'Oh, quick, quick, Harry, quick!' But no one could hear down there for the roar of the building and the rumble of the flames now pouring out of the lower windows and the door. All the men and the spectators crowded back. Harry reached the ground.

'Run!' Baber shrieked.

In the cleared place Harry ran with the bundle. Beyond, silhouetted against a sudden brilliance of the sun, the crowd stood frozen, and one of them was kneeling with a black box camera held in front of his face.

The bundle slipped from Harry's shoulder and fell heavily. For a fraction of a second he hesitated, half turning to stoop and pick it up. Then he ran on, alone. The high, many-windowed wall, embellished with gods and demons, leaned out over him, breaking like a wave of ocean, like the crest of the Matterhorn above him. The bundle rolled, stood, and was revealed as a young girl, her face split by a cry of terror. She took one limping step and then stood frozen, while Harry ran. The house fell and engulfed the girl, and a great cloud of reddish dust, lit by flames and smoke, licked at Harry's heels and hid the crowd beyond, and the man with the camera.

Emily turned away, feeling sick. 'I've got to find Peter,' she mumbled. She began to run. The groom was beside her in a moment. Yes, yes, the horse! She scrambled into the saddle. Peter had gone away to hide from all the decisions. Where? She'd try the bungalow first.

She could go no faster than a trot through the ruined streets, and it took her nearly twenty minutes, and a dozen detours, to reach the bungalow. The groom took the bridle as she dismounted. She climbed slowly up the veranda steps, stepped over a score of sleeping bodies, and walked into the drawing-room.

He was there, on the sofa, staring out at his city and the sunshine and shadow that swept slowly across it. It was strange that no one had thought to come here to find him – but the place was deserted except for the refugees and ayah and the children, and even ayah probably did not know he was here.

She went to him and said: 'Peter, you've got to come down to the kutcherry – at once.'

He stood up, and she prayed that she would feel a wave of anger, terror, even hate, come out against her. But there was nothing, only the limpid reasonableness of the past four years.

She said: 'It's Harry.'

'Oh,' he said. 'Is he hurt?'

'No,' she said. 'He was rescuing a girl from a building. It fell down, and he left her so that he could run away faster to save himself. Purshottam Dass took a photograph of it.'

Purshottam Dass was the local correspondent of the *Patriot*, a nationalist newspaper published in virulent English in Lahore. He was also Harnarayan's right-hand man in the extremist wing of the local Congress group.

'Harry – ran away to save himself,' Peter said slowly. 'I don't believe it.' He did not speak in a puzzled tone at all.

'It's true,' she said, her voice rising. 'Just as true as that you're sitting here, doing nothing, when Rudwal needs you more than it ever did or ever will.'

'Did Peggy see?' he asked.

'Yes. Everything. She had just been telling me to watch because he was so brave – and asking where you were, in the same breath.'

Yar Khan stumbled in. 'M-memsahib,' he stammered, 'the watchman at the river says it is beginning to rise fast, much faster. It will be over the bund in four hours if it goes on at this speed.'

She said: 'The Harab dam, whatever it was! It must have broken.'

Peter said: 'That will flood the whole of the Gujarabad sector to about three feet.'

She said: 'The last time I saw Smythe he thought there were about a thousand injured people, living, trapped in the debris down there. We couldn't get a quarter of them out in time. Oh, Peter, what can we do?'

'Harry,' he muttered. 'Oh, my God! I'll come down. Harry can help. That's it. Harry can do it. Quick – get that horse. We'll go down on it together. Yar Khan, run to the kutcherry!'

CHAPTER 35

Peter held the pony to a smart trot all the way to the kutcherry. Clinging round his waist, she wanted to yell in his ear: 'Faster, faster, the river's rising!' Tragedy spread around them, but she was in a comedy, bouncing up and down on the rump of a small horse.

Peter guided the pony rapidly over the piled wreckage in the streets. 'Harry!' he cried once, as though he had seen Harry in a dangerous place and wanted to warn him. She knew he was not thinking of the rising river, or the fires, or the shattered city, or the people dead by thousands and set out by hundreds for death, or the pale corpses, or the plagues which must be gathering even now, like the river, ready to flow in and overwhelm all that remained of Rudwal. He was thinking of the sorrow and final defeat, in his own fields of courage and self-control and self-sacrifice, of one man.

The fallen house now blocked the street beyond the kutcherry, towards the Gujarabad sector. She marvelled that so many storeys of height, containing so many rooms and so much living, now stood only a foot or two above the earth, with beams pointing up and flames running like lazy rats in and under the rubbled bricks and a thin diseased smoke writhing up to dull the farther view down the canyon of the street.

Baber had gone somewhere with most of his men. Most of those that remained were standing in a group under the kutcherry wall. The tent where they had made tea all night stood alone and, alone in it, Harry and Peggy. Even the khansamah had left. Emily could not believe that he would desert them at this time. Then she saw him sprawled asleep under the wall a few yards off; but the effect was the same, whether it was fatigue or duty or disgust that had sent the rest away. Harry and Peggy were alone.

Peter reined in, and Emily slid down, and he in his turn. Peter walked up to Harry. 'Harry, do you know anything about explosives?'

Harry said: 'A little.' Peggy had shrunk, like the fallen house, like the corpses, the material envelope fallen in about the emptied spaces of the spirit. If Emily had not recognized the grey dress, stained and torn but still showing the perfection of its style, she would hardly have recognized her. Age had come on Peggy. The hate that had smoothed her skin and the courage that had put a new bloom on her cheeks had gone. She had become, in an hour, a woman old before her time, and even the eyes were lacking in life of any kind.

Harry was different. Emily had expected to find him trembling, or possessed by some tautly silent neighbour to insanity, like the young men back from France, whom she had occasionally seen walking the sands below Harlech while they convalesced from the mysterious new malady of shell shock. But Harry was calm and the eyes, which had wandered like birds before, to fasten

513

and suck and dart away, were still and steady on Peter, and, as Peter's used to be, without depth.

Baber and Smythe appeared together. They were utterly weary, and silent with the realization that they had done all they could and it wasn't enough.

Peter said: 'I'm going to send Yar Khan to Shamoli, Harry. It's a mile upstream, on the other bank. There is an old bed of the Maghra there. Shamoli stands in it. I want the bank blown in, so that the Maghra flows down its old course. Yar Khan will be in charge of the demolition, and Baber's men will do the spadework. Baber, how many men can you get within five minutes?'

Baber croaked, cleared his throat, and tried again. 'Thirty.'

'Good. Get across the river at once. Go yourself and get everyone out of Shamoli on to the high ground to the north, at once, by force if necessary. Yar Khan, take all the explosives you've got out of the stores, and all your men, and get to Shamoli. Harry, you're in charge of the whole thing. See that it's done.'

Harry said: 'I can't do that.'

Peter said: 'Why?'

Baber had already gone, his cracked voice raised in urgent shouting. A moment later the villagers began the high-pitched chanting with which they called their sons from distant fields.

Harry said: 'I lost my nerve just now. I killed a girl. No one will listen to me.'

'Has anyone said anything to you about it?' Peter asked, lighting a cheroot.

Oh, hurry, hurry, Emily whispered. Hurry – for the fires crackled, and the city lay at the door of death, and the silent river climbed out of its bed. How can you waste time arguing with him? Go yourself! Go, go, go!

Harry said: 'No, they're all pretending it didn't happen. They feel sorry for me. But I know what they're really thinking, because I'm thinking it myself.'

Peter said: 'That's done, Harry. There are a thousand lives to save now. Go on.'

Yar Khan was there, panting a hundred questions... 'Where can I get a cart to transport the explosives to Shamoli?... How long before the last bridge over the Maghra goes?'

Peter said: 'Go to the tonga stand outside the station. Take my horse. Smythe, find me four constables to go with Mr Walsh.'

Smythe snapped: 'All the police are busy.'

'Take four off the cordon. Quickly, please.'

Smythe turned angrily and spoke to the policeman at his heels. The man ran off, stumbling and heavy-footed. Smythe said: 'The Gurkhas are on their way – two companies. They should be here by three this afternoon.'

Peter nodded. Harry still waited, his mouth a little open. Peggy said: 'He can't go, Peter, can't you see? He can't! Can't you see, he's afraid it'll happen again!'

Peter said: 'He must, and it won't. Go on, Harry.'

Now it was there in his voice and eye, force from the past. He did not speak loudly, but he never had; his eyes were the colour of icebergs, as they had always been, but not cold now; and all the power came together to focus on his friend. As though electrical wires had been connected inside him, Harry began to walk after Baber and his men. They were running, and Harry began to run, and so running faster and stumbling harder they all clambered over the burning rubble which covered the dead girl, and disappeared.

Abruptly Peggy turned and walked away. Emily watched her go and turned to Peter. 'Don't you think you ought to go to Shamoli, Peter? Yar Khan always needs a lot of speeding up, and if they don't hurry they–'

Peter said: 'It will help Harry to do it himself.' He turned away and began pouring himself a bowl of tea. A nurse from the hospital was struggling down the street at an awkward run, her sari hampering her movements. Emily repeated to herself: 'It will help Harry.' It meant nothing to Peter that a thousand people might die if Harry failed. She could not believe he had made a good decision – but he had made one, for the sake of someone who he thought was in a more miserable state than his own. Perhaps that was what had been needed all these years – that he should meet, as he walked numbly through the world, a being who felt worse, lower, more useless than he did.

The nurse was talking quickly to Peter, waving her hands – they had run out of anæsthetics, and one of the doctors had fainted from exhaustion. All the beds at the Lady Curzon had been full since an hour after the shock, but now the grounds were full too, and there was not a spare inch of space in which to put the moaning men and women whom the police and the growing army of volunteers kept bringing. Emily waited anxiously when the girl finished with the inevitable, heart-wringing question: 'What are we to do?'

Peter stared at the nurse, and Emily thought for a moment that he was going to cry. Then he said: 'You'll have to tell them to do the best they can for now… I'll send a telegram to Manali, Sister. The soldiers are coming, and they will certainly have sent down their doctor and all the anæsthetics they can spare.'

Emily cut in eagerly: 'Yes, Sister, and tell Doctor Dhayal to have all new patients sent to the maidan. The Meru expedition's doctor is working up there.'

She sat down on a wooden box that someone had placed behind the table where they had been serving tea. Eleven o'clock in the morning. September 14, 1920. Things were getting organized; the wooden box showed it. The news of the disaster ought to have reached Lahore sometime during the night. How? By carrier pigeon? There were none. But bad news always travelled fast. Help could be expected to reach Rudwal during this coming night or the following morning. The hours had passed in a wave-like rhythm: first the huge shock of the earthquake; then a quiescence, and during it the gathering together of individual and collective will, the feeble beat of that little wave expending itself in the stanching of wounds and the rescue of neighbours; then that too dying away in a long suspiration as men and women sank down under walls and in dark fields and went to sleep, and the helpers dozed over their tasks, and no man moved fast, and few moved at all; then again the gathering, in secret places, of man's power to organize against extinction, and the rising sound of crowbar and shovel and falling stone, and the quickening pace of the refugees, and in the city the single, decisive rifle shots, a looter running, hit, turning, astonished, falling under the feet of the grim policeman – all this gathering towards the dawn, a moment of supreme pause, and *crash!* the wave burst down, the house fell, Harry ran, Peggy broke, the girl died.

In the sunlight the city sprawled in front of her, and to the east she could see the gleaming of the sun on the river.

Adam Khan came on a country pony. 'Peter,' he said, 'we're full up on the maidan. I'm sending everyone I can out into the country.'

Peter said: 'All right.'

Adam said: 'I heard about Harry. Harnarayan has already sent Purshottam Dass to Lahore with that photograph, among others. I couldn't prevent him.'

Peter said: 'No. I've sent Harry to Shamoli.'

'What for?'

'To blow down the bund there and put the Maghra in the old bed.'

Adam's weary eyes lit up, and he said: 'Great heaven! That's a stroke of genius. Who thought of that?'

Emily said: 'Peter did.'

Adam said: 'Wonderful! If it can be done in

time you'll save the Gujarabad sector and everyone trapped in it.'

'It will help Harry,' Peter said.

Adam stroked his chin and looked at Emily. After a while he asked: 'Where's Baber?'

Peter said: 'With Harry. His job is to clear the people out of Shamoli. It should be done by now.' He looked at his watch. 'They've got about half an hour more, according to Yar Khan's reckoning, but I don't suppose you can measure things as close as that, really.'

Adam said: 'We're all going to be busy for a good long time, Peter. I want to tell you, before I get swamped with other things, that I'm going to advise Baber to go to Sandhurst. His lady will wait – if she's as good as he and I think.'

Peter nodded but did not speak. Emily said: 'And you? Are you leaving the Congress?'

Adam shook his head. He said: 'No. I think Harnarayan and the rest of them made an appalling mistake here. The fact that you British made one in Amritsar doesn't alter that. I'm going to fight from the inside to make Congress see the way I think they ought to.'

'Why are you encouraging Baber to go to Sandhurst, then?' she asked. It was getting hot now, and she wanted to lie down in a shady place, but this talk held a febrile interest, for it seemed to prove that there would be a tomorrow in which she would awake and find all this gone and a new world waiting.

Adam said: 'This earthquake has altered my set of values a bit – as the war did in its way. Suppose we – the Congress – got everything we were

519

asking for tomorrow, and you all went away on the next boat. Would that mean we didn't need an army or a police force or engineers or judges? Harnarayan says Baber is a traitor to work for you – but it seems to me that he and people like him are strengthening our legs so that when we are free to walk alone we'll be able to.'

Peter nodded again. The street was full of people, and she realized dully that it had been so all night and all morning – people moving, dragging, dying, eating. There was an incredible litter of blankets, boxes, sacks, beds, scraps of food, firewood, carts, and everywhere the gleam of cooking pots.

'I'll be getting back,' Adam said. 'About half the Congress people here are working with me. A hundred and fifty others came to help during the night.'

A brown stain rose slowly into the sky above the city, wide and low-spread over the houses to the east. Dully she watched. Adam jerked to a stop in mid-stride. A heavy shudder shook the earth and rattled the skeletal walls of the house across the street. Adam was shouting an urgent question, but nothing could be heard under the continuing roar of the explosion.

Peter grabbed her elbow and said exultantly: 'Harry's done it!'

Smythe came scrambling down the street towards them. 'Everyone who can be moved is out of the Gujarabad sector,' he said. 'We haven't been able to check properly into all the fallen houses, but we counted seven hundred and sixty people alive, trapped in the houses. About half of them are going to die anyway – injuries, shock. Was that the Shamoli bund going?'

'I think so,' Peter said.

Smythe said: 'It'll back up later on. The old course is silted right up about twelve miles down, remember? Christ, they've been growing crops on it for thirty years!'

Peter said: 'Yes, but it'll give us at least another twenty-four hours to dig in the Gujarabad sector.'

'The water's in to a few inches now,' Smythe said, 'and it was coming up fast when I left. That was before the bund went, of course. Now what?'

'Why don't you rest for an hour or two?' Peter said. 'This is going to go on for a long time.'

'Rest!' Smythe snorted. 'How the hell can I rest? Where's Lady Margaret?' He glanced round and lowered his voice. 'Did you hear about Walsh?'

'Yes,' Peter said abruptly. 'And I don't want you to mention it to anyone, or let it slip into your conversation.'

Smythe exploded. 'Christ, Peter, tomorrow it's going to be all over the front page of the *Patriot* and every vernacular paper in India! We can't pretend it didn't happen.'

'We can pretend it wasn't Harry Walsh that did it,' Peter said, 'because it wasn't. It was what's left of him after France. *You* weren't in France.' He looked grimly at the red-faced policeman.

Smythe mumbled: 'All right.'

Peter said: 'As soon as he comes back I'm going to send him down to work with you in the Gujarabad sector. See that he's put in charge of something, without supervision.'

'Right,' Smythe said. 'I'm off. By the way, we've shot nine looters so far. That's pretty good, that there have been so few, considering.'

Peter agreed, and after a while the two men began to discuss the disposal of the huge pile of corpses. Emily sat down again, her head rocking dully from right to left, then forward and back. The sun had gone, and it was grey, damp, and hot. Her head ached with a slow, throbbing rhythm. She thought it was going to rain, and she thought it would not be enough to put out the remaining fires. What would happen to the people in the open fields? Were her children all right? Who was looking after them?

She awoke with a start. She was lying on the ground against the wall, and someone had put a rolled blanket under her head. She heard strange voices and saw Gurkha soldiers and officers. Baber was there, and Smythe, and another English police officer. Down the street, near the pile of corpses, a thick mass of red-and-blue turbaned policemen was falling into rough lines. The Commissioner was there, a little apart, talking with Peter. Harry Walsh was there.

How many hours had passed? She struggled to her feet. The rhythm of the disaster was still working, for after the quiet ebb there was gathering now this new wave of effort. Soon the wreckage would be only of material things, like buildings, and the ways of thought would be back in familiar channels. Peggy had returned, her face bloodless, as surely filled with pent emotion as the scene around them was filled with latent movement. The rhythm was working in her too.

Peter turned to Harry. 'Are you feeling up to it?'

Harry muttered: 'Yes. I'm not tired.'

The Commissioner said: 'You look it.'

'I'm not,' Harry repeated.

Peter said: 'Then go ahead.'

Peggy broke in. 'Where are you sending him now?'

Peter said: 'There's a big fire in the Hardial sector. It's been smouldering all day, but now it's beginning to spread.'

'You can't send him to a fire,' Peggy said, her voice high and brittle.

'I must,' Peter said. 'He's the only man who can do it.'

Harry stood hang-shouldered between them. The Commissioner said: 'I don't want to interfere, Peter, but I really think Walsh is dead beat.'

'He is not,' Peter said sharply. 'Baber, you'll go with Mr Walsh?'

Baber nodded. Emily saw that the young man knew exactly what Peter was doing, and why. His look, as he glanced at Peter, was different from anything she remembered since he had been a small hero-worshipping boy. Peter said: 'Get a move on, Harry.'

Peggy turned to the Commissioner and said: 'Don't let him go. Haven't you heard? He...'

Peter drew back his arm and with an effortless gesture struck his open hand across her face, so hard that she sprawled back, staggered, slipped, and fell.

'Peter!' Emily cried, aghast, stooping to help

Peggy to her feet.

'Get a move on, Harry,' Peter said. 'There's no human life involved, so I don't want you to allow any unnecessary risks. The buildings were cleared hours ago. Just get the fire out and, if you can't, demolish the houses around it so that it won't spread.'

Peggy leaned like a sack against Emily, whispering: 'Oh God!... Oh God!'

'Come away,' Emily whispered. 'I'll look after you. Come on.'

She put her arms under the other's elbows and half lifted, half dragged her along the street, past the corpses and the carts slowly loading there, over the rubble, and towards the bungalow.

When they reached it she found Rodney carrying water in the camp mugs to the refugees on the lawns, and ayah screaming at him to come in or he would catch fever from them. She gave Peggy twenty grains of aspirin and put her to bed in the spare room. Then she sat down on the sofa to wait, and at once fell asleep.

She had no idea what time it was when Peter came back; only that she struggled awake, and it was almost dark, and the two of them, Peter and Harry, were standing in the middle of the room. Harry's voice was hard as he said: 'Yes. Good night.'

'Peggy's in the spare room, Harry,' she said, sitting up.

'Oh. Thanks.' The door closed. She was alone with Peter, but the room was full of the whispering and muttering of two hundred people camped on the lawn and along the veranda.

'It's begun,' Peter said. His face was dim, and then a match flared and a strong yellow-red light lit his face and died and flared again, as he pulled on his cheroot.

'What?' she said dully. 'What's begun? Isn't it nearly over?'

'Oh, the emergency... That's over, in a way. We've got more helpers here now than we know what to do with. The Commissioner's taken over till the morning, and I'm a hero. The Commissioner says so. Smythe says so. Even Harnarayan says so – because I had the Shamoli bund blown in.' He sat down beside her. 'No, I meant that Harry has begun to feel again. Only bitterness so far, but perhaps the rest will come.'

'With you, too,' she said, putting her hand on his.

'I think so,' he said after a while. 'I can only see through Harry's eyes now, feel what he's feeling – but there's something else at the edge. It's like looking at something – a mountain, for instance – and knowing there's something else at the borders of vision, but you can't see it without focusing on it, and when you try it moves farther out and is still at the edge.'

'That always means that the thing, whatever it is, is in your eye and not outside it,' she said.

'Yes,' he said. He knelt down, and she saw the cigar arc into the empty fireplace. She held up her arms and held him tight, tighter, till she thought her arms would crack, but all her strength was nothing to the gradually increasing heat of his mouth on hers, and the salt taste of her own flowing, released tears.

CHAPTER 36

On this sixth morning after the earthquake the Lieutenant-Governor returned by the early train to Lahore, taking the Commissioner with him. Emily stood by the windows of her drawing-room and looked out at her lawn. The grass was gouged and ridged like a battlefield, for it had rained twice in those five days, and many thousand feet and hoofs had battered the soil. The *mali* was standing out there in the middle of it, the strong sun beating down on his bowed head as he glowered at the wreckage of his pride. Emily felt a stirring of guilt that she should be worrying about the lawn at a time like this – but the veranda was empty again, and the children were playing in the nursery.

The rhythm of surge and gather, of break and ebb, that had been so prominent a feature of the hours immediately after the shock, had gradually subsided, like any ocean storm, and instead the effort of re-establishing the city and its life had taken on the sound of a motor car or a railway engine. Men worked day and night in shifts, and there was a steady puttering noise, and the night and its memories and sights were sliding back in the distance.

The corpses had gone from the empty lot. Men on horseback could move anywhere through the city, and narrow carts almost anywhere. There were few houses in the Gujarabad or other sectors that had not been cleared of their dead. Five hundred Gurkha soldiers guarded the approaches to the city at a distance of two miles. Military engineers had set up emergency water supplies, and the Maghra had sunk to its normal level. The old bed was full, from its beginning by the shattered bund to the silted fields twelve miles down, and now formed a long, dirty lake. Seven people had lost their lives in that sudden flood. The province's organization for famine relief had been put into action, and had set up half a dozen camps outside the city; hundreds of able-bodied citizens marched in every day from these camps to work at the clearing of the city. Communications had returned to normal, and the story of the Rudwal earthquake and flood had covered the front page of the *C & M* for the past three days.

Mr Peter Savage was the hero of the hour, partly because the blowing down of the Shamoli bund had caught the public imagination and partly because the English community and the government were desperately anxious to find someone who could be held up as a shining antithesis to General Dyer.

Peter was sitting in his chair, reading a sheaf of telegrams. She turned when she heard him tell the waiting chuprassi he could take them back to the office. The chuprassi left the room.

He said: 'I think you'll have to go to England at once.'

The half-smile, secretive and proud, that had been on her face these five days whenever she looked at Peter, now faded away. On the third day they had mentioned this possibility, but she had deliberately put it aside. Now she thought about it again and at once knew that there could be no argument. Life here would be lived on an emergency basis for the whole of the cold weather. There were signs that an outbreak of amœbic dysentery among the refugees might turn into a full-fledged epidemic, and the heavily chlorinated water made Elizabeth sick. The rebuilding of Rudwal would be an exciting thing to watch, even if merely being with Peter had not been all her desire; but she must go.

'I'll stay a year,' she said, 'and then leave Rodney in a prep school and come back with Elizabeth and Gerry.'

He said: 'Yes – unless I can get home leave in nineteen-twenty-two. You'll have a bad time on the ship with Peggy and Harry, I'm afraid.'

She looked up in surprise. It had never struck her that they too would be returning to England; but of course they would be; and, watching the calmness of his profile as he sucked slowly on the thin black cigar, she knew that this was why he had said: 'You'll have to go' – not for the sake of the children or herself, but so that she could accompany Harry Walsh.

She said: 'I'll do my best, darling – if they'll let me.'

'Even if they won't, you must,' he said. 'Harry will try and hide in his cabin. Peggy will take part in everything. You can't drag Harry out and tell Peggy to hide – but if you're there, showing them and everyone else that they're our friends, it'll make a difference. A little... If only I'd been there!'

She didn't have to ask where. Peter, the old Peter, brought back to life by Harry's tragedy (and how much more suddenly, more explosively, if he had seen the thing himself!), would have caught Purshottam Dass and broken his camera; if necessary he would have shot him. There were other hostile witnesses, and there would still be black headlines in the Indian newspapers, and Harry would still be fighting his own private battle, but nothing could have been as bad as that terrible photograph, because that had brought in ten million strangers as overwrought spectators of a struggle that should have been fought out in Harry's private soul.

But perhaps Peter would not have destroyed the plate at all. Perhaps he would have taken Harry at once into some even more appalling situation and had him photographed in the act of rescue. She could only be sure that, if Peter had been there, things would not be the same.

There had been a good result too, though. Peter had slept little during these nights since the earthquake. Because he had been absent at the moment of the disaster, and had not been able to influence the immediately succeeding events, she knew that he had brooded over what was and what might have been. Somewhere in those silent hours, while he chastised himself for the sullen despair that now weighed on the spirit of a brave man and mountaineer and friend, the awakening current of his emotions had spread from the particular of Harry Walsh to the general of his relation to herself, his children, his work, and the world they lived in. Every morning she saw him more drawn and tired, the lines cut deeper into his forehead and the skin tinged more deeply blue around his eyes; and every morning the tide of his interest flowed deeper and more wide across the stricken city.

He said: 'The Lieutenant-Governor's promised to get passage for all of you on the *Hoshiarpur*. She's sailing on the twenty-fifth.'

'And today's the nineteenth,' she said. 'We'll have to leave here on the twenty-third. It will be a rush.'

'I'm afraid so,' he said.

Peggy came in. 'I hear we're being sent home on the *Hoshiarpur*,' she said loudly. 'Harry's just told me.'

Peter said: 'I told him yesterday that we wouldn't have much chance of getting passages at such short notice unless we got H.E to help. He agreed.'

'Well, I don't,' Peggy said, still loud, but flashing a large, hard smile. 'I've told him he ought to go on with the expedition to Meru. There hasn't been an earthquake up there. If we turn tail people will say he's running away from that too.'

Peter said: 'That's impossible, Peggy, and Harry knows it. For one thing all your stores were taken by Adam Khan to feed his refugees.'

'Who gave him authority to do that?' Peggy said. 'Anyway, we can get more. They've got enough food here to feed London, and more coming in on every train—'

'It's out of the question,' Peter said patiently. 'H.E withdrew the expedition's permission to go into the Northern Tehsils.'

'Why?' Peggy said. 'Oh, I know. You'll go next year, now that you're a hero again. A hero at Harry's expense.'

Peter said: 'The Chakdi bridge at Harkamu is down, and so are half a dozen others. Besides, there are no men for you up there. Most of them are working on the road.'

Harry had entered silently. He said: 'Of course we can't go, Peggy.' He sat down, his hands stiff at his sides.

Peter said: 'I got H.E to promise that you would get permission for another expedition next year.'

Harry said flatly: 'Now it's you who are being stupid, Peter. You know the Joint Committee aren't going to choose me to join any more expeditions even if anyone would go with me. I'm in the same boat as you were after nineteen-thirteen – only different – and you always had Gerry. It's a pity he's not alive.'

Emily said sharply: 'Don't talk like that, Harry.'

But Peter said: 'Gerry would have liked to come with us.'

'Us?' Harry said, anger suddenly flaring up in his taut face. 'Don't you remember what I said to you in 'thirteen, at Camp Two on Meru?'

Peter said: 'I remember, but I think it's time we forgot.'

Peggy's brittle loudness was dissolving into a kind of blotchy, shapeless rage. Since the disaster this had happened whenever she tried to talk to one person for more than a few minutes on end.

Looking at her, Emily thought she had been drinking. Now she whipped a small square of folded paper out of the pocket of her dress and waved it in Peter's face.

'How the hell are we going to forget this?' she screamed.

Emily didn't have to look at the paper. There was the building, toppling over against the bright light of the sky, and a single brick seemingly suspended in mid-air as it fell away in front, a forerunner of the leaning mass behind and above; in front, dark, but as vividly realized as a knife held to the face in the night, the girl, her face to the camera, on one knee, her arms out; closer, Harry, running straight at you, a shaft of light frozen in the sweaty sheen of fear on his face.

'Peggy!'

Emily snatched at the photograph, but Peggy jerked it back and put it away. 'It's n-no good trying to pretend it didn't happen,' she stammered hysterically. 'That's what you want, isn't it? So that we'll try to go on just as if it hadn't, and then face year after year of being rebuffed, of people sneering and looking the other way.'

Emily snapped: 'It won't happen like that – and even if it does, do you have to harp on it more than Harry's worst enemy would? You're not helping him or anyone else.'

'Oh, yes, I am,' Peggy said. 'I'm making sure that we don't fall into your trap and come to believe it isn't important.'

Emily turned her back wearily. Peggy must

have lost her sanity that day she lost Peter under the Matterhorn, for hatred like hers was surely a form of madness. These ghastly scenes were the natural outcome of fourteen years of festering bitterness, but none the more bearable for that. Peter worried about Harry, but Peggy needed help just as much – and who could give it?

She heard Peter speaking. 'You underestimate people, Peggy. They will be willing to forget soon enough, if you are. You overestimate them, too – their memories. In a year or two not many people will remember, even if they try to. After Harry has led an expedition to Meru, no one will remember the other thing at all. People don't like keeping memories like that in their minds. I ran away from the Somme, and I don't suppose there are a dozen people in the world who remember it now. Also, a lot of people have had experience of shell shock and know it isn't the same as cowardice.'

Harry sat there as though the conversation had nothing to do with him; but his face, over which he usually kept tight control, had perceptibly closed and hardened. Now he spoke harshly. 'I don't want your sympathy, Peter, and I don't believe in shell shock. I know it isn't the same as cowardice, but I saw too many men use it as an excuse for cowardice... It turns out I've got a yellow streak. I wouldn't have believed it if I hadn't seen that picture. That's why we keep it... I've got five copies, to remind myself. Oh, I've been afraid, on mountains, in the war, but I used to think I had control over myself – not like you. You didn't know what fear was, that was why you didn't have any control. And don't talk nonsense about your running away from the Somme. I know and everyone knows that you were running away from it because you found it too easy.

'Look, everything's finished, like the world, like France, like the two thousand men of my own battalion I saw killed between Neuve Chapelle and the armistice... We all had such high hopes in our own ways, and now we're all broken. You aren't going to be Viceroy of India, because Gerry broke you. And you broke Gerry. And the earthquake found me out.' He rose stiffly to his feet. 'What we've got to do now is get back in our shells and tell the rest of the world to go to hell and leave us alone. I'm a stockbroker, and you're a colonial administrator. You keep your memories of Gerry, and I'll keep that piece of newspaper.'

He walked out quickly. Peggy followed him with a last bitter stare at Emily.

Peter lit a fresh cigar. When it was drawing well he said: 'I'm not going to stand for that. Nor's Harry. Well, if it's hurting as much as that we needn't feel too badly yet. Come on, let's have tiffin. After that I'll give you a hand with the packing – but I'll have to go at four. I'm meeting Harnarayan and the rest of the District Board.'

'All right, darling,' she said. He put down his hand to pull her to her feet, and she swung up and in the same motion into the crook of his arm. He kissed her on the tip of the nose, and the half-smile came back to her lips. It should have been an unhappy house, but she could not feel unhappy, or even doubtful, for long.

CHAPTER 37

The day of the twenty-third crept early upon her, with the sun not yet up, and already the sounds of men dragging heavy boxes along the veranda, and the squeak and grind of ox-cart wheels on the gravel, and Peter not beside her in the wide bed.

'Peter!' she called quietly; but he was not in the bathroom. She pushed aside the mosquito net, wrapped her dressing-gown about her, and went to the children's room. They were jumping up and down on their beds, ayah trying to dress Elizabeth, the bearer helping by making a face of appalling severity at Rodney.

'*Sahib kiddar hai?*' she asked.

'*Daftar-men, memsahib.*'

She walked quickly to the office and put her head in. Peter was there, standing by the window, and with him Adam Khan. Peter waved to her – he too was in his dressing-gown – and said: 'I'll tell you later.'

She went back to the bedroom. The train left at half-past ten. There was no sound from the spare room, but the bearer assured her he had called the Walshes with their *chhota hazri.*

She was sure Peter had not sent for Adam. Therefore Adam had come with news of importance. It might delay her departure. She would stay another few days with Peter!...

Foolish, foolish hope. It would be something quite different – drains, processions, rates of 'earthquake pay.' She could think only of Peter. After four years the man she loved had come to her with a love to match, even surpass, her own. Love flowered inside her and surrounded her like blossoms climbing a wall – and over all, the brilliant sun. His physical presence had sprung up from the well of darkness so that now, as she stooped over a trunk, she saw the light ripple of the long muscles of his thighs. She was a garden, watered again, and the husbandry was a wonder of living, as it had never been even in the beginning; but it filled now an exact and true proportion of the whole love, taking its place between the poetry of the day and the music of the stars. Taking a glass of wine from his hands was a sensual pleasure, the sound of his voice an invitation to ecstasy, not physical but universal. Beyond him, seen only in and through him, life promised the rewards and efforts of a great mountain, but with all the harshness tempered by the new light. She felt that she had been walking for a thousand days without cease on a gravelled plain, her feet sore and her heart numbed, where there was no end, nor ever would be; and then *he* came, riding, burnished arrows in his hand, and suddenly she knew, as the first arrow pierced her, that the plain of her misery had been a mirage, for now in front the mountains rose from there to there, frost and fire and running water – and the wildflower under the rock.

Now she must leave him. She thought of him in

the study and tried to hear the words passing between the two friends who had been enemies and friends, and were now to each other more than either knew. The big house sang to the shouts of the excited children, and a bullock lowed softly, insistently between the shafts.

Peter came in and took off his dressing-gown. 'Harnarayan has organized a demonstration against Harry,' he said. 'At least five hundred people are going to line the road near the station as he goes by. They won't boo – just stand, silently.'

'Harnarayan!' She gasped. 'Oh, no! He – he isn't as mean as that.'

Peter took his razor and went into the bathroom. 'No,' he said, 'but he's not thinking of people. He's thinking of politics.'

She said: 'What are you going to do? Go and see him and ask him to call it off? Can't you forbid it?'

His voice came muffled from the bathroom. 'I could, under the earthquake emergency powers – but I'm not going to. Adam and I are going to go with Harry, on foot. We'll take Rodney.'

She hurried to the bathroom door. He was in his pyjama trousers, his face covered with soap. 'You mustn't, Peter, not even for Harry's sake. Rodney will never forget it till the day he dies. You'll ruin him.'

'I don't think so, darling,' he said. 'At least he'll probably remember it, but not for the reason you think. I believe Adam knows the people of Rudwal better than Harnarayan does. I believe I do, too.'

'You're going to use their love of children to shelter Harry?' she asked. A moment ago she had been almost angry with him, for this threat to her child had seemed unnecessary and cruel. But the man there so close to her was not the old Peter. This Peter had strength and gentleness. She must and would trust him.

He answered her: 'If you want to put it that way – yes. In another way, we're going to remind them that some people are more vulnerable than others. I'd like you and Peggy to follow in the trap a few minutes after us, so that you don't reach the station until we've got there.'

She took off her gown and nightdress. Suppose he had said that she must go with them, and walk slowly down with them between the contempt. This was how she would feel – naked, vulnerable, trembly at the knees. Oh, dear, this was what touched every moment with gold, that even so she *would* have to do it, for another's sake.

The Walshes joined them, unsmiling, at breakfast. At half-past nine Adam Khan returned. Peter put on his white topee, and Harry his big khaki one. They all chatted a moment on the front steps, now bare to the sun where the *porte cochére* had been demolished and removed. Rodney came out, in khaki shorts and shirt and bare legs and sandals, his small, thin face almost hidden under the huge topee.

'Well, good-bye, Mummy,' he said. 'See you at the station. I'm walking there with Daddy and Uncle Harry.'

'I know,' she said. 'Don't jump in any puddles.'

They set off down the curving drive, Rodney

walking in the middle, at first solemn and long-striding, but after a few moments leaping up and down and skipping ahead, but never turning to wave. They disappeared.

Peggy was beside her. 'What good is that going to do?' she said. 'Do you think Harry doesn't know he's being escorted by a hero and a little boy – the Saviour of Rudwal and his eldest son?'

Emily caught Peggy's hand convulsively, for she was full of fear again. She cried: 'Haven't we got enough to worry about without fighting each other, Peggy?' Peggy tried to pull her hand away but Emily held it tight and went on. 'I believe Peter wants to show Harry that people aren't as censorious as he thinks – that they don't want to be judges.'

Peggy glared at her, frozen-faced, for a long minute; then the familiar breaking-up began, and ugly blotches dappled the fair skin, and the classical lines blurred and smudged. But this time there was something different about the change, for the end point was not a desperately bitter woman but a woman spent, pared down at last to the simple bones. It was this woman, a being Emily had not known even in their childhood, who whispered: 'Oh my God, Emily, I still love him.'

Emily put her arms around Peggy's shoulders and gently led her inside and left her in the drawing-room.

She went about the last occasions. Nothing left unpacked in the bedroom. Peter would sleep alone here tonight. The study, to see again where he worked. The three men would be half-way to the station by now. Five minutes more. The drawing-room, so many thousand hours of loneliness, of longing this side of despair, and worse thereby; and all those hours wiped away by a few score since the earthquake.

'*Sab tayyar hai memsahib,*' the bearer said.

They would be walking down the street now, between the silent people. Peggy joined her on the steps; the horse tossed its head and jingled its bit; the trap was polished like the morning; the syce's white teeth gleamed in a proud smile.

A thin, high sound came to them from the south-east. The wind lay in that quarter, and the station, and the street where the bitter people waited. Peggy's new-made face began to tremble. The sound increased.

'They're booing,' Peggy whispered.

Filled with anguish for all their sakes, Emily could not speak; but it was Peggy with her, and Peter had put Peggy in her charge, so she gathered her strength, stepped up into the carriage, and said: 'Oh, I don't suppose so. *Achcha, Daulat, chalo!*'

Near the bungalow the streets were full of police and soldiers, and there were men at work in huge gangs, and grinding bullock carts in close procession, and thunderous Army lorries. Farther on, where the street widened and ran straight towards the baroque turrets of the station, there was another type of crowd – men mostly, here and there the brightness of a working woman's bodice and skirt, one rich sari, a few policemen. The people were dispersing and most had their backs turned to the street, the clopping horse, and the gleaming carriage. Peggy stared straight ahead, her hands clenched in her lap. Here and there a man turned and glanced indifferently at them. Emily relaxed a little. Surely everyone would be more excited if there had just been a demonstration.

At the station she walked at Peggy's side on to the platform, Smythe and a foot-constable clearing a path for them through the crowds of prospective travellers. The train was waiting, for this was the terminus of the branch. Peter was there, and Harry, and Rodney, standing with his legs apart and his hands in his pockets, talking importantly to Baber. (Were they all made of stone, to be so unconcerned? Even to be able to hide such a hurt?) Baber was magnificent in his Punjabi clothes, smiling down at Rodney, talking earnestly.

There was the Old Captain, his left hand shaking these days so that he could not hold the sword in it any more, but let it hang in its scabbard at his side; and a manservant supporting him; and Adam Khan, unsmiling, his eyes alight.

Emily took Peggy and led her into the compartment next door to the one reserved for herself and the children. Harry looked dazed. The conductor was there with a big railway watch in his hand. It showed the time for good-byes.

She caught Peter's arm and took him aside. The others fell back to respect their privacy. 'What happened?' she asked urgently.

'They cheered us,' Peter said.

'They – cheered!' She gasped. 'Oh, Peter! How wonderful! They were cheering you.'

'No,' he said, 'we were all together – Harry, Rodney, myself, and Adam. They meant to be silent, I'm sure, even to boo – but we were all together, so they cheered us.'

'How did Harry take it? Did he think it was just for your sakes, the rest of you?'

'No. It wasn't like that. I don't know how you could tell, but you could. I think that if the cheers were for anybody in particular, they were for Harry.'

After a time she said: 'Aren't Indians extra-ordinary!'

'It isn't because they were Indians,' he said. 'It's because they were people. What happened to them was exactly what happened to Harry, and they knew it. Something broke.'

They were hovering nearby now – one after the other, hands shaking her own, faces smiling, in tears, carefully composed. 'We'll be back,' she said over and over again. 'Good-bye, good-bye, good-bye.'

Peter was in the compartment, kissing Elizabeth, holding Gerry's hand, teasing Rodney. She followed him in. He took her gently in his arms, and the children fell quiet, watching with concern and instinctive understanding. There was nothing more to say and no words to say it with. Good-bye meant the beginning of a new journey. As his lips touched hers she felt their separate persons, bodies and souls, fuse with an annihilating flash into a single being. He left her, but alone she could not stand and sank on to the seat. The train started, but she could not go to the door and wave.

She sat, wanting to smile, crying steadily, until Rodney said: 'Don't cry, Mummy. It makes you look like Aunty Peggy.'

Then she dried her eyes. Harry and Peggy were next door, and what had been begun must be finished.

CHAPTER 38

LETTERS FROM INDIA

D.C's CAMP
RUDWAL, PUNJAB
November 26th, 1920

Dear Admiral,

Thank you for your letter of October 31st which has just reached me. This letter will confirm the cablegram I sent off this morning, and which read as follows: HONOURED TO ACCEPT LEADERSHIP OF JOINT ROYAL GEOGRAPHICAL SOCIETY – ALPINE CLUB EXPEDITION TO MERU 1921 SUBJECT TO EXIGENCIES OF SERVICE HERE STOP WRITING SAVAGE.

The last sentence of my cable refers to the state of emergency caused by the September earthquake. The city is rising from its ashes more quickly than I would have believed possible even a month ago, and only some new and unforeseeable emergency should prevent me being able to get away by next April. I may say, in confidence, that H.E the Lieutenant-Governor of the province told me last week that he would send me on leave next hot weather whether I wanted to go or not; but of course any serious situation in our recovery operations here would compel me to stay.

I will certainly be in a position to supervise the transport and other administrative arrangements at the end, but presume your Joint Committee will act as executive and buying agent for stores and equipment that must be brought from England. In a day or two I will prepare and send to you a detailed list of requirements for your consideration.

As to the membership of the expedition, I am of course out of touch with the new generation of mountaineers and will be happy to accept your judgement and selections. However, my own experience in Parasia suggests that the number of climbers should be kept to a minimum, as each extra man adds a disproportionately unwieldy tail to the expedition. When the approach march is so long and presents so many problems of its own, this is a decisive factor. I suggest that the maximum number should be seven, including a 'climbing' doctor. Personally, I would prefer four, including myself and the doctor, plus a deputy leader who can climb or take charge of administrative matters as the leader thinks best. The selection of this deputy leader is a matter of great importance and I am sure you will agree that no English mountaineer is better suited for the post than Harry Walsh.

I would like, in closing, to express again my gratitude to you and the Joint Committee for your generosity in selecting me. Much has happened since we met briefly in Zermatt in '09, little of it conducive to faith in me as leader of such an expedition. I will do my best to justify your trust, and whether or not we succeed in climbing Meru I hope we will write a story there which will make an example for generations to come, and not only to mountaineers.

Yours sincerely,
Peter Savage

To: Admiral Sir Alexander Ingraham, K.C.B,
D.S.O,
Chairman, Joint Committee, Meru, 1921,
1 Kensington Gore, London.

D.C's CAMP
RUDWAL, PUNJAB
December 22nd, 1920

Dear Admiral,

Your cablegram of December 20th reached me this morning, and I replied as follows: YOUR LIST OF MEMBERS OF EXPEDITION AGREED EXCEPT FOR OMISSION OF WALSH AS DEPUTY LEADER STOP HAVE WRITTEN HIM TODAY URGING HIM TO ACCEPT STOP IF ANY MEMBER UNWILLING TO ACCEPT HIM THIS CAPACITY MUST INSIST THAT MEMBER BE DROPPED STOP ALTERNATIVELY HAPPY TO OFFER OWN RESIGNATION TO BE USED AT YOUR DISCRETION IF THIS WILL RESOLVE IMPASSE LETTER FOLLOWS SAVAGE.

I am sure the above is self-explanatory, but would like to emphasize that I cannot under any circumstances accept leadership of this expedition if Harry Walsh is omitted (unless he is physically incapable or finally determined to refuse to come). The ascent of Meru will indeed be the greatest feat yet recorded in the annals of mountaineering;

546

and it is true, as you point out, that the selection of Walsh as deputy leader will, at least at first, make for dissensions and conflicts within the party and so lessen our chances for a successful attempt. But I have come to believe that the spirit of mountaineering and the spirit of the mountains lie in what we do for each other and in what we give to the mountains (in the way of sacrifice, appreciation, and controlled passion) rather than in what we do *on* the mountains. We will do a fine thing to climb Meru; we will do a finer by far if, through our attempt, Harry Walsh is reinstated in his proper place in the world that he values – and, more important still, in his own eyes.

The other members will of course have heard of his tragedy here, and will perhaps have seen the picture, but once we are launched on the expedition I am sure they will forget all that and see only that we, and Meru, can do something for Harry that no one and nothing else can do. I have confidence in my ability to achieve *this* object at least.

I realize you cannot tell the Joint Committee that its painfully collected funds are in effect to be used for this purpose, with the ascent of Meru a secondary consideration (except that a determined effort on the mountain is an inherent part of the other), yet I am sure that you and every other real mountaineer, alive or dead, will agree that Harry Walsh, or any man, is more important than a new 'first,' and that mountaineering can have no higher purpose than to raise a human being's capacities for feelings and giving.

I realize also that the recent announcement in the press that I am to lead the expedition will make it difficult for me to be replaced without awkward explanations. I cannot pretend I am sorry, as I am sure that what I am doing is good and right, and I welcome every circumstance that will help to ensure my – *our* – success. However, I do mean exactly what I said in my cablegram – that my resignation is in your hands, to do with as you think best.

Yours sincerely,
Peter Savage

Cablegram sent December 22, 1920, to Harry Walsh, 43 Ives Street, London W, England:

ADMIRAL INGRAHAM CABLES THAT YOU HAVE REFUSED OFFER OF PLACE AS DEPUTY LEADER MERU EXPEDITION 1921 STOP I HAVE PLACED MY OWN RESIGNATION IN HIS HANDS TO BE MADE EFFECTIVE IF YOUR DECISION FINAL STOP PLEASE UNDERSTAND THIS IS NOT TO EXERT PRESSURE ON YOU BUT BECAUSE I DO NOT WANT TO GO TO MERU WITHOUT YOU STOP WOULD PREFER COME HOME ON LEAVE TO FAMILY AND SUGGEST WE MIGHT ALL SPEND SUMMER ZERMATT STOP IF ANYTHING ELSE BUT LACK OF DESIRE IMPELLING YOU REFUSE INVITATION I AFFECTIONATELY INVITE YOU TO REMEMBER OUR LAST WALK TOGETHER.

PETER

Dear Harry,

A brief note to follow up my cablegram of the 22nd – cables aren't the best place to say things one feels deeply.

First, I want to add to more personal reasons the fact that I will need your experience on the expedition. Of the five other climbers (the committee turned down my suggestion that it be kept *very* small) only Hutton, who is thirty-five, has ever seen or climbed in the Himalaya, and his experience is limited to one season in Garhwal, where conditions are quite different from Parasia. Of the rest, Robin Granger, the doctor, is the oldest, at twenty-nine, and though I am sure they are all good, even superb climbers, they must lack judgement – where can they have learned it during the war? The leader cannot be in two places at once, and I must have a deputy whose judgement I can rely on entirely, and in whom the rest of the expedition have or will soon learn to have the same implicit faith.

Finally, I have a long memory, and it is full of bright experiences and wonderful things seen and done on the mountains. The true wonder of much that I saw did not come to me till recently – but I owe it all to a night in June eighteen years ago when Gerry and I watched you come down from King's Chapel. If I go to Meru next year I am going to take one of Gerry's old ice-axes that I have here, and I hope that you and I can leave it on the summit, to remind us at least, and the

549

world perhaps, that we three have made a strange web of our lives – and, I think, in the end, a good one. This may sound foolish to some, but I don't think it will to you, who have known Gerry and myself for so long.

At all events, though Meru will be climbed eventually, it will not be climbed by me unless you are with us next year, because I do not want to go alone (on Meru, there can only be two companions I can recognize, and one is dead); and because I shall not go again to that mountain.

Please cable me.

Yours,
Peter

D.C's BUNGALOW, RUDWAL, PUNJAB
January 14th, 1921

My darling,

Yes, I heard a few days before the New Year's Honours were published that I was going to get a C. It's no use grumbling because it's only a C.I.E. They do that so they can give you a C.S.I later. If they give you the higher one first, they can never give you the lower. Such are the laws of the Most Holy Secretariat, on Whom be Praise, in Ordered Files. The Lieutenant-Governor – sorry, he's a full-blown Governor now – sounded out Adam Khan about an O.B.E, but he refused. Baber got an M.B.E, which ought to give him a certain cachet at Sandhurst. You may not have seen that Smythe got a King's Police Medal – well deserved.

Harry is coming on the expedition – his cable reached me today. I presume you will see it in

The Times before this reaches you. I had the devil of a fight with the Joint Committee and Harry himself before it was done, but the Admiral supported me behind the scenes (before the war I know he used to hold up Harry as a model of everything a mountaineer should be, and so had an interest besides his natural generosity in having his judgement vindicated) and we got it done. I lay awake a good deal at night wondering whether I was doing right – there was something about the business reminiscent of Gerry, a forcing of events, or at least of a person's character, that was not happy to remember. But I cannot feel that I am doing wrong, or that any wrong will result this time. I do not think Harry would have accepted, though, if you had not been able to gain Peggy's trust again, and enlist her help. I am sure you have not forgotten to remind Peggy that mountaineering on Meru cannot be divorced from physical danger, and that in gaining some spiritual end we may injure or lose our physical beings – to be a little less high-flown, in the process of putting a sparkle in our eyes we may break our bloody necks.

H.E has told me that I will be approached again, next year, about a post in the Secretariat. I have told him there is little chance that I shall accept. With care we can manage on my pay, and I do not want to leave Rudwal, even to become Commissioner, which is also a possibility within a couple of years. H.E grumbled that the days of the patriarch who spent forty-nine years in one district and left a legend, or at the least a hundred new culverts, were over, and that I would be under increasing pressure to 'broaden my outlook' for the good of the service, etc. I told him I thought I would be able to resist the pressure; and so I will as long as I know you love Rudwal as much as I do and will be coming back to me to share it all, including the bed-bugs I found in our bed last night. Heaven knows where they came from, but I have given Ghulam a piece of your mind.

H.E also threatened to move me to another district if I didn't co-operate with their schemes to promote me, but his heart was not in it. He knows as well as I do that at this period above all, when the reforms are beginning to move forward and the Secretary of State has at last solved the problem of why we are in India at all (viz: to get out), India needs from us not brains but understanding. Privately H.E agreed with me that even a bad collector who stays a long time in one place will do more good than a series of brilliant collectors who stay for so short a time that they are practically tourists.

Rodney will have to stay at home when you come out in '22, darling. I know it's cruel for all of us, but there is no better alternative. For one thing I think we now need each other more than he needs either of us. Do you think Harry and Peggy can act as his 'parents' while you are out here?

Few nights go by without my dreaming of you, fewer still without my cursing myself for a selfish fool not to give up Meru and come to England next summer – but if I did that I think you would send me out again as soon as I arrived, and that is one reason why I love you so much. Some of my night-time dreams of you are very frustrating (I caught myself licking my lips over the female shape of a blowsy bazaar harridan the other day) but you are also at my side during all the sunlight hours, and sitting opposite me at the breakfast table (making the same face at Sharif's unspeakable coffee), and riding at my side when I go out on tour. In point of fact I do not ride, but walk or run, carrying a heavy pack. I feel a considerable fool, but it is as well to remind myself by these painful means that I am 40 years of age and Meru is 27,141 feet high!

Good night darling, and sleep well.

Your loving husband, Peter

D.C's BUNGALOW
RUDWAL, PUNJAB
April 16th, 1921

My darling,

Harry arrived a couple of days ago, very much on his guard, because of course the membership of the expedition has been known for some time, and I think he expected Harnarayan to have organized another and more cold-hearted protest group – but there was no one at the station except myself and Adam Khan, Adam just out of prison from the six weeks I sentenced him to in February (for sedition).

Granger, Norris, de Heurteville, and Barnes were with him, leaving only Hutton to be accounted for. He's on his way with some stuff they had difficulty with at Bombay. My relief – it is Greene, as I thought it would be – has been

553

here for a week, and we ought to be able to get away on the 23rd as planned. Young Barnes has pointed out that that is St George's Day and the anniversary of Zeebrugge, implying that we also will make a most high and gallant endeavour for the sake of Merrie England. I suppose that is true enough but I do not feel that patriotism is or ought to be the driving force behind this expedition. I reminded Barnes that April 23rd was also Shakespeare's birthday. Barnes is only 20 and feels, I think, that he must show on Meru what he would have done for England in the way if he had been old enough. He was out in France for three months, as a matter of fact, but his colonel wouldn't send him to the front.

Their collective attitude to Harry is non-committal, as far as I can judge. They respect him for the hours of instruction and discussion he had with them on the boat coming out, but they are waiting to see what happens when we face the big moments. I am rather depressed to find that Barnes and the Count (de Heurteville) have been hero-worshippers of mine since the first attempt in 1913, when they were in their teens. They hint that I was let down by my fellow climbers that time, and that now I am going to lead them to the top, come hell or high water, *at all costs*. This attitude to my exploits of those days is quite new, and is due to the war, I imagine – but it will lead to some loss of confidence in me from the moment I make the first decision actuated by caution or mountaineering tradition rather than by sheer will-power. Well, all it means is that they will have to learn to be mountaineers rather than climbers, as I have had to do, and forget the image of me that they have been preserving in ignorance of all that has happened since they were schoolboys.

I am very glad you could take young Rodney to see Grandfather several times before he died. If there is any further help you need in dealing with the will, don't forget that you can count on help from Charlie Harrison at Lloyd's.

I fear the Old Captain will not last long now. Somebody – probably Harnarayan, who has the vivid sentimentality of the true revolutionary – is sure to say that his and Grandfather's deaths are symbolic of the end of the era they lived and thought in, but it is not so: I prefer to think of facts rather than symbols, and their era did in fact bleed to death, in Flanders and also, somehow, in the Jallianwala Bagh at Amritsar, and Adam and I are in the saddle now and Baber and young Rodney getting ready to take over – so they had nothing more to live for, and so one has died and the other will shortly join him.

But do not let Rodney forget him. Keep a picture in his room – that portrait my step-grandmother painted of him as he looked just after the Mutiny.

Now everything seems to be done and cleared away, and there is only Meru in front of me – us, all of us. In the past I might have thought of it as a challenge, as an enemy, or just as a beautiful mountain, but now I see it as an opportunity, and I am not afraid that I shall fail to take it.

All my love,
Your husband
Peter

555

MERU EXPEDITION
c/o P.O
RUDWAL, PUNJAB
May 6th, 1921

My dear Peggy,

We are resting two days here at Parasia. Your Harry is very fit – as we all are, except the Count, who has sunburned the end of his nose. Harry has gained the confidence of all the men except Billy, who is very brilliant, fiery, and very young. I think our first day above 20,000 feet will show young Mr Barnes that Harry has forgotten more about climbing than he has yet learned. He was quite noticeably subdued – a miracle for him! – when Harry and I did a rather spectacular traverse of a wet cliff to rescue a clumsy ass of a porter who had slipped and would not leave his insecure perch in case he lost his load – the porters' rum!

Give Emily my love–

Peter

PARASIA
May 8th, 1921

Darling,

The post orderly is waiting, the tent has been taken down over my head, the wind is blowing. We are off in twenty minutes, and I love you.

Peter

CHAPTER 39

The expedition arrived at the old site of Juniper Camp late in the afternoon of May 16. There were many traces that men had been here before, notably the rock in which Gerry and he had scratched their initials on their first reconnaissance in 1911. At the time he had thought the action a foolish concession to Gerry's sentimentality, and even Gerry had had doubts on æsthetic grounds; but they had done it, and the dry air of the Parasian plateau had preserved the hard edges and pale scratches as though it were yesterday that they had stood together and turned the rock into a monument: 'P.S – W,' it said, but gave no date.

It was a reassuring sight, as were the gleaming tin cans left by somebody from the 1913 or Harry's 1914 attempt, a piece of torn canvas anchored under a stone, a worn-out pair of Rudwali sandals – human debris which would have annoyed him if encountered in London or even on the top of Cader Brith; but here, in a place that was wild and lonely, yet not 'dedicated,' they were positive enhancements to natural beauty.

There was a lurid sunset that evening. The sky lay in horizontal bands of garish colour across the pale desert, and the great southern or Gendarme Ridge of Meru swept down black against the

colours out of a feathery sky somewhere un-
imaginably higher above. The porters were in the
best of humour; the climbers had loosened up on
the long trek; nothing serious had gone wrong,
nor had anyone suffered more than a stomach-
ache and one case, among the porters, of
something which Robin Granger diagnosed as
pink-eye.

In spite of all his care, Peter had not been able
to prevent the expedition from reaching an
unwieldy size. Apart from a large caravan of
Rudwali horse-copers from the Northern Tehsils,
whose ponies had carried the bulk of the stores
up to this point, they had a small band of
Rudwali porters and six men from an obscure
valley in north-eastern Nepal. These last were
called Sherpas and were reputed to be excellent
climbers, with the ability to carry heavy loads
and the willingness to learn techniques of
climbing that would enable them to carry the
loads on ground which untrained men, however
strong, could not have passed.

The Sherpas were likely to play an important
role because, if the expedition had to commit its
main effort to the south-east ridge, it would again
have to surmount the Needles. Given reasonable
luck with the weather, Peter felt confident that
they could 'prepare' the Needles – with pegs,
fixed ropes, and even rope ladders (they had
brought several with them) – so that climbers
could get over them without much difficulty. But
his experience in 1913, reinforced by Harry's in
1914, made it clear that if they were to achieve
success by that route they must put three camps,

not two, on the south-east ridge, and must also establish another camp above the Needles, from which the climbers would make their attempts on the summit.

It would therefore be necessary for tentage and stores of all kinds, sufficient for at least four men for three days, to be carried over the Needles. He felt certain that the Rudwalis from the Northern Tehsils could not do this. They were sure-footed and strong of back, but at heart they were essentially shepherds, and he had never encountered among them any 'desire' for mountains in general or for Meru in particular. They regarded mountains as fearsome enemies to be left alone, not as friends, still less as playgrounds, battle-fields, or jousting lists. (All these latter attitudes were represented among the climbers.) The head Sherpa was a small, gloomy man called Garakay.

The heavy work below the snow line and on the easier stretches just above it would be done by the band of foot-Rudwalis, under their leader, who was a brother of the headman of Harkamu. The pony-Rudwalis were going to stay at Juniper as long as the expedition was on the mountain, and Peter had no doubt that they would organize some fine carousals, quarrels, and fights to while away the time.

Finally, they had a young Indian medical graduate from Rudwal City who had volunteered to come along and help Granger; and, in immediate charge of the details of discipline and administration, Subadar Tilakbir Lama from the 13th Gurkhas' depot at Manali. Peter would have liked to have Harkabir again, but his ashes lay in a plot of earth behind Neuve Chapelle.

The Joint Committee of the societies sponsoring the expedition had done them well in the matter of food, and though Peter personally ate chupattis most of the time no delicacy seemed to be lacking that could tempt their appetites when altitude or weakness made them lose the desire to eat. He thought privately that the climbers would find strawberry jam and condensed milk, or some similar revolting mixture, what they would most like to have once they got above 20,000 feet.

The summit of Meru hung alone in the sky, pink and black in a shimmering night, when they gathered in the big dining tent to discuss their farther progress. Nine of them were seated there when the talk began – the seven climbers; Zaman Khan, the young doctor; and Tilakbir. The last-named spoke no English, but Peter explained things to him when necessary, and he made notes; he was a great note-taker, of the slow, pencil-licking type.

Peter had already decided what would probably have to be done, and amply discussed it with the rest of them, but everything depended on the weather and it would not have been wise to make firm decisions before arrival at Juniper. But now they were there, and the lone tree after which the spot was named stood just behind the tent, and the tinkle of the thinly running stream made sweet music to his ears after the long trek across the immense sweep of Parasia. (He had seen two spotted fork-tails in that stream just after his arrival, but the bustle had frightened them away.)

Peter now confirmed what had been tentatively arranged. On the eighteenth they would split into three parties, each accompanied by two Sherpas. George Norris and himself would reconnoitre the south-east ridge; Oscar Hutton and the Count would move round the mountain to the west and try the north face. (Aloysius Roggevin de Heurteville was too much of a mouthful for anyone, and since his prep-school days he'd always been known as the Count.) Harry Walsh and young Billy Barnes would move round the mountain to the east and try the Great Chimney Glacier, and, if they could surmount that, the Great Chimney itself. Robin Granger would stay at Juniper. Peter set May 28 as the day by which they should all meet again here.

Barnes could not quite hide a small tightening of the lips when he heard that he was to go with Harry, but he did not say anything aloud. He was an extremely energetic blond young man, twenty years of age, about six foot three, beautifully built, hard as nails and seemingly possessed of a stamina which didn't usually come to men until they were a few years older. Peter had wondered that the Committee included anyone so young, but after he had seen Barnes on the road – and scrambling up cliffs every evening, just for exercise, when the rest of them were glad to lie about and drink tea in the tents – he saw that the Admiral had known what he was about. Barnes's hero-worship was distressing, for it was based on an admiration of actions which, although they had perhaps been inevitable, Peter no longer thought of with pride. Also, Barnes was too ready to despise Harry Walsh, not so much for that unhinged moment which had caused the furore but because he knew that Harry had been Peter's bitter enemy after the 1913 expedition.

The rest of the climbers had maintained a cordial neutrality towards Harry until they had had the opportunity to see what kind of man he was. By the time they reached Juniper they not only accepted but admired and respected him. Nevertheless, Peter thought he had detected a deep-lying layer of distrust and he wondered once, while ruminating on his problems late at night in the tent he shared with Oscar Hutton, why grown and experienced men, all of whom had fought through the war with great gallantry, should keep even this deep, almost completely hidden layer of reserve against a man whose only lapse had been caused by circumstances and strains that they could understand better than any other men on earth. It did not take him long to appreciate that though such men can understand a man's lapse they are too tough-minded, too honest with themselves, to pretend it has not happened. They had no blame for Harry, but they were mountaineers and they had been soldiers; they had simply recorded, deep down: 'Harry Walsh *can* crack.' When you expect to spend several hours or days with a man on a rope under extreme strain, in places where any failing might cause instant calamity – and not only for you two – this is a piece of knowledge that it is folly to wipe out of your mind.

Barnes probably thought he had been paired with Harry in order that he should show up

Harry's caution. What Harry thought, Peter did not know, for Harry kept a reserve with him. In fact Peter's reason for sending the two of them on the Great Chimney reconnaissance was only that he thought they would make an excellent pair – Harry's wisdom, technical skill, and experience complementing Barnes's fire and sheer strength. He was willing to stake his own life or anyone else's on his conviction that Harry would not crack again, and he hoped that a week of 'big' climbing would give young Billy, at least, the same faith.

Harry seemed to be in excellent shape both physically and psychologically. His manner was quiet, but that was natural to him; he avoided no one and sought no one; he didn't shrink and he didn't push. Peter had had no intimate talk with him but he felt sure that the Joint Committee's acceptance of him, even at his own urging, had begun to show Harry that the outside world – particularly that part of it whose opinion he valued – had forgotten or brushed aside memories which still occupied so large and gloomy a part of his mind. The attitude of the other climbers had further reassured him, and the complete normality of his return to Rudwal had finally convinced him.

That left Harry with only the more fearsome enemy, the most persistent that any man can possess – himself. He knew the world had forgotten, or understood, or forgiven. Now it was only he who had not forgotten, did not understand, and could not forgive. At the same time, and because of this, Harry seemed to be reappraising his sense of values. He had taken it for granted, like most of their generation, that an unobtrusive, well-balanced, but unfailing physical courage was the highest single quality any man could have, and the only one a gentleman *must* have. The war had reinforced that ingrained belief until it, along with the courage itself, was a part of his nature. Now the thought faced him that if what he believed was true, he was of no value; but the world assured him that he was, and his own common sense and revived self-pride concurred. Therefore it must be the ideals that he had lived by that were wrong. But they couldn't be, for they were laws of nature… These were the premises he was debating with himself, and since in this area logic is illogical unless it is personal, no one else could help him.

As for himself, Peter had almost forgotten, in the choral joys of rediscovering himself, his wife, his children, his work, and the mountains, that he had been such a controversial figure in other times. It was brought home to him, though, as soon as he had his first meetings with the expedition. He was made aware – not by words, for the men were much too well-mannered, but by his own new sensitivity – that Hutton, Norris, and Granger had distinct reservations about him. He suspected that the Admiral had had to do a lot of persuading before those three would agree to join any expedition led by him. The Count voiced his nonchalant *nil admirari* appreciation of some of Peter's pre-war feats in Switzerland, and Barnes was a hero-worshipper. Peter had not made any attempts to alter this state of affairs either at the time or, as a deliberate act, at any time; but he felt, as they rode on day by day through the inner chains of the Himalaya, over the passes, and finally across the Parasian plateau, that the three 'hostiles' had modified their opinions, or at least put aside their hostility until such time as he should live up to his evil reputation.

The members got on well with one another, except for the antipathy between Barnes and Walsh, and that was one-sided. Oscar Hutton was thirty-five, and a schoolmaster; he'd joined up in the London Scottish in 1914, won a D.C.M in '15, been commissioned, and fought the rest of the war in Palestine. He was a short, strong man with a battered face and a passion for cricket which bordered on the monomaniacal and would have been far over the border if he hadn't occasionally allowed Vergil to creep into the boundary of his small talk. Robin Granger was a country doctor from Sussex, tall, thin, bespectacled; he had got his V.C at Cambrai rescuing wounded men under fire; he spoke seldom and then usually of gardening. The Count was a scion of a penniless family of landed gentry in Durham, and wild as a hawk; Peter suspected that only the war had saved him from being sent down from Oxford; his talk, which was ceaseless and covered every subject under the sun, indicated that he knew more about wine, women, and song than an ordinary young man could possibly have learned in the few pre-war adult years available to him; he was an enthusiastic cynic, about five foot ten, slender to the point of thinness, and nothing like as volatile as he pretended; Peter was sure that he had walked into his scrapes with his eyes open. George Norris was a thickset man of five foot nine, quiet, almost taciturn; an R.F.C pilot during the war; he'd lost his wife the year before, and Peter thought he might tend to treat the mountain as though he could somehow wreak vengeance on it for his misery. Robin, the count, and Billy Barnes were bachelors, but Robin had a fiancée, a young woman whose picture showed that she intended to put the scatterbrained fellow's practice in order in double-quick time.

There had been some publicity to the effect that the objects of the expedition were scientific as well as mountaineering, possibly to give the solicitation of various sorts of aid an aura of respectability, possibly as a sop to the guilt complex often suffered by learned men when they set out to enjoy themselves. At all events Oscar Hutton had equipped himself with a large book on geology, a small hammer, and a smaller fund of enthusiasm for knocking chips out of the rocks that they passed. The Count held charge of a battery of anemometers, rain gauges, barometers, and wet- and dry-bulb thermometers. His readings were not as accurate as they might have been. He put the anemometer in the lee of any available cliff because, he said, the sight of the damned thing spinning madly round and round in the perpetual Parasian gales made him dizzy. Also, he had found towards the end of the march that some of the porters regularly urinated in the rain gauge. Norris supervised the workings of a wireless set actually operated by two Survey of India havildars.

As for Peter himself, he was the expedition's expert on bird and animal life. He was supposed to shoot and skin the rarer birds for the British Museum, but his aim with the light rifle was deliberately bad and with the special collector's gun even worse. He had, however, taken some good photographs, collected and pressed two hundred different flowers, and recorded forty-four species of birds, three of them never before reported in Parasia, and one probably a new variety of the Desert Wheatear.

Now it was time to try and sleep. He had not been going to sleep easily on this journey. Sometimes Oscar heard him turning over in his sleeping-bag, or was awake when he scrambled out at two in the morning, and asked him whether he was all right or urged him to take an aspirin. Oscar thought he was wrestling with various plans in his mind and worrying over his responsibilities; but he was not. He found it hard to go to sleep because it required of him a definite act of sacrifice to give up the joys of waking realization. As long as he got enough sleep to keep his full strength of mind and body, he was not willing to make the sacrifice. He could not bring himself to clear his mind of its wonders: the understanding of what Emily was, had been, and would become; the meaning of love, total love – there it was now, flowing through his being like a river of gold, carrying him forward on its flood; the sheer animal beauty of this world – the aloneness of the birds that flew with large wings, slow-beating, across the immense plains; the wild ass wheeling at the rim of the salt lake; the mountain called Meru, which he could not think of as an inhuman block of stone and ice but as a part of their endeavours, for it stood beside the golden river, just as it had towered over the slow-traversed and painful desert.

He had started to call this south-east ridge on which Norris and he would start work the day after tomorrow, the old route – the Wilcot Ridge of Meru. Billy Barnes took up the name with enthusiasm and went further, to suggest that the mountain itself be renamed Mount Wilcot. The others pointed out to him that it was against Survey of India policy to name a mountain after a person. The local name was always applied; or if there was none – which was often the case in really wild areas – then a name was made up in the local language. Only two great Himalayan mountains had been named after people, Everest and Godwin Austen – both of whom had been Surveyors-General of India – and the latter mountain was increasingly being spoken of as K2.

But it was time to take the velvet curtain in both hands and draw it firmly across his mind for the night, that he might sleep. Hutton had a tendency to snore, but he did it in a harmonious key – B flat, Peter thought, and he liked it. Emily was not above snoring occasionally, but hers was a kind of sighing whistle, and he liked that too. It proved again that she was human. There would be little magic in her character if her superb qualities had been, so to speak, gifted to her instead of achieved by her, just as there would be little joy in contemplating her when she was dressed and perfumed and moving like a young queen about their house if he could not also think of her in unashamed earthy lust. There was a wide range in human experience, as wide as from the Ganges, with its muddy stream and its bloated, bobbing corpses, to the summit of that mountain whose soaring peak and silver banner he could see through the crack of the tent-flap.

CHAPTER 40

The reconnaissance produced much the results that he had expected. He and Norris, with two Sherpas actually with them and four Rudwalis in support, readily climbed the south-east ridge as far as the Needles. They found nothing changed, and confirmed what was already known: that, as far as the Needles, the ridge route was arduous but not difficult. They did not attempt to climb farther because it was not part of the plans at that time; but on two exceptionally clear days they had a good look at the Mirror Wall, Walsh's Fault, the Bowl, and at the Needles themselves, from below. The Mirror seemed even more impossible than Peter remembered it, a face of ice that presented to them the glittering indifference of the utterly unassailable. Nothing had altered there, and though the risks of getting up and over the Needles were as great as ever, they were still less than those of any other course possible from the Wilcot Ridge.

On their way down Peter saw through his binoculars two tiny dots far down in the Great Chimney Glacier – in the high-altitude glare their dark clothing showed up well against the glacier – and he knew that Harry and Billy were in position. He had little hope that they would discover a feasible route. Looking from their higher angle, down the frightful sweep of the ice wall below the Mirror, he had a momentary thought that he must have been mad to send anyone even to glance at that approach.

He found Norris an excellent climbing companion – sound and strong, careful to avoid unnecessary risks, but armed with the mental and physical equipment to deal with bad situations when they were met. He spent a lot of time looking hungrily at the summit, or the clouds that hid it, or the snow banner flying down-wind from it. Somehow, without more than a hundred words being said between them for a week – and those no more intimate than a request for more sugar, please – Peter thought they had become close friends by the time they returned to Juniper.

Harry and Billy Barnes, and Oscar and the Count, came in from opposite directions two days later, on May 28. That night, in the big tent, the latter pair reported that they had spent forty-eight hours at maximum effort merely getting to the foot of the North Wall, one hour deciding that the wall was impossible, and seventy-two hours extricating themselves. When Peter asked their formal opinions of the route Oscar said: 'No.'

The Count said: 'Even the bloody eagles get vertigo there. We saw one dead at the bottom. Crushed to *pulp*, boss. Pulp! Let's go, though. Oscar would make a lovely, juicy mess and we could take him home in a sack and spread him over the Test wicket at Lord's.'

Oscar said sourly: 'It was a Himalayan griffon, not an eagle. And would you mind giving me another batting partner next time? The Count's humour makes me laugh so much that my ribs are sore.'

Peter turned to Harry, who began a careful report on their reconnaissance. They had found that the Great Chimney Glacier offered fair enough going in its lower section, roughly from 16,000 to 20,000 feet. Then they reached the foot of a place which they described as being more like a frozen waterfall than the conventional picture of an ice-fall. There the glacier moved over a cliff about 1,000 feet in height. That too they had surmounted, and so reached the savage trench where the glacier began, at the foot of the Great Chimney itself. They had climbed on, finally reaching a height of about 23,000 feet among severe cliffs and ice chutes somewhere beyond and below the far edge of the Mirror Wall.

During Harry's story Billy Barnes sat silent, occasionally yawning or puffing at the huge pipe he affected. Harry's unemotional report of what they had done and seen made it clear to Peter that there was no sense in launching the expedition on that route, but before giving his decision he asked Barnes if he had any opinion. Barnes said: 'The Great Chimney won't go – but I thought there might have been a route out of the glacier on the north-west, just short of the fall. That would lead us on to a big ridge – this one.' On the map spread out between them he pointed with the stem of his pipe to the Yangpa Ridge, roughly north-north-east of the mountain.

Peter glanced questioningly at Harry. Harry said: 'Yes. There might, just possibly, be a way up to the Yangpa, though I estimate the chances of its being passable for porters as twenty to one against.'

'We didn't try it,' Billy said.

Harry said: 'There wasn't time. Even if there had been, I wouldn't have tried it, because the ridge it leads to, the Yangpa, is impassable for climbers as well as porters.'

'How do you know?' young Billy Barnes said, and this time his sneer, though slight, was unmistakable. It was on the tip of Peter's tongue to give him a short answer, but Harry spoke first and, Peter was glad to see, with some heat. Sweet reasonableness and tenderness for the susceptibilities of the young were all very well, but mountain-climbing was not a sweet or reasonable affair, and passions, angers, and loves were not only inevitable at high altitudes but desirable and actually necessary for the accomplishment of its aims.

Harry said: 'I know because Lyon and I traversed the lower part of the Great Chimney trench in nineteen-fourteen, and reached the Yangpa at twenty-two thousand feet. That snow, which you thought looked so inviting, is a cornice, and it overhangs nearly a hundred feet on the other side, where it's flat. On this side, where you thought the porters might move along on the firm snow, the angle is eighty-five degrees, and it's just under four inches deep. In other words, there's no anchorage. In other words, only a bloody fool would try the Yangpa. As I told you

573

at the time.'

Billy flushed angrily and got up from the camp chair. 'Do you want me any more, Peter?' he asked stiffly.

'No thanks, Billy,' Peter said. 'For God's sake get some rest or you won't be fit enough to be considered for the summit.' The young man paled then, and went out. Peter thought that his evident fatigue had been caused by the secret conflict with Harry as much as by the tremendous work they must have done; but he had meant what he said, and Barnes knew it.

The rest trailed out, and then Harry and he sat alone for a time, listening to the murmur of the porters and a song the Sherpas were singing as they split a bottle of rum. Harry said: 'He's a good climber, Peter – one of the best. But try not to pair him with me again, will you? As you see, he disapproves of me.'

Peter nodded. There was no sense in pushing Billy against Harry any more. He had hoped Billy would be more receptive, but no one can be so obstinate as the very young and, after all, it was Harry he was primarily concerned with, not Mr William Barnes.

Two days later they began the advance up the Wilcot Ridge. He and the Count went ahead to mark out Camp I on the old site, and Robin Granger came with them to stretch his legs. Oscar, George Norris, and Billy were to lead the whole body of porters up the ridge, and Harry was to stay at Juniper to supervise that end of the work.

They reached the camp site at about ten in the

morning and sat around in the sun, waiting for the porters to struggle into view. It was a beautiful day. Robin went off to sleep, and Peter sat in a contented trance, his back against a rock, while the Count, who had never been on the Wilcot, stared up at the Needles and said: 'Boss, are we going up those ruddy things?' Peter grunted affirmation, and the Count said: 'Mind if I go back to the North Wall?'

Robin mumbled: 'Shut up.'

The leading porters should have been up to them by eleven. By half-past, Peter was becoming impatient. At twelve he asked Robin to go down at once – he was going back anyway that evening – and tell Harry to get a move on, or report what was wrong.

Robin had hardly disappeared down the ridge when he reappeared with Oscar Hutton. When they reached Peter, Oscar said: 'Porter trouble, Peter.'

'What?' Peter jumped up, wrenching his pack on to his shoulders. The porters had been in such good humour and had worked so well that he could hardly believe it.

Oscar said: 'They're on strike – the whole lot of them, except the Sherpas. Billy hit one of them. Knocked him for six.'

'That's not porter trouble,' the Count drawled from behind him. 'That's climber trouble.'

'Harry asked you to come down,' Oscar said.

Peter nodded and led off at a fast pace. As no tents or sleeping-bags would be brought up to Camp I now, none of them could stay there for the night. He was furious, and as he ran down the ridge he told himself that he would send Billy back to Rudwal immediately, with or without escort. If Billy wanted to prove his bravery he could walk alone to Harkamu across the Parasian plateau, among the occasional bandits who wandered into it from Tibet. Let him knock a few of *them* down with blows from his big fists, instead of picking on a poor bloody porter who'd left his wife and home and come into this wilderness from nothing but a wish to help them – specifically, he knew, to help him, Peter Savage.

'Did you see what happened?' he asked Oscar as they hurried down.

Oscar said: 'No. None of us did. I was just going to leave Juniper with a party when the man came tearing into camp, without his load, blood streaming from his forehead. His name is Pahlwan. And hot on his heels were all the rest of the porters, and Billy.'

'Hot on *their* heels and yelling blue murder at them to come back, I'll bet,' the Count said.

Oscar said: 'Yes. Then Harry came up and took them both inside the tent – Billy and Pahlwan. After a while he told me to come up to you.'

Peter said nothing more, and in an hour and a half they reached Juniper. The Rudwalis were standing about in two or three large groups, all talking as loudly as though the incident had happened five minutes instead of four hours before. He went straight to the big tent and found Harry in there. Harry confirmed Oscar's outline, and added that Billy's story was that he'd found the porter, Pahlwan, baulking at a steep pitch quite low on the ridge and persuading the others to refuse to face it until ropes had been fixed for them to hold on to while they walked up. Pahlwan's story, as far as he could make out, was only that a rope would be a good idea at that place, not that he wouldn't go up it without one.

Peter recognized the spot from Harry's account: it was a rock slope, quite steep and about twelve feet high, tricky but not dangerous.

'Where's Billy?' he asked.

Harry said: 'In his tent, sulking. I think we can settle the whole thing out of hand if he apologizes to Pahlwan – but he refuses to. Shall I call him in?'

Peter nodded, and in a moment the young man was with them, standing opposite Peter with his hands working at his sides and his sunburned face heavy with a mixture of defiance and misery. Peter asked him to sit down and tell what had happened, and he did. It was just as Harry had said.

At the end Billy said: 'I had to do it, sir. *You* know how quickly that sort of thing spreads if it isn't nipped in the bud at once.'

Peter groaned inwardly. Billy had been reading the Dyer debates. Perhaps he'd heard of the Punjab Tradition, of instant action by juniors and unfailing support by seniors – and that was a good tradition, too, in its time and place. Certainly he had read accounts of the ferocious climbs of Mr Peter Savage, and so he believed he knew what the model of a mountaineer should be.

Peter said: 'Do you understand the Rudwali dialect, Billy?'

Billy said: 'No – but I could understand his

577

gestures. He was telling them not to go up.'

Peter sent for Pahlwan and the Rudwali head-man and Subadar Tilakbir. Pahlwan was a small, weaselly fellow of about forty, thin, wiry, and sharp of feature. Dr Zaman Khan had put a huge and probably very satisfying plaster cross on his forehead, but otherwise he was not hurt. He explained curtly in the vile Northern Tehsils patois, which contained many Tibetan words and inflections, that he had thought the slope tricky; that he was sure the *Bara Sahib* (meaning Peter) would order a rope put there if there had been enough rope; but he knew there wasn't enough rope, because it was needed higher up where only the evil-smelling *Bhotias* (the Sherpas) would be going; so the rest of them would have to do without, and of course they could because only the evil-smelling Bhotias would *need* a rope on such a place as this. All this he had been ex-plaining to the other porters during a brief pause. Then the *chokra sahib* spoke angrily to him and would not listen to his explanation and finally did a great *zulm* on him by hitting him; so he threw down his load, his heart having been made small and his face black, and returned to seek justice.

'Did you urge the other porters to come with you?' Peter asked coldly.

Pahlwan looked at him for quite half a minute without speaking, and then said: 'Yes.'

'Why?'

Pahlwan did not answer.

Subadar Tilikbir said: 'This man has been the cause of any trouble we have had since leaving Harkamu.'

Possibly, Peter thought, but there had been no trouble. On an expedition as large and long-lasting as this no sensible man called minor bickering 'trouble.' Something about the man's recital stuck in his mind as being out of character. Obviously Pahlwan had been doing a little lead-swinging, stretching a minute's breather into a five-minute rest by his dissertation on the rope, the rock, and the evil-smelling Bhotias. Ah – perhaps that was it. He'd look into it as soon as the immediate cause of the trouble had been dealt with.

He turned to Billy, explained Pahlwan's story, and said: 'I'd like you to apologize to Pahlwan for hitting him.'

Billy licked his lips twice and tried to say something. Finally he got it out. 'I can't, sir ... it was for the sake of the expedition... I was in the right.'

Peter said: 'I don't think so, Billy, and it would have saved a lot of trouble if you'd said you were sorry when Harry asked you to.' Billy shot Harry Walsh a scowl of pure hatred. Peter said: 'Harry, come outside. Stay here and talk to Pahlwan, Billy. You haven't got any money in your pockets, have you?'

'No,' Billy said, puzzled.

Peter said: 'Good,' and went out, taking the others with him.

Soon enough Pahlwan emerged and said: 'It is settled. It is not right that a man of Harkamu should hold a grudge, even though he has been wronged.'

'Not like the evil-smelling Bhotias?' Peter said.

'No,' Pahlwan said quickly. 'One of *them* would have stuck a knife in the young sahib's back while he slept at night, even–' He stopped suddenly and looked at Peter suspiciously, suspecting that he had fallen into a trap.

Peter said: 'So you wanted to make everyone think the trouble was really the Sherpas' fault. Answer me!'

Pahlwan stood glowering at him. Peter said: 'Why should I not send you back to Harkamu?'

The man did not speak. Peter was weighing in his mind whether to send him back or give him some lesser punishment. Harry spoke quietly beside him. 'Peter, I think he wants to go high.'

The suggestion wrenched Peter into an opposite channel of thought. He looked at the little man with new eyes. He was jealous, yes. But suppose it was not because of the Sherpas' extra pay but because of the extra trust the climbers were putting in them? He was sure, suddenly, that Harry was right. In dealing with this affair he had been thinking too much of the large consequences to the expedition, and not enough to the individual feelings of this one unimportant man – but an expedition is composed of individuals, and he had been stupid.

He said: 'Pahlwan, do you want to go high, like the evil-smelling Bhotias?'

Pahlwan said gruffly: 'I am not fit to do so. Only the Bhotias can climb with you on the upper slopes of our sacred mountain.'

Peter said: 'That's what we have found.' Billy Barnes was there, standing stiffly a little aside from the group. The Count and Oscar Hutton had joined it.

Pahlwan said: 'I can climb. I have practised, carrying loads up the peaks above Harkamu. I stole a rope from the sahib in nineteen-fourteen.' He jerked his chin at Harry.

'So that's where it went,' Harry murmured.

'Are you still using it?' Peter gasped.

'Yes,' Pahlwan said. 'It broke two or three times, but I have knotted it together, and parts of it are still sound. But of course we Rudwalis are no good.'

Peter said: 'You can join the Sherpas. Subadar sahib, see that Pahlwan gets the Sherpa pay, and give him boots, crampons, and a sleeping-bag... It would have been better to come to me before we set out, Pahlwan, and tell me what you wanted, rather than sulk and pretend you are being deliberately insulted. How can I know that one Rudwali has tried to fit himself to work high on the mountains?'

'I am the only one,' Pahlwan said. 'But three others want to go at least as far as the Needles. They too will need boots.'

'Good,' Peter said. 'Go, then, and prove yourselves.' The man salaamed and went off, carrying his back very straight.

'Pheew!' the Count said. 'Scratch a bolshie and you find George Mallory... I'll play you poker for a pound ante, Oscar.'

'No, you won't,' Oscar said.

'Dot cricket, then?' the Count insisted.

'We-ell,' Oscar said, 'all right. I'll be the Gloucestershire side of nineteen-seven.'

Peter turned to say a word to Billy, but he had

disappeared. 'He went to his tent,' Harry said, 'looking very sick.'

'About Pahlwan being promoted, I suppose?' Peter said.

'I suppose so,' Harry said.

Peter wondered a moment whether he should go to Billy's tent and try to reason with him, but he decided not to. The young man was not in a reasonable frame of mind, and it was pretty sure that he would hold his misfortunes and mistakes not against Peter but against Harry. In these circumstances a discussion would do no good.

Peter arranged to speak to all the porters that night, to reproach them for their sudden action, which was part reasonless panic, part sympathy, part herd instinct, and to ask them to work harder still now, as the expedition could not afford any more delays.

The talk went off well; the porters murmured their apologies and promised full support, and everyone went to bed. The next day they began again on the Wilcot Ridge, and established Camp I by the second evening. Then came three days of bad weather, a howling wind and dust storm that lasted twenty-four hours and was succeeded by dry snow. On June 7 they began moving stores up to the new Camp II at 21,690 feet, and on June 9 to Camp III.

Camp III was to be placed on the same ledge as the Camp II of 1913. It was to consist of three small tents, and as soon as it was established Peter intended to send most of those who had done the work down to Camps II and I, while George Norris and he, working alone, put the

Needles in a condition where loaded Sherpas could safely traverse them. This, he estimated, would take three hard days.

On June 9, Peter was therefore at Camp II, and the establishment of Camp III was in the hands of Oscar Hutton, while Harry Walsh was working between Juniper and Camp I to keep the supplies flowing evenly up the mountain.

At three o'clock in the afternoon a mild snowstorm suddenly descended on the Wilcot Ridge. Peter scrambled out of the tent, where he was writing his diary. He could not see more than a couple of hundred feet up the ridge, and thought that the snow would be a good deal heavier at Camp III (23,600 feet) than it was down here at 21,690 feet; but he had confidence in Oscar's judgement and returned to finish his work.

At half-past three he heard a muffled shout from outside and went out again. Robin Granger joined him from the other tent. One of the Sherpas was there, beating his gloved hands together against the bitter cold. They leaned together while the Sherpa shouted that one of his comrades and two Rudwalis had fallen off the ridge on the north side – that is, down towards the Great Chimney Gulf. Robin didn't stay for more, but dived back into his tent to get ready. Peter's heart sank as the Sherpa, almost beside himself with his exertions, the effort of shouting against the wind, and making his Gurkhali-Tibetan dialect understood, said five of them, one cordée of three and one of two, had set out in fine weather from Camp III. Then it began to snow, and they were just going to stop because the visibility was getting bad, when it happened. The three had gone too far to the north on a smooth patch of snow, and it had given way under them.

A few more questions – they were by now crouched inside Peter's tent while he struggled into his climbing gear – and Peter knew that a snow cornice had given way under them; that Barnes and Hutton, at Camp III, should by now have learned the news from the other member of the cordée which had not gone over; and that Pahlwan had been first on the other rope and had led the way on to the treacherous place.

He could spare a thought for Pahlwan, and berate himself for allowing him to join the Sherpas; but he knew he would have done it again. Sherpas had no inherent knowledge of mountaineering, the difference between them and other Himalayan peoples being mainly a desire to climb for some object deeper than just getting paid for it. Pahlwan and his three volunteers had shown that they too wanted to climb and though they lacked even the small technical experience of the Sherpas, the Wilcot Ridge below the Needles was as safe a place as any to gain that experience – in good weather. Oscar had put Pahlwan as Number 1 on the rope coming down – quite correctly, as another Rudwali was Number 2 and a Sherpa, presumably the best climber of the three, and the 'commander' of the rope, was Number 3. If anyone was to blame it was this last man, who should have stopped moving as soon as the snow began to fall, especially as he must have known he was near the only dangerous place on the ridge, that smooth expanse of snow about half-way between Camp II and Camp III.

Peter conjured up pictures of the Gulf as he had seen it from various places along the Wilcot Ridge. He did not know exactly what it was like below the point of the accident, because no one had gone out on the treacherously smooth snow of the cornice. He had seen it from lower down the ridge, though, and knew that the cornice overhung about twenty feet in a beautifully curved and thinning parabola, like the arching of some swan-necked bird. There might be a ledge or platform of snow not too far down, but there might not. Three hundred feet down there was certainly a band of greenish rock that ran horizontally along the mountain, jutting out of the sweep of ice and snow, until it ended directly below the west end of the Mirror Wall. Below this band, a thousand feet lower, there was another band, and below that rocks, cliffs, scattered snow patches, ice chutes, rock funnels, and the final direct fall into the head of the Great Chimney Glacier. There was little chance that the men could have survived.

He was ready, and Robin Granger waited outside. Peter sent the Sherpa on down with in-structions to Harry Walsh and started up the ridge.

The snow fell thicker as they climbed, but he did not think it would last beyond nightfall, about three hours off in that latitude and season. The problem would be to get the rescue party down on to the cliffs below the ridge. Unless examination showed something different the site of the collapse itself would probably be the best place. He thought of taking Oscar with him to find the men or what had happened to them but Robin said, as if he had read his thoughts: 'I've got to go, Peter. They may be injured.'

Now – should he go himself? In spite of everything, he was the best climber in the party, and as his thighs drove him up the ridge, at a pace that he knew he could have bettered if the weather were not imposing a hard caution, he could feel an exultant resurging of his old at-all-costs power.

He put the problem aside, having decided he must wait till he got to the site of the accident, and concentrated on climbing. They reached the place in fifty-eight minutes; Hutton, Barnes, Garakay the Sherpa leader, the three remaining Sherpas, and the two remaining Rudwalis were there. The snow towered in great spirals above and around them, a sure sign that the storm would not last long. Robin Granger's breath was coming in great sobs, and he had thrown himself down on the snow to recover after the effort of their climb.

Oscar said: 'I've been up and down the ridge, Peter. This is the only place to go over. I've got a rope anchored. I was going to go over and break the cornice back to the rock. Do you want us to start now? There's only an hour and a half of daylight left.'

'We must go now,' Peter said. 'Robin and I.' Now that he had seen, he knew that he ought to go.

He examined the rope and saw that it was well anchored to an ice-axe driven into the snow. Oscar shouted in his ear, 'Two hundred feet.'

Good. He would force himself to the end and crawl out towards the edge. Soon his weight would break the cornice, and he would fall through. Some of the cornice on either side would fall away, on and around him, so much so that he might disappear under it, like a man being dragged through a high, thin sand dune. Still, he had plenty of men to work him gradually up and down while he slashed away with his ice-axe. Sooner or later the cornice would be broken back until what was left was firm and deep enough to hold the rope.

He stepped forward. All the heads were turned towards him, and he could feel the concentrated intensity of all those eyes behind the dark goggles. At that moment Oscar shouted in his ear – but muted, so that probably no one else heard – 'I'd rather you sent Billy and myself, especially Billy.' Billy stood there, a little back from the rest, hunched like a young tiger, his jaw stuck out.

Peter thought quickly. That was best. Billy should go, because he was a good climber and because he wanted desperately to recoup his own opinion of himself. Would anyone think that he himself was avoiding the duty if he changed his mind now? He dismissed the thought. It had no bearing on the problem.

He stood back and said: 'Oscar, take charge. Robin and Billy, with him – one first, to be lowered on the fixed rope to see if he can see anything, and report whether the three of you can move by yourselves once you've reached the end of the rope.'

Oscar raised his hand, fastened himself quickly into a loop at the end of the rope, and got his ice-axe firmly in his glove. Garakay watched the anchored ice-axe, everyone else hung on to the rope, and Peter stepped a little back, as far towards the edge of the broken cornice as he judged safe. Oscar slipped to his knees and began to crawl backwards away from the group, towards the edge of the cliff, while the men paid out the rope. The strain came suddenly, but very lightly, as Oscar reached the edge and went over. The rope cut about six feet into the cornice. The men hauled up against a tremendous strain. Oscar, dangling in mid-air just below the swan-neck of snow, hacked away at it with his ice-axe. After five minutes he reappeared and reached the flat again. Once more he crawled backwards, and again dropped off the edge; again the men hauled while Oscar widened the channel the rope had cut into the snow. After twenty minutes he shouted that it was as firm as it was going to get, and that so far he could see nothing below him.

'Lower away,' he said.

They lowered away gently. At a hundred and twenty feet the tension came off the rope and it twitched twice, the signal that Oscar was on firm footing. Peter signalled to the men, and they let out a foot or so of slack so that Oscar could move, but not so much that if he slipped there would be enough slack to break the rope when his weight came on it. Peter moved close, took off one glove, and held the rope in his bare hand just in front of Billy Barnes, the lead man of the anchor team. By feeling the tension in it, and giving signals with his other hand, he could ensure that they gave Oscar just as much rope as he needed but no more.

He waited tensely. The rope slid through his bare hand and moved back and forth in its channel in the cornice. He reckoned he had about twenty minutes before he'd get frostbite in that hand. The falling snow thinned, and a dull bluish pall began to darken the murky, howling sky. To the west, behind the summit cone, it was purple and dark red; then that faded.

The rope twitched three times sharply, and the men began to haul up. Peter put on his glove and took off the other. If they were not careful they would jam Oscar into the underside of the cornice, where he could do nothing with his axe, and might break the rope. But it went well, and soon Oscar appeared, holding on to the rope with one hand and walking up over the edge of the cornice, his body almost horizontal.

'Couldn't see anyone.' He gasped. 'Saw a headband – one boot, with crampons. The slope's damned steep... Thought I saw fall marks... If they started an avalanche, they were behind it, not in it – or there wouldn't have been any marks.'

Now there was less than an hour of daylight. Peter said: 'Over you go, then. Who's going to take your rope? And a spare. We'll leave this one dangling at full length. Make sure you can always get back to it. There'll be a tent and a party here.'

He wanted to say a whole lot of other things –

if you find them stay with them until daylight and then bring them out this way, or down, or along, whichever is best; if you don't find them, try again in the morning, but whatever you do, don't try to find this rope-end in the dark once you've left it; dig yourselves into the snow; (to Robin) take an extra ice-axe in case you have to set a leg... But all that would have been a waste of time. They knew, and he could trust them absolutely.

He said: 'Good luck.'

In less than ten minutes, going over one by one, they had all gone. Now Peter could see nothing, nor could the rope tell him anything. It ran across the snow and over the cliff, but it had no life. The three had roped up on the slope below and were moving down and across the mountain in the fast-fading light.

He sent Garakay and two others up to Camp III with orders to bring down a tent, a Primus, tea, sugar, and as many sleeping-bags as they could carry. That left one Sherpa and two Rudwalis with him at the head of the rope. The minutes passed, and soon he had to admit that it was dark. They stamped up and down to keep warm, the wind shrieked, and a large star came out in the west, hovering like a golden coin over the high shoulder of the Gendarme Ridge. Garakay returned about midnight with the tent, and they all tried to scramble into it. It was impossible. The Rudwalis refused to take turns, as he suggested, but grabbed ice-axes and made a deep hole in the snow outside. By the time they were satisfied with it it was half-past three in the morning. Then Peter thought that he slept for an hour, while Garakay held the rope between his hands. Then he held the rope while Garakay slept – and somehow the dawn of June 10 came, as dawns had come before to him on lonely mountains. An hour and a half later Harry Walsh reached them with an army of porters and supplies and everything else that might be needed in the rescue. They had been climbing all night.

Harry said: 'I hear Pahlwan was leading.'

Peter nodded. Harry said: 'I'm sorry I suggested you promote him.'

Peter said: 'Don't be an ass. Wouldn't you be sorrier if you hadn't?'

Harry began to take off his goggles – they were inside the tent. After a while he said: 'Yes – I was feeling what I ought to feel, not what I do. It's a hard habit to get out of.' He seemed pre-occupied.

CHAPTER 41

That had been on June 10. Only today, June 15, had Camp III been established, five days late. Well, it was done at last and here they were, he and George Norris and a stack of pegs, crampons, hammers, and extra rope.

Of those who had fallen over the cornice, Pahlwan was dead; the Sherpa had pneumonia, a broken leg, and severe frostbite of the other foot; and the other Rudwali was sound and actually back on the mountain – though he had agreed to stay below Camp II in future.

Apparently Pahlwan had insisted on going on after the snow began. 'This is not enough to worry a Rudwali,' he'd said. The Sherpa, stung by pride, had allowed himself to be overruled. Pahlwan went too far out, taking a short-cut across the cornice, or losing his way, and fell through. The second man was also on the thin part, and he too had gone through. The Sherpa at the rear had some sort of grip on firm ground and was able to delay the fall of the others before their combined weight snatched him from his place. They shot over the first green rock band, and here the rope broke behind Pahlwan. The others never saw him again. The other two rolled and fell another thousand feet to the second green band. Here they stopped, and Oscar's party did not find them until eight o'clock the following morning. Both parties had spent an appalling night out on the side of the Great Chimney Gulf, not very far from each other. When the rescuers reached them Robin set the Sherpa's broken leg, and then the real problems began. It was Gerry's ice-axe that Robin used to set the leg, so it went down to Juniper and did not see the mountain again. Peter thought that on the whole this was the most fitting end for it.

The five men had had to face the severest trials before they reached safety. They could not get back to the foot of the rope, and instead had to traverse the ice wall for nearly a mile before they could strike up towards the Wilcot Ridge above Camp I. This took them the inside of a full day, since they had to do it twice, once with each man.

By mid-afternoon Billy Barnes had come up the ridge to tell Peter what was happening, and Peter and George Norris went down to help. The next day Walsh, Granger, and Billy Barnes went down into the Great Chimney bowl to find Pahlwan. They searched all day and did not turn back till they had found him and Robin had made sure he was dead. By then it was dark, so they spent the night with the corpse in the Gulf. The next day they tried to bring his body back, but after fruitless and dangerous attempts they gave that up. Instead Robin, who had been an attentive listener to Peter's occasional dissertations on the Rudwalis and their life, cut off his hand and brought that up in his rucksack in order that it might be burned and some portion of Pahlwan's ashes thrown into waters that would eventually reach the holy Ganges and the sea.

Then Peter had ordered a day of rest for everyone, and now it was June 15. The weather was turning uncertain and supplies were low, though still enough, with care, to allow for two attempts on the summit unless there were more delays. Of the climbers, George Norris and he were in the best shape, and they would need to be to surmount the Needles and make them fit for semi-trained Sherpas carrying heavy loads. They were together in a narrow tent at Camp III, its canvas flapping and booming like the sound of distant war, and, beyond again, the wind moaning a slow melody. It was bitterly cold. All the rest of the climbers were at Camps I or II, except Robin who was at Juniper, wrestling for the Sherpa's life against the pneumonia that had stricken him.

On the sixteenth, George and Peter began on the Needles. They worked for three days and did it. The rock was in fair condition for the most part, the snow bad to very bad. They found verglas most mornings on the north sides of the cliffs. The wind never fell to less than forty miles an hour, and for hours on end would hover around sixty or seventy, with gusts that were considerably heavier. Camp III marked the end of anything that could be called Alpine climbing, or even pleasure. As far as there the Wilcot Ridge led gradually up; one climbed; there were wide views; the wind howled, but it was only wind. Above Camp III, as soon as one dug one's crampons into the slope below the Needles, it was different.

The cruel air jabbed into the lungs like icicles; clouds boiled around the rocks and occasionally lashed volleys of huge hailstones into their faces; chunks of rock fell off as they hammered the pegs in; the wind ceased to be wind and took form as a third and utterly evil member of the rope. The views, when they saw them, were always suddenly expressed and as suddenly gone, like curses spoken against them in a deserted cathedral. As they clung to the cliff, wholly absorbed in the microscopic texture of the rock under their hands, the clouds would boil away, and there was the great gulf – and they two – and under them the livid green light of high altitudes.

The only good result that Peter could see, apart from the stupid-seeming fact that they were getting the job done, was the change in George Norris. His taciturnity broke down against the evil silence of the Needles, and he left his misery as an extra coating over the black verglas of those bitter dawns. By the third day he was almost voluble with fatigue and bad temper, most of it directed against Peter. He had done great work, and the Needles had proved to him that though his wife was dead love and hate were not.

So they did it and on the third evening, just before dark, stepped down from the last pitch on Needle One and staggered slowly towards Camp III. Extra tents had appeared there during the day, and Peter saw all the uninjured Sherpas, plus the two Rudwalis who had proved themselves. He also saw several climbers coming out to greet him, but he could not be bothered to register even who they were. Their presence meant the arrival upon him of the next problem, and he didn't want to think about it. It was something to do with who was going to climb the bloody mountain and who was going to do some other bloody job.

He didn't want to climb Meru any more. For three hours George Norris and he had been quarrelling, in single long-spaced words thrown at each other like darts, about the placing of a peg he had hammered in the day before. He didn't want to see George again, and he didn't care where George went or what he did. There would be a crowd in the tents that night, which would not mean extra warmth, only more discomfort, a thicker layer of greasy sweat and congealed breath on the underside of the canvas in the morning. The wind droned and roared, and neither of the Primuses would light.

He opened a tin of sweetened condensed milk and began to force some down his throat. One of the Sherpas was trying to take off his boots and massage his feet – no, it was a Rudwali, Baldev. He told the man that he had no intention of allowing him up the Needles and he could bloody well go down to Camp II the next day. Baldev said nothing but went on with his work.

After about half an hour Harry said: 'Who's to go to Four tomorrow, Peter?'

'I'll decide in the morning,' he said.

'That'll be too late,' Harry said gently, insistently. 'They'll have to leave early.'

Peter scowled at him, but it was true. Four climbers had to go over the Needles tomorrow. Two would bring the Sherpas back the same day, weather permitting. Two would try for the summit the following day.

'Robin and the Count, to begin with,' he said. He knew perfectly well that Robin was at Juniper and the Count had a bad eye. He only wanted to annoy Harry.

Harry said: 'The Count's eye is worse. I've sent him back to Juniper.'

Oh, God, how he hated the mountain Meru! Hate and fear formed a numb, terrifying pain, like a rock crushing a frozen finger. These past three nights he had dreamed about the mountain, and in the dreams it was leaning over his son Rodney, and Gerry was there (they ought to have brought that ice-axe up again somehow), and so was Emily, all as it had been during real life; but the dreams were more unpleasant than the reality, for all its tragedies, having many elements of the grotesque and the sordid.

Harry's voice reached him. 'You must decide now, Peter.'

Slowly he began to think. First he looked around at their faces. Baldev had gone, and Billy Barnes had come in to take his place. Harry Walsh was here. No room for any more.

'Who else is up here at Three?' he asked.

'Oscar and George,' Harry said, 'in the other tent.'

The Count at Juniper with a bad eye. Robin at Juniper with the sick Sherpa. Five of them at Camp III. That made seven, the total.

Billy Barnes seemed tired, and his eyes were wild. His scruffy blond beard made him look like a probationary Viking or a young albino Sikh. 'How are you feeling, Billy?' Peter asked him.

'I'm all right,' Billy said and shut his mouth

with a snap.

'I don't think Billy's really fit,' Harry said quietly – 'quietly' meant that Peter could just hear him against the wind and the raucous tent, though he spoke loudly enough. 'I think he ought to have another day's rest. He took a lot out of himself in the rescue.'

'We'd all be a lot fitter if you hadn't recommended Pahlwan to be promoted,' Billy said, and shut his mouth again with the same snap.

'That was my decision,' Peter said.

'He pushed you to–' Billy began, but Peter cut him off – 'Shut up, Billy… Well, George and I will take the Sherpas up and down. We know the Needles better than anyone… Harry, you and Oscar follow us at noon and try for the top the next day. No, come with us. We'll need all the help we can get with the porters. Billy, you stay here. Then, the next day, you'll go up to Camp Four with whoever's the fitter of George and myself, and try for the top the day after, if Harry and Oscar fail.' He stopped, panting from the effort of the long speech.

'They'll fail,' Billy burst out angrily. 'Oscar can't make it by himself.'

Peter turned slowly then and stared straight at him. 'What do you mean?' he asked. 'Are you suggesting – that Harry isn't even going to try?'

'Yes – yes, I am,' Billy stammered. 'That's just what I'm suggesting, sir. I knew Walsh would let you down! He isn't going to try – because he's windy. He's afraid.'

Peter said: 'You'd better go down the mountain tomorrow, Billy. When you feel better, you can tell Harry you're sorry... There'll only be one attempt, Harry, unless both George and I are feeling strong enough the day after tomorrow ... very unlikely.' He had a splitting headache and would have liked to shoot someone.

Harry began to speak then. He said: 'Billy's reason is wrong – but his fact is right. I don't want to climb Meru.'

'Good God, nor do I,' Peter snarled. 'Everyone's feeling the same.'

'*I'm* not,' Billy cut in with a grim satisfaction.

Harry said: 'I meant to wait ... until you said who was to go in the summit parties ... and only speak if you included me. You did ... but I should have spoken sooner ... in any event. That's what I've been finding out.'

'What the hell are you talking about?' Peter snarled.

'I don't want to climb Meru. Don't want to get to the top,' Harry said.

Peter thought that he himself was going mad with the headache, the three terrible days on the Needles, and his dreams of the mountain and Emily and Gerry. But Billy's haggard, angrily triumphant face told him he was sane enough.

He screamed at Harry: 'You don't want to climb Meru? Why wait till now, tell us? You've taken our food, used the money, people have collected ... now, when we need you, you don't want to come.'

'He's got the wind up,' Billy Barnes said with that venomous happiness, his eyes glowing red in the dim light of the guttering lantern.

Peter's eyes burned with pain. Where had he

seen an expression, heard a voice pitched that way before? ... Peggy, in the bad times. Gradually the physical pain in his head and the sense of baffled frenzy in his mind ebbed away. He looked at Harry, a foot away, and saw that he was perfectly calm, though sorry that he should have had to do this.

He said: 'Tell me, Harry.'

Harry began at once, as though he had been waiting for Peter to join him on the platform of new understanding he had just reached. He spoke slowly and gathered his breath between the clipped, telegraphic phrases. He was as tired as the rest of them. He said: 'I don't think Meru ought to be climbed. So I am afraid, if you send me, I will be looking for excuses, to turn back, without knowing it. Not muscles that give in first, up here, but will. My will, not there, to begin with.'

'This is a sudden change, isn't it?' Peter said, and he couldn't help the bitterness creeping into his voice. 'Remember our talk, by the blue lake?'

Harry said: 'Look, why don't I think Meru ought to be climbed? – I believe, some mountains should never be climbed, but should be left. Symbols of the unknown thing, we strive for, altars to the Unknown God – Everest. This one. The Matterhorn. Whymper was wrong, to keep on and on, at the Matterhorn. Like seducing a special, proud, untouchable kind of girl. If you finally succeed – and you always will, if you go on – you make the girl, into a woman. But if you don't, if you deny yourself, after you've found, that she's different, special, then she stays different. She has a different meaning, greater. Has any wife, whore, courtesan, lover, meant – what Joan of Arc, means?'

Peter listened carefully, torn by unwilling anger and unwilling understanding. Harry Walsh was announcing that he had a mystic-romantic strain in him; but he had chosen a bad time to do it. This attitude towards certain mountains that had come to be regarded as symbols of the mountaineer's craft and art was not rare. At least a quarter of the people who said: 'Everest will not be climbed,' secretly meant 'Everest should not be climbed,' but were too afraid of mysticism to say so. Peter had also noticed that there seemed to be some obscure mechanism linking the ability to climb with the desire to preserve, so that it was only those mountaineers sensitive to this virginal quality of the highest peaks who were capable of ascending them. But most of them climbed on anyway, and if they had been forced to reconcile the two points of view they would probably have said what he would have liked to say now: It is not for *us* to set certain mountains apart; *they* must do it, by remaining inviolable. They had all discussed the subject one evening on the march up, in a camp by a blue salt lake, and Harry had agreed with the 'rational' point of view – but mountaineering is never truly 'rational.' They had been talking about some of the comedies and mishaps of the preparations at the London end, and in particular the character of a rural dean and first-class Alpinist who had written to *The Times* regretting their expedition as a desecration of this particular sacred high place. The letter

601

was written with great charm and out of deep love for the mountains, but with a kind of pagan theology and metaphysical tortuousness which, they had decided, must have made the good cleric's bishop blow his nose with more than episcopal force when he read it.

Now Harry had struck them with the same mystically phosphorescent but nevertheless beautiful thunderbolt, and Peter's sympathy dissolved in anger. By God, Meru *would* be climbed, in spite of Harry. He grated: 'You don't mind, us trying for the summit? I mean, you won't cut the ropes, file the pegs?' As soon as he had spoken, while Harry was still looking unhappily at him, the bitterness passed. 'Sorry, Harry,' he said. 'Of course I accept your position. Work between Camps Three and Four–'

'Haven't finished, Peter,' Harry said. 'Why am I here?'

'Because Peter wanted to give you a chance – to make people forget that photograph,' Billy said.

'Not people,' Harry said. 'Me. People are all right. It was me, I couldn't come to terms with.'

Outside the wind had lessened, and Harry realized he had been shouting needlessly loudly. He paused and collected himself, leaning his head down as though gathering his strength for the ascent of a long, steep pitch. Peter eased his own position in the crowded tent. Now that the wind had slackened there seemed more room, for the wind had been like a physical presence in here with them, and now it had gone away for a moment. It would be back. Meanwhile, he could breathe more easily.

Harry spoke more rationally, though still slowly. 'Somewhere, before I came out this time, I started looking at myself. I had been a coward. I ought to feel I was a cur. I didn't. Not when I really tried. What I'd been standing on, all my life, was cracked, and down below, where I had to look because everywhere else was so – inexplicable, was the idea that cowardice did not disgust me.'

Young Billy Barnes snorted aloud. Peter said: 'Keep quiet, Billy, or go into the other tent.'

'Stay, Billy,' Harry said. 'It didn't matter *what* I found down there, only that it was different from what was on top. I tried the same with other things – gluttony, greed, honesty – all kinds of things, that I *knew* I either admired or despised. Sometimes, in the lower layer, I found the same feeling there was on top. Sometimes I found something different. I tried saying aloud what I really felt, but to myself. I began with the easy ones – "Shyam Singh eats till he's sick. *I don't mind.*" Slowly I got most of the lower level uncovered. I wasn't strong enough to show it to anyone else yet...'

He was looking at Peter and speaking very slowly, partly from fatigue and partly as though it were a difficult lesson and Peter a willing but slow-witted child.

Peter said: 'It took a lot to split the outer case.'

Harry said: 'The whole war, and then the earthquake, and what I did there... I came to the conclusion that people – parents, Eton, Kings, the Alpine Club – had been building a cocoon round me, from the day I was born. It was hard.

603

It couldn't give. It could only crack, split.'

'You didn't find you were a coward?' Peter said.

'No. Only that I didn't really abhor cowardice. That was enough – to make the crack really happen in that place, when the pressure got too great, I suppose... For a couple of months I've been throwing the top layer away. The one that I've lived by all my life. After that talk by the lake I began to think about mountaineering... Hadn't dared before, but then I had to. Was my mountaineering inner or outer layer? It's taken a long time, and I'm really sorry, Peter, but, during the rescue business, I finally scraped away the plaster – and found – what I told you.'

'You're not going to give up climbing?'

Harry shook his head. 'No. But I'll be unhappy when Meru is climbed, and I've got to live, by what I've found, I really believe... By God, Peter, already I feel – as if I'd just been let out of a strait-jacket.'

They were all quiet for a long time, while the rising wind whistled a querulous commentary on man's fitfully splendid soul.

At length Peter said: 'Billy, go and tell George and Oscar that they're to make the first attempt. You and I will make the second. If there's any need.'

'I'll be fit enough by then,' Billy said. He turned in the low doorway of the tent and said: 'I still think Walsh has got the wind up.' Then he went out.

Peter prepared to sleep, bade Harry good night, and lay down. A pair of smelly socks were under his nose, but his headache had gone. He brooded

604

morosely on Harry.

There was nothing to be ashamed of in his attitude, except that when it came to the point – Do, or Not Do – most mountaineers of the class capable of climbing such a peak as this finally overcame or suppressed their qualms... But that *was* Harry's point. He had found that he had been living in a plaster case of correct emotions and proper, even noble, sentiments. He could no longer pretend.

Well, then, why hadn't his damned truth come out quicker? He should have spoken earlier, and then he could have been used more in the rescue and on the lower ridges, instead of being saved for the high work. He had a barefaced gall, to make his announcement now, of all times, when they needed him most! When Billy Barnes, his only enemy, was in the best position to lay it to cowardice and throw the accusation in his face!

Peter stiffened with a jolt of understanding more painful than an electric shock. By God, he was a fool! He was not fit to be charged with the supervision of two corporation dustmen, let alone the activities of these highly strung, magnificently fit, and dedicated men – examples, as he believed, of the highest that his race or any race could produce. Harry was sleeping already; Peter could hear his regular breathing, an occasional stertorous groan and snore, sound asleep for these altitudes. He had called Harry 'traitor' and hinted that he was mad, and worse; Billy had flung the photograph at him; Harry had turned away his face from the mountain that had meant so much to him for so long – and he was sleeping soundly.

The first object of the expedition was accomplished. Harry had solved the problem that the evil moment at Rudwal had set him. He had been a great gentleman; he could now become a great human being, for he had found and demolished the barriers. What kind of priggishness was it to complain that Harry's solution had been wholly unexpected?

Peter decided, groaning, that he had been a pompous ass. He had somehow imagined that there could only be one solution – that Harry would find his old armour, new-burnished, by his feats of endurance and courage on Meru. How much greater was this quiet denial, and how much more powerful a proof of inner contentment! Almost anything else would have been easier for Harry to say and do than what he had said and done. So strongly were the circumstances set against him, so perfectly did his surmounting of them prove his new, supple strength, that Peter wondered whether his sense of the inviolateness of Meru could not have been created by him from what he had found of his real character – not already existing in it – in order to put himself to just this test.

It was possible, but that was an area Harry could investigate, if he cared to, in the company of Viennese doctors with black beards and blacker notions about their mothers.

For himself, he had Meru to think of, and, unfortunately but unavoidably, the bruised personality of young Billy Barnes, who might have been a post-war version of himself when young.

CHAPTER 42

At half-past six the next morning the four of them set off with the five Sherpas and Baldev. Some snow had fallen during the night, and the wind was blowing with its usual maniacal fierceness, whipping the snow like frozen sand into their faces. They were roped into four cordées, each climber with one Sherpa, except that Peter and Harry took two each. They were all heavily loaded, climbers and Sherpas alike, for the whole of Camp IV had to be made ready in this one trip, and they were carrying tentage, stores, bedding, and food sufficient to last two men for three nights, plus a reserve in case the weather grew worse. Certain types of weather – an ice storm, for example – would make the Needles absolutely impassable for two or three days on end, and then whoever was at Camp IV would have to stay there until conditions changed.

It was mountaineering of a different dimension from anything any of them had done before. Though Peter, at least, by now knew the Needles as intimately as a man knows every loathsome wrinkle and malicious mannerism of a hated wife, they were still full of venomous surprises. He did not think he had ever felt such a continuous heat of admiration as he did for the Sherpas. Indeed it was the fervour of his admiration for them that kept him warm and enabled him to lead up and over the whole five-hour ordeal without a mistake.

It was microscopic work all the way, and the vastness of Meru resolved itself into an infinity of grains of rock, crystals of snow. Climbing was not climbing, but painful minutes of placing the foot and supporting the body in exactly the right balance on each of a thousand narrow holds; of levelling ice on which to place the gloved hand; of exerting exactly the right amount of force from the thighs, pressing up just so fast, no faster, holding each rhythmic move to the fineness of a pendulum's swing... The surface of the rock crawled, minute by minute, downward past his face, an inch, a foot, a yard away from his goggles. He forgot the shape of the Wilcot Ridge, but he knew the facets of each tiny excrescence round which he anchored the rope, and knew the exact tone of each grey and green fleck in the stone, the texture under his gloved hands of the two-inch cracks in the cliff – but once a blue vein of ice had filled the cleft, and there was no hold. He leaned against the mountain and groaned. A whole length of fixed rope was useless, for it depended on the climber's being able to put his fingers in that crack. Minutes later he unroped, went up alone, hammered out the peg, refixed the rope. If he had had to think, he could not have done it; but he was inwardly prepared for any and every evil device of that mountain, and moments of thought were rare and painful.

They moved, of course – someone, on one of the four ropes, was always moving – but whenever he looked down he saw the same scene: nine men, blind-goggled and still as tortoises, and as heavily bowed under the huge carapaces of their loads, dark-green-clothed, mottled with white for the snow 'drifted' against the lee side of each man as he climbed, as though he were a small fang of rock. The four lengths of rope fell straight, successive narrow streams of light, from man to man. Cloud was the far floor, and then came the sensation of falling, of a swooping, endless dive into space as the floor opened and the green light played like water below him, swimming down, down, bottomless, no stillness of earth or land or water or life to hold it, only the plunging air.

He didn't think they spoke a dozen words among the ten of them in the whole ascent, and at half-past eleven, as slowly as they had climbed, they came off the foot of Cleopatra's Needle, and it was done. Slowly they began to pitch the camp. They meant to work as fast as possible, because there was no time to waste, but the altitude and the rhythmic slowness of the passage of the Needles had taken possession of them, and that was how they moved and thought and acted.

In three-quarters of an hour the work was finished. For another half-hour they rested, pushed chocolate into their mouths, and tried to swallow, chewing endlessly on the tasteless mush. Listlessly they tried to melt snow, and failed... Couldn't wait any more. The compulsion was on him to continue the slow, hypnotic crawl. A little before one o'clock he and Harry made ready to begin their descent with the Sherpas.

He said: 'Good luck, George. Good luck, Oscar. Billy and I will be up here by noon to-morrow, weather permitting.'

It was a fine afternoon by then, for Meru, and the summit seemed very near – up the névé, up a ridge, some dark rock, up ... up ... about 2,500 feet. Nothing much, after a night's rest. Oscar said suddenly: 'Look here, Peter, let me go down with Harry. You try with George tomorrow.'

Peter shook his head. He had thought of this, but there were two sound reasons why he should not go in the first party. One was that he was the leader of the expedition, and they had still not quite used up their 'leeway of decision.' In the main he had been keeping to the middle of the expedition during the early stages, because there were choices to be made, decisions to be pondered – they could go by this or that route; they could rest a day or move on; they could launch either X or Y on such-and-such an attempt or reconnaissance. He had kept himself in a position where he could receive information from all sources, ahead and behind, above and below, and make the decisions. As they progressed up the mountain the number of choices, in terms of time and place and personality, gradually lessened, and as gradually he worked his way nearer the front. They had now almost reached the end of all choice – but not quite. Someone still had to decide whether the second attempt should be launched – what to do, what risks among many to take if there were a day's delay up at Camp IV, who to send if the Count, his eye healed, suddenly appeared at Camp III.

Tonight, or the following morning, he could afford to spend his own last effort, but not before.

Secondly, and considerably more important, was the fact that the vital task before them at that instant was not the ascent of Meru but the safe return of the Sherpas to Camp III. For this he would choose the best men available, and those were himself and Harry Walsh. If Harry had been in bad shape Peter would not have hesitated to leave him at Camp IV, thus preventing any attempt on the summit the following day. But fortunately he was going strong, and in a fine, loose way that made even his slowest movements a joy to watch.

Oscar said: 'Well – we'll do our damnedest... Want us to bring a piece of rock down from the top for you?'

They shook hands – again the slow-motion movements. Then Peter turned and began to plod through the thick snow towards the towering ice sheath of Cleopatra's Needle.

They were in two cordées this time, Harry and himself each behind three Sherpas. Four was an uncomfortably large number sometimes, especially in the ascent of a really severe pitch with few anchor points, but on this journey Peter thought it might have its advantages. He gave plenty of rope between each man, thinking that when conditions allowed he would keep the last three on the rope anchored close together while the first went down the whole length of each pitch; the three of them could hold him if he fell. Number 2 would follow in the same way;

Number 3 was the danger position, since there were several places where the anchor man alone could not hold him if he fell. In such places Harry would join Peter and they'd send them all down one by one. Harry and himself, of course, like any last man on a rope, *could not* fall. If they did they were not, and would promptly cease to be, mountaineers. This was a hard rule of mountaineering – one of the few there were – and, once understood, it forced a man into a very mature relationship with his capacities. Peter thought grimly that he had never understood the rule better, and had never been less sure that he could obey it.

On the first pitch he made everyone go up and come down again, as though they were on a practice slope in Wales. He did this because he had suddenly felt very queer in the balance and realized only when his first man was launched on the slope that his rucksack was empty. His centre of balance had shifted, but work and the dull rhythm of it at Camp IV had so numbed him that he had not noticed it; so he tried to make sure that everyone consciously thought about his new balance during the first few pitches. Then they began in earnest.

The descent took four and a half hours. They moved fast enough when they were moving, but the times seemed endless when they were changing positions on the rope. Harry and he took the rear only when the general direction of a pitch was downwards; when the general direction was upwards, they led; when a single pitch went both up and down, they prayed. Three times they unroped and took the Sherpas down really dangerous pitches between them, one at a time. The descent was made possible, in these circumstances, only by the great strength and steady nerves of the Sherpas. Whatever happened now, the experiment of using them had succeeded. With further technical training, there was no limit to what they could do.

There was one near-accident, when the third man on Harry's rope, who was the strongest climber of the three, slipped on an easy hold and hurtled out over the Bowl. From above Peter heard the faint scream, looked, and thought that Harry and the Sherpa were both gone – and perhaps the lower two as well, unless the rope broke. But Harry's work with his rock and body belay was instantaneous and faultless, so that although he was jerked half off his hold, and the rope must have stretched to the fullest it was capable of without snapping, he held the man and held his own position. The Sherpa broke his nose as he swung back against the cliff, and then the three of them managed to lower and haul him to safety. Peter thought that that one act more than wiped out any debt Harry may have owed them for his decision of the night before. Next time they were together again, about half an hour later – there were not many places on the Needle Traverse where a whole party could meet – and after he had looked at the Sherpa's broken nose, he croaked to Harry: 'I suppose ... you realize that fellow will be responsible ... for raping the Goddess Mother of the Snows ... someday?... Why didn't you let him fall?'

Harry grinned wearily, and Peter translated the joke to the Sherpas. If they had had the energy to laugh, they would have. They knew about Harry's decision, of course, and thoroughly sympathized with it. The sanctity of high peaks, especially Chomolungma (the Goddess Mother of the Snows, Everest) was nothing strange to them in their own country, and they felt a new bond with Harry that his ignorance of their language had prevented from forming before; also his good manners had not been able to conceal from those shrewd and open souls this 'outer layer' of race pride, which made him feel that they were inferior. Now they regarded him much as they might have regarded an old-fashioned lama in their own high valley. *They* were emancipated; *they* knew it was all right (so they reassured themselves) to tread the summits of the great peaks; but there was still, as there usually is, an even greater respect for the man who sticks to the old beliefs.

Then they went on down, and about half an hour before the end were joined by Billy Barnes. Peter reprimanded him with what energy he had left, but there he was, and he did useful work on the rope for the rest of the way down.

At a quarter to six they reached Camp III after the hardest day's mountaineering in Peter's experience, and found Subadar Tilakbir and Dr Zaman Khan. The latter had a severe headache, was green with exhaustion, and vomited every hour with the regularity of a clock; but he was wildly proud and happy to be here and Peter could not find the heart to send him down.

Tilakbir saluted, and reported bluntly that all was well below and that he had come to help climb the mountain now that two of the sahibs were out of action.

That was impossible, but Peter could still feel pleasure that they had disobeyed his orders. He knew that he wouldn't have been pleased ten years before; and that they wouldn't have done it. So he berated them soundly, asked Harry to take charge of anything that needed attention, and retired to one of the tents. There he struggled out of his boots and gloves and curled up in his sleeping-bag. He felt very tired, and tomorrow he and Billy Barnes would have to reascend the Needles. Up at Camp IV Oscar and George would be sleeping already – well, they would be trying to; sleep was as hard to catch as appetite at high altitudes.

Next morning at dawn he had a brief conference with Harry about the arrangements for the retreat from the mountain. This was June 20. The first attempt would be made today, the second and last tomorrow, June 21. There were decisions to be made about who was to bring down what, what to do in case of bad weather. Finally all was settled, and Peter thought: Those are my last decisions – except one.

At nine o'clock he set off with Billy Barnes. Conditions on the Needles seemed to be almost imperceptibly better about eleven each morning than at any other time, and there was a nice balance to be attained between getting too little rest at III and too little at IV; yet they must be up at IV in good time, in case Oscar and George

615

were in trouble.

Billy's day of comparative ease at Camp III had done wonders for him. None of the rest of them would have benefited so much, but he had the resilience of youth, and after an hour Peter asked him to lead. He was still enough of a schoolboy to flush at the implied compliment. (Peter supposed he flushed; nothing was visible through the blond beard and the sun-blackened skin: but he bridled and stammered: 'If – if you think so, Peter. Thanks.') The climbing itself seemed to be almost easy after the two trips with the Sherpas, and their loads were light, yet Peter did not feel cheerful. His legs felt like thick cylinders of dough, and he had lost the precious rhythm of his breathing. He continuously prayed that Oscar and George had reached the summit, so that he would not have to go. Yet that would be a most bitter blow for young Billy, who had set his heart on climbing Meru, and with his hero. The mountains were a glorious battleground to him, lit by scenes of heroism and treachery. *He* would not betray Peter, as Peter's own best friend had done. *He* would not leave him, as others had done time and again in the legendary days before the war, when Peter Savage and Gerry Wilcot did twenty-four major peaks in fourteen days and Geoffrey Winthrop Young went from the Schönbühl hut to the Hörnli hut, over the summit of the Matterhorn, in four hours, fifty-seven minutes…

They came down the north face of Cleopatra's, going very carefully, at noon. The tents of Camp IV were tucked against the leeward side of a small crag about two hundred feet from the base of the Needle. A heavy snowfall would have caused them to be buried under five or six feet of drift, but the only alternative, the windward side of the same crag, was made impossible by the force of the wind itself. It was an awesomely barren sight – the steep slopes of snow and ice ahead, the black and green rock patches jutting out among them, the two tents whipping and banging, the R.G.S and Alpine Club pennants, already frayed, streaming from the ridge poles.

They spent ten minutes scanning the slopes that led towards the summit, and then crawled into one of the tents.

Peter lay uncomfortably on his back. He should have clumped round collecting snow. He should have lit the Primus and had water on the boil against the return of the summit party. He should have taken off his boots... He did nothing. After an hour Billy, who had dozed off, scrambled to his feet and set to work, leaving Peter alone.

He wondered fitfully whether Oscar and George had succeeded. He prayed that they had; then hastily invited God to cancel that last prayer. Gerry wanted *him* to climb the mountain, because Gerry must understand by now that it was not he who had shot him dead on the summit of Monte Michele. Emily wanted him to climb it – because *he* wanted to. But he didn't. Yes, he did... Even Harry wanted him to climb it – no, he didn't. But Harry would prefer it to be he if it had to be done. When rape is inevitable, hope it's your friend who does it. That applied.

Billy put his head through the flap and shouted: 'I can see them – five hundred feet up – coming very slowly.'

'Do they want help?' he asked.

'Yes – no, I don't think so. It looks a simple slope, but they – they're coming very slowly. Mind if I go and give them a hand? I'm ready.'

'All right,' Peter said. The head vanished. Cursing, Peter found his gloves and crawled out into the shrieking wind.

Billy was trudging slowly away from him, towards two motionless dark shapes on the névé to the west. The sun flashed on something at the summit of the mountain and glared slowly into Peter's goggles. Had they left something up there? He felt a slow welling-up of horrible disappointment. His legs trembled.

The two shapes were moving, like black snails – slower than that. Three hundred feet an hour, downhill, on an even slope. At that rate they couldn't have gone far. But they'd have started out faster.

The group seemed to move a little more quickly when Billy joined them. It was over an hour before they reached the tents. By then Peter had cocoa made, and he knew they had failed.

Oscar was in slightly worse shape than George, but both of them were finished. Tomorrow, Peter thought, he'd be like that.

'I couldn't go on,' Oscar muttered.

About half an hour later, when they'd drunk a little cocoa, George said: 'We went up ... easy ... but slow. Got to the crest of the névé ... there ... about ten-thirty.'

Oscar said: 'I was sick ... vomiting.'

'Had to wait half an hour.'

'Went on.'

'There's an ice slope ... we were doing a hundred feet an hour there ... half-past twelve ... at the top of that ... I was feeling rotten.'

'I couldn't go on,' Oscar croaked, staring at Peter. 'I couldn't...'

'We'd got to a rock ridge...'

'Couldn't make it. Sorry.'

Peter thought that must be the place where the rope broke in 1913 – the invisible rope by which he was dragging Gerry up the mountain and through his life.

They continued to try to eat. Peter made some sort of arrangements for the next day. The others would stay here in case Billy and he got into trouble. There was little that could be done about it if they did. The weather looked promising. A bright evening ascended stealthily on them from that unknown and unreal world below their platform, the pale sky darkening, glowing in fire and ash behind Meru.

George Norris said: 'It's the height. Nothing really difficult up there. Next time we'll have to try oxygen.'

Peter shook his head numbly.

'We will,' George repeated with indomitable anger. 'It's impossible up there. You can't breathe. How did you feel in 'thirteen?'

'All right,' he said. But he had been using Gerry's heart as well as his own in those days. 'I won't use oxygen,' he said.

But this was going to be his last expedition to

Meru, so it was an easy thing for him to say. He thought wearily: Here's another pulpit in the theology of mountaineering. He had hardly thought about it before, but now he knew he did not intend to use oxygen to climb this or any mountain. Why not fly over the summit and jump out with a parachute? Or be lowered from a hovering dirigible? Better still, why not stay at home and read about someone else flying over the mountain and taking a photograph of it?

'You use crampons and pegs, don't you?' George snarled. 'Damn it, you used them first, on Meru.'

'That's different,' Peter said.

Perhaps it was a valid retort; perhaps it wasn't. There were as many pulpits as there were mountaineers. Why didn't he insist that all mountains must be climbed stark naked, without the use of any artificial equipment of any kind? If that were done he would in fact be joining Harry Walsh and his sect, because all the great mountain peaks of the world and most of the lesser ones would hold their inviolability until some cataclysm turned men back into sapient monkeys. A hairy ape could shin up Meru in no time, but would that make him a mountaineer? He must ask Harry...

'We'd better go,' he said to Billy.

They crawled into their own tent and lay down, side by side.

Peter dozed fitfully and awoke in starts. His breathing came as unevenly as though he had just run up Cader Brith while out of training. He thought that if the wind did not stop for a moment he would go mad; then he thought that if the wind did stop he would *be* mad.

Young Billy Barnes was to be his companion, then. It was a pity Billy hated Harry Walsh so much. It was a pity he divided the world so readily into good and bad, friend and enemy. Mistakes were crimes to him, and differences of opinion, heresies. Peter had seen, while they were jammed into the other tent, that the talk about oxygen had worried him. Harry's decision was too far from 'common sense' for Billy to waste thought on it. Besides, it was Harry's, and that was enough to condemn it. But George Norris was a great climber and a good man; and Peter Savage was a great climber and a good man; and they disagreed. Worse, they disagreed in an area where there was no practical test to decide 'rightness,' as there might be in the choice of a route or the placing of a peg. In other words, their mountaineering 'soul' – the thing that made them mountaineers and not climbers – had cast around the clean, concrete, and lovely shape of the mountains a dimly defined and only half-luminous veil of spiritual values. Billy understood, of course, the particular value that had made them risk many 'expensive' lives on the off-chance of saving three 'cheap' ones, for it was an extension of a code he had been brought up with and probably had real faith in. The value that had yesterday sent Peter down with the Sherpas rather than up towards the summit was more difficult for him, especially after the war, when they had all been forced to decide such things and usually to choose the heroic course. More difficult still was the value that had made them give Pahlwan a chance to become a better mountaineer than he was. For one thing, it had turned out tragically. For another, many sound men would not have agreed with what was done, just as there was the disagreement about oxygen.

All these values and many others constituted the fabric of their mountaineering souls. Peter hoped that Billy would find his own, because...

'Metaphysics, at twenty-five thousand feet!' he mumbled aloud.

'Wha'?'

'Nothing,' Peter replied, and cursed a huge stone under his hip.

He remembered the sense of destiny that had once been the mainspring of his life; and he remembered telling Gerry of his mistrust of God because He was liable to change the rules, so that one could only be ready. Well, it looked now as though he had lived his whole life, and all its triumphs and tragedies, only so that he could be an indirect and clumsy instrument in the remaking of Harry Walsh... There was a little more than that. Somewhere in the blundering act of giving, though separated from Emily by seven thousand miles of desert and sea, he had finished the act of union begun in the liquid depths of her body under the Matterhorn.

It didn't seem much, when he remembered that he had been ready to become Viceroy of India and improve the lives of three hundred million people; or to lead huge armies and alter the face of the world for generations to come; to climb higher, farther, more boldly than any man had done before, and from a dozen 'unconquerable' peaks wave the banners of national pride and the symbols of man's indomitable will.

It didn't seem much, but it was enough.

Sleep, sleep, come to me!

He had to work it out somehow, or he would never sleep. Was there a parallel between mountaineers and monks? The difference would be that the monk devoted his tested and improved soul to the abstract glory of God, while the mountaineer, living among people, going out from people to the mountain and returning from the mountain to people, was bound to use his soul in the pursuits of his ordinary way of life. (Would a man who spent his entire years alone, climbing mountains, be called a mountaineer? He thought not. He would be called a monk.) Then the ordinary lives of mountaineers, their families and works and loves, contributed equally with the mountains in the formation of them? Yes. He had an example of that here in the same sleeping-bag with him. Himself. It was not on the mountains that he had developed the value which condemned the 'unfair' conquest of great peaks; it was in his relationship with Emily, and perhaps with Gerry. Between them those two had convinced him that victory was not enough. Again, it was not his mountaineering skill that had blended this expedition into such a wonderful stew of enthusiasm, friendship, self-sacrifice, and human determination; it was something that others, off the mountain, had given him – Harry, Adam, the Old Captain, his grandfather, young Baber, Emily again. And when he returned from

Meru – if he did – surely he would find that these icy forges, which had steeled his mountaineering soul to a new suppleness (and, he hoped, grace) had also tempered him as a husband, father, and friend.

The air was getting rarefied up here. He must add to that last thought – 'and as the Deputy Commissioner and District Magistrate of Rudwal.' It brought the speculations back to earth – although it was true, damn it!

He would try again, keeping a firm footing on the ground. Mountaineers did not like to bare their souls, even to themselves, and he was a mountaineer...

One: The people he had worked with and the people he had loved, as well as those with whom he had climbed on the mountains, had made him a mountaineer. Two: Whatever the mountains had wrought in him was a part of him, and would influence those he worked with and those he loved. Three: Mountaineering consisted of people, including himself, and only incidentally of mountains.

Three – no, four: All those statements were also true of the manufacture of sewing machines. But not as beautiful.

Five: He was glad that Harry was all right again.

Six: He hoped Billy Barnes turned into a mountaineer. Why? Because there was nothing greater. Better. Higher.

Seven: He, Peter Savage, was a person (see Statement Number Something-or-other, above), and he was homesick for Emily, Rodney,

Elizabeth, baby Gerry, Adam, Baber, Old Uncle Krishna Harnarayan, and all.

Eight: There remained only the small matter of climbing Meru tomorrow.

The wind was shrieking across the mountain, and they were very high – four of them alone. He was frightened. He would not be anywhere else.

CHAPTER 43

Nagging wakefulness haunted the hours when he should have slept; cold lethargy dominated the hours when he should have worked. He looked out at six in the morning, and found a powder snow blowing about the mountain and the wind in the north-east. The temperature was eight degrees below zero Fahrenheit. He could only estimate the wind strength, since they had no anemometer. He put it at seventy-five, with gusts up to a hundred.

That gave him a torpid satisfaction. Wind such as that welded the impalpable cold into steel razors which slashed through clothing, skin, and flesh, into the heart of the marrow. An attempt on the summit would not be feasible in these conditions. But he must wait for an hour or so before he could decently cancel the effort. Billy lit the Primus.

He tried to eat. Against his will, he found himself weighing the problems, for he was now approaching his last decision. Should they – or could they – make the attempt? Billy respected his silence. What few words had to be said struggled like heavy birds against the noise from outside, and landed, *plop*, sometimes where they were noticed, sometimes not.

At eight o'clock he crawled outside and took a long look round the horizon. The sky immediately overhead was pale, cold blue. Arabesques of thin mare's-tail cloud streamed across the zenith twenty and thirty thousand feet above him. To the south, over the edge of the Bowl, with the Needles to his left, he saw a mass of heavy, dark clouds, tinged with iridescent blue, high-banked along the line of the Himalaya. There the monsoon was in full torrential strength. The land between was pale gold to match the pale sky, without haze, but the angle of the light and the great distance combined to smooth out lakes, lesser mountains, and desert into one sweep of featureless, golden pallor.

The wind had dropped. Forty now, with gusts to sixty. Backing into the north. Visibility still good for distance, when you could see over the blown snow; not so good for close work.

It was just feasible. He groaned, went into the tent, and said: 'Are you ready, Billy?'

George and Oscar came out to see them off. There was no handshaking, and twenty minutes after he had made up his mind they began the ascent of the first névé. They were roped. It was not necessary on the névé, but he did not think they would be able to rope up when they reached the harder sections ahead. His hands were already frozen inside the heavy gloves, and he opened and closed his fists slowly as he trudged up, in the lead.

There were many ways of surmounting that névé, for it was wide and even, like a triangle, the sides closing to a narrow crest on the rolling ridge nine hundred or a thousand feet higher. Camp IV was near the centre of the base of the triangle.

He led because he believed that his longer experience of all types of snow and ice surface would enable him to choose the smoothest route. The total saving of effort would not be more than the equivalent of another thirty feet, presuming he never made a false step or induced Billy to make one. Thirty feet might be the difference, in the end. Camp IV was only 2,441 feet below the summit if their measurements were accurate. He could feel his strength flowing out, as on this same nevé eight years before it had flowed in. It was best that he should use himself in these early stages, leaving Billy, who was moving well and breathing more easily than he, in better shape to go on alone in case he failed.

The light glared and wavered against his goggles. The glittering surface of the nevé disappeared for seconds on end as the wind drew a screaming curtain of powder snow across it and whipped it on to tower over the southern gulfs in those spiral columns he knew so well. The familiar sludge of invisible lead gathered under his crampons and gradually sifted inside his boots, filling them up, squeezing his feet out of existence, then his calves, then...

Rodney's schooling was a big problem. There were schools in India that could give him the actual education, but that wasn't enough. In the conditions of India as it was, he would never have his nose rubbed in the mud by the butcher's boy. That was important... Surely he had detected signs of a musical sense in Elizabeth? It was a little early yet to be sure, though. Nothing could be more harmful than to sit the child down at the piano and to teach her to hate music. Baby Gerry. Ah, he was just a baby. No good making plans or even thinking much about him at this stage. Just love the little beggar. He was too gentle for his own good. But you couldn't be too gentle... Just enjoy him while he was a baby and see that he stayed gentle.

They reached the crest of the nevé. Half-past eleven. Three hours. They must have stopped several times during the ascent. Several times? All the time, to suck in groaning breaths of air. He didn't remember any moving, only the stopping.

'How are we going, Billy?'

'A little slowly, Peter.'

Good boy. Honest. Honesty is the best policy, absolutely essential in a mountaineer.

'Are you sure you're all right?'

That was Billy speaking.

'Of course.'

That wasn't honest. Better amend it. 'I think so. I can go on. For a bit.'

Oxygen. He'd tried some in one of those Italian hospitals. Wonderful stuff. He was sucking a malted-milk tablet, sitting, his head bowed forward. Not in an Italian hospital. Here.

Now what was there? A ridge, green-black rock. The windward side clear, the leeward dense with blown snow.

'Ready?'

'I can't hear,' Billy shrieked.

He'd lost his voice, then. Perhaps his vocal cords were frozen, or frostbitten. You had to breathe in through the mouth, however much it hurt. Otherwise you never got enough oxygen to keep a fly alive. Oxygen.

He motioned for Billy to take the lead, and Billy set off. Billy was going slowly now. Better than himself, but very slow. This was painful work here. It was a temptation to take off the goggles to see where he was putting his feet. Rock slabs, with dry crystal snow, now in a thin layer, now whipped away and curling and coiling and writhing like ghosts on the left hand. There was a sheer fall on the left, where the nevé had reached and then fallen over a sharp edge. Two thousand feet down began the battleship prow of ice that surmounted the Gendarme Ridge. There was a little snow close under this knife edge, though, on the left – steep, and overhanging that drop, but packed. A strip, three, four feet wide, a foot deep. On the right, he didn't know. Yes, he did. He'd looked over that side while they were coming up here in '13. It was a more gradual slope that side, but it was murderous, because it was this rock slab, bare of ice, snow, verglas, anything you could cut into, sloping down towards the Yangpa Ridge. Very dangerous.

'Keep to the left side,' he called. 'In the snow strip.'

Billy didn't hear him. Next time Billy stopped, Peter whispered and pointed until he understood. The left looked worse, but there was something to cut into. The right looked safe, but it was death.

All this had been different in '13. Not really, just a little. Wind blowing, snow falling, eight years passing. How had he got up here so wonderfully then? Levitation? Leap frog? Divine afflatus? *Hubris,* translated into terms of horse-power?

Billy began to cut steps, the axe-blade swinging up, falling of its own weight, a wedge of snow jumping silently out. About 26,400 feet here, probably.

Surely there was something a man could do to show Harnarayan that young Baber was not a criminal and a traitor? Another thing – what Harnarayan and Adam were doing was good in its way, but in essence it was English, not Indian. The democratic revolt, the revolution, complete with slogans and catchwords, was an English idea. European, anyway. If they abolished the Old Captain's India, they'd be sorry. But the widows had to eat better, and Dr Dhayal needed another forty beds, and everyone could do with a new heart... They'd have to understand that Peter Savage might be a fool, but he wasn't malicious. Adam did understand. One thing was sure – no one was going to get exactly what he wanted, however bitterly he struggled (using lies, might-is-right, oxygen). The way they met each other was going to matter more than who won, because victory was impossible – and, also, it was not enough.

They had reached the place where Gerry threw away his axe. He could remember that time very clearly. Now what would happen? Would he be stopped again, by an unseen hand?

He got over it, Billy leading. He felt no desire to throw away his ice-axe. He was just too tired, for one thing.

'It's past one,' Billy said a little later.

A little later again he saw Billy's face very close to his – obscuring the goggles, as a matter of fact – and his neck was twisted round. He took off his goggles to see better, but Billy put them on again and pulled him half upright.

'You fainted,' Billy said reproachfully. Reproachful because he hadn't told him he was going to.

'I didn't know I would, you bloody fool,' he said furiously.

He got up, Billy trying to push him down, but he won and jerked his legs into action. About twenty steps, he thought, and then the rock rose slowly, levitating.

When he thought he was conscious again he asked: 'Where are we?'

'Twenty-six thousand eight hundred. About.'

Three hundred and forty-one feet to go. At this rate, two hours. Billy alone, an hour.

He leaned against the rock fang on his right and motioned Billy on. Billy stayed, hunched over his axe, numb, gasping, his huge, black, round eyes catching the light. Goggle-eyed. *That's* what it meant!

'On!' He was speaking into Billy's ear, through the fur helmet, parka, and all.

'No.'

'Look. Let me rest. I'll never come again.'

That unsettled Billy, because he had enough energy left to think. Billy knew this was his mountain. But Billy could see he had reached the end. The will was there, but every time he tried to make it work his legs, he fainted. He said: 'I'm sorry.'

Billy understood then that he could not go up there, and never would. So Billy could never go with him, his hero. Billy was young, so Peter said: 'That's an order.'

Not good mountaineering. Bad 'soul' to order people to do things you can't do yourself. Bad 'soul' to give any order, come to that.

He said: 'Use your judgement. As far as you can. Not more than one hour up – then turn back, wherever.'

Billy helped him settle against the rock, and disappeared. Peter lay back, supporting himself with his ice-axe dug into the snow at his feet, the haft in his glove, the glove tight against his belly. Waiting was as exhausting as moving. Physical effort to force himself to wait. Very hard, hard…

Emily had no business on this mountain, no business at all. True, he'd taken her up the Zmutt Ridge that day to show her that nothing was impossible, but Meru *was* impossible, because she was a woman. Just the same as he couldn't have a baby. She should have stayed at home and let him tell her, one way and another, what kind of things there were on Meru.

'Go down at once,' he said angrily. 'You haven't brought Rodney and the babies with you, have you?'

'Of course not,' she said tartly. 'How on earth do you think they'd get up here?'

He was glad to see she'd had the sense to put on mountaineering clothes, good modern ones, with trousers, not the impractical stuff they used to wear when she was a girl.

The wind backed another two points, and he

knew he was done for. Now it was blowing directly on him, and he was freezing to death, not slowly. Death reached in, those razors in hand. He had to move to keep alive. There was no place to move to, except up or down. He had no strength to do either. What he had was a faint power to cling, like a shell on a rock, something left over from ten million years ago.

That was dribbling out as the wind slashed deeper. He slipped down, his feet sliding slowly away from under him. Very slowly. No danger of going over the edge, of course, just of going, lying in the snow under the ridge, and going on somewhere from there without further movement. Nothing swift or catastrophic at all.

Billy was there again, his goggle eyes in front of him.

'What's the time, Billy?' he asked; but his teeth were clamped tight together and would not open at all.

'The wind changed,' Billy said. 'I thought you'd be cold.' He was rubbing snow into Peter's face, slapping him lightly with his gloves, pushing, pulling.

'Did you...?'

'No. Only a hundred, hundred and fifty feet up. Twenty minutes.'

'You could have done it?'

'Perhaps. I don't think so. Next time... Gendarme Ridge looked a little easier from there. Better to meet the bad stuff low down, eh? Come on, Peter ... Peter ... Peter!'

Peter's legs began to move, very slowly, down the ridge. He had failed.

CHAPTER 44

They were a hundred and seventy miles away when he saw Meru for the last time. They were all standing outside the big tent when she came out of far cloud, sailing up against a dark sky early in the night, starlight on her southern precipices.

I shall not see her again, and do not want to...

The publishers hope that this book has given you enjoyable reading. Large Print Books are especially designed to be as easy to see and hold as possible. If you wish a complete list of our books please ask at your local library or write directly to:

Magna Large Print Books
Magna House, Long Preston,
Skipton, North Yorkshire.
BD23 4ND

This Large Print Book for the partially sighted, who cannot read normal print, is published under the auspices of

THE ULVERSCROFT FOUNDATION

THE ULVERSCROFT FOUNDATION

... we hope that you have enjoyed this Large Print Book. Please think for a moment about those people who have worse eyesight problems than you ... and are unable to even read or enjoy Large Print, without great difficulty.

You can help them by sending a donation, large or small to:

**The Ulverscroft Foundation,
1, The Green, Bradgate Road,
Anstey, Leicestershire, LE7 7FU,
England.**
or request a copy of our brochure for more details.

The Foundation will use all your help to assist those people who are handicapped by various sight problems and need special attention.

Thank you very much for your help.